Behind
Closed Doors

Susan Lewis

Behind
Closed Doors

CENTURY

Published by Century 2014

2 4 6 8 10 9 7 5 3 1

First published in Great Britain in 2014 by
Century
Random House, 20 Vauxhall Bridge Road,
London SW1V 2SA

www.randomhouse.co.uk

Addresses for companies within The Random House Group Limited
can be found at: www.randomhouse.co.uk/offices.htm

The Random House Group Limited Reg. No. 954009

Coventry City Council		
CEN*		
3 8002 02179 007 8		
Askews & Holts	Aug-2014	
CRI	£9.99	

ISBN 9781780891767

A CIP catalogue record for this book is available from
the British Library

The Random House Group Limited supports the Forest Stewardship
Council® (FSC®), the leading international forest-certification
organisation. Our books carrying the FSC label are printed on
FSC®-certified paper. FSC is the only forest-certification scheme
supported by the leading environmental organisations, including
Greenpeace. Our paper procurement policy can be found at
www.randomhouse.co.uk/environment

Typeset in Palatino by Palimpsest Book Production Limited,
Falkirk, Stirlingshire
Printed and bound in Great Britain by
Clays Ltd, St Ives plc

To James,
with love

Behind
Closed Doors

'Where are you going?'

'*Out*. All right?'

'Not before you've cleared this table, you aren't, and there's plenty to do round here.'

'I'm not your bloody slave.'

'Don't speak to me like that, and stop arguing all the time. Now, there are the dishes . . .'

'No way!'

Heidi Monroe's normally soft brown eyes sparked anger out of their tiredness, while her milky caramel skin flushed into the crinkled halo of her chaotic dark hair. 'Sophie, I've had about as much as I can take of you today,' she sighed. 'I'm shattered, I've got a headache, Archie'll be awake any minute . . .'

'So? You're the one who decided to have a baby, not me. *You* take care of him . . .'

'I intend to, but I need your help. I've got a stack of work to get through tonight . . .'

'It's Sunday, for God's sake. Normal people take Sundays off, but not *you*. Or me, thanks to you and this bloody place. I'm not the one who took the job, so I don't see why I have to work as well . . .'

'Most girls your age would love to earn some

1

pocket money, so why don't you think yourself lucky instead of bitching about everything?'

'I'm *fourteen* for God's sake. I want to have a life like . . .'

'From what I hear you have *more* of a life, and you know what I mean by that. Have you heard what people are saying about you?'

'I don't *care* what they say. They're a bunch of losers . . .'

'I hope it's not true, Sophie, that's all I can say, because if your father ever hears about it . . .'

'*Shut up! Just shut up.*' Sophie's pretty, stricken face was a fiery red oval inside her purple-streaked hair; her lavender-blue eyes were darkened by confusion and anger. Nothing was ever going right in her life, *nothing*, and it just wasn't fair.

'Stop shouting, or you'll wake Archie.'

'You're the one shouting, and I don't care if I wake him up. I'm going out.'

'No you're not . . .'

'I worked all day, for God's sake, I deserve to have some time off.'

'You can go when you've cleared the table and tidied up that tip of a bedroom.'

'I'm going now!'

'Sophie, get back here.'

'I said, *I'm going now.*'

They stood staring at one another, months of bitterness and bewilderment ticking like a time bomb between them. It was as though they'd stopped knowing one another, were challenging the monsters each had become to strike first or back down.

Sophie's lip trembled as she glared at Heidi. 'You can't make me do anything I don't want to,' she choked angrily.

'Do you want me to tell your father about the way you speak to me?'

'Tell him what you like, he couldn't give a damn anyway.'

'You know that's not true.'

'Oh God,' Sophie spat in disgust as thirteen-month-old Archie started screeching, 'I'm getting out of here right now,' but as she tore open the kitchen door she walked straight into her father.

'What the heck's going on in here?' Gavin Monroe demanded. 'I can hear you two halfway down . . .'

'It's not me, it's her,' Sophie yelled over him. 'She's picking on me again. Always picking, picking, picking . . .' She was thrusting her face towards Heidi as though daring her to come and slap it. 'Why don't you go and shut your stupid child up!'

'Sophie!' her father barked, shocked and angered.

She wasn't listening; she was already storming along the hall.

'If you leave now you don't need to bother coming back,' Heidi shouted after her.

'Thanks for making me want to kill myself,' Sophie yelled out, and flouncing through her bedroom door she slammed it so hard behind her that a poster fell off the wall.

She hated them! Really, really hated them and it would serve them bloody right if she did leave home, or better still if she killed herself. In fact she might just do that, at least then she'd be out of this house and would never have to put up with them again. Why were they always so mean to her, making her feel useless or stupid, or like she was a waste of space that was always in the way?

Grabbing her iPod she jammed it into a speaker and turned up the volume. She didn't want them to hear her sobbing, no way was she going to give them the satisfaction of knowing they'd got to her, even though they had, because she could hardly catch her breath.

Throwing herself down on the bed she grabbed her old rag doll and squeezed it tightly to her chest. Sometimes this doll felt like her only friend in the world. She'd had her since she was a baby, and she'd never let her go, *not ever*. It had been a present from her mum, and for a long time after she had died Sophie had cried into the doll's corn-coloured hair, sure she could still smell her mum's perfume and even sometimes hear her voice.

'It's all right, my darling,' her mum would whisper, 'I'm still here. You just can't see me, that's all.'

'I want you to come back,' ten-year-old Sophie would sob.

'I know you do, sweetie, and I would if I could, but you're my big, brave girl . . .'

'No, I'm not brave. I want to be with you, please Mummy, please let me be with you.'

'But what would Daddy do without you? He'd be so lonely, and you know how much he loves you.'

Her dad used to love her, she was sure about that, but he was much more interested in Archie now. So was Heidi. Everyone was fixated on Archie, and in truth Sophie wanted to love him too because it felt really terrible not to when he was just a baby. The trouble was all he ever did was cry and eat and poo. He never laughed, like other babies, or did cute stuff, and he even looked a bit weird, though she'd never said that to anyone. She didn't even like admitting it to herself, it felt so bad. One thing was certain though, he definitely didn't like her. If she went anywhere near him he started howling the place down, and it made her feel like howling too.

The really upsetting part of it all was that she and Heidi had been like best mates before Archie had come along. It hadn't been as good as having her mum again, nothing would ever be as lovely as that, but she and Heidi used to go places together, do each other's hair, and practise their make-up. Sophie hadn't even minded when her dad had said he was going to marry her, because it was definitely better having Heidi around than when she used to lie in her bedroom at night listening to her dad crying and not knowing what to do to make him feel better. Heidi changed all that. Right from the off she'd made him laugh and suddenly he wanted to do things again. Sometimes he'd say it was like having two daughters instead of one, since Heidi was only thirty, sixteen years younger than him, but she'd never really acted that old. She did now, since Archie, and the way she'd changed, withdrawing from Sophie and stressing out all the time, had made Sophie start longing for her mother all over again.

If only it could still be just the three of them the way it used to be, her, Mummy and Daddy, living in Devon, singing in holiday camps and at children's parties and in church. She'd still have her lessons at home, although her mother had always said she'd have to go to proper school when she was eleven, so perhaps she wouldn't.

The thought of school swelled another painful

misery in her heart. In less than three weeks the summer holidays would be over and she'd have to go and face those horrible girls again. They were forever picking on her, calling her names, pulling her hair and even punching her when she went past. At the end of last term they'd started telling everyone she had an STD so they ought to steer clear. It wasn't safe to be near her, they warned, and it seemed everyone had listened, because she'd ended up more or less isolated, with only Estelle as her friend.

'They're just jealous because you're much prettier than them,' Estelle had insisted, 'and the boys like you better.'

Sophie didn't think she was prettier, and as for the boys . . .

Tears were streaming even faster down her face now. She didn't care about boys, or school, or anything else; all she cared about was how it wasn't fair that she didn't have her mother any more, when everyone else had one. It made her feel like a freak, as if she wasn't worth staying around for; even though she knew that was nonsense, it was just how it felt.

'You have to be brave, sweetheart,' her mother had whispered the day she'd told Sophie she couldn't hold on for much longer. 'I know it won't be easy at first, but you're a big girl now, and Daddy's going to need you to help him.'

'But I don't want you to go,' Sophie had wept. 'Please, please don't go.'

'I promise you, my love, I'd stay if I could, just for you, but there's no more they can do for me.'

'What about if we say our prayers?'

'We've said them, my darling, but I'm afraid

they haven't done any good. So what we're going to do, you and me, we're going to start filling this book with all our memories, and after I've gone you can carry on putting things into it, anything you like, flowers, words, postcards, photographs, locks of hair, wishes, dreams, and it will be as though we're still sharing it.'

The book was next to Sophie's bed now, but it wasn't like they were sharing it at all. Even though she'd carried on sticking things in and writing about her feelings and her days, a bit like she was talking to her mum, she could tell she was on her own. Her mum hadn't even come when Sophie had started to write things to shock her. It was like she didn't care any more.

Suddenly jumping to her feet Sophie yanked up her mattress and stuffed the book underneath, as if she were burying it, like her mother. She didn't want to see it again, ever. It was just stupid and childish filling it in all the time, like she still believed in Father Christmas or the tooth fairy. She was a grown-up now; she knew very well that when people were dead they were dead. Her mother wasn't coming back, and her father wasn't interested in her any more, so she might as well be dead too.

Grabbing her phone, she turned the music up even louder and went to push open the window. The salty scent of warm sea air engulfed her, along with the flashing lights of the funfair across the street and a cacophony of screams and laughter that wafted and whipped down from the rides. Since they lived in a bungalow at the edge of a holiday park sneaking out was easy; she simply had to climb on to the ledge and jump down on to the grass below.

Minutes later she was running through the cara-vans, heading for the beach. She wasn't sure how long she'd stay there, or if her dad would come to find her. He usually did, sooner or later, but he was going away tonight, so he might not bother. He'd just knock on her bedroom door on his way out, shout cheerio and when she didn't answer he'd assume she was inside sulking.

'Give me a ring when you're in a better mood,' he'd call out, or something along those lines, and off he would go. He wouldn't realise she wasn't there. No one would until morning and by then . . .

'Hey! Sophie! What're you doing?'

Her heart suddenly lit up. Was that . . . ? It had to be. She was sure she recognised the voice.

She turned round quickly, breaking into a smile. God was on her side after all. He was going to make everything just the way she wanted it . . .

Chapter One

Andrea Lawrence had taken a wrong turn in life. She'd known it for a long time now – it was impossible not to know it when it kept her company like a shadow, or stepped out of nowhere to trip her up with a reminder. It could even make her feel like a stranger when she looked in the mirror, or force her to ask herself what she was doing when right in the middle of something serious. The trouble was, it was too late to turn back. All she could do was keep following the road she'd chosen at a time when she really hadn't been thinking straight at all, and hope it would all come right in the end.

How was it going to do that when so much had already gone so horribly wrong? She wasn't in proper control, was taking decisions that even she didn't agree with, and pride – yes, she had to admit it – *pride* was making it impossible to back down. And professionalism was playing its part, she mustn't forget that, since she wasn't bad at what she did, some even said she was made for it, but she knew that wasn't true.

This was what was going round in her mind when a tentative voice said, 'Hi, I don't suppose you've got a minute?'

Looking up from the case notes she was supposed to be reading on her laptop, Andee's aqua-green eyes, behind the frames of her varifocals, showed impatience, wariness, reserve, until she saw who was asking the favour. Barry Britten, one of her oldest friends and, as of a year ago, a colleague. She liked him, a lot. He was honest, funny, direct when he needed to be, and sensitively discreet. He was also one of the world's best dads to his adorable year-old twins.

'As it's you, I'll make it two,' she replied, removing her feet from the chair they were resting on and putting the laptop aside. Though she was a woman who rarely turned heads at first glance, a second look might arrest attention, in spite of her efforts to blend into the world unnoticed for anything beyond her presence. Each morning she strained her shoulder-length ebony hair into a brutal ponytail, unadorned by anything more than a plain elastic, wore thick-rimmed glasses instead of contacts, and, to her teenage daughter's dismay, almost never used make-up. The way she dressed, at least for work, in a plain white shirt and loose black pants, invited no one to admire her slender legs or to try stealing a glimpse of tempting cleavage. It wasn't that she didn't appreciate male attention, in the right place and the right way it was welcome; it was simply that she had no time for those who seemed to think looks counted more than personality.

'I've just been over to Paradise Cove,' Barry told her, sinking into the easy chair her feet had freed for him. His normally merry brown eyes were showing concern; his mole-dotted cheeks seemed pale. Unusually they were the only ones in the Stress & Mess, aka the old canteen, which these days had no kitchen, merely a microwave, two-ring burner, sink, fridge and temperamental coffee-maker.

'And?' Andee prompted, glancing at her watch. The thought of the workload waiting upstairs on her desk, and all it entailed, made her groan inwardly.

'A girl's gone missing,' Barry replied, his eyes coming directly to hers. 'Stepdaughter of the caravan-park manageress. Aged fourteen.'

Feeling the immediate rise of demons stilling her breath, Andee waited for him to continue.

'I wanted to tell you before all the fuss kicks off,' he said. 'Assuming it does. Obviously it won't if she turns up.'

Andee nodded, and encouraged him to go on.

'Her name's Sophie Monroe,' he elaborated. 'On the face of it it's looking like she's a runaway. Her computer's gone, so's her mobile phone, a few clothes, toiletries, that sort of thing.'

Since taking off into the blue beyond either to punish or to escape parents wasn't unheard-of behaviour for girls of that age, Andee kept her personal feelings in check as she said, 'Some kind of upset at home?'

'Things have been a bit tense lately, according to the stepmother.'

Stepmother. It was a sad truth that steps always rang alarm bells, in spite of the fact that they could often be the best of all parents. 'What about the father?' she asked. 'Is he around?'

'Yes. He's blaming himself, says he should have taken more notice of how unhappy she was.'

Yes, he probably should. 'What did you think of him?'

Barry shrugged. 'He seems a regular sort of bloke, worried out of his mind . . . They both are.'

If the father turned out to be on the level Andee knew she'd have all the time in the world for him. She always had time for fathers who cared. The father of her children cared a lot, about them, if not about her, but that was behind her now, she was moving on. 'How long's she been gone?' she asked.

Clearly expecting the question, he said, 'They think about a week.'

Andee's eyebrows rose. 'So not that worried,' she commented drily.

'Apparently the stepmother thought she'd gone with her father – he's a long-distance lorry driver, and was away most of last week. And he thought she was at home.'

'Didn't they speak to one another during that time? It surely didn't take an entire week for them to realise the girl wasn't with either of them.'

'No, but when it did become apparent they assumed she was hiding out at a friend's house to try and put the wind up them, so the stepmother tried to find her. Then the father received a couple of texts from the girl telling him to stop looking.'

Andee's eyes narrowed. 'When was that?'

'He received the first one last Wednesday, just after the stepmother turned up at the best friend's house to see if she was there. It seems reasonable to assume this visit prompted the text, although the friend is swearing she doesn't know where Sophie is.'

No surprise there.

'The second text,' Barry continued, 'was sent the next day. In it she's claiming to be with friends

12

he doesn't know, so he might as well stop looking because he'll never find her.'

Imagining how well that had gone down, Andee said, 'So what prompted them to get in touch with the police now, rather than straight after receiving that text?'

'Apparently they kept calling her and sending messages, certain she'd give in eventually and tell them where she was, but she hasn't. The father got home last night, half expecting her to turn up once she knew he was back, but still no sign of her and no more texts.'

Andee sat with it for a moment. 'Do they know exactly when she disappeared?' she asked.

'They can't put a precise time on it, but it was last Sunday night.'

Andee checked her watch again. She ought to be back at her desk by now, and as if acting as a reminder her boss, Terence Gould – Terry's All Gold as most of her colleagues called him – put his head round the door. He was a good-looking man in a severe sort of way, with a gaze that seemed to cut straight through a person's defences and a bark that could be every bit as fierce as his bite. Though his demotion from a higher rank had happened before Andee's time she knew all about it, everyone did, and no one considered it deserved.

'Am I getting an update on these robberies this afternoon?' he enquired, his flinty eyes fixed on Andee.

'I'm on it,' she assured him.

'Three o'clock, my office.'

As he left Barry murmured, 'You know he's got the hots for you, don't you?'

Pretending not to hear, Andee said, 'So your girl – Sophie, was it?'

He nodded.

'I'm guessing the Force Incident Manager isn't ranking this any higher than medium risk.'

'Correct. No sign of foul play, no history of abuse in the family – although that's still being checked.'

'Has she ever run off before?'

'Apparently not for more than a few hours.'

'What did your instincts tell you about the parents?'

He inhaled slowly. 'They seem pretty much on the level, but I'm still worried. A week's a long time and if it drags on . . .'

'If it does it'll be recategorised as high risk and you'll get all the backup you need. For the time being I'm guessing you've got the door-to-door inquiries under way?'

He nodded. 'Of course. I'm just about to go back there.'

Andee picked up her bag. 'I'll come with you.'

He hesitated.

Knowing what was on his mind, she said, 'I'm coming.'

'But Andee, with your history . . .'

'Why don't you let me worry about that? All you have to do is talk me through it again as we walk down to the car.'

Twenty minutes later Andee was at the wheel of her Ford Focus following Barry's patrol car through the Waverley housing estate, heading for the caravan parks that cluttered the sandy coastline like an unruly crowd with nowhere to go. As she often did when progress was slow, she surveyed her surroundings and reflected to herself how like a library the world was. Each house, office, shop, trailer, car, just about everything, had a door, and behind that door, much like inside the covers of a book, lay a story or indeed, many stories. They could be sad or joyful; embarrassing, shameful, shocking or downright scary. There were weird ones, tall ones, short ones, incredible, full-on intriguing, silly, horrific, heartbreaking and sometimes desperately tragic.

More often than not she found herself involved in the latter few.

Flipping down the sun visor as they turned on to Wermers Road, home to Kesterly-on-Sea's edge-of-town retail superstores, she ignored the fact that she was supposed to be investigating a series of robberies here, and turned her thoughts to Sophie Monroe instead. She began painting a happy picture for herself of how this chapter of Sophie's story was going to end. Wherever she was hiding she'd soon get lonely, hungry, cold, frightened, and make contact with her parents. They'd then go to pick her up from wherever she was and all would be forgiven and if not forgotten, then at least put aside for the time being as they all tried again.

This was the denouement Andee and her colleagues most frequently encountered when it came to teenage runaways, though Andee was personally and painfully aware that not all families were quite so lucky when a child disappeared.

Hers was amongst those who'd not been blessed.

Perryman's Cove, known locally as Paradise Cove, or simply the Cove, was an area of Kesterly-on-Sea she hadn't visited since she was a child, and by the look of it, as they approached through Waverley, it hadn't changed all that much. Perhaps a few dozen more houses on the surrounding estate, most sprouting satellite dishes like some sort of fungal outbreak, or signs proclaiming themselves B & Bs, or Guest Houses, or Family Run Hotels with Sea Views.

Sea views, from here? Give her a break! OK if you happened to be a seagull, or a pilot, or zoning in via Google Earth, but in these parts you were lucky to spot the sea from the beach, never mind from a mile inland.

Taking a right turn at Giddings roundabout she kept behind Barry as they inched with the traffic through a tangle of scrubland and copses, past the Fisherman's Arms and Albert's donkey retreat, until they were plunging into the coast's glittering, flashing, throbbing mayhem of a holiday resort.

Kesterly's answer to Vegas.

She smiled inwardly as a wave of nostalgia swept her straight back to her childhood. Though she hadn't come here often, four or five times maybe, and never to stay in one of the caravan parks (worse luck), the sudden thrust back in time to those heady, hot summer days was having quite an effect on her. It was suddenly all too easy to remember how she, her sister Penny and cousin Frank used to steal out of their grandparents' house, up on the headland, and cycle full speed down to the grassy sand dunes of the Cove where they'd abandon their bikes, never thinking for a minute they might be stolen (and they never were). Once in the Cove they hardly knew what to do first, they were so excited, hit the funfair to ride the Octopus, or shoot ducks, or bump round the dodgems, or stay on the beach to trot up and down on donkeys called Fred or Floss or Frank, which they'd found totally hilarious. An ass named after Frank! The biggest thrill of all was going in search of new friends in the holiday parks who were visiting from all over the country. How they used to envy those kids being able to spend a whole two weeks *in a caravan*.

As she rounded the first bend past an old shack calling itself Saucy Spicy Ribs, a crazy-golf course and a crowded café, her memories became so clear she could almost taste the candyfloss and toffee apples of bygone years, and hear the squawk of Punch and Judy. Certainly she could smell fish and chips, and the blare of music punctured by shrieks, bells, sirens and laughter seemed almost as thrilling with the memory doors open as it had in reality over twenty-five years ago.

How could she have been back in Kesterly for more than a year without coming here once? She knew her kids had been down, probably more often than they told her, but though she passed the place almost daily, generally out on the ring road on her way to the notorious Temple Fields estate, or to the motorway if she was heading further afield, surprisingly nothing had brought her here.

'Wouldn't it be brilliant to live in this place all the time?' Frank used to gasp during their escapades, when they'd help their new friends struggle huge urns of water back to their caravans for washing or cooking. If it rained they'd play snap or old maid or spoons, all snugged up in the cosy banquettes of someone's holiday home, or go to watch a magician, or a fire-eater, or a clown with cute dogs at one of the Entertainment Centres. (It turned out their grandparents had always known where they were, and since the world had been a rather different place back then they'd trusted the stallholders, park managers and various other adults to keep a watchful eye on the adventurers.)

It was hard to imagine allowing young children such freedoms today. In fact, Andee would rather not try, given how many more predators there seemed to be out there now. As far as she was aware, though, there had never been any trouble, or certainly not of that sort, in Paradise Cove.

Which brought her back to Sophie Monroe and exactly who the mysterious friends she'd mentioned in a text might be.

Passing three banners for Eli Morrow's Dare Devil Show Tonight at 6.30 and a huge blue elephant inviting all takers to eat as much they could for a fiver, she followed Barry into the recessed entry of Blue Ocean Holiday Park. Had she been told it was called Golden Beach she'd have known exactly where it was, but it had apparently changed names since her day.

It had also, she noticed, as they drove under what appeared to be a permanently upright security barrier, acquired some fancier caravans than those she remembered, and a rather quaint red-brick bungalow near the entrance which, she knew from Barry, was home to the manager, Heidi Monroe, and her family.

Pulling into a reserved spot outside the dwelling, while Barry and Simon Lear, who was with him, drove on to the site offices and entertainment complex, Andee turned off her engine and was about to gather up her bag when her mobile rang. Seeing it was her mother, she clicked on. 'Hi, everything OK?' she asked.

'I'm fine,' her mother assured her. 'Just wondering what time to expect you this evening.'

'Hard to say. Why, do we have something on?' Please don't let her have forgotten her mother was entertaining, she managed to let her down often enough as it was.

'No, not us, but I've been invited for drinks at the Melvilles' and I wondered if you'd like to come with me.'

'As your date?'

Her mother's laugh rarely failed to make Andee smile. What a sweet, beautiful, courageous woman Maureen Lawrence was. How could life have treated someone so gentle so cruelly?

'How about as my significant other?' Maureen suggested, having recently learned the phrase from her grandchildren and been tickled to bits by it.

Still smiling, Andee asked, 'When do you have to let them know?'

'Oh, you can just turn up,' Maureen assured her. 'They'll be delighted to see you.'

Since she was fond of the Melvilles, who'd been friends of her grandparents when they were still around, Andee said, 'What are the kids doing, any idea?' Since Luke was seventeen now, and Alayna fifteen, they were making serious claims on independence, so it wasn't unusual to find out where they were or what they were doing after, rather than before, the event.

'Alayna's here,' her mother replied, 'and Luke's gone into Kesterly with his friends. Oh, I'd better go, someone's at the door. Call me when you're on your way, and Alayna said please don't forget to buy her a strapless bra at M&S, she needs it for tomorrow night,' and adding an habitual 'love you' she rang off.

After texting Alayna for confirmation of her bra size, Andee dropped her phone back into her bag, and checked her Airwave radio was on before getting out of the car. She had got no further than opening the door when her mobile rang again.

This time it was Graeme, the antique dealer she'd recently started seeing, and feeling a pleasing warmth swell inside her she clicked on the line. 'Hi, how are you?' she asked.

'The short answer is fine,' he replied, his tone lilting with the humour that had attracted her to him in the first place, 'the long one is in a hurry to get back.'

'But I thought you loved Italy.'

'I do, and I'm still hopeful that the next time I'm here you'll be with me. As you're not at the moment, I'm finding myself rather keen to get home to Kesterly.'

Though she was pleased by the words, she couldn't help wondering if they were moving too fast. But why was she thinking that when they'd had *six* dates and had progressed no further than a romantic kiss the night before he'd left? And she couldn't deny how much she'd enjoyed that. Anyway, she was surely allowed some fun after all the heartache she'd had to go through. 'Are you on schedule to come back tomorrow?' she asked.

'I'm afraid not,' he groaned, 'which is why I'm calling. I'm having to delay by a day, but if you're free on Wednesday evening I'd love to cook for you.'

She liked the sound of that. 'At your place?'

'Unless you've got somewhere else in mind?'

Smiling, she said, 'I'll bring the wine.'

'Just bring yourself.'

And an overnight bag? She wouldn't ask, of course, but she wondered what he'd say if she did. More to the point, what would she do if the answer was yes? Why, she'd take one, of course, and tell her mother and the children she was going . . . She couldn't think of anywhere off the top of her head, but she'd come up with something. 'I should go,' she told him. 'Call me when your plane gets in.'

After turning off her personal phone, she got out of the car and paused for a moment to take in her surroundings. Though there was no sign of life inside the bungalow, crowds of holidaymakers were milling around, coming and going from the camp, chomping on ice-creams or toffee apples, while the shop, only yards away, was like a giant cake bursting with people and prizes. Citrussy-coloured beach balls, buckets, spades, luminous inflatables, surfboards, wetsuits, flippers, snorkels (*snorkelling in Kesterly!*), everything the self-respecting camper could wish for, plus throbbing disco music.

And across the street was the pulsing, whirling, psychedelic monster of a funfair.

'The owners of the site are currently in Spain,' Barry had informed her earlier, 'but the Monroes have let them know what's happening and apparently they're keen to co-operate in any way they can.'

This was good, Andee always liked people who co-operated, though in the case of Jimmy and

Jackie Poynter it could be a first. Not that she'd had any dealings with the couple herself, but several of her colleagues had, so one thing Andee could be certain of was that the Poynters weren't regulars at the policemen's ball.

'Mrs Monroe? Heidi?' she smiled when an anguished-looking woman with beautiful Afro-Caribbean features and a shock of glorious dark hair answered the door. She'd be around thirty, Andee guessed, though the purple shadows under her eyes were making her seem haunted and older.

The woman nodded and stammered, 'I – um . . .' She pressed a sodden tissue to her mouth as her voice caught on a sob. 'If you could go to the office,' she said, 'it's next to the shop . . .'

'I'm Detective Sergeant Andrea Lawrence,' Andee explained, holding up her badge and feeling for the strain this woman was under – provided it was genuine, of course, and she had no reason to think it wasn't when she clearly hadn't been expected.

Heidi Monroe was frowning, as though not quite understanding. 'I wasn't . . . They didn't say anyone else was coming.'

Still smiling, Andee said, 'Can I come in?'

For a moment Heidi seemed at a loss, then a voice called out from inside, 'Who is it?'

Stepping back, Heidi opened the door wider for Andee to enter. 'I'm afraid we're not very . . .' she began, but didn't finish as she led the way along a dimly lit hallway with doors on either side, into a bright, open-plan kitchen-cum-living room at the back. It was cosily furnished with downy sofas and a thick pile carpet, and looked out on to a small garden with a large pebbledash building

22

beyond that blocked any other sort of view. It smelled of oranges and used nappies.

'It's the police again,' Heidi announced.

A stocky man with not much hair and a tattoo on his left arm turned from whatever he'd been staring at outside, which was probably nothing. The anguish in his eyes was so stark it was almost palpable, and the tight white line around his mouth showed the inner struggle with his conscience. *Was he to blame for his daughter running off? What should he be doing to try to find her?* No sign at the moment of the infant Archie whom Barry had mentioned, though the smell, jumble of toys scattered around the place, and cute clothes hanging on the washing line outside firmly established a baby in residence.

Andee moved forward to introduce herself. 'You must be Gavin,' she said, shaking his hand. His grip was firm enough, but there was no colour in his face and she could almost feel the worry that was weakening him.

'I take it you haven't heard from Sophie since my colleague was here?' she asked.

Gavin swallowed and shook his head. With a glance at his wife, he said, 'I keep checking my phone, and sending texts, but she's still not answering.'

'It's not like her,' Heidi put in. 'I mean, it is, sometimes, if she's upset or angry with us, but never for this long.'

'What about the rest of your family?' Andee asked. 'I take it you've tried contacting them?'

Heidi looked embarrassed as she said, 'We don't really have anyone, or no one she'd go to. Gavin's an only child and his parents are both gone, and mine, well, they won't have anything to do with us, and I don't have any brothers or sisters.'

Wondering if it was the mixed marriage that had alienated Heidi's parents, Andee gestured towards the table, and Heidi rushed to move a high chair out of the way.

Once all three were settled and Andee had taken out her notebook, she said, 'I hope you'll bear with me if I repeat some of the questions you were asked earlier. We just want to get everything straight.'

'Of course,' the Monroes said in unison.

'Anything that'll help us find her,' Gavin added hoarsely.

Having seen the school photo they'd given Barry in which the wide-eyed, blonde-haired Sophie looked rather like a young Scarlett Johannsson, Andee was trying to find a likeness to her father. For the moment it was hard to detect one, though chances were Sophie didn't resemble the photo much anyway, since most girls that age totally transformed their appearance once out of uniform.

'Can I start by asking about Sophie's mother?' she said. 'Is there . . .'

'Her mother died four years ago,' Gavin told her.

Andee regarded him with interest. As far as she was concerned this was as important as what Sophie looked like, or what she'd been wearing the last time anyone had seen her, since losing a parent in early life could have a profound effect on a child's behaviour. 'Does she have family on her mother's side?' she asked.

Gavin shook his head, 'Jilly had a brother, but he was killed in the same accident that took her parents. It happened before I met her, so I never knew them.'

'I think Sophie still misses her mum,' Heidi commented sadly. 'I mean, I know she does.'

How could she not? Losing the centre of her world at the age of ten wasn't something a child was ever really going to get over, especially if she hadn't received the right counselling.

Had she?

Deciding this part of Sophie's background could be pursued at a later date, should it prove necessary, Andee changed course. 'OK, perhaps we can start with when you last saw her. When was that, exactly, and what happened?'

Heidi's hands clenched and unclenched on the table. 'She was here with us last Sunday night. We had tea together, about seven, then Gavin had to pop out.' She took a shuddery breath. 'As soon as he'd gone Sophie said she was going out too. I told her she couldn't until she'd cleared the table and we ended up having a silly row about me picking on her all the time . . .' She glanced at Gavin. 'It was the usual stuff, you know what it's like when we ask her to help out around the house.'

'I don't think she means to be difficult,' Gavin told Andee, 'it's just a phase she's going through.' His mouth twisted wryly. 'They're all the same at that age, aren't they? Think they're already grown up. Can't tell them anything . . .' His voice trailed off as his inner struggle got the better of him.

'Do you row a lot?' Andee asked Heidi.

Heidi pushed back her hair as she shook her head. 'We never used to, but lately . . .'

When she didn't elaborate, Andee simply nodded her understanding. 'So what happened after the row?' she prompted.

Heidi shrugged. 'She took herself off to her

room, the same as she always does. Before she slammed the door she said . . . She said thanks for making her want to kill herself.' Her eyes closed as the memory of the words seemed to cut right through her. 'I didn't take any notice of it at the time,' she said brokenly.

'She didn't mean it,' Gavin put in quickly, clearly trying to reassure himself as well as his wife. 'She's always saying stuff like that . . . It's just with her disappearing after . . .'

Knowing that suicide was one of the favourite threats of worked-up teenagers, Andee asked, 'Has she ever made an attempt on her own life?'

Gavin's face was ashen as he shook his head.

'Or talked about ending it in any serious way?'

Again he shook his head.

'OK. So she went to her room . . .'

'And then she must have sneaked out,' Heidi continued. 'We didn't hear her go, but when I looked in later and saw she wasn't there I assumed she'd gone over to the entertainment complex, or maybe to her friend's, Estelle Morris.'

'Did you call Estelle?'

'Not that night, but I did when Sophie still hadn't come back the next day. Estelle said she hadn't seen her. I didn't know whether to believe her or not, so I tried ringing Gavin. When I couldn't get through I left a message for him to call me back. I didn't say anything about Sophie in the message because I didn't want to worry him. I kept telling myself she was with him, that she'd waited for him to leave the house and had gone running after him. Of course he'd have let me know if she had, but it's . . . Well, it's what I kept telling myself until . . . until we finally got to speak.'

'Which was when?'

'On the Tuesday. We talked about the baby first . . . I kept waiting for him to say Sophie was with him, but then he asked how she was and if she was over her paddy yet . . .' She glanced at her husband, her breath catching on a sob. 'That was when we realised that neither of us knew where she was, so I immediately rang Estelle again. She kept swearing she hadn't seen her, or heard from her. I still didn't know whether or not she was telling the truth . . . I wanted to believe she was lying, because if she was at least it would mean Sophie was safe. Then Gavin got a text from Sophie telling him to stop looking for her.'

'Can I see it?' Andee asked Gavin.

Opening up his phone he found the message and handed it over.

Dad, will you please stop looking for me, it's embarrassing. I'll be back when I'm ready, not before.

Glancing up, Andee said, 'So you stopped looking?'

Heidi shook her head. 'No, except . . . I mean, the problem was I didn't know where else *to* look. Of course I asked people around the camp if they'd seen her, trying not to make too much of a fuss. I was afraid if I did and she found out she'd stay away longer.'

'Had anyone seen her?'

'Not since Sunday. Then Gavin got another text . . .' She nodded to the phone.

Scrolling to it, Andee read, *I know you're not really bothered, but just in case I'm staying with some friends that you don't know, OK. They're really cool and they're going to help me get a job so I can take care of myself from now on.*

Andee's eyes narrowed thoughtfully. 'Do you believe this about the friends?' she asked.

'We don't know what to believe,' Heidi told her. 'You only have to look at where we live to realise how many people she's coming into contact with. She's meeting new people all the time.'

'Have you noticed her taking a particular interest in anyone lately, or vice versa?'

'Not especially, no. I mean, she mixes with some of the punters, but most of the time she's with Estelle.'

'And what about Estelle's parents? Have you spoken to either of them about where Sophie might be?'

'To her mother, yes, and Sophie's definitely not there. Which I realise doesn't mean Estelle's not covering for her, but . . .'

'They do that, don't they,' Gavin came in raggedly, 'make up stories or alibis for one another without realising how much worry they're causing, or how much danger they could be putting themselves in.'

Andee could hardly deny it. 'Do you think Sophie could be in any danger?' she asked carefully.

He flinched. 'I don't want to think it, but it's – it's hard to make yourself stop when you don't know where she is.'

Andee knew from experience that it was next to impossible. To Gavin she said, 'So where exactly were you last week?'

'On a job,' he replied, sounding as wretched as he looked. 'I do some driving now and then for Pollards, the haulage company, based out at Frimsey. I had a big load to take down to Toulouse last Monday, but I decided to drive to Portsmouth on Sunday night and sleep in the cab so I'd be ready to get the early ferry in the morning.'

'Did you see Sophie before you left? I mean after the row.'

His misery was apparent as he shook his head. 'I knocked on her door and shouted out that I was leaving, but she didn't come out or turn her music down, so I realised I was still in her bad books. I know what she's like when she gets in one of her moods, she won't speak to anyone. You have to allow her time to get over it, so I told her to give me a ring when she was ready and I left.'

'So you don't know if she was actually in the room at that point?'

'Her music was on, so I presumed she was, but I guess it's possible she wasn't. She thinks we don't know how she sometimes sneaks out of her window and takes herself off to the Entertainment Centre or over to the funfair. With it being the summer holidays we're not so strict about what time she has to come home.'

Andee nodded. 'So the last time you heard from her was this text, sent last Thursday? Nothing since?'

His face turned greyer than ever as he shook his head again. 'As I said, we keep trying to get hold of her, but she's either ignoring our messages or . . .' His breath caught. 'I don't know why she's doing this. It's not like her to stay angry for so long.'

Andee's eyes dropped to his hands, resting emptily on the table. They were oil-stained, strong and touchingly helpless. 'The job you were on,' she said. 'It took you to France, you say?'

'That's right. I was carrying aircraft parts down to Toulouse.'

Knowing how much traffic went between various West Country manufacturers and the main Airbus factory in the Haute Garonne, Andee said, 'And you got back last night. Is it usual for a trip to take so long?'

'It's about normal for a delivery like that. There are lots of restrictions on the hours we can spend at the wheel and the speed we can go . . . Well, you'd know all about that, being a police officer. Everything's in my log. They'll have it at the office.'

Andee nodded and sat back in her chair. 'OK, so she's taken her computer, some clothes and toiletries. Would she have had any money?'

As Heidi started to answer a loud wail swept down the hallway like a lasso claiming her attention. 'She might have had something left from her wages,' she answered, getting to her feet. 'She works around the camp sometimes, you know, cleaning, or serving meals at the caff or the carvery. I'm sorry, I'd better go and see to him.'

'Of course.'

After the door closed behind her, Gavin said, quietly, 'I didn't want to say anything in front of her, but before I left there was fifty quid in the pocket of my good suit.'

When he didn't continue, Andee said, 'And it's gone now?'

He nodded.

'Why don't you want your wife to know?'

He shrugged. 'I suppose I ought to tell her. It's just. . . I don't know, I guess neither of us is thinking very straight at the moment. I keep getting it into my head that she's gone off and won't ever come back. You hear about that, don't you, how some kids disappear and aren't ever seen again . . .'

Andee's heart contracted. Yes, she knew all about that.

'. . . I don't think we could bear that,' he ran on. 'She means everything to me. She's my princess, my special girl . . . I'm not saying she doesn't have her faults, show me a child that doesn't, and I don't mind admitting there have been times lately that I could blinking throttle her . . .' His eyes widened with alarm as he realised what he'd said.

Holding his gaze and speaking very gently, Andee said, 'Have you ever been physical with her, Gavin?'

He shook his head vehemently. 'No, *never*,' he cried in a tone that sounded very like the truth. 'It was just one of those things you say, you know, like you could murder a burger, when what you really mean is you're hungry.'

'It's OK, I understand, kids can be maddening, especially teenagers.'

Clearly reassured by her reply, he said, 'I don't know what happens to them, I swear it. One minute she's singing and dancing about the place like an angel, all skinny legs and freckled nose, the next she's stomping about with an attitude big enough to fall over, and flirting . . .' His voice cracked with despair. '. . . flirting with blokes like she knows what it's all about.'

Taking the simplest part of that first, Andee said, 'So would the photograph you gave my colleague this morning be a true representation of how she looks now?'

He shook his head. 'Not when she's out of school, anyway, and she's gone and put purple streaks in her lovely blonde hair. She thinks it makes her look sophisticated, or trendy, or something, but when

31

she's all got up in her miniskirt and a top made for maximum exposure . . . I'm sorry, I know I shouldn't say it about my own daughter, but it makes her look, well, you know what I'm saying . . . and she's not like that, not really. It's just a front she puts on, like she's trying to make herself seem more grown up than she is. I keep trying to tell her it gives the wrong impression.'

Knowing better than to take a father's word for his daughter's morals, Andee said, 'Do you have any photographs of her when she is made up? Or some video, perhaps?'

He was shaking his head. 'I don't know. There might be something in her room, I suppose. Shall I go and look?'

Guessing if there was anything it would almost certainly be on Sophie's phone, Andee said, 'In a moment. First of all I'd like to ask about money again. Does she have a bank account?'

He nodded. 'I don't think she's got anything in it though, she's always broke.'

'Does she have use of a credit card?'

'No. I've told her she's too young for that. Not till she's earning her own money.'

'And what about her passport? Have you checked whether she took it with her?'

The anguish in his eyes was terrible as he looked at her. Apparently he hadn't considered the possibility that Sophie might have ventured beyond British shores. 'Heidi keeps them in the drawer,' he said, pointing to a dresser.

Realising he was afraid to know the answer, Andee went to open the drawer herself, and finding three passports she held up Sophie's for him to see.

If he felt any relief it wasn't evident as he rubbed a hand over his balding head and tried to steady his breathing.

Returning to her chair, Andee went on, 'We need to talk about boyfriends. Do you know if she had one?'

As he looked at her he flushed with what appeared to be embarrassment. 'I'm not sure she'd have told me even if she did. You're probably best to ask Heidi about that.'

'OK, so why don't you tell me what you can about her as a person. What sort of changes have you noticed in her lately?'

Bleakly he said, 'Like I told you just now, she's suddenly trying to be all grown up, which I suppose is to be expected at her age, but her attitude . . . She can be as sweet as you like one minute, and the next she's got all this hostility pouring out of her. If you didn't know us you could be forgiven for thinking she came from a bad home, the way she carries on. She doesn't seem to realise how lucky she is compared to some.'

'When did all the hostility begin?'

His eyes drifted to nowhere. 'About nine months ago,' he said quietly. 'We kept putting it down to changing hormones and all that, and I expect that's a big part of it, but I can't help worrying that her nose has been put out of joint since Archie came along.' His eyes flicked to Andee. 'She doesn't ever bother with him,' he sounded hurt and bewildered, 'her own brother, and if we ask her to do anything for him . . . Anyone would think we'd asked her to pull out her own teeth.'

'And before he was born, you were close, the three of you?'

'Definitely. Well, me and her always were, and she got on brilliantly with Heidi when we were first together. Actually, right up until Archie . . . Heidi's always been really good to her, and if Sophie was being honest she'd say the same. They were forever in each other's pockets, went everywhere together, and when Heidi got the job managing this site . . . Well, you should have seen Sophie. Over the moon she was, thought all her Christmases had come at once to be living on a holiday park. I think she still likes it here, but it's not so much about magicians and playgrounds now, as discos and crushes on the punters or the cabaret acts.' He shook his head despairingly. 'I should have listened to her more, tried to understand that Archie coming along was a bigger change for her than she knew how to handle.' His eyes were wet with tears as they returned to Andee's. 'I just hope it's not too late to put things right,' he murmured brokenly.

Taking a tissue from a box on the table, Andee passed it to him and waited for him to blow his nose. On the face of it, this really was looking as though the girl had run away, but to where, and who she was with now were questions still very much in need of answers.

'Tell me,' she said, deciding to return to the deeper aspects of Sophie's state of mind, 'does Sophie talk about her mother much?'

His sadness was hard to watch as he shook his head. 'Not really, but I know she thinks about her a lot. I have to admit, I do too. She was a lovely woman, good and kind right through to her soul.'

Andee was about to continue when Heidi came in with a teary-eyed, runny-nosed Archie perched on her hip. One glance at him was enough to confirm whose son he was, since he'd taken on his father's features in a way that made him appear strangely old for a baby.

'He needs a bottle,' Heidi said, going to the fridge.

Andee smiled at the child and received a solemn stare in response.

'We were talking about boyfriends just now,' Gavin told Heidi. 'I said you'd know more about that than me.'

Heidi sighed heavily as she planted a baby's bottle into a pan of water to heat. 'She didn't confide in me any more,' she admitted regretfully, 'but I . . .' She glanced awkwardly at her husband. 'I never told you this,' she said, 'but I found some birth pills in her bedroom, a few months back.'

Gavin's eyes closed as if he couldn't take much more.

'I tried talking to her about it,' Heidi said to Andee, 'but she went off on one about me snooping round her room.'

Having no trouble imagining the scene, Andee said, 'Do you know if she took them with her?'

Heidi shook her head, and shrugged. 'They're not here any more, so I suppose she must have.'

'Have you ever seen her with anyone in particular?' Andee asked.

'Not really. She messes about with boys around the camp, the ones here on holiday, and those who work at the club or the office, but I don't think there's anyone special.'

'So you can't think of someone she might have gone off with?'

As Gavin's head came up, Archie started to wail.

'All right, I'm coming,' Heidi soothed, going to pick him up.

'Why would she just run off with someone?' Gavin demanded, as though the concept made no sense at all. 'Especially someone we don't even know.'

Andee watched him, waiting for him to answer his own question.

In the end it was Heidi who said, 'We haven't been keeping a close enough eye on her . . . I know it's my fault. I wasn't expecting motherhood to be quite the way it is. My job's suffering, everything seems to be . . . I keep telling myself to spend more time with Sophie, but it just never seems to work out.'

'You can't blame yourself,' Gavin told her. 'She's more my responsibility than yours. I should have talked to her more, carried on doing things with her the way we used to.'

'We weren't prepared for the baby to take over our lives the way he has,' Heidi added miserably. 'I suppose that sounds naïve, but other parents seem to manage when a second one comes along. There's not always such a big age gap though, is there, and Sophie was used to being the apple of her daddy's eye.'

Having seen several families break down in just this sort of situation, Andee brought them back on track as she said, 'Please think hard about this: has anyone left the site in the past week, casual workers, visitors, members of staff, who she might have gone off with?'

Heidi shook her head. 'We have a changeover of guests on Saturdays, but that would have either been the day before we last saw her, or six days later.'

36

'And the workers?'

'No one's left that I know about, but we can check the staff records.'

Knowing that sort of information would be automatically gathered by the uniforms who were over at the office now, Andee decided she'd probably heard enough for the moment, and began packing away her notebook. 'I know my colleagues carried out what we call an open-door search while they were here,' she said, 'but would you mind if I took a look at Sophie's room before I leave?'

Heidi's eyes were on Gavin as she replied, 'I don't see any reason why not. I mean, we've searched it ourselves looking for something that might tell us where she is, but there's no note, no anything that even gives us a clue.'

Andee got to her feet. 'One last question,' she said, shouldering her bag, 'have you ever suspected Sophie of taking drugs?'

Gavin's face darkened, while Heidi shook her head.

'I'd say booze is more her thing,' Heidi offered. 'She's got totally wasted a few times lately, to a point where she practically passed out when she got home.'

Happy to be spared further detail of that, at least for now, Andee said, 'OK, if you could show me her room?'

Leaving Heidi to cope with Archie, who'd begun screeching at the top of his lungs, Gavin led the way back down the hall to the last door on the left. As she followed Andee was trying to get a sense of the place that might offer some sort of insight into what this family's life was really like. Not that she was particularly doubting anything she'd been told, so far there was no reason to, but the Monroes wouldn't be the first parents to have thrown their daughter out, or worse, only to regret it later.

The first thing Andee noticed on entering Sophie's bedroom was a beautiful poster, actually a portrait, hanging next to the bed of a six- or seven-year-old Sophie with her parents. All three were wearing white, and Sophie's mother, a slight woman with flowing honey-coloured hair and gentle eyes, was holding a guitar while Sophie, in a calf-length lacy dress and white ribbons, was perched on her daddy's knee smiling shyly. The image was so captivating that Andee found herself going towards it.

'Heidi got someone to do it, from a photo,' Gavin told her gruffly.

'It's lovely,' Andee murmured, noting the sweet freckles on Sophie's nose and the way one of her hands was curling into Gavin's.

'This is Jilly's guitar,' Gavin said, picking it up from beside the bed. 'Jilly is Sophie's mother. I keep trying to get Sophie to take up her lessons again, but she won't. It's a shame, because she used to show a lot of promise.'

'And the CDs?' Andee enquired, noticing a small bookcase full of them.

Swallowing, he said, 'They're mostly of me and Jilly, back in the day. Some have got Sophie singing with us, or on her own. We used to have a bit of fun listening to them, but I can't seem to get her interested any more.'

Andee continued to look around. On the whole, the room was much like any other fourteen-year-old girl's, with posters of boy bands cluttering up the walls, mostly of Westlife, Andee noted, which seemed curious given her age. Perhaps her mother had been a fan. A couple of shelves were loaded with semi-retired soft toys, while untidy piles of clothing and shoes were scattered about the floor, and a hanging rail acted as a wardrobe. The dressing table was littered with cheap cosmetics, gaudy jewellery, various hair accessories and a bag of bird food.

A glance at the window showed a feeder hanging just outside.

On the single bed fairy lights were trailed round the headrail and furry cushions lined up against the wall, while a limp rag doll with tatty clothes and red felt cheeks was smiling up from the pillows. For some reason it made Andee feel sad. Except it wasn't just the doll that was affecting her, it was the room itself, she realised, though she couldn't quite say why. She wondered what secrets were harboured within these walls, what scenes they had witnessed, what loneliness, as this young girl struggled to accept that her mother was never coming back. And there had been a struggle, Andee was in no doubt about that.

Going to the window she pulled back the nets and looked out on to the campsite's entrance. Since the room was on ground level she could see how easy it would be to climb in and out without anyone hearing, especially if they were in the kitchen at the back of the house.

She turned to Gavin, who was rummaging in a drawer.

'I can't find any pictures of her,' he declared sadly. 'Nothing here apart from underwear and sweet wrappers and stuff. Oh hang on, what's this?' and pulling out a four-strip from a photo booth he regarded it bleakly. 'That's her all over,' he murmured as he gazed down at it.

Going to look, Andee saw a teenage girl with the same pretty face as in her school photo, languid violet-blue eyes, a full-lipped mouth, but in these shots her silky blonde hair was streaked with purple, as though she'd deliberately tried to spoil it. In place of the sweetest of smiles were various scowls and gestures that Andee guessed were meant to be funny, or perhaps offensive.

'Can I keep these?' she asked, as Gavin let the strip go.

Still looking down at them, he said, 'I don't see why not. I wouldn't want you putting them on the telly or anything, though. She wasn't like that really, or she never used to be.'

'It's OK, we won't do anything without your consent.' There was no point telling him the media wouldn't be interested at this stage, not when the case had all the hallmarks of a stroppy teenager trying to frighten her parents into giving her some attention.

So why were her insides knotting with the sense that there was more to this than she was seeing right now?

You should step back from it, a voice inside was urging. *Don't do this to yourself. Let someone else take it on.*

Casting a last look around the room, she thanked Gavin, told him she'd be in touch soon and returned to her car. For several moments she sat motionlessly at the wheel staring at Sophie's window, imagining her pouring seed into the feeder and watching the birds come and go. Or clambering in and out in the moonlight. Or closing the curtains to shield herself from the rest of the world.

In the end she took out her Airwave and went through to Barry. 'Where are you?' she asked.

'Just leaving the clubhouse. How did it go with the parents?'

'I'm worried,' she admitted. 'Did you know the mother died four years ago?'

'Yes, they told me. Is it relevant?'

'It could be. What have you come up with over there?'

'Nothing conclusive. No staff, casual or otherwise, have left during the past month. The changeover of visitors could prove a nightmare to follow up, but the residency manager is getting the records together.'

'Did anyone see her that Sunday night?'

'Several people are claiming to have. Apparently she was at the Entertainment Centre until quite late, which puts her there after the row with her parents. We haven't found anyone yet who's heard from her since.'

'Did anyone see her leave?'

'Not that we've come across, but there are still a lot of people to interview.'

'Sure. Do you know if she mentioned the row with her parents to anyone?'

'Not that we've come across.'

'Drugs? Sex?'

'Bit early in the day,' he responded, 'but if you insist.'

Andee rolled her eyes.

'Nothing significant on the first, mentions of the second, if we're to take gossip as gospel.'

Since plenty of girls Sophie's age were sexually

41

active there was no reason why she wouldn't be, especially in light of the birth pills. It saddened Andee to think that Sophie might have been using promiscuity to reclaim the attention she'd lost from her father, or to blot out the pain and loneliness of losing her mother. 'If she is sexually active it makes her high risk,' she declared. 'She was on the pill, apparently, but no steady boyfriend, unless you've come across one.'

'No one so far.'

'OK, I have to get back to the station. I'm already late for Gould. If nothing's changed between now and five I'll meet you at the friend's house? You can text me the address.'

'You mean Estelle Morris? Easier said than done. She's gone up to Bristol for the night with her mother, back sometime tomorrow.'

'OK, we'll talk to her then. Meantime I'm going to try to get this reclassified as high risk,' and after ending the connection, she continued to stare at the window to Sophie's room. From this angle the nets were as impenetrable as the walls either side of them, making the truth of how, why, when she'd left, as elusive as the secrets locked inside her young girl's heart.

Where are you? she whispered silently, feeling the chill echo of the words rising like ghouls from the darkest caves of the past. *Where did you go? Who are you with?*

Please God let her be somewhere safe, because the alternative wasn't one Andee was prepared to contemplate, not when she knew what hell it could bring.

Chapter Two

Kasia Domanski was loving living in England. Just about everything thrilled her about it: from the people, to the colours, to the luxury of shopping for anything she wanted, to the funny traditions such as driving on the left and cricket. She even enjoyed the climate, though so much rain and gloom had made her sad at first; the summers in her country were much longer and hotter than they were here, with the exception of this one, which was the best she'd known since arriving.

Kasia was a small, slender woman, only five feet two, weighing fifty-one kilos, with wispy blonde hair, sky-blue eyes and a pretty mouth that always seemed about to quirk into a smile. On her next birthday she was going to celebrate becoming thirty and now that she had so many friends in England she was planning to throw a splendid party.

She knew that not all her fellow countrymen had settled in as well as she had, but it hadn't always been easy for her either. When she'd first arrived, five years ago, she and her children, three-year-old Ania (now eight) and one-year-old Anton (now six) had shared a small flat with her sister in the northern zone of Kesterly's Temple Fields estate. It was an area fraught with racial tensions and kids who hung around in gangs, either trying to sell other kids drugs or settling scores with their rivals. Speaking English very well, she'd often wished she didn't understand the names she was called, and it was awful the way some people had spat at her in the street for scrounging off the state or taking jobs from the locals. The truth was she'd never once gone to the government for a handout. She'd come into the country with enough money to get her through the first weeks without having to worry, and during that time her sister, Olenka, who was a nurse at the Greensleeves Care Home close to Kesterly seafront, had helped her to secure a position there that had been vacant for several months.

Those first two years had been so terrible that hardly a day had gone by when Kasia hadn't longed for her mother, and her home in the valley of islands in the south of Poland. Indeed, she would have returned were it not for the fact that she had more to fear there than she did in England. In her country they didn't have the kind of refuges that existed in just about every town in the UK to protect women and children from violent men, and Kasia had desperately needed that protection. Her husband, the children's father, had beaten them so regularly and so badly that in the end, the only way to escape him and his wretched alcoholism had been to leave. With Olenka already in England it had been decided Kasia must join her, so her parents, who were by no means well off, had used up all their savings to send her.

Kasia had paid them back long ago, and she continued to send money; their family home in the mountains now had an indoor toilet instead of a wooden box at the side of the house. Her mother could even pay for help harvesting the raspberries that grew on the slope of their hill, and her father had bought a reconditioned tractor. Despite welcoming these new luxuries, they still insisted Kasia should spend her money on the children. It was hard for them to comprehend that she had enough these days to make sure none of them went without. She was even able to buy small gifts for the old folk in the care home when their name days came round. They seemed to enjoy this Polish tradition that most had never come across before.

Though she and Olenka both still worked at the home, they now lived on the much friendlier Waverley estate, Olenka in a spacious apartment over the newsagent's on Seldon Rise, and Kasia in a smart terraced house with a bay window and climbing wisteria on Patch Elm Lane that she and Tomasz rented from his employers.

Tomasz. His name alone could cause ripples of happiness to float up from her heart and form in a smile. He was her handsome, talented, generous, gentle bear of a partner who stood over six feet tall, had muscles as hard as the rocks in Kesterly bay and eyes that made her melt every time she looked into them. They'd met three years ago when he'd come to Greensleeves to sort out a plumbing problem, and if it hadn't been love at first sight then Kasia didn't know what was.

She'd soon discovered that the whole world loved Tomasz once they got to know him; it was hard not to when he was so full of humour and kindness and always made time for someone in need. Like Kasia he'd been in England for two years by the time they met, and also like her, he still sent money home to his mother.

It wasn't long after they'd first got together that Tomasz's fortunes had taken an amazingly happy turn. The Poynters, who owned two of Perryman Cove's biggest caravan parks and several other businesses besides, had put him in charge of all their maintenance needs. Not only that, they'd guaranteed him at least two performances a week during high season at the Blue Ocean Entertainment Centre. Since Tomasz loved to sing almost as much as he loved to laugh he'd leapt at the opportunity, and these days, having learned just about every English popular song in existence, he often topped the bill during the summer months.

Now, as she hurried in through the gate of their caramel-coloured house with its pots of topiary each side of the porch and colourful stained-glass panel in the front door, she was rummaging in her bag for keys while talking to Tomasz on the phone.

'So where are you now?' she was asking, pushing open the door and stooping to pick up the mail. How she adored this place with its rich red wall-to-wall carpets, dishwasher in the kitchen, family photographs on the walls and feeling of safety.

'I've just left Blue Ocean,' he replied. 'By the way, the police were there today asking about Sophie Monroe.'

Kasia frowned. 'Do you mean Heidi and Gavin's daughter? What about her?'

'Apparently she's gone missing.'

Kasia stopped in her tracks. 'Missing?' All kinds of terrible images were flashing through her mind.

'That's what's being said. I don't know the

details of it yet, only that the police have been asking everyone if they saw her last Sunday night.'

'And did you see her?'

'Not that I can remember, but the cabaret room was full so she could have been around without me noticing.'

Closing the front door, Kasia started along the hall, pushing shut the understairs cupboard as she went. 'Is that the last time anyone saw her? Eight days ago?'

'I think so. Glyn reckons she had some kind of bust-up with her parents and now she's paying them back by hiding out somewhere.' Glyn was Olenka's live-in partner and head chef at Blue Ocean Park.

'That's terrible if it's true,' Kasia murmured. 'It's terrible anyway. Heidi and Gavin must be so worried. Have you seen them?'

'Not today. Ewan the deputy manager was running things, as usual.'

As she entered the narrow kitchen Kasia dropped her bag on a worktop and cast a quick look through the mail. 'I wonder if I should call Heidi,' she murmured. 'I don't suppose there's anything I can do, but I want her to know that we care.'

'I expect all her friends are calling,' Tomasz replied, 'but I'm going back there later. If I see her, or Gavin, I'll make sure they know we'll be happy to help if we can.'

'OK. Please do that. Now, what time should we expect you home?'

'Probably around seven. Are the children in this evening?'

Kasia consulted the whiteboard that dominated the wall over the small table they used for breakfast.

It charted everyone's commitments for the week, though as school was out it wasn't as cluttered as usual. 'Ania's got dance at six and Anton's starting his karate lessons at seven.'

'Of course, and I promised to be home in time to take him. OK, I should ring off now, I'm just turning into Seaview Park.'

'Did you remember to call your mother today?'

He laughed. 'Do you think I would dare to forget her birthday? She was happy to tell me what a terrible son I am and she said thank you for the perfume and chocolates.'

Knowing the thanks would have been only for him, since his mother was a devout Catholic who disapproved of her only son's relationship with a married woman, Kasia said, 'I'm glad they arrived in time.'

'They did. Now I really must go. Call if you need anything, otherwise I'll see you before seven.'

After ringing off Kasia poured herself a cold drink and ran upstairs to slip out of her uniform before taking a shower. Olenka, whose shift at the care home didn't start until eight this evening, was minding the children, and since she wasn't due to bring them home for another half an hour there would hopefully be time to check emails before chaos broke out.

However, when Kasia went into the spare room where Tomasz had set up their computer she found, to her confusion, that it wasn't there.

'Our computer has disappeared,' she told Tomasz when she got through to his mobile.

'What?' he cried. Then, seeming to connect with her words, he laughed. 'Sorry, I forgot to tell you. I took it in this morning to get everything transferred on to a new laptop. I thought it was time we upgraded.'

Having no argument with that since they'd been discussing it for weeks, she said, 'So when do we get the new one?'

'Hopefully today. I'll call into Curry's on my way home to see if it's ready.'

'OK. I hope you're in the mood for zrazy tonight?'

His sigh was all pleasure. *'Kochanie,* I am always in the mood for zrazy – with kasha on the side?'

Since it sounded very like her name, she murmured teasingly, 'You are making this sound very indecent.'

Laughing, he said, 'I will save my reply for when we are alone.'

Kasia was still smiling to herself a few minutes later when Olenka let herself in downstairs with the children.

After dishing out kisses, admiring Ania's new hairslide, cowering from Anton's scary dinosaur and cuddling her eighteen-month-old nephew, Felix, Kasia opened the back door for them to go and build castles in the sandbox Tomasz had created next to the playhouse.

As they settled she turned to her sister, and speaking in Polish, said, 'Did you hear about Sophie Monroe?'

Glancing up from the tea she was making, Olenka said, 'You mean that she's disappeared?' At five foot four Olenka was taller, plumper and darker than Kasia, and being three years older and two longer in Britain she considered herself more sophisticated and streetwise. 'I reckon Glyn's right, she's hiding out somewhere to try and scare her parents.'

Sighing, Kasia said, 'It would be a cruel thing to do, but let's hope that's all it is.'

Slicing through a lemon, Olenka dropped a wedge into each mug and handed one to Kasia. 'It's Heidi I feel sorry for,' she commented. 'She's never done anything to deserve all the crap that girl gives her.'

Since she knew very little about the family, Kasia merely shook her head sadly.

'From what I hear,' Olenka continued, 'she's been throwing herself at half the blokes who come to the camp. It doesn't matter whether they work there or are just visiting . . . Some of the campers have complained, apparently. Wouldn't you if she was coming on to your husband or son?'

Accepting that she wouldn't like it very much, Kasia said, 'She's still quite young and probably doesn't understand half of what she's doing. We didn't when we were her age.'

Olenka cast her a look.

'Well, we didn't,' Kasia insisted. 'OK, we lived in a very different world to Sophie's, but you must remember what it was like when the hormones started to change, and how mad we suddenly were about boys.'

'That might be true, but we didn't do anything about it, unless you're telling me you did.'

'Of course not. I'm just saying that girls Sophie's age aren't always aware of how they're coming across. Anyway, let's change the subject – would you and Glyn like to eat with us this evening? There's plenty here.'

Olenka watched her unwrapping the steaks. 'If you're making zrazy it always tastes better the next day,' she commented.

'I know, but I'm serving it tonight.'

'I see you have the best cuts.'

Reaching for a rolling pin, Kasia said, 'Would you like to bash them, help get rid of some of whatever's eating you?'

Olenka had to smile. 'OK, I'm jealous. Not that I'd swap Glyn for Tomasz, or maybe I would . . . No, no, I'm not serious, it's just the way Tomasz has got in with the Poynters . . . You're living like royalty, you two.'

Kasia gasped a laugh. 'I hardly think a terraced house in Waverley compares to Buckingham Palace, and it's not even as if we own it. We pay rent, the same as you, and the reason Tomasz earns more than Glyn is because he has more than one job. You should get Glyn to turn himself into a cabaret act as well.'

Olenka's eyes danced. 'I promise you, he wouldn't be allowed to demonstrate his other skills in public, and may the good Lord save us from his singing.'

Giving her a playful nudge, Kasia gestured for her to get started on the pounding as she reached for the phone.

'Hi, it's me,' Tomasz told her. 'I've just had a call from Curry's; apparently the computer won't be ready until tomorrow, and the kitchen at Seaview's lost power. I've no idea how long it'll take to sort, but I don't think I'm going to be home by seven. Is Anton there so I can speak to him?'

Used to the unscheduled demands on his time, Kasia called out to her son. 'Any more news on Sophie Monroe?' she asked as they waited for the boy to amble up the garden.

'I don't know, I'm not at Blue Ocean, but Jimmy

51

Poynter rang just now. He's worried about what it'll do for business if she doesn't show up soon, especially if it goes public. The campers won't like having the police crawling all over the place.'

Kasia's eyebrows rose. 'I think they'd like it a lot less if they found out something had happened to the girl and no one had bothered to look for her. Anyway, here's Anton,' and planting a kiss on her son's unruly dark hair she passed him the phone.

'Sorry, Andee, it just can't happen.'

Detective Inspector Terence Gould was shaking his head with a regret that Andee understood, but was still finding hard to accept. 'You know as well as I do that we don't have the resources to start running a wild goose chase for a fourteen-year-old who took money, a computer, mobile phone . . .'

'Which hasn't been used since last Wednesday,' Andee interrupted.

'But it has been used, to tell her father she's with friends . . .'

'Who she failed to name. What if someone's forced her to send those messages?'

His frown deepened. 'Is there any evidence of that?'

'No, but frankly I find it odd that she's suddenly cut contact.'

'With her parents, maybe, but you haven't spoken to the best friend yet.'

'We've checked with the service provider. The phone hasn't been used at all since last Wednesday.'

'So she's got herself a pay as you go. You know how savvy kids are these days.'

'She hasn't been on any of the social media sites

either, or not that we've found so far, and she was a regular Facebook user up to a week ago.'

His eyes held hers in a level gaze. 'Has she threatened suicide in any of her postings? Is there any suggestion of stalking, bullying, trolling, grooming?'

'OK, none of the above, but that doesn't mean we should rule them out.'

'You need to speak to the best friend. What's her name?'

'Estelle Morris, and Barry Britten's already spoken to her on the phone. She swears she doesn't know where Sophie is.'

His eyebrows rose incredulously. 'And you're taking her word for it?'

Andee stared at him hard, knowing it was a reasonable point. 'Let me tell you why this case should be categorised as high risk,' she said forcefully. 'It's extremely likely she's sexually active. At fourteen that makes her . . .'

'Andee, you know what it makes her, a bloody nuisance, exactly like half the other fourteen-year-old girls out there . . .'

'Who haven't been missing from home for over a week. What if she went off with someone who was staying at the campsite and now he's holding her somewhere?'

'Unless you tell me differently there's nothing to say that's happened.'

'Nothing *yet*.'

'When there is, we'll review the situation, until then let uniform deal with it, while you get back to the burglaries on Wermers Road. We've got Wickes on the list now, Debenhams, Curry's . . .'

'How can stolen electricals be more important than a missing girl?' Andee cried angrily.

His jaw tightened, reminding her that he didn't appreciate insubordination, even from her. 'We need to know how the hell anyone's getting this stuff out of the stores undetected,' he continued, as if the offence hadn't occurred. 'It's looking very like we have a crime syndicate operating on our patch, and if we have we need to let them know they're not welcome. So now, do me a favour, make them a priority and leave the missing girl to the boys in blue.'

Andee held her ground. 'I'm sorry, I can't do that,' she stated boldly.

His face darkened. 'That wasn't a request.'

'I realise that, but, sir, there's more to this . . .'

'Andee, you're forcing me to say things I'd really rather not.' Ignoring her challenging look, he went on, 'OK, we both know you can't see straight where missing girls are concerned.'

Though her face tightened she said nothing. He continued, not unkindly, 'You're letting your own experiences colour your judgement, but no matter what shade you paint it, Andee, finding that girl isn't going to bring your sister back.'

Andee's heart caught on a beat. He was right, of course, but that wasn't what this was about.

'Burglaries,' he said quietly. 'Make some arrests. Show us country bumpkins what you girls from the Met are made of.'

Though she knew it was meant to be a self-deprecating joke to defuse the moment, she couldn't quite manage a smile as she left his office and returned to her desk.

'I get the feeling it didn't go well,' Leo Johnson commented, looking up from his computer. He was a striking young man with a shock of wiry red hair, a wrestler's physique and an enthusiasm for his job that could be as entertaining as it was sometimes annoying. However, he was certainly the DC she preferred to work with, along with Jemma Payne, a newer recruit, though she had to admit she was privileged to be part of the entire Kesterly CID team. They watched each other's backs in a way she hadn't experienced with the Met, willingly weighed in on cases when further help was needed, and stood together whenever the proverbial hit the fan.

Sinking into her chair, she sighed heavily.

'For what it's worth, I'm backing your instincts,' Leo told her.

Groaning in frustration she let her head fall into her hands.

Since it was the end of the day most desks in the main office were empty. There were just a couple of other DCs poring over a map spread out between them, and an admin assistant talking to someone on the phone.

She turned to Leo. 'Do you know about my sister?' she asked bluntly.

His hands stopped on the keyboard.

Of course he did. It had no doubt been the first bite of gossip to be chewed over when news had reached Kesterly CID that Andee Lawrence was being appointed as one of the new detective sergeants. And the reason they'd know her name was, in part, because her father's family were from Kesterly, though he'd been a detective chief super-intendent with the Met at the time Penny had disappeared. Those terrible days of searching, praying, constantly fearing the worst might have been pre-email, pre-computers as they knew them now, but stories of that time, and what had happened to her father as a result, had spread round the force as fast as any virus without cyber assistance.

And like a grisly sort of heirloom they reverberated down the years.

'Anything from social services?' Andee asked, returning to the Sophie Monroe case.

'Still waiting,' Leo replied.

Unsurprised by that, since social services were rarely speedy, she got to her feet. 'OK, talk to CAIT,' she said, referring to the Child Abuse Investigation Team, 'find out if they've had any dealings with the Monroe family. I'm going home,' and grabbing her bag and phone she swept out of the office.

'On my way,' she told her mother's voicemail as she steered her car from the station car park on to the leafy quadrant where Kesterly Police HQ was located. A drink at the Melvilles' might be just what she needed this evening. Better still would be a drink with Graeme, and a whole night with him would be best of all, but that wasn't going to happen until Wednesday at the earliest.

Would she really go through with it? She'd never slept with anyone but Martin.

Slowing up behind the tourist train on Kesterly seafront, she found herself wondering what her father would advise were she able to discuss the Sophie Monroe case with him. In a way she was glad she couldn't, since she knew only too well how deeply the subject would distress him. It was having much the same effect on her with all the memories it was bringing back, though this wasn't the first time she'd been involved in a misper since joining the force. She could handle it, she felt sure of that, even though this was the first case of a missing fourteen-year-old girl to come her way.

Penny had been only thirteen the first time she'd taken off without a word. They'd been living in Chiswick then, where they'd always lived from the time Andee was born, though not in the same house. They'd moved to the four-bedroomed semi, just off the high street, a year after her father's promotion to DCS, which was about a year before all the problems began.

Andee understood, now it was too late, that her sister had started to suffer from depression almost as soon as she'd hit puberty. The trouble was, as a family they were always so busy – her father with his job, her mother with her small estate agency, Andee, who was two years older, with studying, boys, socialising, all the usual mid-teen stuff – that Penny's change of behaviour, if it was noticed at all, was invariably put down to 'a phase she was going through'.

Andee's memories of Penny back then were always darkened by the way she, Andee, used to yell at her for crashing into her room without knocking, or for her constant complaining and whining.

'What do you mean you're not pretty?' she used to snap at her. 'Just because you've got a few spots doesn't mean you're ugly. Get over yourself, will you, and go and annoy someone else.'

Penny would return to her room, but then she'd come back again, saying something like, 'I wish I was as clever as you. I'll never be good enough to go to uni.' Or, 'Mum and Dad love you the best,

I can tell.' Or, 'I don't have any friends. Nobody likes me.'

And Andee would shoot back with, 'Stop feeling so bloody sorry for yourself and grow up.' Or, 'I don't have time for all your crap, so get out of my way.'

Andee's insides still churned with shame when she recalled how cruel and impatient she'd been with her sister, and the pain of it had burned deeper with time. She'd never stopped tormenting herself with the private tears Penny must have shed over the way no one would listen to her. Her fragile young heart must have fractured into thousands of pieces under the strain of longing to be understood. There was nothing Andee wouldn't give for the chance to make it up to her, to be able to tell her how pretty, intelligent, loved and popular she was, to make her the very centre of her world, but fate, God, whatever it was, had never allowed it.

The first time Penny stayed out all night, causing her parents to frantically ring around all her friends, even to go out searching the streets into the early hours, she'd shown up again the next morning saying she'd been at Mia's, a recent arrival at the school whom she was getting to know. The second time, a few weeks later, there was less of a fuss and afterwards it hadn't taken the family long to get caught up in their hectic lives again. Eventually they'd stopped worrying when Penny went off in 'one of her funks'. They assumed she was at Mandy's, or Kelly's, or Mia's, and because she always came back after a night or two no one ever checked.

Then one day she didn't come back. She'd been

gone for an entire weekend by the time Andee and her parents began ringing everyone they knew, searching the streets, the local shops, refuges and hospitals, but they'd found no sign of her. The police were alerted, neighbours' gardens were trawled, everyone was questioned, but no one could throw any light on where she might be.

It was impossible for Andee to think of that time, even now, without feeling the same surging panic and fear; however, over the years, she'd learned to quickly bury it and move on. She knew that Sophie's disappearance was going to make this emotional control more difficult if she didn't show up soon.

Worse though, far, far worse than not knowing where Penny might be, was the letter that had turned up after she'd been gone for almost a fortnight, bearing a local postmark. Andee knew that in all her life she would never again find anything so painful to read.

Dear Mum and Dad, I probably ought to say sorry for leaving the way I have, but maybe you already don't mind very much that I'm not around any more, so instead I'll say sorry for always being such a disappointment to you. I know Dad wanted a son when I was born, so I guess I've been a let-down to him from the start, and I don't blame him for always loving Andee the most because she's much nicer-looking than I am and likes sports, the same as him, and is really clever so it stands to reason that he'd be really proud of her. I know I shouldn't say this, but sometimes I hate her for being so much better than I am at everything. No one ever seems to notice me when she's in the room. It's like I become invisible and I know she wishes I would go away. So that's what I'm going to do.

I don't know what else to say, except sorry again. I expect you'll all be much happier without me. Please tell Andee she can have whatever she likes of mine, although I don't expect she'll want anything at all.

Your daughter, Penny

The shock, the fear and grief that ripped through the family was only surpassed by the desperate need to find her. More police were drafted in; friends, neighbours, even strangers from far and wide came to join in the search. It was all over the news for weeks, but Penny was never found.

Andee remembered her mother being sedated throughout that time, while Andee herself had wanted to die rather than live with the fear of what might be happening to her sister. The question she kept asking herself, that everyone was asking themselves but never spoke aloud was, *had Penny committed suicide? Or was she still out there somewhere waiting, needing to be convinced she was loved?*

No body was ever found, and they never received another letter.

The disappearance had proved the beginning of the end for her father. Not knowing what had happened to his daughter tore him to pieces, over and over, ceaselessly. That she hadn't believed he loved her when he had, more than his own life, wasn't possible for him to deal with. He'd never had a favourite, he swore it, but how could he tell Penny that if she didn't come back?

It soon became clear that he was finding it increasingly difficult to focus. The sense of despair, shame and guilt was so consuming that he could hardly relate to anyone, either at home or at work. In his heart and in reality he was still looking for her. Everywhere they went his eyes were searching faces, doorways, alleyways, desperate for a glimpse of his girl. Within a year he'd become a shell of the man they used to know. Though he went through the motions of his everyday life at work, at home it was obvious that he was struggling to carry on the pretence. Hardest of all, it seemed, was sharing any sort of closeness with Andee. It was as though he was afraid Penny might be watching, ready to accuse him again of loving his elder daughter more. So the easy banter that had always existed between them had fallen into silence. They no longer joked and bickered over issues as they came up on the news, he stopped asking how she was doing at school, and he almost never laughed.

It was two years after the dreaded note had arrived that the cottage next to his parents in Kesterly came up for sale. After discussing it with Andee and Maureen, he put in for early retirement and moved the family to the West Country. Though Andee knew that her parents shared her fear that Penny would come back and find them gone, like them she was also glad to be out of the house that Penny would always haunt.

However, being in Kesterly wasn't any easier for her. In some ways it was worse, since every corner she turned, everywhere she looked, every scent that carried on the breeze seemed to hold a memory of Penny. She could see her leaping up as she found a crab in a rock pool; laughing her head off as she trotted along the sands on a donkey; coming up from the waves gulping for air as she learned to surf. It wasn't the same for her parents;

they hadn't spent their summers here, so for them it was something of a fresh start.

Even so Penny was always there. She was the tragic hole in their lives, the one that could never be bridged until she was found; the one they always had to step around to find one another.

Penny, Penny, Penny. The cry rose silently, inextinguishably from their very existence.

Though Andee completed sixth-form college in Kesterly, as soon as it was over she returned to London to begin her police training. She knew it was crazy even to think this might be a way to find Penny, but having no real closure where her sister was concerned was at the very centre of who she was back then. Not only that, she'd felt a burning need to try to restore the connection with her father that she so desperately missed. Maybe becoming a detective would go some way towards encouraging him to take an interest in life again.

To a small degree it had worked. Certainly he'd stopped passing the phone straight to her mother whenever she rang, and during her visits he would invariably sit quietly listening as she told Maureen about street situations she became embroiled in, or serious cases she was helping to solve. The biggest breakthrough came when she was seconded to CID during her second year in uniform. Her father began asking questions, even occasionally offered advice, though before long his conscience almost always seemed to suck him back into his shell, as though he could feel Penny watching with accusing eyes.

In spite of his inner torment he'd seemed proud when Andee had taken the detective's course at Hendon and officially made it into CID. 'Just don't go getting yourself promoted out of policing into politicking,' he'd cautioned. 'It was what happened to me, and I always regretted it.'

'Everyone says you were one of the best DCSs,' she told him, truthfully.

Though he'd cocked a dubious eyebrow, he'd seemed pleased by the compliment, and as she settled into her new role as a DC she could tell that he was gradually bringing himself to enjoy a second career through her. And he continued to do so all through her twenties and into her thirties, approving or disapproving all the new techniques and procedures, or chuckling at the gossip about old colleagues, or puzzling over the complications of ongoing cases. It wasn't that he was always on the phone, or urging her to come to Kesterly, he simply waited for her to contact him and when she did it was as though he had new air in his lungs, new blood running through his tired veins.

She never troubled him with the mispers. She handled them alone and always hoped, prayed, that one of them would somehow lead her to Penny.

They never had.

Her father's greatest joy, her mother's too, was without question her children when they came along. She'd given birth to Luke, her eldest, during her time on the beat, and Alayna, the darling of everyone's heart, two years later. Her parents quite simply adored them and were never happier than when they came to stay for the summer, just as she, Penny and Frank used to stay with their grandparents when they were young.

It was at her father's suggestion that Andee had taken her sergeant's exam, a little over two years ago. Though she'd passed the board (he'd decided, jokingly, to take all the credit), there had been no positions available to apply for at the time unless she'd wanted to move out of London, which she hadn't, then, so she'd had no choice but to continue as a DC.

She'd still been a DC eight months later when Martin, the father of her children and her partner of almost twenty years, since sixth-form college in fact, had decided he'd had enough and left.

Three months later her father suffered a massive coronary and didn't survive.

He'd died without ever knowing what had happened to Penny.

This was a truth Andee had never been able to bear.

More than a year after his passing, Andee was still, in a very private sense, suffering terribly. It was hard to say who she missed most, him or Martin, though she guessed it had to be Martin, considering what a major role he'd always played in her and the children's lives. In truth, he still did, at least in the children's, since they saw him often, and during major family events it was as though they were all still a family. Whether he'd ever realised how painful she found those occasions she had no idea since she'd never told him, and he'd never asked. They simply went through the motions, as though they were friends used to being around one another, and when it came time to say goodbye they'd hug and promise to call soon. They always did, of course, since there was always something to discuss about the children, but that was as far as it went. She didn't want to hear him repeat his reasons for leaving – she'd heard them at the time and didn't need to have it rubbed in. Over the years, while running the home and taking care of the children, he'd built up a highly successful Internet security company, and when the US government had got in touch to offer him a contract in Baghdad he'd taken it. Just like that. It was his time, he'd said, so he wasn't going to turn it down. He'd only be gone for three months, four at the most, and perhaps they should use the time apart as a trial separation. That had come as an even bigger shock than the job offer. She hadn't understood why they needed a trial separation when as far as she was concerned they were happy together.

He'd always sworn there was no one else, but she was never sure she believed him. She only knew that without her cousin Frank and his wife, Jane, she'd never have been able to cope with the children and her job during the months that Martin was away. After his return it had become easier, though he hadn't moved back into the house, he'd rented a flat in the next street so he was always on hand for the children.

A part of her had longed for him to come home, at times had nearly begged him to, but her pride had never allowed it. After all, if it was what he wanted he'd ask, and the reason he didn't ask was because he was clearly perfectly happy with the way things were. He didn't even object when she applied for the detective sergeant's job in Kesterly, having decided she couldn't carry on leaving her mother to cope on her own.

So now, here she was, living in her grandparents' cottage that had become part of the bigger property her parents had created by knocking the two places into one after her grandparents had passed. Luke was a student at the same sixth-form college she and Martin had attended, while Alayna was at Kesterly High. Since Martin's parents were in Westleigh, on the south side of town, and his sister, brother-in-law and their daughter were in Mulgrove, one of the outlying villages, they had plenty of family around, and it hadn't taken either Luke or Alayna much time at all to make a whole host of new friends. They were exactly like their father in that respect, warm, open, gregarious and invariably the life and soul.

How blessed she was in them both, but how hard it could be when they reminded her of him the most.

She was over it now though, thank God. She'd finally moved on and how much better she felt for it.

From the seafront it took no more than twenty minutes to drive up on to the northerly headland, where the hamlet of Bourne Hollow formed an irregular bowl of craggy rocks and green pastures with just two dozen dwellings, a pub, and a small convenience store-cum-café at its heart. It was such a picturesque little spot that it was often overrun by tourists and hikers, many of whom her mother got chatting to while out tending to the flowering pots around the green. On a clear day, such as today, it was possible to climb up to Seaman's Spit, a monument at the top of the hollow, and see as far as South Wales in one direction, and Exmoor in another.

As Andee pulled up outside Briar Lodge, the name her parents had given to their extended home, she was about to get out of the car when Leo came through on her Airwave.

'CAIT have no record of Sophie Monroe,' he told her, 'and I've just heard back from social services. Apparently she hasn't crossed their paths either.'

'OK,' Andee replied, taking a moment to process it. On the one hand it suggested the girl had come to no harm in the home or at school; however, way too much abuse went undetected for initial inquiries to be conclusive. 'Check that backgrounds are being run on both parents,' she instructed, 'and on the caravan site, in case something's gone on there in the past that might be relevant.'

'Already happening.'

'Good. I take it you're still at the office.'

'Yep.'

'Has Gould left yet?'

'Nope.'

'OK, best try to keep him happy, so see if you can dig up something about these robberies. Better still, I'll get a couple of the other DCs to go over to Wermers Road in the morning to take statements. I want you free to come with me.'

'Oh, yippee! And we would be going where?'

'Probably back to Blue Ocean with Barry and the uniforms.'

'Sounds like a sixties pop band.'

Smiling, she said, 'Run those checks, then haul yourself out of there and get a life.'

'But what would I do with it if I found one?'

'Your problem,' and ending the connection she got out of the car in time to wave to a young couple who'd recently moved into one of the cottages next to the shop, as they strolled across the green towards the Smugglers.

'Hey everyone, I'm home,' she called out as she stepped in through the rose-covered front porch.

Receiving no reply she crossed the hall with its wood-panelled walls and colourful paintings of Kesterly Bay, mostly done by her father, and pushed open the kitchen door to find her mother standing behind the table looking so troubled that panic hit Andee like a blow.

'What is it?' she demanded. 'Where are the children?'

'They're upstairs,' Maureen Lawrence hastily replied, her attractive features showing more concern for her daughter now than for whatever had upset her. 'I'm sorry, I didn't mean to scare you. It's . . .'

'Is it Martin?' Andee cut in, feeling suddenly sick.

'No, no, it's his father.'

'Dougie?' Andee could already feel herself backing away from it.

Her mother nodded. 'Carol just rang. He had a stroke this morning . . .'

Andee became very still. 'Please don't tell me,' she murmured, her eyes searching her mother's – and finding the answer she didn't want to hear she put a hand to her head. 'He didn't make it, did he?' she whispered, realising she had to have it spelled out.

Maureen took Andee by the shoulders and drew her into an embrace, but she was the one shaking.

'Ssh, it'll be all right,' Andee whispered softly, though why she would say that when obviously it wouldn't she had no idea. 'Have you told the children?'

'Yes. They're very upset. I said I'd take them over to see Carol when you got home.'

'Of course.' Andee glanced along the hall at the sound of both children coming down the stairs.

'Oh Mum,' Alayna wailed, pushing past her brother to get to Andee. 'I can't bear it, it's so awful. Poor Grandma Carol, she's going to miss him so much.'

Clasping her tightly, Andee held out her other arm for Luke. He was taller than her now, with a typical sportman's physique, and was becoming so like his father in looks and mannerisms that it could sometimes take her breath away. The only way he resembled her was with his thick dark curly hair.

'Are you OK?' she asked softly, as he wrapped his arms around her and Alayna.

He nodded, but she could tell he'd been crying.

'Dad's on his way,' Alayna said, looking up. She was her own version of Martin, with the same stunning blue eyes, long dark lashes and captivating smile. She even had his tousled blonde hair, though hers tumbled halfway down her back while his only infrequently got below his collar.

'Have you spoken to him?' Andee asked.

'Not yet,' Luke replied, going to hug his grandma, typically making sure she didn't feel left out. 'I expect he'll call when he gets to Heathrow.'

'Where's he coming from, do you know?'

'Cyprus, I think. It's where he was yesterday, on his way to Beirut.'

Of course, Beirut, or Damascus, or Cairo, anywhere his clients sent him to help set up the security system he'd devised.

'I'll make some tea,' Maureen said, going to the kettle. 'You've probably had a difficult enough day . . .'

'It's been fine,' Andee interrupted, taking Alayna's new bra out of her bag and handing it over. Never in a million years would she tell her mother about Sophie Monroe now. With any luck Sophie would turn up before anything went public, so Maureen wouldn't have to live through the reminders of what it had been like when her own daughter had disappeared all those years ago.

The daughter she knew her mother still wondered about every day, saw on buses, crossing the street, playing with children in the park, because she did too. The daughter they both secretly prayed might miraculously walk in the door one day and complete them again.

'Have you rung the Melvilles?' Andee asked.

Maureen nodded. 'Yes, they were very sweet. They knew Dougie, of course.'

Most people in Kesterly did, since he'd been mayor for a while, and had long served on the town council. By trade he was a builder with a company that was as well known and respected as he was. He'd even, at his own expense, restored the local cinema ten years back and to everyone's surprise and delight it had recently started to turn a profit.

'Will you come over to Grandma Carol's with us?' Alayna asked, keeping her arms round her mother.

'Of course,' Andee replied. She'd always had a close relationship with Martin's parents so she definitely wanted to be there for Carol now. 'I should go upstairs and shower first. Mum, why don't you take the children, and I'll follow as soon as I'm ready?'

'What about your tea?' Maureen protested.

Feeling in need of something stronger, Andee said, 'I'll be fine.'

'Shall I wait for you?' Alayna asked, tilting her lovely face up to Andee's.

Cupping it in her hands, Andee gazed into her eyes. How she adored her children who'd never, for a moment, doubted they were loved, not even by their father. Perhaps especially not their father. When he was around he saw them every day, and when he wasn't he called or texted regularly, sent them emails, snapchatted, FaceTimed, or instant messaged, whichever was the easiest, or perhaps whatever took his fancy, that day. He'd known what it had done to Penny, feeling her father didn't care about her as much as he should, and in spite of not loving their mother any more Martin wasn't prepared to let either of his children doubt their father's love.

Andee's head was starting to spin.

Dougie was dead.

Martin was on his way home.

A fourteen-year-old girl was missing.

It was as though the world was tilting off its axis, forcing the past to collide with the present in a way that was making her feel oddly nauseous and distanced from herself.

'Mum?' Alayna prompted.

Remembering the question, Andee said, 'No, it's OK. Grandma Carol will be wanting to see you, and I have a couple of calls I need to make before I leave.'

After they'd gone, she poured herself a vodka and downed it in one. Then picking up her phone she carried it outside. Not surprisingly, since he was in transit, she found herself going through to Martin's voicemail, but she couldn't let these moments pass without at least leaving him a message. 'Hi, it's me,' she said, quietly. 'I've just heard about your dad and I wanted to say how sorry I am. The children are on their way over to your mum's now. They're looking forward to seeing you.'

As she ended the call she stood staring along the length of the garden with its neatly clipped roses on one side, all kinds of vegetables on the other and washing line down the middle. There was no sea view from here, it was facing inland, though the salty-scented air and screeching gulls left no doubt it was close.

She could feel Martin's grief almost as though it was a part of her own, though his would be deeper, more consuming. He'd loved his father, there was no doubt about that, and he would feel the loss in more ways than he would yet be aware of, though what would matter to him most right now was that he was there for his mother, and the children.

Who would be there for him?

Deciding not to dwell on that now, she pushed it out of her mind. A girl was missing, that was what really mattered, and Dougie would have been the first to say so. Actually, so would Martin.

Going to her bag she took out the four-strip shots of Sophie and stared at them closely, as though trying to see past all the make-up and attitude to who the girl really was inside. She was out there somewhere, she had to be, and for all anyone knew she was crying behind her mask, feeling afraid, lost in a world that had become too much for her.

Thanks for making me want to kill myself.

Andee couldn't allow herself to believe she'd

meant it, not when she'd taken her computer, phone and some clothes. It didn't make any sense.

So had someone helped her to run away?

It seemed most likely.

So where had they taken her?

Where was she now?

Why wasn't she using her phone or computer?

Was someone hurting her?

Was anyone listening as she cried?

Who really cared about Sophie? How often had she slipped down her parents' list of priorities? How desperately did she still long for her mother? Andee had no answers to those questions, but what she did know was that she wasn't going to allow a shortage of police resources to stand in the way of finding her. Sophie Monroe needed someone to care, to listen and to put her first. She was already first for Andee, and it was where she was going to stay until the day she was found.

And please God, please, please, let that day come soon.

Chapter Three

Suzi Perkins was so grateful to have her job at Blue Ocean Park that she spent ten minutes each morning uttering a chant of thanks to the universe, in the hope that it would be transmitted to those who'd helped her get it. Top of that list was Jackie Poynter, one of the campsite's owners, whom Suzi had met for the first time at the interview two years ago. As soon as Jackie had heard why Suzi wanted to leave Essex and start a new life she'd hired her on the spot and had even named the tanning salon she was to run in her honour.

It wasn't usual for Suzi to tell anyone her story; the only people on the site she'd confided in were Jackie, because she'd had to, and Heidi, the manager, who was probably Suzi's closest mate these days. Whether they'd ever told anyone else Suzi had no idea, certainly no one had ever brought it up if they had, but there again, it wasn't something anyone would feel comfortable mentioning. After all, what did you say to someone who'd lost her husband and three beautiful kids in a fire started by her husband's psycho girlfriend while their mother, Suzi, was out clubbing with her mates? Suzi hadn't even known the girlfriend existed until the police had told her the blaze was arson and that they had the probable culprit in custody.

How could she have deserved such a punishment for a night out with her friends, especially when it was something she'd hardly ever done?

Though the tragedy had taken place three years ago, Suzi's heartbreak remained almost as raw as the day it had happened. Losing all three of her precious girls had been like losing all the vital parts of herself. It wasn't right that she was no longer a mum; it never would be, because her hormones still made her that person, her instincts kept reaching out for them and her memory was never going to let go. Her angels should still be with her, and they would be if their father hadn't screwed around with a nutjob.

He'd deserved to die, everyone had said so except Suzi who thought he should have been made to stick around suffering, longing, forever grieving for his kids and knowing they'd be alive if it weren't for him.

She didn't like being bitter, it didn't help anyone, least of all her, but all the same she hoped he was rotting in hell.

It was her mother who'd found the vacancy at Blue Ocean Park. She'd been scouring websites and newspapers for months, wanting to help her daughter get started again, and then this job had come up. With Suzi's background in beauty therapies it would be perfect, her mother had declared, and perhaps being far from everything and everyone who reminded her of what she'd lost would be a good way to go.

Suzi hadn't argued. She had to do something, so why not this?

Her brother, Gary, had driven her down for the interview. He'd been going through his own set of troubles at the time, stuff she should have been more supportive over, but she just hadn't been in the right frame of mind. He'd come through in the end, but not unscathed, which was why she was trying to help him now. No one had to know about his past, he was only here for the summer, so it wasn't like he was setting down roots or anything, the way she was. He'd be gone when the season was over, back to his usual haunts in London, or most likely to their mother who still had her house in Harold Wood, where Suzi and Gary had grown up.

'Blimey, they're all over the place,' Gary was grumbling as he peered through the blinds of Suzi's Suntan Salon, watching a handful of uniformed cops swarming around the nearby caravans.

Receiving no response, he glanced over his shoulder to where Suzi, a large blonde bronzed woman in her mid-forties, was creating a buy one, get one free poster to hang outside. This was the trouble when the weather was good, she found, business was always slow, and it wasn't forecast to rain again until the weekend so she had to try something to get the punters in.

'Shit, they're coming this way,' Gary muttered, standing back.

Without looking up she said, 'Then you'd better make yourself scarce, hadn't you?'

'They'll see me leave.'

'So? For all they know you've been having a treatment. Anyway, you're one of the lifeguards for God's sake, they're going to want to talk to you at some point . . . Unless they find her first, of course.' Her eyes narrowed questioningly as they met his.

'I don't know where the fuck she is,' he cried, throwing out his hands.

'Then you've got nothing to worry about, have you?' she said tartly.

His handsome face flushed with hurt. 'That's just great,' he grunted, 'even my own sister suspects me . . .'

'I don't suspect you of anything,' she cut in hastily. 'I'm just saying if you start acting suspicious they're bound to think you've got something to hide.'

His colour deepened, reminding her that of course, he did, which was why it was probably a good idea if they didn't interview him yet about Sophie.

'Go in the back,' she told him, 'I mean right in the back, not where the beds are, and stay there till I come and get you.'

'What if they want to search the place?'

She blinked in amazement. He might be hunkier than the Hoff, but he was definitely a few miles short of the beach at times. 'Why would they want to search it?' she demanded. 'No one's going to think she's hiding here. They'll just want to talk about the last time I saw her, and if I might know anything that can help find her.'

'So what are you going to say?'

Getting up from her desk, she replied, 'If you want to hang around you'll find out.'

He didn't. The cops were some of his least favourite people, so scooting swiftly across the reception he disappeared through the beaded curtain, while Suzi grabbed a watering can and went outside to soak the geraniums. If it turned out her brother knew anything about Sophie Monroe, where she was, how she'd got there, why she hadn't come back yet, then Suzi didn't want the cops finding out before she did. Damage control was what she was calling this little exercise, a way of trying to safeguard everything she had here before her brother could bring it down round her ears, because it would just about destroy her to have to leave it now.

'Hi, mind if we have a word?'

She turned round with a friendly smile and saw, to her surprise, that neither of the officers was in uniform – all those she'd spotted about the site up to now had been. These two, a bloke and a woman, were in plain clothes, which had to make them detectives, and if detectives were asking questions they must be taking this case more seriously than she'd thought. 'Sure,' she answered cheerily to cover a clench of anxiety. 'What can I do for you? To be honest,' she ran on, before the ginger one could speak, 'I wouldn't advise any treatments for someone with your sort of skin.'

'That's not why we're here,' he replied, holding up his badge. 'DC Johnson. This is DS Lawrence.'

So definitely detectives. Another horrible thud on her heart. 'Oh, you'll be wanting to ask me about Sophie Monroe,' she responded helpfully.

'Could we go inside?' Leo Johnson suggested.

Leading the way, she gestured towards the leatherette sofas that formed the salon's waiting area. 'Would you like a drink?' she offered, going to help herself from the cooler.

Leo held up a hand. 'We're fine, thanks,' he

replied with a smile. 'We'd just like to know what you can tell us about the last time you saw Sophie Monroe.'

Her eyes flicked to the woman cop, who hadn't yet sat down. She was busy reading all the notices on the board and posters on the walls. She had a nice figure, Suzi couldn't help noticing, and great hair too, if she bothered to do something with it. Some women just didn't know how to make the most of themselves. 'Well,' she began, turning back to Leo and wishing she didn't feel so nervous when she had nothing to be nervous about, 'it's hard to be sure when I last saw her. I mean, she's always around the site, especially with it being the school holidays, you know, in and out of the Entertainment Centre, working at the arcade, or mucking about in one of the warden's golf carts.' She chuckled fondly. 'Bit of a prankster she is at times, but there's no harm in having some fun is what I always say.'

'Indeed,' Leo agreed. 'So do you remember when you last saw her?'

'Let me think. You know, I'm sure it was on the beach last Saturday, with a group of other kids. That was probably the last time.'

'So you didn't see her on Sunday?'

She shook her head slowly. 'Not that I can remember.'

'Did you know any of the kids she was with?'

She was still shaking her head. 'All I can tell you is they looked quite a bit older, maybe in their twenties, and I think they were staying in one of the yellow zone caravans, that's the economy end of the park, but I couldn't swear to that, and I definitely don't know them.'

'Boys and girls?'

'Mostly boys, I think. Her mate, Estelle, was there. I definitely remember that, because I saw her running up to one of the vans to get an ice cream. Frankly, you couldn't miss her, the way she was bursting out of her bikini.'

'And you don't remember seeing Sophie again after that?'

As she shook her head she glanced at the woman detective again – DS Lawrence, had they said? She was leaning against the wall now, hands in her pockets, ankles crossed as she listened. Why didn't she say something? It was creeping Suzi out the way she was just standing there like some sort of mind-reader who could get to all the things not being said. 'No, I don't think I saw her after that,' she replied, turning back to Leo. 'But I did hear . . .' She stopped, deciding it wasn't her place to tell them about the row Sophie had had with Heidi on Saturday night. Anyway, Heidi had probably already told them herself, and since Sophie hadn't gone off until late Sunday night it was hardly important, especially when those two were forever at each other's throats. She might say God spare her the stress of teenage girls, but he had and actually she'd give anything in the world to have a humdinger with one of hers, anything rather than nothing.

Leo's eyebrows were raised, apparently waiting for her to go on.

Realising she had to say something or she was going to give the impression she was holding stuff back, she said, 'Well, I heard that she was helping out in the Carvery on Sunday, and that something went on with one of the waiters. She tripped him up for a laugh, or something, and he didn't find it very funny.' That had happened, just not last Sunday, but at least it had given her something to say.

'Do you know which waiter it was?'

'No, I'm afraid not.'

'Do you happen to know if she had a regular boyfriend?'

Suzi shrugged. 'This place is holiday-romance central, and with the way kids go in for friends with benefits these days . . . I mean, she's a bit young for that, obviously,' she added hastily, 'and I'm not saying she was into it, but it's kind of what they do, from what I hear.' She was conscious of her brother out back. Was he listening to any of this, or had he climbed out of a window to go and bury his head in the sand?

Taking another direction, Leo said, 'How well do you know Sophie's parents, Heidi and Gavin?'

Suzi smiled. 'I'm quite good friends with Heidi.'

'Does she talk to you much about Sophie?'

Realising it would sound bizarre if she said no, Suzi rolled her eyes as she answered. 'Show me a mother – or stepmother – who doesn't talk about their kids – and I have to be honest, it sounds, from what Heidi says, that Sophie can be quite a handful at times. But being Heidi she's always finding excuses for her, saying she's going through a phase, or she's feeling left out because of the baby, or it's her time of the month.'

'And her father?' Leo prompted. 'Does she seem to have a good relationship with him?'

'As far as I know she thinks the sun shines out of him, and he thinks the same about her.' She was aware of DS Lawrence's eyes on her, so penetrating they could be going right through her skull to thoughts even she didn't know she had. 'I know what you're thinking,' she suddenly blurted, 'everyone always blames the parents when kids go off the rails, or do something daft, but they're good people, Heidi and Gavin, two of the best.'

There was something about the way the detectives looked at each other that turned Suzi hot inside. She'd said too much, or they'd read something into her words that she hadn't meant to be there. 'I'm just saying,' she ran on, 'if Sophie's taken it into her head to leave home, well obviously she has, I don't think you should be looking to blame the parents.'

Leo smiled and got to his feet. 'Thanks, we'll bear that in mind,' he told her.

Pushing herself away from the wall, Andee said, 'Is there a back door to this place?'

Suzi's heart skipped a beat. 'Yes, but I always keep it locked.'

Andee nodded. 'So the person I saw standing at the window just now is still here somewhere? Listening?'

The colour drained from Suzi's face. 'I – I don't think . . . He's probably on one of the beds by now. He's my only customer so far today.'

'And would he be someone who's visiting the site, or who works here?'

'He – um, well, he's working here for the summer, as a lifeguard at the open-air pool. Actually,' she went on awkwardly, 'he's my brother.' She might as well tell them now, or it would only look odd if they found out later and she'd failed to mention it. *Please God don't let him have been with Sophie Monroe on Sunday night.*

Leo's pen was poised. 'Your brother's name?'

She knew she had to tell them, it would look suspicious if she didn't, but it was all right, Gary wasn't from around here so it wouldn't mean anything to them. Unless they looked him up. All hell would break loose if they did that. 'Gary. Gary Perkins,' she said hoarsely.

DS Lawrence was looking at her again, so piercingly that Suzi felt she was being pinned to some sort of confession she didn't even know she was making. What *was* it about that woman's eyes?

'Here's my card,' Leo said, handing one over. 'If you remember anything else give me a call.'

Assuring him she would, she watched from the open door as they walked down the road towards Alfie's Pie Shop, no doubt discussing what she'd said. Or maybe what she hadn't said, and heaven knew there was plenty of that, but no way was she going to start telling them about the rumours she'd heard concerning some of the foreign girls who'd worked at the park going off to become strippers, or worse, because they had nothing to do with Sophie, even if they were true. And she really didn't believe they were.

Taking herself through to the back she found her brother perched on one of the beds with his head in his hands.

'Did you hear all that?' she asked, surveying him with unease.

He nodded.

'Please tell me you weren't with Sophie Monroe last Sunday night,' she demanded fiercely.

He looked up. His guilty expression was answer enough. Slapping him round the head she cried, 'What the hell were you thinking? You know damned well how old she is . . .'

'Stop it, just stop,' he growled, jumping to his feet. 'It's not my fault she's gone and run off . . .'

Her eyes were flashing wildly. 'You know what this place means to me . . .' Her voice broke on a sob. 'I can't go back to where I was before, spending all my days thinking about how it would be if they hadn't gone . . . if that psycho bitch . . .'

'Ssh, ssh, I'm sorry,' Gary murmured, trying to hug her. 'I didn't mean to cause any trouble . . .'

Pushing him away, she said, 'No, you never do, but you just can't seem to stop yourself.' She looked at him in despair. 'Why did you have to go near her? If they don't find her, they're going to think you had something to do with it . . .'

'I swear, I didn't do anything . . .'

'They will find her, won't they?' she pressed.

'Course they will.'

She wanted to believe him, more than anything in the world she wanted it to be true, but she had a horrible feeling about this. She couldn't put it into words, it was just there, lodged in her like a stone, and she had no idea how to get rid of it.

'What about the girls who used to work here?' she asked. 'Do you reckon Sophie's gone with one of them . . .'

'No, I don't,' he broke in irritably. 'Apart from anything else she's too young.'

'Says who?' Suddenly, not knowing what else to do, she grabbed the phone. 'I have to call Jackie Poynter.'

'What for?'

'I have to tell her what's going on.'

'Do you seriously think she doesn't know that already?'

'Jackie, it's me, Suzi, at the salon,' she gulped as

she made the connection. 'Yeah, I'm good, thank you. Well, actually . . . You know you asked me to keep you up to speed about the Sophie thing . . .'

'She's got everyone doing that,' Gary grumbled.

Turning away Suzi said, 'Yeah, that's right, the police have been at the camp all morning. No, that's just it . . . It was only uniforms earlier, but a couple of detectives are going about asking questions now . . . I honestly don't know how seriously they're taking it, but if CID's on the case I reckon they must be stepping it up. OK, OK, I will. Whatever I hear. Thanks. Sorry to interrupt your holiday,' and ringing off she turned back to her brother.

'You'd better start praying that girl shows up,' she told him, 'because that's the only chance we've got of getting through this without both our lives falling apart.'

Spotting two uniformed officers interviewing the staff at Alfie's Pie Shop, Andee and Leo decided to leave them to it, and turned off down a leafy avenue of the camp's more elite caravans where the sun was sparking off windows and kids were charging about a brightly painted playground. A large notice declared: *Children Must Be Accompanied by an Adult.* This was nothing like the kind of site Andee recalled from her childhood, when freedoms had abounded and the caravans had seemed to rejoice in their shabbiness, each one different to the next, not only in size, shape and colour, but in character too. Back then there had been no tarmacked roads running between them, or smart wooden decks attached like patios, only lumpy grassland and tented lean-tos for shade. These gleaming vanilla boxes were a trailer-park version of Wimpy homes, with each van – or villa as these red-zone residences were apparently called – seeming to have rolled off the same factory line as its neighbour. Given their size she could imagine they were pretty luxurious inside, which was great for those who holidayed this way, but she would always have a soft spot for sofas that doubled as beds, tables that folded away into cupboards and camping stoves that blew off blokes' eyebrows rather than be lit.

'Gary Perkins,' she said, as they strolled into the yellow zone, where the caravans, though still big, bore more of a resemblance to those she remembered. Penny had always liked the blue ones, whereas she and Frank had preferred those with two or more colours. 'The name rings a bell, but I can't think why. Does it mean anything to you?'

Leo shook his head. 'Weird that he was hiding out the back.'

Andee couldn't disagree. 'We'll get one of the uniforms to have a chat with him, if they haven't already. So, what did you think of the sister?'

He shrugged. 'She seemed on the level, I guess.'

'There's something sad about her,' Andee commented thoughtfully. 'Behind all that orange tan and the Bambi lashes is a sad person trying to make her way in the world.'

Leo glanced at her in surprise. 'Her and most of the rest of us,' he retorted.

Andee cocked him a look. 'Are you sad, Leo?' she asked tenderly.

'You don't know the half,' he sighed.

Guessing she probably didn't, she said, 'You

know what bothered me the most about Suzi Perkins – in fact about everyone we've spoken to today – is how unconcerned they seem about Sophie.' She pondered that a moment, wondering if unconcerned was the right word. Deciding it would do for now, she went on. 'It was particularly noticeable in Suzi, considering she's supposed to be a friend of Sophie's parents.'

'So what are you saying?'

What was she saying? 'That Sophie's a human being, a child even, with a heart, feelings that can be hurt, and everyone seems too wrapped up in their own lives to remember that. Given her age she's probably particularly sensitive and is doing her best to hide it with all this promiscuity and aggression we've been hearing about.'

'She wouldn't be the first.'

'Indeed she wouldn't, but running away can be a cry for attention, and if that's what this is then no one, apart from her parents, seems to be reacting.'

'She's not answering the phone, or going online,' Leo reminded her.

'Possibly because she wants to cause a fuss. She needs to know someone has cared enough to call the police, and that the police, in turn, are taking her disappearance seriously.'

Leo arched an eyebrow. 'You might be able to sell that to me, but I don't think Gould will buy it as a reason to up the game.'

Knowing he was right, Andee inhaled deeply.

Bringing them back to practicalities, Leo said, 'The kids on the beach Suzi told us about. Do you want me to find out who they are?'

She nodded slowly. 'They could still be staying here, if not there'll be a record of whoever rented the caravan.' She glanced at her phone as it rang, her heart already tensing in case it was Martin. It turned out to be Gould who no doubt wanted an update on the robberies on Wermers Road, which, according to the DC who'd reported to her this morning, were happening in broad daylight.

How the hell were these people getting out of the stores without setting off any alarms? It had to be an inside job, but in every store?

Deciding to deal with Gould when she returned to the office, she let the call go through to messages, and quickly read a couple of texts that had arrived while she was at the salon.

Dad's just arrived. Staying at Grandma Carol's today so we can be with him. Love you. Axxx

Cancelled my driving lesson tonight so you don't need to take me. Decided to stay here with Dad and Grandma Carol. Probably be home tomorrow. Lx

Clicking off, she tried to gather her thoughts. For some reason she wasn't finding it easy today. It could be the heat, or more likely the memories of Penny that kept causing a pure and present ache in her heart. Or the fact that Graeme was due back tomorrow night and Martin was now in Kesterly. He'd texted last night to say it had been too late to call by the time he'd got her message, but could they meet?

She hadn't replied yet, but she would as soon as they'd finished here.

'Let's find Barry, get the lowdown on what the uniforms have come up with around the camp this morning,' she said. 'Then, presuming the Monroes still haven't heard anything, we should head over to Estelle Morris's.'

*

'Tomasz? What it it?' Kasia asked worriedly, as he clicked off the phone and came in from the garden. She hadn't heard any of the conversation, but from the tone of it, and the worry in his face, it was clear something was wrong.

'It's nothing,' he replied distractedly.

'Then why are you . . . ?'

'Actually, it's my mother. They've taken her to the hospital.'

Instantly alarmed, Kasia said, 'What's happened? Has she had an accident?'

As he shook his head he seemed so agitated that she wasn't sure he'd even registered the question. 'She collapsed,' he muttered. 'In the street. No one knows why, but they're doing some tests.'

'You have to go to her,' Kasia insisted. 'She needs you there.'

He dropped his head in his hands. 'I have so much to do here . . .'

'It doesn't matter. She is your mother. If anything were to happen, you would never forgive yourself if you weren't there.'

His normally gentle blue eyes showed his anguish as they came to hers.

'Everything will be fine,' she told him firmly. 'Mr and Mrs Poynter will understand why you must go, and you have a good team. Wesley will be able to manage them until you get back.'

'You're right,' he said, wiping a hand over his face. 'I have to go.'

Taking his hand she squeezed it between both of hers and held it to her cheek. 'I will pray for her,' she promised earnestly.

Drawing her into his arms he held her tightly. *'Kocham cie,'* he whispered fiercely.

'I love you too,' she whispered back.

After a while he pulled away and cupped her fragile face between his large, workman's hands. 'I should go upstairs and book the flight,' he told her.

Smiling, she said, 'You can use our new computer.'

It seemed he couldn't smile too.

'Would you like me to come with you?' she offered. 'I can ask Olenka if she could mind the children.'

His eyes closed as he shook his head. 'They need you here.'

Of course, but she knew how she would feel if something had happened to her dear *mamia*. She wouldn't want to travel alone, and Tomasz had no brothers or sisters to help shoulder the burden.

'I'll be fine,' he assured her, as though connecting with her concern.

'God and our Blessed Virgin will take care of you,' she said, touching her fingers to the tiny Medal of the Immaculate Conception at her throat.

He nodded, and turned around as Anton came charging in through the door. 'Hey, little man,' he smiled, swinging him up in the air. 'Don't worry, I haven't forgotten you.'

'We're going to build a house for Ania,' Anton told his mother.

Feigning surprise, even though she'd heard talk of nothing else since they'd got up that morning, Kasia said, 'How wonderful. Will she eat all her meals out there and invite friends in to play?'

Anton nodded. 'She promised to invite me in, and you have to keep promises, don't you?' He was looking at Tomasz.

'You most certainly do,' Tomasz agreed. 'Now,

90

I want you to go and make sure you know exactly where we should put the house, while I run upstairs to book a flight.'

Anton's eyes rounded. 'Where are you going?' he asked worriedly.

'To see my mummy in Poland, but I won't be gone for long, and I promise, even if we haven't finished the house before your bedtime, it will be all done and waiting when you get up in the morning.'

As Anton skipped back down the garden and Tomasz went to unpack their new laptop, Kasia returned to folding the washing. Since there were flights to Krakow every day from Bristol, she guessed he would try to get on one in the morning. This would mean him leaving home at around six, and if he received a call-out at one of the Poynters' businesses between now and then he would have to go. Still, even if it meant staying up all night, she knew he'd make sure the playhouse was finished before he left.

The glow of the love in her heart was as precious to her as the gift of her children, as meaningful as the communion she took every Sunday. She had so much to thank God for, so many reasons to feel blessed. She had never thought it possible to find so much kindness in a man after all she'd suffered at the hands of her husband. Thankfully, he had no idea where she was now, her parents would never tell him, nor would he be sober for long enough to try and find out. It was one of the great tragedies of her country, the number of men who drank themselves to oblivion, many of them ending up committing suicide, or collapsing in the snow and dying of cold.

Tomasz was nothing like that. He was strong and honest and brave and had no need of alcohol or anything else to provide an escape, because he had nothing to escape from.

Tonight she would say a special prayer for his mother – and add another for Tomasz to come safely back to her.

Chapter Four

It came as no small relief to Andee to discover that Estelle Morris seemed genuinely worried about Sophie. Here at last was someone, other than Sophie's parents, who apparently cared about the girl and where she might be. This was presuming, of course, that Estelle wasn't putting on an act, and Andee certainly hadn't ruled that out yet.

'I kept saying we ought to ring the police,' Estelle was telling them as she led Andee and Leo into a front room that smelled, as well as looked, as though it had recently undergone a vigorous sprucing. Estelle's mother smiled a greeting as they came in. Andee wondered if she'd ever seen so many ornaments. It would hurt her head to try and identify them all: a china sombrero with matching maracas, three wise monkeys from Tenerife, a wooden camel train from Tunisia, and a boogieing crocodile that snapped at her ankles as she passed the grate was as far as she was prepared to go.

'Did you say that to Heidi Monroe?' Leo was asking as he perched on the edge of a purple armchair, while Andee took its partner the other side of the gas fire.

Estelle flushed awkwardly. She was a sweet-looking girl with similar purple hair to Sophie's – no

doubt an adventure embarked upon together –
and golden-brown eyes that showed how young
she really was. 'No, I only said it to my mum,' she
admitted. 'I mean, I knew there was a chance
she was with her dad, but even if she was I couldn't
understand why she wasn't answering my texts.'

'Did you try calling her?'

'Yeah, loads of times, but I just kept getting her
voicemail.'

Andee said, 'Is there another friend she might
have contacted, or perhaps gone to stay with?'

Estelle's eyes went to her mother, who was
sitting on the arm of the sofa quietly listening. She
was a compact woman with razor-cut hair and the
look of someone who prized neatness and order
as much as her ornaments. 'I thought about Tania,'
she said.

Marian Morris seemed doubtful. 'Estelle and
Sophie were quite close to one of the girls who
worked at the camp for a while,' she explained.

'She left about a month ago,' Estelle added.

'We wondered if Sophie might have heard from
her,' Marian continued, 'but even if she had, I can't
think why she'd go off without letting anyone
know where she was going.'

'Especially not me,' Estelle added.

'Do you know where Tania went after she left
the camp?' Leo asked.

Estelle shook her head. 'She didn't even tell us
she was leaving.'

Leo's gaze held steadily to hers. 'Do you know
where Tania was from?' he prompted.

Estelle didn't seem sure.

'The Ukraine,' her mother provided. 'I'm sure
that's what she said.'

'So she's not English?'

Marian shook her head. 'We enjoyed meeting her, didn't we Estie?'

Estie nodded. 'Definitely.' Then, 'First she goes off without saying anything, and now Sophie's done the same.' She looked so miserable that it was clear she was taking it personally.

'Do you still have Tania's number?' Leo asked.

Taking out her mobile, Estelle scrolled through her contacts. 'Me and Sophie tried ringing it a few times after she went, but she never answered, so we assumed she'd lost her phone or got a new one.'

As Leo jotted down the number Marian suddenly got to her feet. 'Goodness, where are my manners? I put the kettle on ages ago. Would you like some tea?'

Deciding it might be a good idea to talk to Estelle on her own for a while, Andee said, 'That would be lovely, thank you. No milk or sugar for me. My friend here takes both.'

After the door closed Andee turned back to Estelle. 'Staying with Tania for the moment, did she live at the camp while she was working there?'

'Yeah, she did. In the staff quarters.'

'And she would have been what sort of age?'

'Eighteen – and she was dead pretty. All the blokes went after her.'

Suspecting that was why Sophie and Estelle liked to be around her, Andee decided to store the information for the moment, and glanced at Leo, a signal for him to bring the subject back to Sophie.

'So, did you see Sophie at all last Sunday?' he asked.

Estelle shook her head. 'Not Sunday, no. We

were supposed to get together in the evening, but she never turned up, and I couldn't get any answer from her mobile.' Her eyes began filling with tears. 'You don't think anything bad's happened to her, do you?' she asked shakily.

'We certainly hope not,' Andee replied. *If this girl turned out not to be on the level she had a dazzling career ahead of her in Hollywood.*

After waiting for Estelle to dab her eyes with her fingers, Leo said, 'So the last time you saw Sophie would have been when?'

'Saturday,' Estelle sniffed. 'We went to the beach.'

'Did she mention any plans then to leave home?'

'No, nothing. We were having a laugh with these blokes from . . . Actually I can't remember where they were from, Sunderland I think, or somewhere up north anyway. They were trying to get us to go to a party at their caravan on Saturday night, but we ended up not going.'

'For any particular reason?'

'When the time came Sophie didn't feel like it. She'd had another row with Heidi, so we just stayed in her room chatting, and listening to music and making videos and stuff.'

'Videos?' Andee queried.

'On our phones.' She reached for hers, and finding what she was looking for she passed it over.

Hitting play Andee watched Sophie coming to life on the small screen, a slight, captivating girl with a bust slightly too large for her skinny frame and denim shorts slung low on her hips. She was using her heavily made-up eyes and pouting lips to flirt with the camera as she danced and writhed like a true professional.

96

'She's good, isn't she?' Estelle murmured.

If you call a child behaving like a stripper good. Without looking up Andee said, 'Would you mind if I emailed this to myself?'

Though Estelle clearly did mind, she apparently couldn't think of a reason to refuse, as she simply shrugged as if to say, if you like.

After making sure it had gone through Andee handed the phone back. 'Where did you shoot it?' she asked.

Estelle seemed to flinch. 'Uh, I can't remember. I mean, I think it was at Sophie's.'

'Would you like to take another look at the background?'

'No, it's OK. It was definitely in her room.'

'Was anyone else there?'

Appearing more uncomfortable than ever, Estelle said, 'No, it was just us.'

Andee waited.

Estelle's colour flowed into the roots of her hair.

'Estelle, you need to tell us the truth,' Andee insisted.

'I am,' she cried. 'There was just us. We were messing around, you know, dancing to all sorts of stuff.'

Fairly certain there was more to it, Andee said, 'If anyone else was there . . .'

'There wasn't!' Estelle cried. 'I swear it.'

Deciding to sideline it for the moment, Andee resumed, 'OK, you were telling us just now that Sophie had had another row with Heidi on Saturday night. Do you know what it was about?'

Estelle gave a half-shrug. 'Heidi's always having a go at her about something these days. She's been a right cow since the baby was born. She used to be really nice before, more like a mate really than a stepmum. You could tell her most things and she'd be totally cool with it. Now, it's like you can't say anything to her without her going off on one. My mum reckons it's because she knows there's something wrong with the baby and she doesn't want to admit it, so she's all stressed out about it.'

Considering that a fair assumption based on the little she'd seen, Andee said, 'Did Sophie mention anything that night about running away?'

'Not really. I mean she was always saying she couldn't wait to leave home, and stuff like that, but if she'd been serious about running away she'd definitely have told me.'

'So Saturday evening was the last time you saw her?'

Estelle nodded. 'She was supposed to be coming here on Sunday, after tea, but I never heard from her and like I said, I couldn't get any answer from her mobile.'

'What did you think might have happened?'

Estelle glanced down at her hands as a flush spread across her cheeks. 'That she'd probably had another row with Heidi,' she mumbled, 'but if she had I know she'd have rung me . . . So I suppose I thought . . . Well, I wondered if she might be with . . .' Her words ran out and she kept her eyes down.

'With who?' Andee gently prompted.

Estelle shrugged awkwardly and still didn't look up.

'Does she have a boyfriend?' Andee ventured.

'No, not a boyfriend exactly, but there's this . . . I mean, she has this thing about someone who works at the camp. I thought she might have . . . you know . . .'

Andee's eyes went briefly to Leo's. 'Can you tell us his name?' she asked.

Estelle shook her head.

'Why?'

'I just can't. It wouldn't be right. She wouldn't want me to.'

'Is it possible she's gone off with him?'

'No, because I've seen him since Sunday. Anyway, he's married, and she's only fourteen. If her dad was to find out . . .'

Andee stiffened. This was potentially very serious indeed. 'Do you think her dad might have found out?'

'No, because the bloke wouldn't be working at the camp any more if he had.'

'So what does this person do at the camp?'

At last Estelle's eyes came up, wide and worried and once again brimming with tears. 'I don't know what she sees in him really,' she admitted. 'I mean, he's really buff and all that, but he leads people on and . . .' She broke off as the door suddenly opened and her mother came bustling in with the tea.

Biting down on her frustration, Andee waited for Marian to pour and pass out her dainty china cups before trying to steer the conversation back on course.

'I understand you want to keep Sophie's confidence,' she said to Estelle, 'but it's important for us to know more about this man.'

Marian's eyes rounded with surprise. 'What man?' she asked Estelle.

'It's no one,' Estelle answered irritably. 'It was nothing. Just leave it, OK?'

Before Marian could respond Andee said, 'You do want to help us find Sophie, don't you, Estelle?'

'Of course I do, but I'm telling you, she's not with him.'

'With who?' her mother demanded crossly.

'I said leave it.'

'Don't tell me to leave it. If you think she's with some . . .'

'I just said, she's not with him,' Estelle cried angrily.

'Who is he?' Marian insisted.

Estelle stayed silent.

Marian turned to Andee, her eyes burning with frustration.

Raising a hand to still her, Andee said, 'If Sophie's involved with an older man . . .'

''She *isn't*. Not like you're meaning it.'

'Then how is she involved with him?'

'I just said, she isn't. She likes him, that's all.'

'So why don't you tell us his name?'

'Because I can't.'

'You mean because you won't.'

Estelle shrugged.

Andee's eyes went briefly to Marian. She could see the worry for her own daughter and what she might have become embroiled in, but for the moment at least they must keep this about Sophie. Deciding to rewind a little so they could approach the mysterious married man another way, she said, 'Let's go back to Sunday evening. You say you didn't hear from Sophie. I think we should probably check your phone records to make sure she wasn't trying to get in touch . . .'

'Actually, I did get one text from her,' Estelle suddenly blurted.

Marian looked astounded. 'You what?' she demanded. 'Why are you only telling us this now?'

'I forgot.'

'What do you mean, forgot? How can you forget?'

'What does it say?' Andee broke in.

Looking profoundly miserable, Estelle found the text and passed her phone over.

Reading aloud, Andee said:

Sorry didn't ring, had another row with WSM. Ended up getting chased on beach by Shrek. Totally scary. With G now. My hero. T on tonight. Definitely going to go for it.

Passing the phone to Leo, Andee said, 'WSM?'

'Wicked stepmother.'

Of course. 'And Shrek?'

'He's one of the site wardens,' Estelle explained. 'A total weirdo. He's got this thing about Sophie.'

After making sure Leo had noted this, Andee said, 'And would T be Tania?'

Estelle shook her head.

'Then who are G and T? And please don't say a drink.'

Estelle's shoulder raised in a shrug. 'They're just like, mates.'

'So you can tell us their names.'

Estelle's head went down and her mother lost it again. 'For God's sake, Estelle. The police need to know who Sophie was with on Sunday night . . .'

'It won't make any difference,' Estelle cried. 'They're totally cool . . .'

'How can you say that when we don't know where she is? And what did she mean that she was going for it tonight? Had she been planning to run off with them?'

'No!' Estelle's eyes flicked to Andee.

'We need the truth,' Andee told her darkly.

Estelle was seeming to shrink inside herself. 'She wasn't planning to run away,' she muttered under her breath.

'Then tell us what you think has happened.'

'I don't *know*.'

'Would either of these men – can we take it they're both men?'

Estelle gave the briefest of nods.

'Would either of them harm her, do you think?'

'No way. Well, definitely not Gary . . .' Her eyes dilated as she realised she'd said his name.

'Are we talking about Gary Perkins?' Andee came in quickly.

Estelle only looked at her.

'Who's Gary Perkins?' Marian wanted to know.

'He's a lifeguard at the camp's pool,' Leo informed her.

Marian looked confused. 'What, the one whose sister runs the tanning salon?' She turned to Estelle aghast. 'You surely haven't been mixing with him? He's old enough to be your father.'

'No he's not,' Estelle snapped. 'And who said I was *mixing* with him?'

'Was Sophie?' Andee asked.

Estelle clearly wanted the ground to swallow her up.

Since Sophie's text more or less confirmed an association – *With G now. My hero* – Andee said, 'Was Gary Perkins there when you shot the video of Sophie dancing?'

'No!' Estelle muttered fiercely.

Suspecting he had been, Andee asked, 'Who's T?'

'And none of your messing about this time,' Marian scolded. 'We need to know who he is . . .'

'All right, all right, he's the maintenance bloke, OK? She's like totally mad about him, but all he's interested in is one thing.' Her cheeks were so hot now that Andee almost felt sorry for her.

As Marian gaped at her, Leo said, 'Just to be clear, we're talking about sex?'

This was too much for Marian. 'Have those men been taking advantage of Sophie?' she demanded furiously.

'Oh Mum, get over it will you? She's not a kid, and anyway . . .'

'She most definitely is a kid, and if I find out you've been going the same way I can tell you this right now, you'll be straight up that clinic to check for STDs . . .'

'I haven't done anything,' Estelle shouted. 'Get off my case, will you? I never said anything about sex.'

'But you insinuated it.' To Andee, Marian said, 'I'm sorry, I had no idea any of this was going on, and I'm sure Sophie's parents haven't either . . . You little tart,' she shouted at Estelle, slapping her legs.

'Mrs Morris,' Andee chided. 'We really need to calm this down.'

'I'm sorry,' Marian gasped, 'but what do you do? We're going to have words later, my girl, you can be sure of that.'

'None of this is my fault,' Estelle cried. 'I'm not the one who was with them, am I?'

'Maybe not last Sunday, but what about other days? If I find out one of them has laid as much as a finger on you . . .'

'OK, let's try to get this back to Sophie,' Andee broke in firmly. Giving them a moment to resettle, she said, 'The text tells us that Sophie was with at least one of these men last Sunday evening . . . I'm taking it you believe her?'

Estelle blinked. 'Why would she lie?'

'Because sometimes people say things to make themselves look cool, or more grown up than they are, or to get other people into trouble. Is she likely to have done that?'

Estelle didn't seem certain as she shook her head.

Wishing she didn't have to ask the next question in front of Marian, Andee said, 'Have you ever spent time with these men yourself?'

'No, not like you're meaning it,' Estelle protested.

'But you have been in their company?'

'Not in Tomasz's, no.'

'Tomasz being the maintenance man?'

Looking trapped again, Estelle nodded. 'He's a singer at the club too,' she added sulkily. 'That's mainly when we see him, so when she said he was on tonight, she meant he was performing.'

'And the rest of the text? That she was going to go for it?'

'Means she was going to try to get off with him.'

'Do you think she managed it?'

'I don't know, because I haven't heard from her since,' and suddenly breaking into sobs she buried her face in her hands. 'It's not my fault I don't know where she is,' she wailed. 'I wish I did, but I don't so stop picking on me.'

Deciding they probably had enough for now, Andee got to her feet. 'I'm sure we'll be wanting to talk to you again,' she told Estelle as they reached the door. 'In the meantime, if you think of anything else, or if you hear from Sophie I want you to call me right away.'

Taking the card she was being offered, Estelle said, 'I will, I promise.' Her eyes came pleadingly to Andee's. 'Do you think she's all right, wherever she is?'

'I certainly hope so,' Andee replied, and after thanking Mrs Morris she followed Leo to the car.

'So what did you think of all that?' she asked, as she got into the passenger side.

'Well, first up I'd say we need to talk to these two blokes.'

'That's a given. Find out if any of the uniforms have already interviewed them. If they have it'll be interesting to know what they've said they were up to last Sunday night.'

'Won't it just. And whatever it was, I'll put money on the fact that it won't include associating with a fourteen-year-old girl. Where now? Back to the station?'

'Via the campsite office. I want some details for this Tania, and the maintenance bloke. While you're doing that I'll take a wander over to the pool, see if I can have a little chat with Gary Perkins.'

However, when she got there it turned out Gary Perkins was on a day off, and a brief stop at his flat over Alfie's Pie Shop told her he wasn't at home either. Nor did his sister seem to know where he was, if she was to be believed, and Andee wasn't really sure about that.

'I hate being cynical,' she commented to Leo as they drove back through the Cove, 'but when you're lied to more times in a day than the surf hits the shore, it's hard not to be.'

'Are you thinking of Suzi Perkins now, or Estelle Morris?' he queried.

'Both, but more of Estelle. Fourteen-year-olds are notorious for the lies they tell, and something's not sitting right with me about her. I can't tell you what it is yet, but we definitely need to keep an eye on her.'

After a while he said, 'Do you reckon there's a link between this Tania disappearing and now Sophie?'

'We can't rule it out.'

'But you're not convinced?'

'Not yet, but what I do know is that we really need to step this investigation up, because the longer Sophie Monroe is missing the less chance we have of finding her.'

Gould was waiting as Andee and Leo walked into the CID suite, and it was evident from his expression that he wasn't happy.

Before Andee could speak he gestured to his office and followed her in, closing the door so the rest of the team couldn't hear. 'I cut you a lot of slack, Andee,' he began, 'but you're . . .'

'Sir, I know, and I appreciate it . . .'

'. . . going too far,' he growled over her. 'I've just had Jimmy Poynter on the phone demanding to know what the hell's going on at his campsite, disrupting his punters . . .'

'Sir, a girl's gone missing . . .'

'I'm aware of that, but uniforms are on it, and *you* should have been checking out those robberies, not spooking everyone at the caravan site into thinking this is a bigger deal than it is. She's a runaway. We'll find her . . .'

'If you'd hear me out . . .'

'What's more,' he said over her, 'if you'd done as I asked, and focused on the robberies, you'd know by now that three Blu-ray players just upped and walked out of Hunt's Electricals this afternoon, and there were two DCs in the place when it happened.'

Not quite sure what to say to that, Andee opted for a dynamic refocusing. 'We have reason to believe that Sophie Monroe has been associating with men much older than herself,' she declared, 'and that she isn't the only girl to have gone missing from that camp.'

Now she had his attention.

'There's another girl, Tania Karpenko,' she continued, 'who, as far as we know, no one's seen or heard from in the past month. She's eighteen, so she doesn't have to give an account of her whereabouts, but we're checking now to find out if any other girls have, quote vanished unquote, from Blue Ocean Park, or any of the other camp-sites. If they have . . .' She let the sentence hang. He'd know how potentially serious the situation could be if it turned out Sophie's wasn't the only disappearance.

'Did the two girls know each other?' he asked. 'Sophie and this Tania? They must have.'

'According to Sophie's bestie, Estelle, who we've just spoken to, they were good friends with Tania in spite of the difference in their ages. Take a look at this,' and whisking out her phone she opened up the email she'd forwarded from Estelle.

Gould's frown deepened as he watched it. 'Where the hell would a girl her age learn to dance like that?' he growled.

Andee's eyebrows rose. 'It's called twerking,' she explained. 'Try Lady Gaga, Miley Cyrus, Rihanna . . . In fact, look at most pop videos these days, they're way more explicit than this.'

'So what are you trying to say?' he asked, handing her phone back.

'The best friend's denying it, but I reckon someone else was there when this video was shot, or maybe they sent it to someone, like Tania, who might have shown it to an interested party.'

'By interested party, you mean some sort of pimp?'

'It's possible, still hypothetical of course, but the best friend showed us a text she received from Sophie last Sunday night. In it she's saying she was with a man called Gary Perkins, who's a life-guard at the site's pool. There's also mention of the maintenance bloke, Tomasz Sikora, but we're not sure yet whether she was actually with him. Apparently, apart from being a plumber, he's also a bit of a wow in the cabaret room.'

Gould frowned.

'He sings,' she explained.

'Where's he from? The way you're saying the name doesn't sound English.'

'According to the site's records he's from Poland, but we've yet to verify that. Tania Karpenko told Estelle and Sophie she was from the Ukraine, but her staff file has her down as Slovakian.'

'Why would she lie?'

'I've no idea.' She took a breath. 'Going back to Tomasz Sikora, apparently he's been multitasking for the Poynters for the past three years.'

'So you've spoken to him?'

'Not yet. He wasn't around when we were over

there earlier, and apparently the uniforms missed him when they were going door to door.'

'What about this Gary Perkins?'

'No sign of him this afternoon either, but Dan Wilkes was supposed to be running a check on him,' and opening the door she called out to ask if there was any news.

'Right here,' Dan Wilkes replied, getting to his feet. 'You're going to love this, but not a lot. Your bloke's on the sex offenders' register.'

Andee blinked in astonishment. A lifeguard at a holiday camp was on the sex offenders' register! How the hell had that happened? She turned to Gould. 'We need to bring him in right now,' she declared.

Not arguing, Gould said, 'Find this Polish bloke too.'

'Andee, there you are,' one of the admin assistants greeted her as Andee returned to her desk. 'Gavin Monroe rang about ten minutes ago, asking to speak to you.'

Wondering why he hadn't tried her mobile, Andee said, 'Do you know if he's heard from Sophie?'

'All he said was he wanted to talk to you.'

Picking up the phone Andee pressed in Gavin's number. 'Send a couple of uniforms over to the camp to bring in Perkins,' she instructed Leo, 'he can't be allowed to stay, no matter what. Mr Monroe? DS Lawrence speaking. You were trying to get hold of me?'

Sounding clogged, as though he'd been crying, Gavin said, 'I was just . . . Heidi and me were wondering if you'd heard anything yet?'

Quickly pulling back from his despair, she

replied, 'Nothing that's telling us where she is.' Should she mention the older men? Perhaps not yet, and certainly not over the phone. 'Has anything else occurred to you that you think might be helpful?' she pressed.

'Not really. I just wish there was something we could do. It's terrible just sat here, waiting, fearing the worst, thinking of all the things I should have said or done.'

Having been in that very place, Andee was only too aware of how torturous the waiting could be. It still was. 'You mustn't give up hope,' she told him. 'I'm sure we'll find her.' How could she be sure when they'd never found Penny?

This was different.

How?

She didn't know, it just was. It had to be.

'Before you go, is it possible to have a word with Heidi?'

'She's popped out with the baby. Shall I ask her to ring when she gets in?'

'If you don't mind. Or maybe you can tell me. Does she do the hiring and firing at the camp?'

'As far as I know she sits in on the interviews, but I think the final decision is usually Jackie Poynter's.'

'OK, thanks,' and deciding not to distress him with anything about Gary Perkins being hired, apparently in spite of his conviction, she assured him she'd be in touch as soon as there was some news, and rang off.

After reading through her emails she brought the case notes for Sophie up on her screen to begin checking through everything that had been added in the past few hours. Scrolling down, she saw that Slavoj Bendik, also known as Shrek, had seen Sophie on the beach on Sunday night, but she'd run away when he'd tried to approach her. *Ended up getting chased on beach by Shrek*, the text had said. However, it had gone on to say, *With G now. My hero*. So presumably Shrek hadn't caught her. Or maybe he'd been with G too.

Deciding to get everything more thoroughly checked out, she reached for her mobile as it rang and clicked on.

'Hi, it's me. Is this a bad time?'

She turned so her back was to the office. 'I'm afraid it's not good,' she replied, wondering if the sound of Martin's voice would always throw her into turmoil. *Only when it caught her off guard*. 'How are you?'

'Fine, I guess. Bit shocked, but maybe I shouldn't be.'

'I don't think we're ever prepared for the loss of a parent.'

'No, I suppose not. You know he thought the world of you.'

'The feeling was mutual.'

He took a breath. 'The kids seem to be doing OK. They're upset, obviously, but they're being great with Mum. It's good for her to have them here.'

'I'm sure they wouldn't want to be anywhere else.'

'No, probably not. She was glad you made it over last night.'

She knew he was going to ask to see her, and that she'd have to agree. Why was she feeling reluctant? Because of Graeme and the new beginning she'd finally started to carve for herself? Or because of how unsettled she was over everything right now?

'We need to talk,' he said.

Need to talk? Of course, about his dad. He'd want to relive the memories, and as she shared so many of them . . . 'We've got a missing girl,' she told him. 'Things are looking . . . They're not straightforward.'

There was a pause before he said, 'Are they ever in those situations?'

'Not really. She's fourteen.'

'I see.' He would be thinking of Penny now, and perhaps remembering that he was the first person she'd really spoken to about her missing sister when she'd started college. Oddly, it was part of what had brought them closer together, and had helped to form a bond between them that had lasted for over twenty years. He'd understood how tormented she was by never having any answers, and though they almost never spoke of it now, she knew he'd never stopped understanding.

'I'll call, soon,' she promised.

He didn't say anything, and a moment later the line went dead.

Feeling terrible for turning him down Andee toyed with ringing him back, and might have if she'd known what to say. Since she didn't she picked up the phone again and called the officer who'd interviewed Shrek – aka Slavoj Bendik. It turned out the site warden had admitted chasing Sophie, not to harm her, he'd said, but to find out why she was crying. When she'd shouted at him and run off he'd decided to let her go and had gone on to play poker with friends, where he'd spent the rest of the evening. The friends had confirmed this.

A while later, with the case now categorised as high risk, and the press already running the story thanks to Perkins's involvement, she said to Leo, 'If we don't have it already we need the camp's CCTV from last Sunday, and any information we can find on forced prostitution and trafficking in the area.'

Leo cocked her a look.

'We can't ignore it,' she told him. 'You've seen the way she danced, we know there are Eastern European girls coming and going from the camp and she was friends with Tania. We need to know if she's got caught up in something like it. Does anyone have anything to share on prostitution and trafficking?' she called to the office at large.

'We had a case a year or so back,' Karen, one of the other DSs, told her. 'The girls were mostly Somalian, being run by an Iranian in a house on the Temple Fields estate. Immigration ended up taking it over.'

'Anything since?'

'Not that I've heard, but that doesn't mean it isn't happening.'

'I'll get on to it,' Dan Wilkes offered.

'Any reply from the maintenance guy's mobile yet?' Andee asked Leo.

He tried again and shook his head.

'OK, we've got an address so let's go over there,' she decided, and getting to her feet she was about to start for the door when Gould came out of his office.

'I just heard Dougie Stone died yesterday,' he stated.

She nodded. Gould and Dougie had been golfing partners. 'Sorry, I should have said something.'

'It's all right. You know, if you want to take some time off . . .'

Suspecting it might be a ruse to get her off this case, she said, 'Thanks, but it won't be necessary. The children are with their father.'

He nodded, and turned back to his desk. 'Let me know if you change your mind,' he called after her as she left.

Twenty minutes later Leo was ringing the bell of number eight Patch Elm Lane. When a small boy inched the door open Andee gave him a friendly smile.

'Hello?' she said softly. 'Are your mummy or daddy at home?'

'Anton, what have I told you about answering the door,' an accented female voice scolded. 'You never know who it might be.' As the speaker came into view Andee was immediately struck by how lovely she was. She almost seemed to glow, and though Andee wasn't given to fanciful observations, the first word coming to mind about this woman was angel. Funny how some people exuded the very essence of who they were, while others, mostly, were all but impossible to read.

'Can I help you?' the woman asked, looking puzzled.

'We're looking for Tomasz Sikora,' Andee explained. 'I believe he lives here?'

Frowning, the woman said, 'Yes, he does, but I am afraid he goes to Poland to see his mother. She is unwell. Perhaps I can give him a message when he rings?'

Andee smiled as she held up her badge.

The woman's eyes widened with alarm. 'You are the police? Is something wrong?'

Andee looked down at the boy's wide, inquisitive stare and caught a glimpse of Luke at that age. How long ago it seemed, and yet almost like yesterday. 'Is this Mr Sikora's son?' she asked.

'No, he . . . My husband he is . . . Tomasz, he takes care of us now. He is like a father. He is a very good man.'

Andee's eyes returned to hers. *Why had she felt it necessary to add that?* 'May we come in for a few minutes?' she asked politely.

Seeming uncertain of how to refuse, the woman pulled the door wider, and taking her son's hand, she pointed down the hall towards the living room.

'Do you mind if we ask your name?' Leo began when she joined them after sending the boy upstairs.

'I am Kasia Domanski,' she told them. 'I don't understand . . . Why do you want to speak to Tomasz? Is it about Sophie from the caravan park?'

Intrigued by the assumption, Andee said, 'Yes, it's about Sophie. Do you know her?'

Kasia shook her head. 'Not really. I see her around sometimes, if I am there, but I don't go often.'

'So you don't work at Blue Ocean?'

'No. I am a nurse at the Greensleeves Care Home. Sometimes, if it is not too late I take the children to watch Tomasz sing at the club. He is a very good singer.'

'Was he singing last Sunday?' Andee asked.

Kasia fiddled with her necklace as she thought. 'Yes, I am sure that he was.'

'Do you remember what time he came home?'

She shrugged. 'A little after midnight. The same time as he usually comes when he has been singing.'

'Did he say if he'd been anywhere else that night?'

'No.'

'Did he mention seeing Sophie Monroe?'

'No, he say nothing about her.'

'Does he ever talk about her?'

'No, never. Apart from to tell me the day before yesterday that she is missing and the police are helping to find her.'

Andee nodded. 'When did he leave for Poland?'

'This morning on the early flight from Bristol.'

'To where, exactly?'

'Krakow.'

'And when are you expecting him back?'

'I am not sure. It depends what happens with his mother. Maybe a few days.'

'And you're absolutely sure he's gone to Poland?'

Kasia blinked, and appeared offended. 'Yes, I am sure. He would not lie about his mother.'

Allowing Leo to take over, Andee spent the next few minutes watching Kasia's changing expressions as she was asked if it was possible Tomasz had finished early on Sunday and not come straight home; if she was sure Tomasz had gone to Poland *alone*; if she had met many of Tomasz's friends.

By the time Leo had finished tears of anger and confusion were shining in Kasia's eyes. 'I don't understand why you come here saying these things. Tomasz is a good person. You can ask anyone. Everyone they tell you, he is a very good person.'

Knowing she truly believed it, and hoping, for her sake, it was true, Andee smiled reassuringly.

'Perhaps you can give us his mother's number before we go,' Leo suggested.

Kasia immediately looked uneasy. 'I am not sure,' she stumbled. 'She is not . . . She does not like that Tomasz is with me, because I am married to another man. So when he is with her, I always call him on his mobile.'

'Would you mind trying him now?' Leo prompted.

Noticing how she was shaking as she connected to his number, Andee found herself willing the man to answer, if only to restore this trusting young woman's faith in him. It was evident though, when her eyes came to Andee's, that she had been pushed through to voicemail.

'Tomasz, *to ja*,' she began.

'Please speak English,' Leo quickly interrupted.

With her eyes on him, Kasia whispered hoarsely, 'Tomasz, the police are here and they want to speak to you. Please call me.'

Andee waited until she'd rung off before saying, 'Does the name Tania Karpenko mean anything to you?'

Looking more puzzled than ever, Kasia shook her head. 'I don't think so. Why? Who is she?'

'She's someone who worked at the camp until about a month ago. We're not quite sure where she is now.'

As Kasia's hand went to her mouth, Andee looked down at her mobile to check an incoming text.

Mum, you have to call me. Axx PS: If you can't get me try Luke.

117

Wondering what it could be about, Andee pocketed her phone and said to Kasia, 'If you speak to Tomasz before we do, please ask him to get in touch right away.'

'Of course,' Kasia promised. 'I know he will want to help in any way he can.'

Once they were back in the car, Leo said, 'Funny that she doesn't have the mother's number. Who would she call in an emergency?'

'I was wondering the same.'

'Do you think she was lying?'

'No, I think it's more likely he's never given it to her.'

'Because whenever he says he's going to Poland, he's actually going somewhere else?'

'Possibly. Or he's going there, but not to see his mother,' and taking out her Airwave she point-to-pointed one of the DCs back at base. 'Terry, find out if there were any flights to Krakow from Bristol today,' she instructed, 'and if there were, whether Tomasz Sikora was on it. Oh, and check for any fourteen-year-old girls too. We know Sophie's passport is at home, but that doesn't mean she's not travelling under another name.'

'He could be too,' Leo suggested as she disconnected.

'We have to start somewhere,' and going through to Barry Britten she said, 'Have you picked up Gary Perkins yet?'

'Afraid not,' he replied. 'No sign of him at the camp, and the sister's adamant she doesn't know when he's coming back.'

Andee's expression darkened as she said, 'OK, I'll be in touch,' and after disconnecting she went through to Gould. 'Sir, both Gary Perkins and

Tomasz Sikora seem to have disappeared. According to Sikora's wife, girlfriend, Sikora left for Poland first thing this morning to visit his sick mother, but now she can't get hold of him. Perkins we've got no idea about, and the sister's saying she hasn't either.'

'OK,' Gould replied. 'The incident room's already being set up. I'll contact Polsar now to get them on the case.' At last, the specialist search unit. 'You know I ought to remove you, given your history,' he added abruptly.

'But we're driven by performance targets,' she reminded him, 'and you don't have the resources . . .'

'Don't quote my own lines at me. There are still . . .'

'Sir, I promise you, this won't be the first time I've been involved in a missing-person case since joining the force, so I know what I'm letting myself in for.'

'It's not only you I'm worried about,' he informed her, 'it's the rest of us, if you end up letting personal issues get the better of your judgement.'

'It won't happen, you have my word.'

'Where are you now?'

'Just coming into Kesterly, we should be there in about five. If you could . . .' She stopped suddenly as she spotted a familiar figure at a table outside the Seafront Café. Her mouth turned dry as her head started to spin.

'Are you still there?' Gould demanded.

Without answering she ended the call.

Glancing over at her, Leo said, 'Are you OK?'

'Yes, yes, I'm fine,' she assured him.

And she would be, any minute now. She just needed a few moments to get over the shock of seeing Martin with a woman at a table outside the café. Actually, not just with, but holding her hand and laughing at whatever she was saying.

Laughing? When his father had just died?

This, she realised as the shock of it turned to something much deeper, must be why he'd asked if they could talk – and no doubt what Alayna and Luke were trying to warn her about. Their father had met someone else, who was here in Kesterly, presumably to lend Martin her support at this difficult time.

Chapter Five

'I thought you might like some company,' Marian Morris said tentatively as Heidi opened the front door.

As Heidi looked back at her, Marian felt she was watching her collapsing in on herself. It was clear she hadn't slept in days; the circles under her eyes were like bruises, the ashen hue of her skin made her seem like a ghost. Marian could only begin to imagine the fears chasing around in her head, particularly now they were looking for this paedo lifeguard who'd upped and disappeared as soon as the police had started asking questions.

Marian knew she'd be beside herself if she was in Heidi's shoes.

Estelle was still swearing on her own life, her mother's and the Holy Bible that nothing 'like that' had ever happened during the couple of times she and Sophie had been at Perkins's flat, but even if it hadn't – and Marian desperately wanted to take Estelle's word for it – they shouldn't have been mixing with a man of his age in the first place. So, for that alone, Estelle was grounded at least until Sophie was found.

Poor woman, she reflected sadly to herself, as Heidi led her along the hall to the kitchen. She must know that the police were combing the entire cove now; every shop, pub, amusement arcade and fairground ride was being turned inside out. Then there were the pathways snaking from the main road down through the dunes, the mile stretch of beach with all its seaweed and debris, and the rocks around the headlands where heaven only knew what sort of marine life was hanging out.

Overnight, the situation seemed to have gone from a running-away to some kind of abduction. At least that was what they were saying on the news, so Marian could only think that the police were combing the area for some signs of a struggle.

'I saw Gavin out there helping with the search,' she said, as Heidi gestured for her to sit down at the cluttered table. 'It must make him feel better to be doing something.' Should she have said that? What on earth could make him feel better about digging around in ditches and hedgerows for signs of his missing daughter? Marian knew it would tear her to pieces. 'Some of the punters are joining in,' she ran on, 'which is really sweet, isn't it, considering they probably don't know her. And it's disrupting their holiday.'

Heidi didn't answer; Marian wasn't even sure she was listening.

'It can't be easy for you,' Marian sympathised, 'all this waiting, not knowing. It must be terrible.'

Heidi nodded and pushed a hand through her messy hair. 'I keep thinking she's going to walk through the door,' she admitted hoarsely. 'Sometimes it's like I even see her.'

As she swallowed hard Marian squeezed her hand.

'I need to tell her how sorry I am about the silly rows we've been having,' Heidi ran on brokenly. 'I want us to go back to the way we were, you know, friends and everything. Actually, I wouldn't even mind if she didn't want us to be close again, just as long as she was here and we knew she was safe.'

Which was all any parent wanted, to know their child was safe. 'Have the police been to see you today?' Marian asked.

Heidi nodded. 'Someone came first thing to explain what was happening and why.' Her breath shuddered as she tried to inhale. 'She said I made her want to kill herself,' she whispered, almost to herself, as though she couldn't quite believe it.

'But kids say stuff like that all the time. You can't take any notice of it.'

Heidi seemed not have heard, clearly trapped by her inner hell, so to try and distract her Marian said, 'Where's the baby? I expect this has all been quite disruptive for him, hasn't it?'

Heidi looked at her blankly, almost as though she'd forgotten his existence. 'He should be waking up any minute,' she finally managed. 'If it weren't for him I'd be out there looking too. Sitting here, waiting and worrying like this . . . It's doing my head in. And then there's the office. I keep telling myself I should go over there, but how can I think about anything else? It would look like I don't care if I try, and that's just not true.'

As her face crumpled Marian grabbed a tissue and put an arm around her. 'No one thinks that,' she lied on behalf of others rather than herself, since she did believe Heidi cared. In fact she knew it, and she wished everyone else would keep their malicious, uninformed gossip to themselves. 'I'm sure no one's expecting you to go over there.'

'The Poynters are on their way back from Spain,' Heidi announced, her voice thick with tears. 'They're being really nice about everything, but if they start losing business over this . . .'

'You mustn't worry about that,' Marian insisted. 'They understand it's not your fault, and Sophie's going to turn up safe and sound any time now. You wait and see.'

As Heidi looked at her Marian could feel her hopelessness as if it were emptying her own heart. 'Oh, sweetie, you mustn't give up,' she urged. 'It's going to be fine. I promise.'

'The police were asking about Tania yesterday,' Heidi told her. 'Do you remember her? The pretty blonde one from Romania? Or was it the Ukraine?' She jumped as the landline rang. Her eyes went to Marian, showing how scared she was, until hope seemed to whisper from the wings and she lifted the receiver to say a cautious 'Hello?'

Seeing how she was bracing herself for bad news, while praying it might be Sophie, Marian put a supportive hand on her arm.

'No, we don't have anything to say at this stage,' Heidi told the caller, and hung up. 'A reporter,' she explained. 'The police warned us they'd start getting in touch. That's the fourth call this morning.'

'Haven't they given you a family liaison officer?' Marian asked. 'I'm sure they usually do in cases like this.'

Heidi was looking haunted again. 'They said someone will be here today,' she answered dully. 'We don't really want one though.' Her breath caught on a sob. 'They'll be judging whether we're crying enough, or if we're hiding something.' Her voice was fracturing again. 'They always suspect the parents,' she said, 'and everyone knows me and Sophie were rowing all the time.'

Coming straight to her defence, Marian said, 'And everyone knows what fourteen-year-olds are like, so no one's blaming you for what's happened.'

Covering her face with her hands, Heidi said, 'I think Gavin's blaming me. He hasn't said that, but I know he's wondering why I didn't call him sooner when he was driving through France. I wish to God I had . . .'

Marian looked round as the doorbell sounded.

Heidi immediately tensed – if it were at all possible to tense more tightly than she already was, and Marian doubted it.

Since she was clearly fearing the worst, and who wouldn't in her shoes, Marian said, 'Would you like me to go?'

For a moment it seemed Heidi might say yes, but then pulling herself up she said, 'It'll probably be the FLO. Why don't you put the kettle on?'

Left alone in the kitchen Marian cast a dismal eye about the place, and wondered whether it would seem helpful if she tidied up, or interfering. Deciding she could at least load the dishwasher while the kettle was doing its thing, and perhaps wipe down the counter tops, she set about her self-appointed tasks, while keeping an ear open for what was being said at the door.

At first it wasn't possible to make it out, but then Heidi started raising her voice and Marian immediately ran to find out how she could help.

'I don't know how you've got the nerve,' Heidi was shouting.

'I swear he's not a paedophile,' the woman at the door was protesting. Recognising her as Suzi, from the salon, Marian put an arm round Heidi as she growled, 'You need to leave. We have nothing to say to you.'

'Please,' Suzi implored, 'what they're saying about my brother . . . They made a mistake . . .'

'There's no mistake,' Marian cut in waspishly. 'Sophie was with him the night she disappeared, and now no one knows where *he* is. Unless you do, and you're here trying to get information to feed back to him . . .'

'No!' Suzi cried. 'That's not why I'm here. I swear, Heidi, I came because I was worried about you.'

'You need to leave,' Heidi told her. 'I can't talk to you.'

'Heidi please, if you'd hear me out . . .'

'Just go,' Marian snapped, and pulling Heidi inside she slammed the door.

As Suzi turned back towards the salon, passing Fun City, Treasure Island and Mickie's Tavern, all of which were teeming with police and curious punters, she was feeling totally swamped by shame and humiliation. She didn't have to look up to know that hostile, accusing eyes were following her; if only the ground would open and swallow her up.

She understood now how her mother felt each time she left the house: as though she was as guilty as her son. Suzi shivered at the memory of rocks being hurled through their windows, and the graffiti splashed on her mother's car. Was that how it was going to be for her now? Everyone blaming her for her brother's crime, tarring her, who'd never done anything but love kids, with the same brush that turned child molesters into social pariahs? They wouldn't care that she hated paedos too, or that Gary's offence had involved a fifteen-year-old girl who hadn't been a virgin before that night, and who'd ended up writing to him in prison saying she was sorry, could she come to visit. His only crime in his so-called victim's eyes had been his lack of interest in repeating the experience; reporting him to the police had been the unnamed girl's revenge.

Why had the police felt the need to prosecute when there were so many real monsters out there who needed to be caught?

'Suzi?'

Looking up, she frowned as she saw someone she recognised, but couldn't immediately place. Then she remembered it was the detective who'd come to see her the day before.

'I was hoping to find you at the salon,' the detective began.

'I'm on my way there,' Suzi replied stiffly. Why didn't this woman with her X-ray eyes go away and leave her alone? 'If you're about to ask me where my brother is, I can tell you now, I don't have the first idea.'

Apparently unruffled by the hostility, the detective said, 'Have you heard from him since . . . ?'

'No, I haven't,' Suzi cut in angrily. 'And yes, I've tried ringing, but wherever he is, he's not picking up. Is that OK? Have I answered your questions?'

Still managing to look friendly, when in her shoes Suzi would have wanted to give the stroppy cow a good slap, the detective said, 'Did you know he was with Sophie on the Sunday night she disappeared?'

For a long moment Suzi was tempted to lie, but in the end she felt her shoulders slump as she simply nodded. 'Yes, I did,' she admitted, 'but he *swore* to me he didn't know where she went after.'

'After?'

'After he saw her,' Suzi mumbled lamely.

'Do you know if they were at his flat?'

Suzi kept her eyes on the caravans they were passing. If anyone looked out of their window now would they have any idea what was going on between these two very different women? One in a seersucker beach dress, the other in black trousers and cream shirt. If they knew this woman was a police officer and she was Gary Perkins's sister they'd soon work it out.

'Do you?' the detective prompted.

Suzi shook her head. 'He didn't tell me where they were,' she answered truthfully.

'Do you know if anyone else was with them?'

Suzi shook her head again.

A moment or two passed as they skirted the recycling bins and continued on towards the salon. 'How well does your brother know Tomasz Sikora?' the detective suddenly asked.

Confused, Suzi said, 'You mean the singing plumber?' What bearing did this have on anything, unless Gary and Tomasz had got into something she knew nothing about? 'I suppose he knows who he is,' she said carefully, 'everyone does, but they're not mates, or anything like that, if that's what you mean. Or not as far as I'm aware.'

'So he didn't mention anything about Tomasz

being with him and Sophie on the night Sophie disappeared?'

Suzi came to a stop. 'Why? Was he?' she asked.

Still appearing friendly, the detective said, 'It's possible.'

'So have you spoken to Tomasz?'

'Not yet. It would appear that's he's vanished too.'

Not knowing what to say to that, Suzi took out her keys and unlocked the salon door. 'Tell me,' she said, before going in, 'why did you have to make my brother's previous conviction public? I thought someone was supposed to be innocent till proven guilty? He's hardly going to be that now, is he?'

Managing to sound regretful, the detective replied, 'I'm afraid we can't withhold that sort of information when a young girl is known to have been with him the night she disappeared.'

No, Suzi supposed they couldn't. Nevertheless, it still didn't seem fair.

Nothing did any more.

'If you do hear from your brother,' Andee said, as Suzi started inside, 'you will contact us, won't you?'

Though Suzi nodded, she couldn't be sure that she meant it. She guessed it would depend on how the search went, and what Gary said when, *if* he got in touch.

God help the good women who protect bad men, Andee was thinking gloomily as she walked away from Suzi's Suntan Salon. It was a tragedy to see and an absolute headache to deal with, especially when the men concerned so rarely deserved it.

In spite of Suzi Perkins's prickliness it had been plain to Andee just how wretched she was feeling inside, how cruelly torn between loyalty to her brother and . . . and what? Coming clean with what she actually knew?

Undoubtedly Kasia Domanski was experiencing the same inner struggle, although she didn't appear to share the same doubts about Tomasz that Suzi clearly had about her brother. If anything Kasia was proving unshakeable in her belief that Tomasz was a 'good person', in spite of the police knocking at her door to question her about his connection to a missing girl.

Possibly three missing girls if they included Tania Karpenko, and another name had come to light this morning, Michaela Reznik. No one seemed certain about where she was from, or where she might have gone after leaving the camp.

Personnel records, along with criminal record checks, were definitely not a strong point at Blue Ocean Park.

'I am very worried,' Kasia had insisted, when Andee had dropped in earlier on her way to the campsite. Kasia's puffy eyes had been sore evidence of a sleepless night. (Join the club, Andee had thought grimly to herself.) 'Always he calls when he goes away,' Kasia had told her earnestly. 'I don't understand why he doesn't this time. Something must have happened to him . . .'

Of course, it could all be artifice, but Andee didn't think so. If appearances – and her own instincts – were anything to go by, the woman really didn't have a deliberate untruth in her, and certainly no calls had been exchanged between the telephone numbers being monitored. Which didn't mean Tomasz and Kasia weren't using other phones, though Andee was a long way short of being convinced about that.

What she was far more convinced of, in fact was in no doubt of at all, was how truly devastating it would be for Kasia Domanski to have her trust in Tomasz shattered.

He had not been on a flight to Krakow.

Andee hadn't told Kasia that this morning. First she wanted to be sure that he hadn't taken another flight from another airport, and she wouldn't know that until the passenger manifestos of all flights to Krakow over the past couple of days had been fully analysed. Far more problematic was going to be tracing the other girls, who didn't appear to have any health, dental or even proper employment records, at least not here at Blue Ocean Park. On the other hand, until someone actually reported them missing she knew Gould wouldn't agree to commit any resources to finding them.

'Hey, Andee, there you are,' Barry Britten called out, coming down the steps next to Alfie's Pie Shop just as Andee reached them. His jacket was off, and due to the heat large patches of perspiration were blooming under his arms. 'We've found an interesting little stash up there in Perkins's flat,' he informed her. 'I mean quite literally. He's only got his own hydroponics outfit installed like a second oven.'

Andee wondered why she wasn't surprised. 'A sex offender is growing cannabis in the middle of the campsite? It makes me wonder what we're going to find next. A terrorist running the firework display? No sign of the man himself, I take it?'

'None,' Barry confirmed. 'We're waiting for the

electricity board to come and disconnect his little grow tank, so we can take it away. The CSIs have got everything else bagged and tagged, ready to go.'

'Any obvious signs Sophie was there?'

'No, but we've taken plenty of prints. I can also tell you that the twerking video was almost definitely shot there. The backgrounds match.'

Andee's expression flattened into dismay. 'I don't want to think this,' she said, 'but I can't help wondering if there's some sort of procurement going on here. Three girls disappearing from this site . . .' She sighed, not liking the way this was looking at all.

'Did you pick up anything from Sikora's place this morning?' Barry asked.

'You mean for DNA? I left Leo to go through the dirty laundry.' Enjoying Barry's laugh, she said, 'Incidentally, did you hear there's a question over another girl who's worked at the camp? A Michaela Reznick.'

Barry nodded. 'Yeah, I did. I've also heard the Poynters are on their way back from Spain. Have you ever met them?'

Andee shook her head.

He grinned. 'You should talk to your fellow DS, Carl Williams, when he gets back from leave. He's come that close to nailing them on at least half a dozen occasions.'

'For what?'

'You name it, they've been up for it, but somehow they've always managed to slither free. I thought the last time our Carl was going to walk across the courtroom and punch the smirk right off Jimmy Poynter's ugly mug. I don't think anyone would have blamed him if he had.'

'Mm, looks like I'm in for a bit of a treat,' Andee commented wryly, 'unless Sophie shows up before they do, of course.'

Sobering, Barry said, 'Let's hope she does.' Then, 'By the way, I spoke to Martin last night. You know, to say sorry about his dad.'

Andee's eyes drifted to where a couple of Polsars, watched by a small group of holiday-makers, were using mirrors on poles to search under nearby caravans. She wondered if anything of significance had been discovered yet, either here, out on the main drag, or on the beach. If it had she'd have been notified. 'I'm sure he appreciated that,' she said. Had Martin told their old friend about the new woman in his life?

Did it matter if he had?

Changing the subject, she said, 'Has the FLO turned up at the Monroes' yet?'

'Should have by now. Do you want me to check?'

'It's OK, I'll do it. What are you doing when you've finished here?'

'Loading up and heading back to the station.'

Leaving him to it she set off in the direction of the Monroes' bungalow, checking in with control as she went. After being told that no one had reported any suspect brothels or trafficking in the area over the past six months, and that Tomasz Sikora's computer, which had been seized that morning, had a virtually empty hard drive, she clicked off her Airwave and took out her mobile.

'Hi, it's me,' she said, when her mother answered. 'Are you still at Carol's?'

'No, I got back about an hour ago,' Maureen replied. 'The children are still there, but I think

133

they're planning to come home later. Is everything OK with you?'

From the mildness of her tone Andee could tell that she hadn't seen any news over the last twelve hours, which was actually no surprise, since she knew only too well how the death of someone close could transport a family from the everyday world to a place where only the past and memories existed or mattered.

Having no intention of telling her mother about Sophie's disappearance over the phone, Andee simply said, 'I'm fine. I spoke to Luke and Alayna last night.'

'They told me. They're worried about you.'

'I know, and they shouldn't be. I'm fine with their father meeting someone else. It was always going to happen . . .' She was surprised by how matter-of-fact she was managing to sound when inside she was annoyed, upset, possibly even jealous, though she wasn't prepared to run with that. 'Have you met her?' she asked.

'Only briefly,' Maureen replied. 'She flew in yesterday, apparently, and is staying at a hotel in town. Martin thought it might be a bit much for her to stay at Carol's, especially while the children are there.'

Relieved he'd had the sense to realise that, Andee said, 'What's she like?' and immediately wished she hadn't.

In a voice that conveyed little warmth, Maureen told her, 'She seems very pleasant. She's a translator, by all accounts. They met in Cairo a few months ago when they were both working there.'

'It sounds as though they're well suited.' How bizarre, bewildering, it felt to think of Martin being in any way suited to another woman, when she couldn't even begin to imagine herself with another man. Apart from Graeme, of course, who she was imagining herself with all the time lately, and actually liking the way it felt. How perverse her feelings were, unfathomable, contrary, downright unpredictable from one minute to the next. 'Is she going to be at the funeral?' she asked.

'I'm not sure. Carol doesn't want her there. Between us, she's not happy about her being here at all. She thinks it's wrong for someone Dougie didn't know to show up, almost like a member of the family, and I'm afraid I have to agree.'

Deciding not to get her mother any more worked up by saying that she did too, Andee simply said, 'I'll talk to Martin later, but I should go now. I just wanted to check in to make sure everyone's all right.'

'We're as well as can be expected, given the circumstances, but it would be nice if you could take some time off to be with us all.'

She'd understand once she knew about Sophie, but for now all Andee said was, 'I know, and I'll try. I'll see you later, OK? Love you,' and ending the call she quickly refocused her thoughts to matters at hand, since she had no intention of allowing them to be hijacked by Martin and how angry she felt with him for just about everything.

Finding the Monroes' front door open and hearing raised voices coming from the kitchen she paused, not wanting to intrude, but curious to know what the shouting was about.

'. . . I don't know what you're expecting to find out there,' Heidi was yelling. 'Why are you doing it? You're just tormenting yourself . . .'

'I can't just sit around here doing nothing,' Gavin

135

protested. 'We don't know what she might have dropped, or if . . .'

'Stop it, just stop,' Heidi yelled over him. 'I can't take much more of this. I want them to find her as much as you do, but we . . . Oh Archie, I'm sorry, my love, I didn't mean to scare you. Sssh, don't cry. Mummy's here.'

Continuing along the hall, Andee knocked on the kitchen door and pushed it open. The baby was screaming so hard that no one heard her. She glanced around at the mess, open cupboard doors, crockery piled in the sink, food packets strewn over the counter tops. The place stank of dirty nappies and was so hot and stuffy it was hard to breathe.

Turning as she rocked the baby, Heidi almost shrank back when she saw Andee standing at the door. Her fear of the worst possible news was so evident that Andee immediately assured her that that wasn't the reason she'd come.

'The front door was open,' she told them.

As Gavin lifted his head from his hands she could almost feel its weight. He clearly had no idea what to do with himself, how to drag his mind out of the depths and allow hope to keep him afloat.

Hope, the great saviour with its positive and believable scenarios, and the great tormentor when it wouldn't go away, even after twenty years of nothing but false leads and no contact at all.

What would be Gavin's worst fear?

It surely had to be that someone had taken Sophie and used her horribly before dumping her body, but was that really the worst that could have happened? How often had she, Andee, wished she could be told that Penny was dead rather than think of her in the kind of living hells she'd come across at the most heinous of all crime scenes. She'd had to deal with victims who'd been imprisoned for months, sometimes years, their emaciated bodies riddled with scars, burns, all manner of abuse. In one particularly gruesome case two mentally deficient youths had had their fingerprints burned off, teeth extracted, even their tongues had been removed to stop them from talking. Wasn't death better than that? The victims would surely have thought so.

She'd forgotten until now how her father used to try comforting himself by pretending he'd been told Penny was dead.

They'd all done that. Andee realised that in a very deeply buried place inside herself, she still did.

'Do you mind?' she said, going to open a window.

No one objected, apart from the baby, who screamed louder than ever as he watched her.

'Ssh, it's all right,' Heidi tried to soothe, but it was clear she was close to tears too.

'I'll go and lie him down,' Gavin said, getting to his feet.

As she handed him over Heidi seemed to lose her balance, making Andee wonder when she'd last eaten. They clearly weren't coping well. They needed some serious support, which, in part, was why she'd come. The FLO was turning up this afternoon apparently, but meantime what the Monroes needed more than they realised were details of the various organisations and charities that served as a vital backup for families in their situation. So she'd brought a handful of leaflets and factsheets herself.

'I take it you haven't found her.' Heidi sank into a chair at the table.

'I'm afraid not,' Andee admitted, going to sit down too.

Heidi seemed to twitch as she looked at her. 'No news about Gary Perkins?' she asked.

Andee shook her head. 'I'm afraid not,' she repeated. There was no point getting into the fact that Perkins would never have been anywhere near the campsite if the proper criminal record checks had been carried out. It clearly hadn't happened, and reminding Heidi, as manager, that she was responsible for the oversight wasn't going to help anyone now. 'We still don't know for certain if Sophie's with him,' she said, 'but as he's disappeared too, along with Tomasz Sikora . . .'

'Tomasz Sikora?' Heidi echoed. 'Oh yes, Tomasz Sikora. Why aren't they saying anything about him on the news?'

'We have nothing, at this time, to connect him to Sophie's disappearance. I know she mentioned him in her text to Estelle, but it doesn't actually place them together at any point that evening, and so far we have no witnesses to say they saw them together either. We're hoping to speak to him though, obviously.'

'So where is he?'

'We're told that he's visiting his sick mother in Poland. The local police are checking this.'

Heidi began chewing her nails. 'I can't believe . . .' she murmured, her focus clearly drifting. 'I mean it's not . . .' Her eyes suddenly shot to Andee's. 'Does Tomasz Sikora have a record?' she asked hoarsely. 'I mean like Gary Perkins?'

'Not that we're aware of, but we're also pursuing that with the Polish authorities.'

'I knew she had a crush on him,' Heidi mumbled, almost to herself. 'She was always in the cabaret room when he was on. Never liked to miss a show.'

'So if he'd asked her to go away with him, do you think she'd have gone – willingly?'

Heidi pondered this. 'I don't know. I suppose it's possible. But where would he take her?'

Since she wasn't in a position to answer that, Andee said, 'Are you aware of any sort of friendship or alliance between him and Gary Perkins?'

Heidi shook her head. 'They must know each other, because they work in the same place and there's always something needing attention at the pool. Tomasz has to be over there at least a couple of times a week.'

Andee looked round as Gavin came back into the room, and listened quietly as Heidi filled him in on what had been said about Tomasz Sikora.

'But you're looking for him?' he pressed.

Andee nodded. 'Of course, but we can't go public with his name or his picture until we know for certain that he's disappeared.'

'You don't know where he is? Isn't that enough?'

'We're still waiting to hear from the Polish authorities.'

He seemed suddenly agitated, unsure what to say or do. 'I should have kept a closer eye on her,' he croaked shakily. 'I knew she was going off the rails . . .' He clapped his trembling hands to his face. 'This is all my fault . . . I should have stopped her going out so late . . .'

'She used to sneak out,' Heidi reminded him. 'Half the time we never knew she was gone.'

His eyes went to Andee. 'How serious, how violent is Perkins's history?' he asked, 'because if he lays . . .'

'Not violent at all,' Andee came in quickly.

Seeming to accept that, he looked at Heidi, but turned away again. 'They're so much older than her,' he declared. 'What was she thinking, getting involved with them?'

Deciding not to get into the obvious answer, that Sophie had lost her father's attention so was seeking it elsewhere, Andee said, 'Do you recall two girls who used to work at the camp? Tania Karpenko and Michaela Reznik?'

Heidi frowned. 'Yes, why?'

'We can't seem to find any record of where they went after they left here.'

Heidi's frown deepened. 'They don't always tell us where they're going,' she said. 'Some of them only stay for a few weeks . . . Are you saying you think Sophie might be with them?'

'We can't say anything for certain at the moment, but we'd like to trace them. Are you aware of any friendships or relationships that might have existed between them and Tomasz Sikora or Gary Perkins?'

Heidi looked blank as she shook her head.

Gavin hardly seemed to be listening.

'It's still very early in the investigation,' Andee reminded them. 'There could be a lot more to uncover.' She regarded them both expectantly, but neither seemed to have engaged with her meaning. 'Is there anything else you want to tell me?' she prompted gently.

Heidi's eyes rounded with shock as Gavin's head slumped forward.

'What are you saying? Do you think we're hiding something?' Heidi cried.

'I think it's possible you might know more than you realise,' Andee explained.

Heidi was baffled. 'Then how would we know it?'

'After you've had some time to reflect on what's been said today it might come to you.'

They all looked up as Barry Britten tapped on the door and put his head round. 'Sorry to interrupt,' he said to Andee, 'could I have a word?'

'Have you found something?' Gavin wanted to know.

'Sorry,' Barry responded.

Getting to her feet, Andee dug out the literature she'd brought from her bag and put it on the table. 'I think it would help you a lot to take a look through these and maybe get in touch with one or two of the organisations,' she told them. 'They have a great deal of experience in supporting families who are going through what you are now. Some are actively involved in helping to trace the missing child. Take your pick, go online and have a look at their websites, see which ones you think will work for you.'

Picking up a factsheet from The Child Exploitation & Online Protection Centre, Gavin said, 'I just can't think what they would want with her.'

Realising he was meaning Perkins and Sikora, Andee squeezed his arm and followed Barry outside.

'What's up?' she asked, checking on the messages that had come in over the past half-hour.

'No details,' he replied, 'but I've been told to let you know they're ready to show you some CCTV.'

Chapter Six

'Tomasz! Where are you? Please tell me what is happening?' Kasia cried into the phone. 'The police have been to the house. They take away . . .'

'Stop, stop,' Tomasz urged. 'What are you saying? Why did they come to the house?'

'They are asking about Sophie. They want to know where you are the night she disappears. What time you come home, and if I am sure you go to Poland. I know you are there, Tomasz. I see by the code, but what is this number? It is not your usual one.'

'I had my phone stolen, or maybe it fell from my pocket. I have only just been able to get a new one. Kasia, please, you must not worry. Everything is fine.'

'But why do they think you know about Sophie?'

'I don't know.'

'You must call them. They said if I hear from you, I must tell you to call. You will do it, won't you Tomasz?'

'Of course. Where are you now?'

'In my office at the care home. I cannot stay long. Tomasz, the police have taken our computer, and other things . . .'

'What other things?'

'Your razor from the bathroom. You forgot to pack it.'

'I know, but I have bought another. What else?'

'Coins from the drawer by your side of the bed. Clothes from the laundry . . .'

'Why do they want that? I don't understand.'

'They didn't explain, but Olenka and Glyn, they are saying it is to get your fingerprints and DNA.'

Tomasz fell silent.

'Please, Tomasz, you must tell me what is going on,' Kasia implored, glancing over her shoulder as Brenda, one of her charges, came bumbling into the room. 'I have the police officer's number here,' she told Tomasz. 'Her name is DS Lawrence. She wants that you call as soon as possible. Do you have a pen?'

'No, but you can text to this number.'

'OK. I must go now . . .'

'First, tell me, are the children all right? Do they know what's happening?'

'They have seen the police, but I have told them that all the houses of people who know Sophie are being searched.'

'So they're not frightened, or worried?'

'I don't think so.' She gave a shaky smile, while trying to take her keys from Brenda. 'It is only me who is those things. I will feel much better when you come home. When will that be? How is your mother?'

'She is doing well. I am still at hospital with her. Kasia, everything will be all right, I promise. You must not be frightened.'

'OK. I'm sorry. I don't want to worry you when you have so much on your mind.'

'I'm fine,' he assured her.

'I must go. Please call me as soon as you know more about your mother.'

After guiding Brenda back to the lounge where a lady from the WI was showing a group of residents how to make paper flowers, Kasia quickly returned to her office and checked the number Tomasz had called from. To her relief it really did begin with 48, the country code for Poland, so he was definitely there. It wasn't that she'd doubted him, it was simply that the police had her so confused she could hardly think straight.

Everything would be fine now. She would text him DS Lawrence's number and when she got a moment later she would call DS Lawrence herself to let her know that if he hadn't been in touch already, he soon would be.

'Alayna, where are you?' Andee asked as she headed into the station.

'At home,' Alayna replied.

Relieved to hear it, Andee said, 'And where's Grandma?'

'As far as I know chatting to Grandma Carol on the phone.'

Of course, they could go on for ever, those two, and now with so much to say about Dougie . . . 'I need you to do something for me,' Andee said, aware this was going to be a big ask of a fifteen-year-old. However, Alayna had been blessed with more sensitivity than the entire family put together, and no one, apart from Andee and Luke, could love her grandma more. 'You might have heard on the news that a young girl has gone missing from around here?'

'No, we haven't seen any news. Oh Mum, that's terrible. Is it anyone we know?'

'Her name's Sophie Monroe. Do you know her?'

'There's someone at my school with that name. She's younger than me, but I think she lives on one of the caravan parks.'

'That's her.'

'Oh my God! What's happened to her?'

'That's what we're trying to find out. On the face of it it looks like she's run away, but we can't be sure.'

'How long's she been gone?'

'Just over a week. You can probably imagine how worried her parents are. Everyone is. And now you know her age you'll understand what kind of effect it could have on Grandma when she gets to hear about it.'

'Of course,' Alayna replied warmly, 'but you know, Mum, I think Grandma handles these things much better than you realise.'

'You could be right, but don't let's take it for granted. I'd really rather she didn't blunder into it on the news, and I can't get home for a while. So if you feel up to having a little chat with her . . .'

'No problem, I'll do it now, but what about *you*? This can't be very easy for you.'

'I'm OK,' Andee assured her, pressing the lift button to go up. How proud she was of this girl who was so considerate of others – and what a struggle she herself was having keeping the agonisingly dark days of the past as deeply buried as they needed to be for her to function normally.

Penny, where are you?

Please, please come home.

Don't you understand how much we love you?

The echoes of despair, guilt, longing – and most of all the fear that it would never end.

And it never did.

'I'm sorry, I have to ring off now,' she said to Alayna. 'Call if you need me. Love you.'

'Love you too.'

Relieved to have got off the line with no mention being made of Martin, Andee exited the lift on the second floor and started along the corridor towards the incident room. As she went she was allowing herself a moment to imagine Alayna holding her grandmother's hands as she broke the news of Sophie's disappearance, her eyes showing a remarkable empathy for a girl of such tender years. She felt terrible for not being there herself, although she knew her mother would understand why she wasn't. Finding Sophie had to be a priority, and because Maureen was always so concerned for others it would be the most natural thing in the world for her to put the Monroes' needs before her own.

How alike her mother and daughter were, their kindness and generosity seeming able to quell the natural reactions of jealousy and insecurity. Even when Andee and Martin had broken up Alayna had seemed more worried about them than she had about herself, although Andee and her mother always kept a close eye on that, wanting to be sure she wasn't suppressing her emotions in order to spare them.

Luke, on the other hand, had taken it hard when his father had gone off and left them in the lurch, as he bitingly put it.

'What about *us*?' he'd cried to Andee, his eyes burning with anger and pain. (At the time he hadn't had the courage to tackle his father to his face, but they'd certainly had the showdown since.) 'Don't we count?' he'd demanded. 'For all he knows you might want to bail out on us as well, but you never would, because you understood your responsibilities when you had children. He's such a bastard. We're better off without him.'

Realising how afraid he was that she might leave them too, Andee had assured him it would never happen. 'And remember, it's only for a few months. He'll be back when the contract's finished.'

'That's exactly what Richard Clash's father said when he went off to Africa, and they've never seen him since.'

Not what Andee had wanted to hear. 'You know Dad won't do that to you,' she'd said gently.

'I never thought he'd take off without any discussion,' Luke retorted savagely, 'but he has. I'm going to be totally screwed up now, thanks to him.'

'You don't have to be. You need to talk to him, to try and understand what's going on with him. You'll find it has nothing to do with wanting to leave you, because I happen to know that was the hardest part of his decision.'

It was true, it certainly had been; leaving Andee, however, hadn't seemed to be difficult at all.

These days an uneasy friendship existed between father and son that Alayna told her more about than Luke ever did. Luke was more inclined to keep his feelings to himself, in part, Andee suspected, to avoid hurting her.

The joys and complications of being a mother, she was musing to herself as she all but collided with Gould coming out of the incident room.

'Ah, there you are,' he said. 'The press office . . .'

'Have been in touch. Don't worry, I'm on it, but I want to take a look at this CCTV before putting together a statement. Have you seen it?'

'Not yet. Is there anything significant?'

'I'll let you know when I've seen it.'

Twenty minutes later Andee was in a viewing room watching selected playback from the security cameras positioned around Blue Ocean Park. With her was Leo, Jemma Payne, Barry Britten and Yaz the technician, who was treating them to the over-powering scent of his manly cologne.

'So, basically, what we have,' she declared, consulting her notes when Yaz brought his edited highlights to a close, 'is Sophie running past the Costcutter shop at seven fifty-two, presumably having just come from her parents' bungalow, then being picked up by another camera at seven fifty-four heading into the lane that leads through the dunes.'

'She doesn't have anything with her,' Leo pointed out. 'No bag, no computer.'

Having already clocked that, Andee nodded and continued.

'The next time we see her is eight thirty-eight going up the steps at the side of the pie shop, which means she's been on or around the beach, or at least away from the site, for approximately forty minutes. Her phone records don't show her making any calls at that time, so it could be she was having a sulk after the row with her parents, or maybe there's no reception there, or she could have met up with someone we've yet to find out about.'

'Pre-arranged or chance?' Jemma wondered aloud.

Since no one had an answer for that, Andee continued. 'Back to the pie shop, and her entry into Perkins's apartment where she remains until nine sixteen, when we see her coming out again. Let's take another look at that, Yaz.'

Finding the relevant footage he hit play and they watched carefully as the large computer screen showed grainy images of Sophie, all willowy limbs and miniskirt, sashaying down the steps and making a jaunty skip on to the gravel at the bottom. Given what they'd found in Perkins's apartment, it seemed a reasonable assumption that she was high. Certainly she seemed in good spirits, suggesting the earlier row with her parents had been all but forgotten.

'The next time we pick her up,' Yaz pronounced as he wound on through the footage, 'she's going into the clubhouse at nine fifty-one.'

'And as it shouldn't take more than four to five minutes to get from the pie shop to the Entertainment Centre,' Jemma put in, 'we have to ask ourselves where did she go after leaving Perkins's flat? Obviously if the camera covering the park entrance had been working, we'd know if she'd returned home, but as it stands, we only know that she went into the Centre at ten minutes to ten.'

'And Perkins was already there,' Barry added, 'because we've seen him leaving his flat at nine eighteen, a couple of minutes after Sophie, and going into the Centre at nine twenty-three. Meaning he must have gone straight there.'

'So did she go home to pack up some things?' Andee wondered. 'If she did, she doesn't have them with her when we pick her up going into the Centre.'

'It's possible she left them somewhere to collect later,' Jemma suggested. 'Or she could have given them to someone – Sikora? – when he drove into the park around nine thirty.'

'How do we know he arrived at nine thirty?' Andee asked.

'We don't for certain,' Yaz replied, rewinding, 'but we do have footage of him driving into the Centre's underground car park at that time. Of course, he might already have been on the site somewhere, but for now it seems a reasonable assumption that he's just turned up for his gig.'

'In which case,' Andee pondered, 'was he in touch with Perkins and Sophie before he arrived to arrange to pick up Sophie's bag?'

Since no one had the answer to that, Yaz fast-forwarded to the footage of Sophie leaving the club at eleven fifty-two, not quite steady on her feet, followed by Sikora's van exiting the car park five minutes later.

'No images of Perkins leaving,' Yaz informed them, 'so chances are he's in Sikora's van – we can't tell from the angle of the camera, although that's definitely Sikora driving. The next time we see him is out on the main drag, having turned left out of the site. It's not possible to see who's in the van with him, if anyone.'

'Left wouldn't be the obvious direction to take if he was going home,' Barry commented, 'although you can get to the estate that way.'

'Is it possible for him to have stopped to pick

up Sophie on the way out of the site?' Andee queried.

'I'd say yes, if she was waiting and ready to hop in. No witnesses to say they saw it happen, but we're still working on it.'

'Is anyone claiming to have seen her talking to Sikora at the club?' Andee wanted to know.

'Yes, we've got a couple of bar staff saying they saw her with him at the side of the stage, just after the show ended.'

'Was anyone close enough to hear what was being said?'

'Apparently not.'

'Did it look like they were rowing, having fun . . . ?'

'None of the above. She was only with him for a few seconds, apparently, then she left.'

Andee nodded slowly. 'I'm taking it there's direct access from the clubhouse to the garage.'

'There is,' Barry confirmed. 'Stairs and lift. Parking for around a dozen vehicles, including the wardens' golf carts.'

'OK, so how many white vans are there like this?'

'Three,' Jemma told her, 'all used by Sikora and his maintenance team.'

'Do we have a registration number for this one?'

'We have for all three,' Jemma replied, 'and as soon as we can confirm which van this is we'll get it circulated.'

'OK, so what this *could* be telling us,' Andee declared, 'is that Sophie left the site with Perkins and Sikora in Sikora's van around midnight. Given that Sikora is supposed to have arrived home shortly after . . . How long would it take him to get there if he took the longer route?' she asked Barry.

'Fifteen minutes, at that time of night,' he replied.

'OK, so presuming we believe the girlfriend and he did arrive home around twelve fifteen, what we need to know is where he might have dropped Perkins and Sophie.'

'Given the timing it has to be somewhere close by,' Leo piped up, 'unless, of course, Sikora's girlfriend *is* providing some sort of alibi.'

Having to accept the possibility of that, Andee glanced at her watch as she got to her feet. 'We need a team over at the bungalow taking what footprints they can from outside Sophie's bedroom window to see if any could feasibly belong to Perkins or Sikora. OK, I know it's a long shot given how much time has passed, and chances are they didn't get out of the van, but let's get it done anyway. Same goes for fingerprints on the sill and around the window. Does anyone know when the Poynters are expected back?'

'Apparently they're flying into Gatwick tonight,' Jemma told her.

'Then you and Leo go and have a chat with them tomorrow.'

A few minutes later Andee was back in the incident room. 'OK, what's new on Perkins?' she called out, checking her mobile as it rang. Seeing it was Martin she felt her heart catch, but now wasn't a good time to talk to him so she let the call go to messages.

'Still no sightings,' Dan Wilkes told her. 'The local police have paid his mother a visit, but she's claiming she hasn't heard from him in a fortnight.'

'When did he last check in under the terms of his order?'

'Four months ago. He was still living in London then.'

'And he didn't tell anyone he was moving. That puts him in violation right there. We do such a grand job of following up on these guys, don't we? All his usual haunts have been checked?'

'As far as I know.'

'OK, let's hope that turning him into a full-on media star manages to flush him out,' and going to the incident board she stood staring at Sophie's photos – the innocently smiling schoolgirl who'd lost her mother at far too young an age, and the purple-haired bundle of frustrations and loneliness who seemed to have been trying all the wrong ways to regain the attention of her father.

Penny's problems had all stemmed from believing her father didn't love her.

Mindful of needing to draft a new statement for the press, she took herself off to a nearby empty office where she could think more clearly as she pulled it together. For some reason she always found it easier to write drafts by hand; once done she'd type it into an email and send it over.

She was only a couple of lines in when her mobile bleeped with a text.

Told Grandma, think she's OK, but give her a call when you can. Ax

Immediately connecting to her mother, Andee said, 'Hi, it's me. Are you all right?'

'Yes, of course,' Maureen replied. 'It's very worrying news though, and I'm not sure you should be the one handling . . .'

'I'm fine, Mum, honestly, and I couldn't sit on the sidelines while the search went on. You must understand that.'

'Yes, I suppose so. I'm just afraid for the toll this is going to take on you.'

'You know it isn't the first misper I've been involved with. I've survived the others, and I'll survive this one too.'

'But if you don't find her . . .'

'We will. This is different, Mum. Sophie wasn't depressed, at least not in the same way as Penny was, and we've got good reason to suspect that she went off with someone willingly. All we need to do now is track those people down.'

'I see.'

Able to picture her mother's troubled eyes, while sharing the devastation of never finding anyone who might have led them to Penny, Andee injected more tenderness in her tone as she said, 'I'm sorry, I have to go now, but I'll be home later. We can talk again then.'

As she rang off she checked to find out who had texted during the call. *Hi, just to say landed on time. Is 7 this evening good for you? Gx*

Reminded of how much she wanted to see him, she quickly tried to think what to do. It should be fine, unless there was some kind of breakthrough with Sophie that would obviously have to take precedence. But there was also her mother whom she'd just promised to see later, and Martin, though she certainly wouldn't see him tonight.

Texting back, she wrote, *Complications with a case, so can we say 8? Might not be able to stay for dinner. Really sorry, but very much looking forward to seeing you. Ax*

A moment later he texted back, *Whatever works for you. x*

Loving him for being so understanding, she put

her phone aside and continued her notes for the press release, hastening back to the incident room as soon as it was done where she found Gould sitting at her desk.

'CCTV,' he stated.

'It's interesting.'

'So I've been hearing . . . Do you want to get that?'

Checking her mobile and seeing a number she didn't recognise she quickly clicked on. 'DS Lawrence,' she announced impatiently.

'Hello, it is Kasia Domanski speaking.'

Andee's eyes widened in surprise. 'Hello Kasia,' she said, as much to let the others know who was on the line as to try and sound friendly. 'How can I help you?' As Gould waved for silence in the room she switched the call to speaker.

'I am ringing,' Kasia began, 'to ask if you have heard from Tomasz yet?'

Receiving a shake of the head from Leo, Andee said, 'No, we haven't, I'm afraid. Have you?'

'Yes, yes, he called me about an hour ago from Poland. He says he is going to call you.'

'Did he say when?'

'No, but his mother is not well. He is at the hospital with her. I think he will be in touch with you today. I just want to let you know this.'

'Thank you. I very much appreciate it. Do you know which hospital he's at?'

'I am sorry, he did not tell me, but I have a number for him. He lost his mobile, so he has a new one now.'

Grabbing a pen, Andree scribbled down the number and noted the country code. So he was in Poland. 'Thanks, I'll try contacting him,' she said.

'If he does not answer, it will be because he is not allowed to have phone on while in the hospital,' Kasia warned.

'Of course.' Realising Kasia was about to ring off, Andee quickly said, 'Before you go, can I ask you to confirm the time Tomasz came home on the night of the seventeenth?'

There was a slight hesitation before Kasia replied, 'Um, yes, I am sure it was his usual time, around quarter past twelve. Maybe a few minutes after.'

Andee's eyes met Leo's. Kasia wasn't sounding as certain as she had when they'd first asked her. 'Is there a chance you might have been asleep and not actually noticed the time?' she suggested.

'I – uh, I am sure it was then.'

No longer convinced, Andee said, 'Just one more question. How long has Tomasz had his laptop computer?'

'Only two days by the time you take it. We need a new one for a long time, and at last Tomasz get round to it. Please, when can we have it back? I need to use for my emails and accounts.'

'I'm sure we can release it in the next day or so,' Andee replied. There was no point keeping it when it had turned out to have next to nothing on it. 'Do you still have the old one?'

'No, Tomasz take it to Curry's so they can transfer everything we need, then I think he throw it away.'

Guessing Kasia hadn't had time to realise that only her personal information was on the new laptop, Andee thanked her again and rang off. 'We need to find the other computer,' she told Leo.

'On it,' he responded.

'OK,' Gould addressed them all, 'let's find

out when/how Sikora arrived in Poland, given he wasn't on the flight out of Bristol.'

'I'll check this morning's passenger list,' Jemma responded, as Andee dialled the number Kasia had given her.

'Include flights that left from other airports yesterday,' Andee instructed. 'Whether to Krakow or Warsaw.' Unsurprised to find herself going through to a voicemail box, she left a message urging Sikora to ring back as soon as he could, and said to the room at large, 'I'm sure we're all asking ourselves the same question: is Sophie over there with him?'

'I'll get some pictures through to the locals,' Jemma piped up.

'Can we ping his phone from the UK, to get an actual location for him?' Leo wondered.

Gould shook his head. 'I don't know if it's technically possible, but even if it is we'd have to get all sorts of clearance.'

'But if we believe she *is* there?' Andee pressed.

'We'd have to offer up some pretty compelling evidence to say she is,' he reminded her, 'and right now we don't have it.'

'So what do we do?' Leo demanded.

As Andee started to answer her mobile rang again, and she blinked with astonishment at the incoming number. 'It could be him,' she announced, and quickly setting the call on speaker she said, 'DS Lawrence.'

'It is Tomasz Sikora here,' he told her. 'I received the message that you want to speak to me.'

'That's right.' Andee was looking at Gould. 'Thanks for getting back to me. I think you're aware that we're concerned for the whereabouts of Sophie Monroe . . .'

'Yes, I am, but I do not understand why you think I would know where is she. She is not someone I know very well.'

'But you do know her?'

'Of course, but she is not a friend or anything like that.'

Since he was hardly going to admit it if she were, Andee said, 'Can you tell me if you gave her a lift from the campsite on the night of August 17th?'

'No, I did not, because I have never given her lift from campsite.'

'What about Gary Perkins?'

'What about him?'

'Did you leave the campsite with him on August 17th?'

'No, I did not, because I have never left campsite with him.'

Andee's eyes were still fixed on Gould. 'Can you tell me, Mr Sikora, why Kasia thinks you were on the Bristol flight to Krakow yesterday morning?'

Sighing, he said, 'This is because I tell her it is the flight I am taking, but it was full when I tried to book, so I drive here instead.'

Andee blinked. 'You drove all the way to Poland?'

'That is correct.'

'So when did you arrive?'

'In the early hours of this morning.'

'Is Sophie with you?'

'*No*, she is not.'

'What about Gary Perkins?'

'I came alone and I go straight to the hospital to see my mother. I stay with her until I go out to buy a new phone today. This is when I call Kasia.'

'What happened to your other phone?'

'I don't know. I lost it. Or someone stole it.'

'Could it perhaps be with your old computer?'

'What?'

'I think you understand the question.'

After a moment he said, 'I recycle the computer with a company who does these things. The phone I had with me after that, so it is not with the computer.'

'Which firm did you use for the recycling?'

'I do not know who it was. The man, he approach me as I leave the store and say he recycle computers to make them good for children with learning problems. So I give him our old one and he take it away.'

How convenient. 'Which store was this?'

'Curry's on Wermers Road.'

Andee's eyes went to Dan, a silent instruction to check out this mysterious recycling man. 'Why is none of your data on the new computer?' she asked.

'I have here, on USB. I am going to upload when I get back, but I ask them to do for Kasia.'

'OK. Tell me, which hospital is your mother in?'

With no discernible hesitation he replied, 'She is at the University Hospital, in Krakow.'

Nodding to Leo to get on to it, she said, 'Going back to the night of August 17th, do you remember seeing Sophie at the Entertainment Centre?'

'Yes, she was there.'

'Did you speak to her?'

'No. Or maybe I tell her thank you for the nice things she say about the show.'

'Is that all?'

'Yes. That is all.'

'Did you see her when you were driving out of the site?'

'No.'

'Why did you turn left on to the main road instead of right, which would take you a more direct route home?'

He sounded confused. 'I – sometimes I go the longer way round to wind down a little after the show.'

Andee's eyebrows arched. 'And what time would you say you arrived home that night?'

'It was probably around twelve fifteen, or twelve twenty. I did not check.'

Glancing up as Shona from the press office came into the room, Andee said, 'OK. When are you intending to return to the UK?'

'I hope in the next few days. I can come to the police station to speak to you if that would be helpful.'

Surprised, she said, 'Yes, it would. One last thing before you go, do you remember someone who worked at the camp by the name of Tania Karpenko?'

Sounding wary, he replied, 'Yes, I remember her.'

'Do you happen to know why she left?'

'No, I do not.'

'What about Michaela Reznik? Is she someone you know?'

'I did when she was at the camp.'

'Do you know where she is now?'

'I am afraid I do not.'

Unable to tell on the phone if he was lying, she said, 'OK. Thanks for being in touch, and please let us know when you're back in the country.'

After ringing off she met Gould's stare with one of her own.

'There's no point releasing the CCTV footage at this stage,' he decided. 'It's not conclusive enough.'

'It is as far as Perkins is concerned,' Andee reminded him. 'We see her going into his flat, coming out again around forty minutes later and they've both been picked up going into the club. OK, they're not actually together, but there's only one flat at the top of those stairs.'

'Right. Get Yaz to sort it,' he said to Leo, and vacating Andee's chair he held it out for her to sit down. 'Copy me in on the statement,' he told Shona as she joined them.

'Of course,' Shona replied.

'Dan, get in touch with the police in Krakow to fill them in on what's happening,' Andee instructed. 'They'll need visuals of Sophie *and* Perkins, and the registration number of Sikora's van. Can anyone tell me if the Monroes have a FLO yet?'

'Apparently Lauren Mitchell's there,' she was told.

'Good. Sir, I think I should talk to the Monroes about broadcasting an appeal.'

He appeared thoughtful as he nodded. 'Sure, provided they're up for it.'

As soon as Shona had returned to the press office with the information she needed, Andee rang Gavin Monroe.

'Not news, exactly,' she replied regretfully when he asked, 'but there have been some developments. CCTV footage from the camp shows Sophie going into and coming out of Gary Perkins's apartment that night, so we know for certain now that she was with him. Later footage shows her leaving the club alone, but Sikora's van leaves the underground car park soon after. Unfortunately, the camera covering the entrance wasn't functioning that night, so the van isn't picked up again until it's outside the camp.'

'So are you saying . . . You mean . . . You think she got into the van?'

'It's certainly possible. We've spoken to Tomasz Sikora and he's claiming he has no idea where she is.'

'And you believe him?'

'Not necessarily, but until we can prove she was with him . . .'

'You know she was with Perkins. Where's he now?'

'We're working on finding out.'

'He could be with Sikora.'

'It's possible.'

'So where's he?'

'We have good reason to believe he's in Poland.'

When there was only silence at the other end she knew exactly what was going through his mind, and wished there was a way she could make this easier.

'Are you still there?' she asked gently in the end.

'Yes, I'm here.' His voice was higher, threaded by the strain he was under. 'If they've done anything to her I swear I'll . . .' He choked back a sob.

'I understand how you feel, but if they do have her, I can promise you this, we'll find her.' Why had she said that when she was in no position to offer such a guarantee? Had her father been told the same when they'd been searching for Penny? What the hell did you say to a parent when you had no proper answers to give?

'We're about to issue another statement to the press,' she continued. 'There won't be any mention of Sikora again, only of Perkins.'

'Why not Sikora?'

'Because we simply don't have enough grounds to implicate him at this stage. Perkins, on the other hand, has already broken the law simply by being at the campsite . . .'

Rage broke through his grief. 'If he's hurt her, if he's . . . I swear I'll kill him.'

'The press are all over this,' Andee reminded him, 'so there's a chance we'll have him by the end of the day.'

'Provided he's in this country?'

'Of course, but there's nothing to say at this stage that he's left.'

'This is a nightmare,' he shouted angrily. 'I can't go on just sitting here, doing nothing . . .'

'Actually, there is something you can do,' she broke in quietly. 'I was wondering how you'd feel about broadcasting an appeal? I'm sure you've seen the kind of . . .'

'Yes, yes, I have, and we were going to ask if we could do something like that. I said to Heidi, it might make a difference if she sees me asking her to come back, but if she's in Poland . . .'

'We really don't know that she is.'

'Will it go out over there?'

'If we have good reason to suspect she's there, I'm sure the local TV stations will run it.'

'It *will* make a difference, won't it?' he gasped. 'I mean, if she sees me . . .'

'I'm sure it will,' Andee assured him, remembering how desperately her father had wanted to believe that when he had made his televised appeals to Penny, or to someone who might have been holding her. She'd never forget the endless, torturous hours of nothing that had followed. *Please don't let that happen to the Monroes. It's too cruel a fate, for anyone.* 'We can talk about it more later,' she told him, 'or you can discuss it with Lauren. Is she there?'

'Yes, she's here.'

'Good.' Then, after a beat, 'I know how difficult all this is, especially now the press are so involved, but Lauren will stay with you and there'll be officers outside at all times. You have my number if you want to be in touch?'

'Thank you. Yes, I have it.'

'I'm as determined to find her as you are,' she told him with feeling, and after assuring him she'd be in touch again as soon as she had more news, she rang off.

'Mum, for God's sake,' Suzi was urging down the phone, 'if you know where Gary is you have to turn him in.'

'Who said I know where he is?' her mother snapped.

'You always know where he is, and you've seen the news. He's all over it. Everyone's looking for him, and if you're hiding him it's only going to make it worse for you.'

'Not if they don't find him.'

'But they *will*. Mum, you can't protect him from this. He was with Sophie the night she disappeared, they've got it on camera . . .'

'She's another one who was throwing herself at him,' her mother came in tartly. 'They're all the same, these little tramps . . .'

'Just listen, will you! You know as well as I do that he's not supposed to go anywhere near a girl who's under eighteen. So the very fact he even has this job could end him up back in prison. Oh God,

I should never have helped him get it. This is all going to end up rebounding on me. Already people are giving me a wide berth, like I'm the one who's on the bloody register . . . And now they're saying they've found a hydroponics machine in his flat. What the hell's the matter with him? Does he want to go back to jail or something?'

'You have to stop getting yourself in a state over this,' her mother told her firmly. 'Whatever he's done has got nothing to do with you.'

'It doesn't have anything to do with you either, but that doesn't stop people throwing bricks through your windows and damaging your car.'

'They're just morons who don't have anything better to do. You've got yourself a good position down there, Suzi, so you just hang on to it.'

Suzi felt like screaming. 'How am I going to do that when his bloody face is all over the news with a fourteen-year-old girl who I *know* he's had some sort of relationship with? You've got to tell me if she's with him, Mum, and if she is, you have to make him send her back.'

'Suzi, I swear to you, I don't know where he is.'

'Hasn't he been in touch with you at all?' She gasped as the salon door suddenly opened and a small plastic bag landed softly in the middle of reception.

'What is it?' her mother cried.

'I don't know,' Suzi wailed, shaking with fear. 'Someone just threw something in . . . Oh Mum, what if it's a bomb?'

'Don't be silly. Tell me what it looks like.'

'It's a plastic bag that's got something in . . . I don't want to look . . .'

'It's probably dog poo. Did you see who it was?

If you did, you just go and chuck it back.'

'What good's that going to do? They're trying to tell me they don't want me here, so hurling dog poo at them is hardly going to change their minds, is it? Mum, please, tell me where he is.'

'For the last time, I don't know, but I can tell you this, if he was with that girl the night she disappeared he's better off hiding, because until she turns up everyone's going to think he's done away with her and next thing we know he'll be up on a bloody murder rap when he hasn't even done anything wrong.'

'But what if he *has* done something to her? She's *fourteen*, Mum. Nearly half his age . . .'

'This is your brother we're talking about, of course he hasn't done anything to her. Now you just calm down and go on about your business knowing you've got nothing to feel ashamed of.'

'Mum! Don't hang up. *Mum!*'

Realising the line had gone dead, Suzi clicked off her end and covered her face with her hands. She didn't know what she'd done to deserve such a terrible life. Why hadn't she realised it would all go wrong as soon as she brought her liability of a brother here? The truth was her mother had always been able to talk her into doing things she didn't want to do – and slipping Gary into this job for the summer had been their mother's idea.

'You have to do something to help him,' she'd been told. 'He deserves a fresh start as much as you do after what he's been through.'

'But you know he's not supposed to be around kids,' Suzi had protested.

'And you know what a load of nonsense that is. He's no more a threat to them than you or me. So you do what you can to get him in there.'

'But they run checks on people who are working with children, so they'll know straight away he has a record, and once it gets out, which it will . . .'

'All you have to do is say it's just for the summer. He's got a good record from when he was working at the pool in Dagenham. I'll have a chat with someone I know there to get him a reference, which you can give to your employer. If she starts talking about CRB checks then we'll say he's found something else. All right? This isn't a big ask, Suzi. This is what families do for one another.'

So she'd done it, and neither Heidi nor Jackie Poynter had mentioned anything about running the usual criminal record checks, so Suzi had to presume they'd never happened.

Thinking of Jackie Poynter, and what she would have to say about all this when she got back, was enough to make Suzi want to run away and hide. If she knew where to go she wouldn't even hesitate, but there was nowhere, and in her heart, in spite of how scared she was, she didn't want to be a coward. Much better to stay and face the music, and if Jackie did end up firing her . . . Well, she'd have to cross that bridge when she came to it, because right now she had absolutely no idea what she'd do if it happened.

Chapter Seven

Much later in the day Andee was finally driving towards home when Graeme rang. Seeing his number was so pleasing that she felt the frown leave her face like a bird taking flight. 'Hi, are you home yet?' she asked cheerily.

'At the shop,' he replied. 'And you?'

'On my way to check on my mother, change after a long day at work and hopefully to make myself presentable in time to see you at eight. Are we still on for that?'

'Indeed we are, if you're sure you can make it. I've just been watching the news. I take it you're involved in the missing girl case?'

'I am, so I'm afraid my evening might not turn out to be my own. But for as much of it as I can control, I'd like to spend it with you.'

'Now that's what I want to hear. So I thought I'd prepare a frittata rather than the more exotic fare I had in mind, and I'll go easy on the wine just in case you have to desert me.'

'I'm sorry I've had to spoil the original plan.'

'Don't be. I know what your world is like, I watch *Midsomer Murders*.'

Laughing, she said, 'I have some other news, but it can wait till I get there.'

'Really? I'm intrigued. Actually, I also have news, but that too can wait. Call me when you get to the gate. Apparently the buzzer's still not working.'

She was still smiling as she ended the call, her mind flying off in all sorts of romantic directions, until the phone rang again and she saw it was Martin.

Why on earth should she suddenly feel guilty about talking to another man, and why was she feeling in the least bit bothered about seeing him with another woman?

Knee-jerk reactions, both, nothing to do with reality.

'Hi, how are you?' she asked, realising too late that her breezy tone was unsuited to someone who'd just lost his father.

'Yeah, I'm OK,' he replied, the low timbre of his voice stirring up feelings she'd tried so hard to defeat. Why wasn't it possible to erase them like chalk from a board, or dead flowers from a garden, when they were no longer required?

'I know you saw me with Brigitte,' he told her, coming straight to the point and pronouncing the name Bridge-eet. Much more exotic than plain old Bridge-it.

'She's very pretty, from what I saw of her,' she responded, finding it easy to speak the truth in spite of not liking it much. Except what difference did it make to her how the woman looked? She'd moved on, she had someone else in her life now . . .

'I was hoping we could get together,' he said.

Her eyebrows arched. 'What, the three of us? I can't imagine why . . .'

'Actually, I meant you and me.'

Swallowing the rest of her protest, she asked, 'And what would Brig-*eet* think of that?'

'She's fine with it.'

Childishly detesting her, Andee said, 'Oh, well then there's no reason for me not to be, is there? Unless, actually, I'm not sure why you want to get together. Is there any point? It'll only be awkward for both of us, and I don't think you need to be dealing with any more right now.' *His father's dead, Andee, you really don't have to be this hostile.*

'I'd like to see you. That's all.'

She'd already taken breath to answer before realising she wasn't sure what to say.

'I miss you,' he told her. 'I miss us.'

Thrown, and almost, for an instant, drawn into it, she quickly reminded herself of how skewed a person's perspective could be after suffering a loss, especially one as close as a parent.

Before she could stop herself, she said, 'So that would be why you brought Brigitte here, to show her how much you miss me?' What the hell was she saying?

Sighing, he replied, 'I didn't *bring* her, as you put it. She came because she wanted to show she cares.'

How nice of her. 'And what about you? Do you care? I mean, about her.' Had she really just asked that? What the heck was the matter with her? 'Of course you do,' she ran on before he could reply. 'She wouldn't be here otherwise. How are the children getting along with her?'

'They've only met her briefly, but I'm not expecting . . .'

'Hang on, hang on, I'm following this now,' she interrupted. 'What you're asking is for me to give your relationship my blessing so the children will feel all right about making friends with her.'

'Andrea, I was hoping you might . . .'

'Don't patronise me.'

He actually laughed. 'How was that patronising?'

'You called me Andrea.'

'And I don't always?'

As a matter of fact he did. 'It was the way you said it. Anyway, when, where would you like to meet?'

'I'm happy to fit in with you.'

A typical response from him, casting the net too wide for her to get out of. 'It's hard to set a date while I'm involved in this case,' she reminded him.

'The missing girl? I just saw it on the news.'

'I'm sure we'll end up getting her back. In fact, I won't let it go until we do.'

'So you reckon she's with this Perkins guy?'

'Let's just say we definitely need to speak to him.'

'What about the other guy, the Pole, they're talking about online?'

'They are?' Of course, how could she have imagined that wouldn't happen when so many questions had been asked around the camp about Sikora? 'We're not sure about him,' she said. 'What sort of things are they saying?'

'That he's part of a gang specialising in trafficking women.'

She groaned inwardly. 'Based on what evidence?'

'I've no idea. There are other girls being mentioned with foreign-sounding names. It's all about procurement, apparently.'

'Well, it's good to know the cyber detectives have

a proper handle on things,' she retorted. 'I thought you, at least, wouldn't be so easily taken in.'

'I'm just asking,' he protested. 'No need to bite my head off.'

No, no need. 'Sorry, I didn't mean to. We don't know anything about those girls at the moment, and as they're not British nationals, and no one from their own countries has reported them missing our main focus has to be Sophie.'

'Of course.' Then, after a beat, 'Will you let me know when we can meet? The funeral's been set for next Monday, by the way, it would be great if you could make time between now and then.'

How could she not? How could she be so cruel as to make him doubt it? 'Of course I can,' she assured him. 'I'll – I'll call when things are a bit clearer.'

After ringing off she called through for an update on the online rumours and was told that they were still being closely monitored, but nothing substantive had presented itself yet. However, they were staying on it, and would report immediately if anything changed. So now she was free to carry on feeling wretched and upset on too many levels over Martin. She remembered how he used to remind her of how important it was for her, the family, even the investigation, that she take time away from it once in a while. She'd fought him about it some-times, but had always ended up loving him for understanding when a fix of her home life and her real priorities had become vital.

How come he'd just stopped loving her? Why hadn't she realised it was happening?

I miss you, he'd said. *I miss us*.

Determined not to think about him any more, she connected to the incident room again. 'Jemma,' she said when she got through. 'Anything new from Krakow?'

'All I can tell you at the moment,' Jemma replied, 'is that the local police have run a blank on the hospital in Krakow. Several Sikoras listed – it's a big place apparently – but every one of them is male, apart from one who's only twenty, so hardly our Sikora's mother.'

'I see,' Andee murmured. 'Have you tried his number again?'

'Yes, frequently and no reply.'

'Any movement on his bank account?'

'None.'

'OK, get on to the girlfriend and find out if she's heard any more. What about Perkins? Any sightings?'

'Plenty, but still nothing positive, and nothing to say he's gone through any of the channel ports, or taken a flight to Poland. We've had a couple of callers claiming to have seen Sophie, one in Hull, the other in Hereford, but it turns out both are known to their local police as regular responders to helplines.'

In other words, time-wasters.

'In light of what's happening in the online community,' Jemma ran on, 'the press office wants to know if they can put out a statement saying Sikora has now been traced and is helping with enquiries, but I've asked them to hold fire on that.'

'Absolutely. We'd look pretty damned stupid if it turns out he's given us the slip again. Is Gould around? Do we know if he's contacted Interpol?'

'Actually I heard just now that he's referred it upstairs, but I don't think we'll hear back on it until tomorrow morning at the earliest.'

'By which time Sikora could be anywhere.' Pulling up outside Briar Lodge, she remained in the car as Jemma spoke to someone at her end.

'Are you still there?' Jemma asked, sounding excited as she came back on the line.

'I am. What was all that about?'

'Apparently someone's just rung to say they think they saw Sophie going into Kesterly station last Monday or Tuesday with a bloke who fits Perkins's description.'

'Do we have the station footage from last week?'

'No, but I'll send someone to get it now.'

'OK, talk Yaz into staying on to view it. I'll come back if it turns out the sighting's real.'

An hour and a half later Andee was in Graeme's stylish Georgian home overlooking the botanical gardens, not quite sure why she was feeling odd about being alone with him, when she'd been so looking forward to it. It had to be some sort of fallout from Martin's call still hanging around to unsettle her; contact with him had a way of doing that, which was extremely annoying when she shouldn't be thinking about him at all.

And she wouldn't be, she told herself firmly, had she not just told Graeme about Dougie's passing.

They were sitting on a plush velvet sofa at one end of the impressive kitchen, and as Graeme's warm grey eyes searched hers inquisitively, but not intrusively, she was reminded of why she found him so attractive. He was a quietly confident and elegant-looking man, with a voice and

175

manners to match, and an unhurried manner that was always calming to be around.

She knew, because he'd told her, that he had two sons, aged twenty and eighteen, and from the photos scattered around the place she could see that they resembled him. Both were at uni, one in London, the other in Edinburgh, and apparently they rang their father regularly. Though Graeme tried hard not to talk about them too often, she could tell when he did how proud he was of them. It was another reason she'd fallen for him. He was clearly a great father, as well as a good, kind, humorous man with a way of making people – her, anyway – feel very glad to be with him.

'I'm sorry my news wasn't . . . Well, a bit happier,' she grimaced.

'I'm sorry too,' he said, 'I mean, for your loss and for how difficult I think you're finding this.'

Feeling herself flush, she said, 'I'll miss him. He was a huge part of our lives.'

'I'm sure. He meant a lot to a great many people.'

Her eyebrows rose. 'Did you know him?'

'A little. Not well. He was a good mayor, that's for sure.'

Andee smiled. 'He enjoyed his time in office. We were living in London then so we didn't get to see so much of him, but we always heard about his accomplishments – and his failures. He could be very loud about them.'

Graeme's eyes twinkled. 'How are your children taking it?'

'They're upset, obviously, but I think having their dad around is helping. It's where they are this evening, with him and their grandmothers. I'm not sure I'd have found it easy to get away otherwise.'

'It's good that your families have stayed close,' he commented. 'It's always been a source of regret for me that my ex-wife refuses to be friends.'

'Why do you think that is?'

'It's a good question, when she's the one who left me. Though I think it probably has something to do with me not wanting to take her back when her new relationship fell apart. However, that's water under the bridge. We speak when we have to about the boys, otherwise we're in very separate worlds. Now, are you ready to eat?'

As though answering for her her tummy rumbled, and they both laughed.

'Come on,' he said, pulling her to her feet, 'I've set up a table on the terrace, and I've even brought out the candles. If you'd care to light them, I'll rescue the frittata from the fridge – do you mind having it cold?'

'Not at all. Can I make a salad?'

'All done. Just tell me if I can pour you a glass of wine.'

She pulled a face. 'A small one, and you don't know how much it's costing me to say that, because I'd love nothing better right now than to kick off my shoes, let down my hair and finish the entire bottle with you. But if something breaks tonight . . .'

'I understand, but I'll hold you to it for another night.'

'Please do.'

'Maybe after the funeral,' he suggested. 'I have a feeling your family is going to need all the spare time you can manage until then.'

Putting her arms around him, she gazed up into his eyes. 'You're probably right,' she whispered, 'but I want you to know that I'd much rather be spending it with you.'

With a smile he pulled her in closer. 'I haven't told you my news yet,' he reminded her.

Since his mouth was very close to hers, she didn't feel in too much of a hurry to hear it.

'I,' he murmured, 'have found a house in Umbria that I'd like you to take a look at.'

Her eyes widened as she drew back to look at him.

'I've brought photographs to show you, and I shot some video while I was there, but you'll get a much better idea if you see it in person. When you're ready, of course.'

Her heart was suddenly beating faster. A holiday in Italy. With him. How different her life could be if things were to work out for them.

Maybe this was the road she'd been meant to travel.

'I'll get that frittata,' he grinned, and pressing a lighter into her hand he turned her towards the terrace.

Much later that night Andee came awake with a start. Sound was thrumming through her ears like a speeding train; her heart was racing, her mind was still clinging to the clouded chaos of dreams. Penny's face undulating in water, her dark hair floating like seaweed. Sophie in a pit of darkness pleading with someone to come. Martin walking away with Sophie. Sophie turning around and staring at her. Her father urging her to find Penny. Sophie's father yelling at her for failing his daughter.

Penny laughing as she skipped down over rocks on to a beach. Sophie crying for her mummy. Alayna running from someone. Martin trying to catch Alayna. Luke turning on his father. Sophie still crying for her mother.

What had happened to the lovely gentle dreams she should have been having about Graeme and Italy?

Taking soft, deep breaths she flipped back the sheet and sat on the edge of the bed, waiting for the jumbled madness to fade. Her pulses continued to race, but the shaking in her limbs was subsiding and the irrational fear flooding her head was slowly draining.

It was only a dream. Nothing she'd seen or heard was real.

Accepting it would be a while before she could sleep again, she put on a robe and let herself quietly out of the bedroom on to the landing.

Seeing both children's doors slightly open, she went to check on Luke and found him sprawled in all his youthful glory on his iron-framed bed, dead to the world. As she moved on to Alayna's room she found herself wondering where Sophie was now, this minute, at this hour of the night. It would be wonderful to think she was safely sleeping somewhere. Or awake and planning her return.

The CCTV from Kesterly station had shown images of two people who, in close-up, were clearly neither Perkins nor Sophie.

Pushing Alayna's door further open, she peered inside and felt a bolt of alarm shoot through her heart. The bed was empty. Her daughter wasn't there.

'Alayna?' she whispered into the shadows.

Turning around she checked the bathroom, but there was no light on.

Realising she was in danger of overreacting, she ran down the stairs, trying to outdistance the voices and images from her dreams, and found her daughter curled into an armchair at one end of the kitchen, munching on a slice of toast while watching a nearly silent TV.

Heaving a secret sigh of relief, Andee said, 'There you are. What are you doing up at this hour?'

Alayna shrugged. 'Couldn't sleep. I just boiled the kettle if you'd like some tea.'

Deciding it was too hot for tea, Andee filled a glass with water and sat down at the table. After a moment Alayna licked the crumbs from her fingers, turned off the TV and came to join her.

'So what were you and Luke chatting about earlier?' Andee wondered, suspecting it was their grandfather.

Alayna frowned in bafflement.

'Your bedroom doors were open,' Andee explained. 'I thought you'd been in together for a while.'

Alayna rolled her eyes. 'That's what it's like having a detective for a mother. We can't ever get anything past you.'

Andee smiled, wishing it were true.

'If you must know,' Alayna said, helping herself to a sip of her mother's water, 'we were talking about you and Dad.'

Feeling her heart tighten, Andee reached up to smooth the silky blonde waves from Alayna's eyes. She knew she was biased, show her a mother who wasn't, but Alayna was growing into quite a beauty and though Andee felt proud of her, she worried that she would be judged on how she looked rather than how very worthy and intelligent a young woman she was.

'Aren't you going to ask what about you and Dad?' Alayna prompted.

Andee shook her head. 'I can guess it had something to do with Brigitte and how you wish she hadn't come, because it's not the right time for Grandma Carol, and because you're afraid it might be upsetting me.'

Alayna threw out her hands. 'See, you know everything.'

Andee smiled. 'Knowing you as well as I do, it wasn't hard to work out, but I don't want you to worry about me. It was always going to happen, Dad finding someone else . . .' How would Alayna take it if she discovered her mother had met someone too?

'Do you know how long they've been together?' Alayna asked.

'No. Do you?'

Alayna shook her head. 'I haven't asked, because I don't want him to talk about her. We'd much rather he came to his senses and realised he's made a terrible mistake and it's you he wants to be with.'

Feeling a familiar churning inside – a throwback, Andee reminded herself, to a time when she'd longed for that to be true – she said, 'I've told you before, you have to put that out of your minds. Dad would never have left if he hadn't been serious about wanting to break up with me . . .'

'But why should he get to make all the decisions? And if he doesn't wise up soon you'll meet someone else. Then it'll definitely be too late.'

Knowing the time wasn't right to mention Graeme, Andee said, 'I think it must be quite serious with Brigitte, or she wouldn't be here.'

'Grandma Carol doesn't want her at the funeral.'

'But if Dad wants her there . . .'

'Luke's going to tell him it can't happen.'

Andee sighed. 'I'll talk to Luke. Falling out with Dad now is the last thing either of them needs when they're both very raw over Grandpa's death.'

Seeming to see the sense of that, Alayna took her mother's hand as she said, 'If you'd just talk to Dad . . .'

'Sweetheart . . .'

'No, I know what you're going to say, but I truly think . . .'

'Stop,' Andee broke in gently. 'This has to be between me and Dad, and things have moved on since. Sssh. Everyone's upset about Grandpa right now, and it's only natural to think back to when things were different. Maybe once the funeral's over and we've all settled down a bit we can have this chat again.'

Alayna's head dropped to one side as she gazed at her mother. 'I just hate to think of you being unhappy.'

'Darling, I'm not unhappy. Sad about Grandpa, of course, and worried about Sophie Monroe . . .'

'That's what I mean. You've got so much going on that you're trying to block out how you feel about Dad, and this business with Sophie has to be bringing it all back about your sister.'

'I won't deny it's making me think of her, but I promise you, I'm handling it.'

Alayna was quiet for a moment, as, loving her

more than ever, Andee stroked her hair. 'Do you really think she's gone off with this paedo guy they're talking about on the news?' she asked.

'It's certainly possible.'

Alayna's eyes were full of concern. 'What will he do to her? You know, some people are saying that she's been sold into prostitution by an Eastern European gang. Do you reckon that's true?'

Andee shook her head slowly. 'There's no evidence of it.'

'I feel really sorry for her, wherever she is. And I hope all those girls who keep being mean to her at school are feeling really terrible now.'

Andee's eyebrows rose. 'Girls are mean to her at school?'

'Yeah, they're always calling her names and picking on her. She fights back, and you should hear some of the names she calls them, but they're always the ones who start it, and they almost always end up making her cry.'

How desperate Sophie's life had become: losing her mother, finding her father more interested in a new baby, being bullied at school . . . More than enough to drive a teenager into running away.

Thanks for making me want to kill myself.

As the echo wrapped itself round her heart, Andee got to her feet. 'Come on,' she said, pulling Alayna up, 'one of us has an early start in the morning, and though you might not need your beauty sleep, I certainly do.'

Tucking an arm through her mother's as they started along the hall, Alayna said, 'Going back to Dad . . .'

'Let's not.'

'But you can't keep hiding from it, Mum.'

Suppressing a smile, Andee said, 'I promise you I'm not.'

'I think he is, though.'

Wondering how she'd worked that out, Andee said, 'You think too much.'

'I reckon I can see things you can't. It's easier when you're looking from the outside.'

'I don't think being our daughter exactly puts you on the outside.'

'You know what I mean.'

'I do, but this conversation is over for tonight,' and dropping a kiss on Alayna's head, she gave her a gentle push into her room and closed the door.

Chapter Eight

'A shoe?' Andee repeated, her insides knotting with the dread of what this could mean. 'What kind of shoe?'

'A girl's shoe,' Leo replied, turning to the incident board. 'Apparently it was found here, in a rock pool.' He was pointing to a spot on the map at the far end of the beach closest to the Kesterly peninsula, where a treacherous area of rocks, caves, jagged reefs and hollows of quicksand was constantly thrashed by the waves. No one could survive a fall from those cliffs into such a maelstrom. A body could be washed away and might never come back.

Thanks for making me want to kill myself.

'When I said what kind of shoe, I meant is it a trainer, a pump, a sandal . . .'

'A trainer,' he provided.

'And we know it's a girl's because?'

'It's mostly pink.'

'Where is it now?'

'On its way here. It's a size four apparently.'

Jemma was checking the case notes. 'According to Heidi Monroe she wasn't sure whether Sophie was wearing trainers or flats when she left the house that night. Apparently she's size six, or thirty-seven, but that doesn't correspond. Thirty-seven is a size four.'

Remembering the CCTV of Sophie coming down the steps next to Alfie's Pie Shop, and later leaving the club, Andee decided she couldn't have been wearing trainers. On the other hand she could easily have changed into them some-time later.

'Get on to the FLO and explain that we need a correct shoe size for Sophie. She'll know how to handle it. Has anyone from the media got wind of it yet?'

'No calls so far,' Leo replied. 'Could be no one's up yet.'

Since it wasn't quite seven in the morning, he could be right.

Andee turned away as once again Sophie's words echoed in her mind.

Thanks for making me want to kill myself.

Had things really been so bad that she'd actually wanted to die? How frequently had she said it? Or even thought it? Was it possible she'd persuaded Sikora to drop her off near the cliffs that night? Had she wandered to the edge and stood staring out to sea, or down at the rocks, feeling they were her only way out?

Her eyes closed as Penny's chalky face from last night's dream rippled before her; she could hear screams, police sirens, sobs, her mother wailing . . . She felt uncomfortably hot all of a sudden, nauseous and in desperate need of air.

'The local police in Krakow have had a chat with Sikora,' Leo announced. 'Apparently they're satis-fied Sophie isn't with him.'

Reading the incoming information over his

shoulder, Andee said, 'Maybe she isn't now, but he could have dropped her anywhere by the time they spoke to him.'

'If she really did go with him. No prints taken from around the window of the bungalow are a match for Sikora's or Perkins's. Footprints under the window were a non-starter, much as we expected. Oh, and the computer recycling guy? He does exist. He hangs around stores like Curry's and approaches those who come out with new computers in the hope of getting their old ones for free. He then turns them around and gives them to local charities.'

'Can he remember what he did with Sikora's?'

'Not exactly, but he says even if he could it would be stripped of all its previous information by now, if it wasn't already.'

Nothing was ever straightforward. 'OK. What are you doing?' she asked Jemma.

'Leo and I are about to go and have a chat with the Poynters,' Jemma reminded her.

'Actually, I want you to go and talk to Estelle Morris again,' Andee decided. 'Leo, see if Barry's free to go with you. While you're with the Poynters keep in mind that you'd turn left out of the camp-site to go to their place, which of course was empty that night, so it could be where Perkins and Sikora took Sophie when they left the campsite. Check to see if there's any CCTV around their property, people like them often have it. It wouldn't take much more than five or six minutes to get there from the Cove, and chances are Sikora has keys to the place. He could have dropped Sophie and Perkins off and been home and tucked up in bed not much later than his usual time.'

'Morning everyone,' Gould greeted them, strolling into the room with a takeout coffee and doughnut.

'I was about to come and see you,' Andee told him. 'A girl's shoe's been found. No positive ID on it yet, but there's a chance it could be the right size. Did you get anywhere with involving Interpol?'

'I've just walked in the door,' he reminded her, 'but I can tell you this much, without actual footage of Sikora driving off with the girl they're not going to take it.'

Annoyed by the truth of that, she took out her phone and tried Sikora's number for the second time that morning. Going through to voicemail she repeated her last message, 'Tomasz, it's DS Lawrence. I'd like to speak to you again so please call me. You have the number,' and clicking off she connected to Kasia Domanski. 'I'm sorry to call so early,' she apologised, after explaining who she was, 'but I'd like to know if you heard from Tomasz overnight?'

'Yes, I did,' Kasia replied. 'He says he called you.'

'He did, but I need to speak to him again. Is he still in Krakow?'

'Yes, but he says he is hoping to be home by Sunday or Monday.'

It would be good to believe that. Kasia clearly did. 'Did he say anything else?'

'Not really, just that he was concerned about the children and was going to bring them presents.'

'OK. If he gets in touch with you again and he hasn't already spoken to me, please ask him to ring.'

After ending the call she stared hard at Gould.

'You know, I keep thinking there's something we've missed,' she informed him.

'Such as?'

'If I knew that we wouldn't have missed it.' Suddenly turning to Jemma, she said, 'Have you spoken to the FLO yet today?'

'It's still a bit early,' Jemma pointed out.

'OK. I'll call the Monroes to tell them about the shoe. We don't want the press getting hold of it first.' Picking up a phone she dialled the number, apologising once more for calling so early when Gavin's gravelly voice came down the line.

'Have you found her?' he demanded. 'Is she with him?'

'We're still checking the information that came in overnight, but there's nothing so far to give us a lead.'

'I see.' His voice was flat, drained of belief in their ability, of hope that he would ever see his daughter alive again.

'The reason I'm calling is because our records are showing a discrepancy in Sophie's shoe size,' she told him carefully.

'Is that important?'

Though she might want to, she wasn't going to lie to him. 'A trainer's been found. I haven't seen it myself yet, but I'm told it's pink and a size four. We're wondering if it could belong to Sophie?'

Knowing this had probably hit his heart like a punch, she gave him a moment to reply.

'Where – where did you find it?' he asked eventually.

'On the beach.' No need to mention anything about cliffs at this stage.

'You mean the beach here?'

'At the Skippers end of the Cove.'

He fell silent.

'Size?' she prompted gently.

'I don't know. I . . . I'll speak to Heidi.' Moments later he was back saying, 'She's a size six and she doesn't have any pink trainers.'

So not likely to be hers. 'Thank you,' she said, feeling no small relief.

'I think we might find her today,' he declared, sounding suddenly upbeat.

Touched by the flare of hope, and remembering only too well how uplifting, energising, those moments could be, she said, 'If you don't mind I'd like to take another look round her room.'

He sounded baffled, thrown. 'I thought you . . . Is there anything in particular . . .'

'Not really. I'd just like to get a feel for it again.' Since the room wasn't a crime scene it hadn't been torn apart during its first thorough search, and it wasn't her intention to do that now. She just wanted to be there to see if she could pick up on some essence of Sophie, a feeling of something she couldn't imagine right now that might turn out to be significant.

'OK. We're here,' Gavin said. 'Come whenever you like.'

Ringing off, she glanced at her watch. 'OK, everyone meet back here at one,' she instructed. To Gould she said, 'Unless something breaks between now and then I think we should set up a press conference for this afternoon, so the Monroes can make their appeal.'

He nodded slowly. 'I'll get on to the press office, and let them know,' he replied.

*

An hour later Andee was driving into the campsite when Dan Wilkes came through on the Airwave. 'We've heard from the police in Krakow again,' he told her. 'Apparently one of their officers paid Sikora's mother a visit, *at home*, and she says she hasn't seen her son since May.'

Andee's heartbeat jarred. 'Go on,' she said.

'That's all,' he responded. 'Still nothing on Perkins.'

More irritated by that than surprised, Andee asked, 'Does Gould know about this latest from Krakow?'

'Yes, he does.'

'So he's pressing harder for Interpol's involvement? We need Sikora taken in for proper questioning.'

'All Gould said was that we still don't have anything that actually connects Sikora to Sophie's disappearance.'

Thanking him abruptly Andee pushed her way through the press scrum outside the bungalow, informing the reporters as she went that there were no further developments at this time. As she reached the front door it opened before she could knock.

'I saw you arriving on telly,' Lauren Mitchell, the Monroes' FLO, explained. The girl was in uniform, minus her cap, and with her silvery-blonde hair and girlishly ruddy cheeks she didn't appear, at least to Andee, very much older than Alayna.

'How are they?' Andee asked, as Lauren closed the door.

'I'd say agitated,' Lauren replied. 'They've been talking about making flyers and posting them around town . . .'

'Her face is on the front of every paper this morning,' Andee pointed out.

'That's what I said, but you have to understand their need to do something.'

Of course – and out of nowhere a terrible memory assailed her of how her father used to ride buses around town, stop strangers in the street and trawl homeless shelters in search of his missing daughter.

How could she have forgotten that? She could see him now waiting at the bus stop for Penny to come home from school, and as though it were happening right now she could feel his wrenching despair when the bus pulled away, leaving him standing there alone.

She glanced down the hall as Heidi Monroe came out of the kitchen. With her plaited hair and fresh clothes she was looking better than when Andee had last seen her, though there was no mistaking the tremor in her voice as she said, 'Would you like some coffee? I've just made some.'

'That would be lovely, thank you,' Andee replied. 'How's Archie this morning?'

Heidi's smile was fleeting. 'Asleep, thank goodness. He's been awake half the night.'

As she disappeared back into the kitchen Andee and Lauren followed.

'I'm thinking about getting the train to London,' Gavin announced as soon as he saw Andee. 'A mate of mine in Kesterly said he'll make some flyers for us. I could post them round the stations and ask if anyone's seen her.'

Realising he'd temporarily detached from reality, Andee let it go as she said, 'We'd like to broadcast an appeal this afternoon.'

His face became pinched as he registered the words.

Passing her a coffee, Heidi said, 'Gavin mentioned you want to look at her room again.'

Andee nodded.

'She's not there,' Gavin said. 'I keep looking.' His laugh had no humour. 'Daft, isn't it? I mean, I know she's not there, but I keep hoping I'm wrong. I tell myself the next time I open the door she'll be lying on her bed, or sitting on the floor, or feeding the birds.'

Remembering doing exactly the same in Penny's room, telling herself it was all a dream and if she looked hard enough she'd wake up and Penny would be right where she belonged, Andee felt almost stifled by pity. 'Would you like to come and look with me?' she offered.

Though he shook his head he was already getting to his feet.

Minutes later they were standing in bright bands of sunlight streaming through chinks in the closed curtains of Sophie's room. They could hear the reporters outside, but it wasn't possible to make out what they were saying. The blare of music from the funfair was horribly jarring.

'Like a Virgin', by Madonna.

She wondered if Gavin had registered it.

'Where do you want to look?' he asked, casting a hopeless eye around the room.

'Why don't we start with her dressing table?' Andee suggested, and putting her coffee down she opened the top middle drawer.

'We've had it all out, so did your lot when they searched the place,' he told her.

'I know. I just want to be sure there's nothing we've missed.'

Finding only hairgrips, elastics, chewing gum and a pack of matches she moved on to the drawers either side.

After closing them too she sat quietly for a moment, not really listening to anything now, or even thinking specifically. She was simply feeling, as though by some process of osmosis she could work out why she'd wanted to come and do this. What was she really expecting to find that hadn't yet come to light?

She'd done this in Penny's room on countless occasions and it had never worked, but that wasn't to say it couldn't now.

Getting up, she went to browse through the hanging rail and shoes piled in a jumble at the bottom. 'How do you know she took clothes with her?' she asked Gavin.

His head came up, almost as though he'd forgotten she was there. 'Uh, I don't know,' he replied. 'I suppose we assumed she'd taken some because her holdall was gone, and her toothbrush and make-up things.'

Andee nodded and turned towards the neatly made bed with the rag doll on the pillow. After pulling back the sheets she lifted the mattress, not expecting to find anything, and indeed nothing was there. However, when she let it fall back into place she heard the sound of something sliding down the wall.

Glancing at Gavin, she dragged the foot of the bed into the middle of the room and stepped round it to see what had fallen. Intrigued, and conscious of Gavin watching her, she picked up a tatty

A4-size book with the single word *Sophie* in large yellow letters on the front of it.

She turned to Gavin. He'd gone almost yellow with shock.

'We searched this place,' he muttered hoarsely. 'When we couldn't find that book we thought . . . we assumed she'd taken it with her.'

Andee began flicking through it. Not only was it filled with Sophie's girlish writing, but with all kinds of cuttings, pressed flowers, ticket stubs, photographs, drawings . . .

'Her mother gave it to her,' Gavin told her. 'They started it together, just after Jilly found out she wasn't going to make it. They filled it with memories and hopes and dreams . . .' Putting a hand to his head, he sank down on a stool.

Giving him a moment, Andee quickly scanned the final entry. Though it offered no insight into where Sophie might be now, it did tell her that this wasn't for a father's eyes. Not yet, anyway.

'I'll have to take it with me,' she said gently.

He nodded. 'You'll take care of it though, won't you?' A sob escaped him.

'Of course,' she promised.

She was back in her car before she opened it again and stared at Sikora's name printed carefully inside love hearts, through the margins and throughout the text.

Kasia hated calling in sick, she'd never done it before when it wasn't true, but she was so worried about the way things were going that she hadn't wanted to leave the children, not even with Olenka. Keeping them safe from the press and away from the Internet was all that mattered when people were saying such terrible things about Tomasz. She could hardly believe it. Even some of their neighbours were turning against him. She wanted to shout at them to remember all he'd done for them without ever charging a penny.

Just because his name had been linked to Gary Perkins they were calling him a paedophile, a child-molester, some sort of monster. It was even said he was part of a gang that trafficked young girls. It was as though they really believed he was involved in Sophie's disappearance and it just wasn't true.

'But you have to face the fact that it might be,' Olenka kept insisting as gently as possible. 'I know it's not what you want to hear. I swear, I don't want to believe it either, but Kasia, admit it, you don't even know where he is.'

'He's in Krakow,' Kasia cried. 'He called me. He says he is coming home soon . . .'

'I know what he said . . .'

'Stop! Please stop,' Kasia begged, bunching her hands to her ears. 'You are not going to turn me against him. He has done nothing wrong. Do you hear me? He is with his mother in Poland, and soon he will be home.'

Watching her sister pace and inwardly pray, Olenka let a few moments pass before saying, 'OK, convince yourself of that if you want to, but at the same time you must ask yourself . . .'

'No! I don't care what you say. Tomasz is a good person. He would never hurt anyone . . .'

'Maybe not you, or the children, but Kasia, you don't really know what he's doing most of the time. He says he is with his mother, but you don't know that for certain. And when he tells you he is working at the campsites, I know of at least one time that he wasn't there.'

Kasia's face was ashen, her hands were shaking as she wrung them together. 'I know why you're saying these things,' she cried angrily. 'It's because you are jealous that he is paid more than Glyn. You want me to believe bad things about him, so you make up lies . . .'

'I am *not lying*. I didn't want to tell you before, because I knew it would upset you, but Kasia, Tomasz is the one who lied about where he was at night. Not every night, but some . . . '

'I am not listening to any more,' Kasia broke in furiously, 'you must leave my house if you do not stop saying these things,' and praying with all her heart that it would be Tomasz on the phone, she snatched it up and managed a ragged 'Hello?'

'*Kotek*, it is me.'

Sinking to her knees in relief, she said, 'Tomasz. Where are you? Are you on your way home yet?'

'Soon, there are still a few things I need to do here, then I will be back.'

Keeping her head down, so she didn't have to look at her sister, she asked, 'What sort of things?'

'I won't go into it now. I just need you to understand that what they are saying about me on the Internet, it isn't true. None of it.'

'I know. I know, but Tomasz, the police want to speak to you again. They rang here this morning . . .'

'Don't worry, I'll call them back. Have you heard from Mr and Mrs Poynter?'

'No, but Olenka says they have returned from Spain. Tomasz, did Gary Perkins leave the campsite in your van that night? That's what they're saying, and that you . . .'

'Kasia, you must ignore it. None of it is true. Now tell me, how are the children?'

'They're OK. They are upstairs playing. There are people from the press who keep trying . . .'

'The press? Kasia, please do not speak to anyone from the press. They will trick you into saying things you don't mean . . .' He broke off suddenly. '*Kurwa!*' he muttered, shocking her because he never swore. 'I must go,' he said, 'but *kotek*, remember, everything will be fine. I promise,' and without saying goodbye he abruptly rang off.

Remaining on her knees with her head bent, Kasia clicked off her phone and tried to make herself breathe more steadily. Tomasz had been in such a rush, had sounded so stressed and afraid that it was as though his adrenalin had whooshed down the line into her veins. She needed to think more clearly, allow God to guide her, because she had no idea what she should do next.

Andee was on her way back to the station when Leo rang. 'How did it go with the Poynters?' she asked, before he could speak.

'Surprise, surprise, they've got no idea where Sophie might be, and they're saying the reason they came back is to do everything they can to help find her.'

'Very obliging.'

'Apparently Sikora does have keys to the place and takes care of it while they're away so they're assuming he did come in, but everything was as they'd left it when they got back. Plenty of cameras around the outside of the property, but apparently they're all dummies, so no record of who's been going in and out.'

'What about an alarm?'

'They have one, but it doesn't work with a digital clock, so nothing to say when it's turned on and off.'

'Great,' she muttered. 'Did they let you have a look round?'

'Absolutely, and you've never seen a place like it. Think Middle East, *Geordie Shore* and fountains. They're very big on fountains. Got them in the kitchen, the bedroom, all the way down the side of the stairs and even in the bathrooms, or one of them anyway. When we got to talking about Perkins she, the missus, went off on one about how disgusted she'd been when she'd found out about his record. Apparently they never employ anyone without carrying out a CRB check first so she's got no idea how it happened, but once Sophie is home safe she'll be speaking to Heidi, whose job it is to do these things.'

Passing the buck, but sensitive enough to hold on to it until Heidi's current troubles were over. 'Did she say if Perkins has ever been to the house?'

'Not to her knowledge. Apparently they don't usually mix with employees.'

'What about Sikora?'

'Nothing but praise for him. Good worker, reliable, honest, a joy to have around. They know he's in Poland at the moment, on compassionate leave, as they put it.'

'Are they in touch with him?'

'They say not.'

'Mm. Anything else?'

'Not really. They look as crooked as Boycie and

his missus, but as we know, looks aren't every-thing. How's it going your end?'

'I found a diary under Sophie's mattress.'

'No way!' Barry shouted down Leo's phone. 'I looked under there myself.'

'It had got trapped between the bed and the wall, probably by the bottom sheet. I guess moving things around for a second time dislodged it. Anyway, no time to read it yet, but Sikora's name is featuring large towards the end.'

'In what context?'

'She had a crush, that's for sure. What I don't know yet is how far it went, or what kind of role Perkins played, but he's mentioned too. I'll have it copied as soon as I get back.'

Suzi was sitting at the salon's reception desk with the window blinds closed and the door locked when Jackie Poynter turned up. She was a tall, large-boned woman in her mid-fifties whose natural Slavic beauty had faded a lot more than her accent.

'It's a circus out there,' she complained as Suzi let her in. 'If it's not the press it's the police and if it's not the police it's some punter wanting to have a go about his holiday being ruined.' She sighed heavily, as though concerned about how to deal with that. Then assuming a breezy smile, she enquired, 'So, where is he?' She was looking around the room as though Gary might be hiding under the desk or behind a pot plant.

'I don't know,' Suzi replied timidly. Despite her shows of friendliness Jackie Poynter wasn't a woman to cross, and everyone knew it. 'If I did, I swear I'd tell you,' she added with conviction.

Seeming to accept that, at least for the moment, Jackie said, 'OK, then tell me, did he have something going with Sophie Monroe?'

Sensing it was best not to lie, Suzi said, 'I'm not sure. Possibly.'

Jackie sighed again and gave herself a moment to think. 'You know the police came to see us this morning?' she asked, fixing Suzi with her harsh amber eyes.

Suzi flinched.

'They were asking if your brother and Tomasz Sikora might have used our house while we were away.'

Suzi still said nothing.

'Well?'

'If they did I knew nothing about it.'

Jackie regarded her carefully, as though deciding whether or not to believe her.

'He doesn't tell me what he's doing,' Suzi insisted.

'But you knew, when you recommended him to me, that he had a criminal record?'

Since she was in no position to deny it, Suzi simply mumbled a sorry.

Jackie's eyes narrowed, as though she were intrigued. 'I'm guessing from looking at you that he never told you it's the reason I hired him,' she stated.

Suzi blinked, not sure she'd heard right.

'Of course, I never expected *this*,' Jackie continued, throwing out her hands, 'but perhaps I should have, given the other girl was the same age as Sophie. He clearly has a thing for teenagers.'

'The other girl was fifteen, sixteen by the time they pressed charges,' Suzi corrected.

'The point is, she wasn't a child, or not in the sense I would mean it. If he'd been one of those creeps who go after small kids he'd never have got through the door.' She shook her head, as if exasperated with herself. 'Jimmy said I was making a mistake when I took him on, and it doesn't please me to prove my husband right.'

'I don't understand,' Suzi said. 'Why would you hire him if you . . . ?'

'He had good references as a lifeguard, and we needed one. And *I* needed someone I could trust to carry out . . . other business. I discussed it with him, he understood what a very big favour I was doing him and was happy to take on his extra duties.'

Knowing she still wasn't following this well, Suzi said, 'Do – do you mean growing cannabis?'

'No, I do not mean that. I had no idea about that until the police found it in his flat. It's a shame, but he's turned out to be quite a liability, and Jimmy is telling me I have to sort it out. Of course, I will, but it's left me with a lot of explaining to do. Not that I'm especially worried. The police aren't anywhere near as clever as they like to think.' Her eyes suddenly widened. 'I'm not saying the fallout won't cost us some business for a while,' she admitted, 'I'm sure it will, but the main thing is that no one learns about the other more private matters your brother has been involved in.'

Suzi didn't know what to say.

Jackie stared at her hard. In the end she said, 'Let's not talk about how I helped you turn your life around by setting you up in this salon, or how I willingly gave your brother a second chance. It would only embarrass me. You too, I'm sure. On the other hand, if you've ever wondered how you might thank me . . . It's a small thing really, because all you have to do is keep to yourself anything your brother might have told you concerning his extra duties here.'

'He's never told me anything.'

'That's good, but if he ever does . . . It wouldn't be good for anyone if the police were to find out, and there's really no need for your brother to go down for anything more than breaking his protection order.' She threw out her hands in a gesture of incredulity. 'Why on earth would he want any extra time added to his sentence? And why would you want to lose all of this when you've worked so hard to build it up?' She smiled pleasantly. 'Do you hear what I'm saying, Suzi?'

Not knowing what else to do, Suzi nodded.

'Good, I'm glad that's clear. Now, I should be going.'

As she reached the door, Suzi dared to say, 'What about . . . What about Sophie?'

Jackie turned round, apparently amazed. 'Really, Suzi,' she chided, 'if you think I know . . . I could take offence at that, really I could, but I'll tell you what, to show what good friends we are, I won't,' and opening the door she took herself off into the sunshine.

'Jemma, are you still with Estelle Morris?' Andee asked down the phone.

'Just about to leave,' Jemma told her.

'OK, ask her what FBC stands for, will you?'

'FBC. OK, hang on.'

As she waited Andee stared down at the final entry of Sophie's diary, written the day before she'd disappeared,

FBC with Gary last night. He said I was amazing. I think he really likes me, which is lovely, and I really like him too, but there's no one to beat Tomasz. Really, really love T, and I know he loves me. Can't wait to see him tomorrow night.

'Are you there?' Jemma asked coming back on the line.

'I'm here.'

'Apparently it means full body contact, as in going all the way.'

Having already guessed that, but needing it confirmed, Andee said, 'So would PBC be partial body contact, as in messing around, foreplay?'

Jemma asked and apparently Andee's guess was correct.

'Thanks,' Andee said. 'I'll see you when you get back, unless there's anything you need to tell me now.'

'Nothing that can't wait.'

After ringing off Andee continued to look through the final entries of the diary in a turmoil of sadness and shock. She dearly wished she hadn't had to photocopy the book to circulate around the team. It seemed such a horrible exploitation of a lonely young girl who'd already been exploited enough.

G gave us some weed. Amazeballs! Totally love it when we get stoned. He had some mates round so loads of PBC. T was supposed to be coming, but he didn't turn up. Went to find him, but he'd already left.

Saw Tomasz tonight. Am totally and completely in love with him. Wish I could run away with him so we could be together and I wouldn't have to put up with the WSM any more.

Had row with Dad about not getting on with Heidi.

Wish Dad would just leave me alone. He doesn't care any more, so why does he bother to pretend? Would love to have Tomasz's baby. It would be so cute and sweet, not like Archie who's totally weird. Feel really bad saying that, but he is.

Going to tell T how I feel about him. I know he'll say I'm too young, but I don't see how age makes a difference. You can't help your feelings. They don't just switch on when you're sixteen. I know he's the right one for me. I can see us together. Estelle says she can see it too. She's the best friend ever.

Dad only went looking for me tonight!!! Thank God I was at Estelle's. He'd have gone totally ballistic if he'd found me at Gary's, or in the back of T's van. (So want to get into the back of T's van right now. Where are you Tomasz? Wish you'd call me.)

The poor girl had completely lost her sense of self-worth and was desperately trying to find it in the attention of these men. Men who'd taken full advantage of her, if these entries were to be believed, and Andee was mindful of how inventive an adolescent girl's mind could be.

Going back to the beginning of the month, she started again. *Party tonight at one of the Red Zone caravans. Few local boys there, couple me and E really fancy. Loads of dope and PBC. Some of them wanted to go FBC and got dead rough when I said no. Really terrifying. Thought I was going to be raped. Feel like crying. Where was T when I needed him?*

Looking at the picture of a younger Sophie on the whiteboard, the Sophie whose innocence and dreams shone like an aura around her, Andee felt the need to find her growing ever more urgently. The angry, confused mass of hormones this poor girl had become wasn't really her; it was a reaction to feeling lost in a world without her mother, confused by the torn loyalties of her father. All she really wanted was to be loved, to feel safe and protected the way she had as a child, and it was all going horribly wrong.

It was almost too tragic to bear.

'Sir,' she said, going through to Gould, 'there's a diary you need to see. It's still not putting Sikora together with Sophie after they left the Entertainment Centre that night, but there are strong suggestions that their relationship was inappropriate, if not sexual.'

Chapter Nine

Though Kasia was in the kitchen she was nervously aware of the enormous black car with tinted windows parked outside her house. She didn't actually know the man in the driver's seat, but she'd seen him before, during a barbecue at the Poynters' mansion up on the hill, and a few times at Blue Ocean Park. Tomasz called him the *goryl* – the gorilla. He drove Jackie Poynter wherever she went, which was why he was out there now, waiting for his boss to come out of the house so he could drive her to wherever she was going next.

It was debatable when that would be, since Jackie had spent the past ten minutes in the garden taking a call on her mobile and there was no sign of her ending it yet.

It was a relief to Kasia that the children were with Olenka for the rest of the day, and overnight while she worked. She wouldn't have wanted them here in case they annoyed Mrs Poynter, who wasn't known for her patience with young ones. Besides, keeping up a front for them was becoming more difficult by the day, especially when they were constantly asking when Tomasz was coming back. They had so much stored up ready to tell him and were so excited about it that they kept arguing over which story belonged to which teller. How it would make him laugh to see them.

'Sorry,' Jackie sighed as she stepped in through the door, 'I didn't think it would go on that long. And you were on your way out?'

'To work,' Kasia told her, 'but if you would like some tea . . .'

Jackie waved it away. 'I just wanted to make sure everything's all right for you here,' she smiled. 'I've heard what they're saying about Tomasz online. Of course we know it isn't true.'

Kasia only looked at her. This woman unnerved her, no matter how friendly she was being.

'Tomasz is a good provider,' Jackie continued, looking around. 'A good worker too. I can't think where any of us would be without him.' She sighed gently and took out a cigarette. 'I expect you think that a lot.'

Kasia wished she had the courage to say she didn't allow smoking in the house, but how could she when it was Jackie's house?

'Tell me,' Jackie said chattily, 'do you ever have any contact with your husband? Antoni, is that his name?'

Kasia's mouth dried as she shook her head.

'That's good. A real *dupek* from what I hear. He used to beat you?'

Kasia nodded, and wondered why Jackie was bringing this up, how she even knew, because she was sure Tomasz wouldn't have told her.

'It's good that he doesn't know where you are,' Jackie ran on. 'The last thing you need is trouble knocking at the door.' She blew out a stream of smoke and gave a laugh. 'It's the last thing any of us needs, isn't that right?'

Kasia cleared her throat. 'Tomasz keeps us safe,' she said softly.

Jackie's eyes were full of understanding. 'Of course he does, but I want you to know that if you're worried about anything, Kasia, if something happens to upset you or if the police start pressuring you in any way, I'm here for you, OK?'

Kasia nodded, in spite of not feeling at all comforted.

'We can always get things sorted, but if you don't call me, there won't be anything I can do.' She looked at her watch. 'OK, it's time I was going. I don't want to make you late.'

After seeing her out Kasia stood in the hallway, pressing her fingers to the holy pendant at her throat as she listened to the unsteady beat of her heart. She was trying to work out what the purpose of Jackie's visit had been, why it had left her feeling as though she'd just received some sort of warning.

'I think,' she whispered into the phone to Olenka as she hurried to catch the bus, 'she doesn't want me to speak to the police.'

'Then don't,' Olenka advised. 'You have nothing to tell them anyway, so you shouldn't have anything to worry about.'

It was true, she didn't know anything that would get anyone into trouble, but she desperately needed to get hold of Tomasz so he could explain to her what Mrs Poynter's visit had really been about.

Andee was driving back to Blue Ocean Park when Luke rang. 'Hey Mum,' he said, not sounding his usual upbeat self. 'Is it OK to talk?'

'Sure. What's up?'

'I just wanted to let you know I'm staying over at Jake's tonight. There's a party going on and it probably won't end till late.'

'Well, at least you're telling me,' she retorted drily. The last time he'd stayed out all night he hadn't even sent a text warning her he wouldn't be back. In truth, she hadn't actually realised he wasn't home until he'd rung to ask if she could pick him up.

Did that make her a bad parent?

He was seventeen, it was time to loosen the reins. It wasn't as though he couldn't take care of himself.

Knowing it wouldn't be quite so easy when it came time to allowing Alayna the same freedoms, she said, 'You're sounding a bit fed up.'

'I'm OK. Have you arranged to see Dad yet?'

Wishing her heart wouldn't contract at every mention of Martin, she said, 'No, not yet, but I will.'

'Mum, I've got to tell you, I think it's totally crap of him letting his girlfriend . . .'

'Luke, I know what you think, and I'm not arguing, but it won't help anyone if you and Dad start falling out, least of all Grandma Carol.'

'Yeah, and that's why I'm not saying anything to him, but if I was you I'd totally blow him out about getting together. I mean why would you want to know about his bloody relationship? He's way out of order even asking to see you. What's it to you who he's screwing? Why do we care what he does?'

Able to picture the angry set of his handsome face, she said, 'I know you haven't forgotten that he's only just lost his father. That's probably what he wants to talk about. Even so, if Brigitte is going to be a part of his life, she'll be a part of yours too . . .'

'No way! It's so not going to happen. And hello, who else has lost their father? He's not the only one.'

'It's not the same, Luke, and you know it.'

'It is from where I'm standing.'

'He loves you, and he's always there for you. OK, I get that you're angry, but honestly, now isn't the time to start dealing with it.'

'But if Alayna's right and he wants to get back with you . . .'

'He wouldn't have allowed Brigitte to come if that were the case, so put it out of your mind. Now, I ought to go. Have a good party tonight, and don't get too drunk.'

'Like as if.'

'Yeah, like as if. Love you.'

'Same here,' and the line went dead.

Moments later she was connecting to Martin. He was the only person she could discuss this with, or the only one who'd be able to make sure things didn't get out of hand between him and his son.

'Hi, it's me,' she said when he answered. 'Unless something breaks on this case beforehand, I can probably meet you on Saturday.'

'OK,' he replied, drawing it out. 'When on Saturday?'

She thought. 'How about an early dinner at the White Hart on Moorstart Road?'

'That's fine. Shall I meet you there, or come and pick you up?'

Realising she couldn't be sure where she'd be,

she said, 'Let's meet there at six thirty. I'll call if anything changes.'

'OK.'

'And Martin?'

'Yes.'

'I really don't want to talk about your relationship with Brigitte.'

'It wasn't my plan.'

'Good, because I think the relationship we really need to discuss is yours with Luke,' and leaving him with that she rang off just as Gould came through on the Airwave.

'They've got Perkins,' he announced.

Hitting the brakes, she quickly swerved into a lay-by. 'Is Sophie with him?'

'No sign of her yet. Apparently he's been holed up in a basement flat in the St Paul's area of Bristol. The local police found him when they were raiding the place for the lowlife who lives there. So far he's claiming not to know where she is.'

'Is someone on their way to get him?'

'They are. He should be back here by one, two at the latest. Where are you?'

'On my way to start prepping the Monroes for the press conference, but I think we should delay until after we've interviewed Perkins.'

'Absolutely. I've read the parts of the diary you highlighted, by the way. Andee, there's nothing there to tie Sikora to her disappearance.'

'I know that, but it's establishing a relationship between them . . .'

'Is it? I think you should read it again.'

'She says at one point that she saw him that night . . .'

'She could have been watching a show.'

212

'And what about saying her dad would go ballistic if he found her in the back of Sikora's van? That's suggesting it's something she does.'

'Or would like to do. Listen, I'm not saying you're wrong about this, but I think you're in danger of overreacting . . .'

'Sir, she's a fourteen-year-old girl . . .'

'Exactly . . .'

'. . . who needs to be found.'

'And chances are we're a lot closer to it now we have Perkins.'

Having to accept that, she said, 'I'll call the Monroes, let them know what's happening. There's no point me going there now.' She glanced at her mobile as it rang. 'Actually, they're calling me. I'd better take it,' and disconnecting she clicked on to her mobile.

'Ma'am, it's Lauren,' the FLO told her.

Wincing at the title she'd never encouraged, Andee said, 'What's up?'

'Mr and Mrs Monroe have just been given an appointment for Archie with the community paediatrician, so they're wondering if it would be all right to postpone the prep for the press conference.'

'It would,' Andee responded. 'Are they still there?'

'Mr Monroe is. Mrs Monroe's already gone to the clinic.'

'OK, put him on.'

A moment later Gavin's voice came down the line. 'I hope we're not causing a problem. We've waited weeks for an appointment, and now this cancellation has come up . . .'

'It's fine,' Andee assured him. 'We're having to

delay things anyway. Gary Perkins has just been arrested.'

There was a beat of shocked silence before he said, 'Is she with him?'

'Apparently he's claiming not to know where she is, but we'll have a better idea of whether he's telling the truth once we've interviewed him.'

'When are you doing that?'

'He should be back in Kesterly within the next couple of hours, so sometime this afternoon. I'll call as soon as there's some news.'

'You've been to see Kasia?'

Jackie Poynter popped two Anadin and washed them down with a large glass of wine. 'Yes, Tomasz,' she confirmed, opening her menthol cigarettes, 'I have been to see Kasia.'

'Why?'

Not much liking his tone, she flicked a lighter and inhaled deeply. This search for Sophie Monroe was turning into a major headache, and she really wasn't in much of a mood to deal with a disgruntled Tomasz Sikora right now either. 'She didn't tell you?' she responded.

'She said you talked about her husband.'

She took another drag. 'Mm, I believe he came up.'

'But why did you talk about him? You've frightened her. She doesn't know anything . . .'

'Then she has nothing to worry about. Is there another reason for this call, Tomasz, because I'm rather hoping there is.'

'Yes. I've been contacted.'

At that her eyes widened. 'Good. So everything's going to plan?'

'Yes.'

'And you'll be coming back with how many girls?'

'None. The police are looking for me. I can't bring anyone or anything with me. Aleksei is organising it.'

'How do we know we can trust him?'

'We don't have much choice, unless we want to cancel the arrangement.'

Her expression turned sour. 'OK. Do I need to know any more than that?'

'It is only important for you to know that I must speak to the police when I return.'

She took a moment to consider that. 'Can you handle it?'

'I think so.'

'Gary Perkins has just been arrested. Did you know?'

'No, I didn't.'

'Jimmy's arranged a lawyer for him. We can do the same for you.'

He didn't answer.

'Are you still there?'

'Thank you,' he said quietly.

'You're welcome, and please stop worrying about Kasia, she'll be fine, everyone will, as long as you keep your head.'

It was late afternoon now, and to Andee's frustration Perkins was still holed up in an interview room with one of the town's most established lawyers. No duty solicitor for him, apparently.

'Piers Ashdown,' Leo murmured, as they helped themselves to coffees in the Stress & Mess. 'Makes you wonder how that connection was made, doesn't it?'

Trying not to check her watch again as they sat at the only clean table they could find, Andee sighed heavily. Though she was impatient to get on with this, she was trying to take her mind off the wait by wondering when, if, Graeme would be in touch. She hadn't heard from him since the night she'd gone round there, and she was sure, when she left, that he'd said he would call. Of course, she could always call him, and maybe she would if he hadn't been in touch by tomorrow. She sorely wished she could see him tonight, tomorrow night, any night, but at least he understood that for the moment her family commitments had to come first.

Realising Leo was talking about Sophie's diary, she quickly refocused on what he was saying. 'It's like it's been written by two different people,' he was commenting. 'She's changed a lot between the time she started it and now. If you ask me, it's like she's trying to grow up too fast. There again, show me a kid of that age who isn't.'

'What about her relationship with Sikora?' Andee asked. 'Do you think it's real, or just a dream?' Though the diary had gone off for analysis now, they wouldn't have the results for at least another week and she couldn't stop wondering about it.

Leo was shaking his head as he thought. 'It's hard to tell. She obviously wants one, but whether or not he took advantage . . . He might have, but there again . . . I was thinking about the local boys she mentioned, back at the beginning of the summer. Her best mate must know who they are.'

'If she does, she isn't telling because Jemma's already asked. All she'll admit to is being at the party and things getting a bit out of hand.'

'Was there an assault?'

'Estelle says no.'

'She's got to know these boys' names.'

'They're already in the case notes. One was called Jason, or Justin, another was Carl, and she's sure there was someone called Rob or Robin. That's all she can remember, she claims. She's got no idea which school they go to, or where any of them live. They met them on the beach and got chatting, like kids do, and when it came out they were all from Kesterly Sophie invited them to a party that night. Are you thinking it has some sort of significance?'

He shrugged. 'They're the only locals around her own age she's mentioned,' he replied. 'Maybe she made a connection with one of them that Estelle knew nothing about.'

Feeling doubtful, Andee looked at her mobile as it rang. At last Jack Trevors, the custody sergeant.

'Apparently Mr Perkins's lawyer has a pressing engagement this evening,' Trevors told her, 'so he's keen to get started.'

'Don't you just love lawyers,' Andee muttered, as she and Leo made for the lift.

On reaching the custody suite they found Piers Ashdown, a portly, pompous man, talking into his mobile. However, he had the grace to end the call as soon as he saw them.

'Piers,' Andee said, not fully disguising her antipathy.

'Good to see you, Andee,' he told her. 'I'm sorry about Dougie. A great shame. He's going to be missed.'

'He will be,' she agreed. 'So, I'm guessing we have a prepared statement.'

Ashdown's eyebrows arched. 'You know, it's your amazing powers of deduction that make you such a good detective,' he teased.

Thinking how happy it would make her to slap him, Andee gestured for him to go ahead and exchanged a roll of the eyes with Leo as they followed him into one of the more spacious interview rooms. Perkins, unshaven and very possibly unwashed, was already there.

After everyone had identified themselves for the tape, and Perkins had been reminded of his rights, Ashdown started to read aloud.

'"I, Gary John Perkins, am issuing this prepared statement to say that I was with Sophie Monroe on the night of August 17th. She came to my flat some time around eight thirty, upset because she'd had a row with her parents, and weirded out after being chased on the beach. She thought it was one of the wardens who'd been chasing her. She stayed for about an hour, maybe less and then said she was going to the Entertainment Centre to watch Tomasz Sikora. I left the flat just after her and went to the clubhouse too."' Ashdown peered over his glasses. 'The clubhouse is the same as the Entertainment Centre,' he informed them.

Andee only looked at him.

Resuming, Ashdown read, '". . . went to the clubhouse too, where I had a couple of beers with whisky chasers. After the show ended I saw Sophie chatting to Tomasz Sikora. I don't know what they were saying, because I wasn't close enough. Just after that I went down to the underground car park and got into one of the wardens' golf carts. I was meaning to take it out and have a bit of a laugh, but I couldn't find any keys. I ended up falling asleep in the back of one and I didn't leave the car park until Rafal, I don't know his surname, but he's a warden, woke me up and drove me out in the morning. That's all I have to say. I will not answer any other questions you put to me.'"

As Ashdown looked up, Andee glanced at Leo before asking Perkins, 'Are you aware of Sophie Monroe's age?'

Sitting back in his chair, Perkins said, 'No comment.'

'Why would she have come to *your* flat after being chased on the beach?'

'No comment.'

'What did you do during the time she was there?'

'No comment.'

'Did you give her any illegal substances?'

'No comment.' He was clearly enjoying this.

'Did she talk about running away while she was with you?'

'No comment.'

'How well do you know Tomasz Sikora?'

'No comment.'

'Did you see Sophie leave the clubhouse?'

'No comment.'

'Did you tell anyone you were going down to the underground car park?'

'No comment.'

'Did you speak to Tomasz Sikora when he came to get into his van?'

'No comment.'

'Did you leave with Tomasz Sikora?'

'No comment.'

'Why did you disappear from the campsite when you found out Sophie had been reported missing?'

'No comment.'

'Where is Sophie now?'

He shrugged. 'No comment.'

'Did you know Sophie kept a diary?'

His eyes turned wary. 'No comment.'

'Have you ever had sexual relations with Sophie?'

'No comment.'

Andee glanced at Ashdown. He surely had to know there was no way Perkins was walking out of this station today, nor would the magistrates bail him when he went before them tomorrow. He was in for the long haul, with absolutely nothing to save him, unless his lawyer did something radical and advised him to be helpful.

It wasn't going to happen, Andee could see that as plainly as she could see that Perkins still hadn't connected with just how serious this was.

In the end she got to her feet and with the tape still running, she said to Perkins, 'I have no more questions for you, Gary, I'm simply going to tell you something that I don't believe your lawyer has bothered to explain. No matter what you're hiding, who you're covering for, or where Sophie is now, the evidence in her diary is going to send you down for life,' and having had the satisfaction of watching her words smack the smugness off his face, she left the room.

She wasn't surprised when Ashdown came hurrying after her.

'You sounded fairly confident about that, Andee,' he declared, joining her at the custody reception desk, 'but as we both know you're going to have a hard time proving those diary entries are fact.'

'Tell it to the CPS,' she advised.

'I shall, but I'm talking to you right now and I stress again . . .'

'I heard what you said,' she interrupted. 'Now you can hear me. If you think you can persuade a jury that the diary entries are made up, all I can say to you is good luck, Mr Ashdown, because you're going to need it.'

'Andee, you're not listening to me . . .'

'No! You're not listening to *me*. The only thing that's going to save your client from a life sentence is if he tells us where Sophie is, and even then there are no guarantees.'

'But he doesn't know . . .'

'Bullshit! He knows. So when you're ready to tell me, you know where to find me,' and leaving the custody sergeant to deal with the charge she got into the lift and took out her phone.

'He's not talking,' she told Gould when she'd made the connection.

'Where is he now?'

'Being booked.'

'OK, I'll get back to you.'

Minutes later Leo followed her into the incident room. 'Do you believe any of the statement?' he asked.

'His timings check out,' she replied, 'up to the point he went down to the car park. We need to find out from the warden if he really did pass out in a golf cart.'

'The warden could be in some way involved.'

'Indeed, so don't rule it out.'

'Jack Trevors just told me something interesting,' he said. 'Apparently when Perkins was brought in he gave his address as Blue Ocean Park, but when Ashdown turned up he changed it to a flat in Kesterly that, by all accounts, Suzi Perkins has just rented.'

Andee regarded him curiously. '*When* did she rent it?' she asked.

'Not sure, but I thought it would be worth looking into.'

'Do that, because it's sounding to me as though she was expecting him to be bailed so she needed somewhere away from the campsite for him to go. Except why on earth would she think he'd get bail? She's got to know it was never going to happen.'

'Ashdown didn't know about the diary until he got here,' Leo reminded her, 'so my guess is he told her there was a chance he could get her brother out.'

Andee was frowning hard as a sixth sense told her there was more to this. 'Find out what you can about that flat, and about Piers Ashdown's clients,' she said, and leaving him to it she took herself off to CID to find Hassan Ansari, one of the DCs, sitting at her desk.

'What's going on?' she asked as he looked up.

'Pressure from on high to get these burglaries sorted over on Wermers,' he told her. 'Anything you can tell me I ought to know?'

'Everything's in the case notes,' she assured him. 'Have there been any more?'

'Not on Wermers, but a couple of stores at the Mall have reported being targeted. Gould was looking for you.'

'I'm looking for him. Where is he?'

'Not sure now.'

Taking out her mobile, she was about to ring him when a call came in. Seeing it was Graeme,

222

her heart gave a pleasing flip. 'Hi, how are you?' she asked, going into Gould's empty office and closing the door.

'I'm good. I see from the news that you've got your man.'

'Mm. Unfortunately he's claiming not to know where our missing girl is, so as it stands we're not any closer to finding her, but that's not for public consumption. How are things your end?'

'Busy, but not too busy to think about you.'

Smiling, she said, 'Well, I'm glad about that, because I'm finding myself thinking about you quite a lot too.'

'Enough perhaps to have dinner with me tomorrow night?'

Her heart sank.

'I know, I know, I'm supposed to be giving you some space over the next couple of weeks, and if it's a problem . . .'

'I promise you, I'd love nothing more than to have dinner with you, but I'm afraid it's not going to be possible.'

'OK, I won't say I'm not disappointed, but I do understand.'

'Maybe we could meet for a drink on Sunday or Monday? Can I give you a call?'

'Of course, any time. Do I have to let you go now?'

'Probably. I'm in my boss's office and he could walk in at any moment. It was good to hear from you.'

'It was good to hear you too. Don't forget to call.'

Still smiling as she rang off, she clicked to open a new text and almost immediately wished she hadn't.

*Dad just told me you're seeing him tomorrow night.
Great news! He's really pleased, I can tell. Love you
both, Ax*

'The alibi's checked out,' Leo told her as she
walked into the incident room a few minutes later.
'The warden's saying he did find Perkins in a golf
cart on the morning of August 18th. I'm still
working on who owns the apartment Suzi's
rented.'

'OK,' she responded distractedly. 'Have you seen
Gould?'

'Not recently. The press office have been on.
They're asking for a statement about Perkins, and
they want to know when the Monroes are going to
make their appeal.'

'I'll pull together a statement,' she replied, sitting
down at her desk, 'and let's set up the appeal for
seven.' She checked her watch and reached for the
phone to call Gavin and Heidi.

'It's Andee Lawrence,' she said when Lauren
Mitchell answered. 'How's everything over there?'

'Not good, I'm afraid,' Lauren replied. 'They've
been told the baby probably has something called
Noonan syndrome.'

'Oh God,' Andee murmured worriedly. 'Do you
know what that is? Please tell me it's not
life-threatening.'

'I don't think so. As far as they know it depends
on the severity of his heart defects, and they still
don't have those results. Otherwise, it means he
won't grow very tall, his eyes will be set quite
wide apart – I guess we can see that already – and
maybe there'll be other deformities or malfunc-
tions along the way. They won't really be sure
about those until he gets older.'

'That's awful,' Andee said with feeling. How the hell would she cope if it happened to one of hers? 'How are they taking it?'

'Quite badly. Mother and baby have hardly stopped crying since they got back and Dad looks like he's gone to a distant planet.'

'OK, we'll put the appeal off till tomorrow. Tell them I'll be there in the morning to go over it – unless, of course, we manage to locate Sophie tonight.'

'Is there any chance of that?'

'I'm trying to remain hopeful. Jemma and Danny are in Bristol working with the local police, interviewing neighbours around where Perkins was found. They haven't called anything in yet, but there's still time.'

'I'll tell Mr Monroe that. He'll want to know.'

After ringing off Andee sat back in her chair and pushed her hands through her hair. Now she didn't have to prep the Monroes tonight she had time to read through the notes that had been added to the database during the day. This would include all the social media reports and Internet rumours that had built up over the past few hours. She wondered if there was a chance she could get away by eight. Possibly, but not likely, so it wouldn't be fair to call Graeme. She didn't want to end up having to let him down again. Besides which, if she did find herself with a free couple of hours this evening she really ought to spend them with her mother; she'd managed no private time with her at all since Sophie's disappearance.

Chapter Ten

Mummy's Favourite Things:
 Sophie, liquorice; kittens; starry nights; singing; playing the guitar; daisy chains; Daddy.
 Sophie's Favourite Things:
 Mummy, bubble gum; kittens, the beach, singing with Mummy and Daddy, making daisy chains; Daddy.
 Daddy's Favourite Things:
 Sophie and Mummy.

Andee could feel her heart aching as she reread the opening page of Sophie's journal, written when she was nine years old. How safe and perfect her little world must have seemed to her then. Such a horribly stark contrast to what was happening now.

Whatever was happening now.

Why on earth hadn't she made contact again? What, who, was stopping her? And why, if she'd had no intention of coming back, hadn't she taken this diary with her? Anger with her mother for dying? Embarrassment for anyone else to see it?

Andee had brought a copy home to read again without all the hullaboo of the office going on around her. Her mother and Alayna were in the next room watching TV. Her mother hadn't wanted to talk about how the disappearance of a

226

fourteen-year-old girl was affecting her, she'd said when Andee had suggested it, unless Andee did of course. Andee didn't; it was best to keep focused on Sophie, and try not to let her own feelings get in the way of things.

Was she succeeding at that? How often was she seeing Penny when it should be Sophie, or her father when it should be Gavin? More often, she knew, than she'd care to admit. But was it affecting her judgement, or skewing her instincts? She didn't think so, but how could she really tell?

Flipping on through the diary, she paused to look at various photographs stuck into old-fashioned paper corners. Most were of Sophie's parents performing on stage, her mother with long wavy blonde hair, sometimes worn in plaits or a ponytail; her father in an assortment of jaunty hats, braces, and for a while with a beard. The Upbeats, they'd called themselves, and judging from the happy smiles and seemingly constant laughter, they'd named themselves well. There were pressed flowers glued on to some pages with their names neatly logged underneath: *bluebell found in Marrin Wood; primrose from our garden; lily of the valley like the one Mummy had when she got married.* There were tickets to special events such as a ride on a steam train; a trip on a riverboat; the Christmas grotto at Longleat; a visit to a petting zoo, plus many others for the various gigs her parents had performed. The shots that moved Andee the most, however, were all of Sophie, as a baby peeking out of a sling worn by her mother; riding her father's shoulders as a toddler; fast asleep with her rag doll (*Sophie aged 5 and Amelia aged 3*).

Why hadn't she taken the rag doll?

Because she'd intended to come back?

Because it would appear too childish?

There were several birthday snaps of Sophie blowing out candles and opening presents, and even more showing her taking part in her parents' shows. Such a tiny girl in some, barely reaching her father's knees. Andee couldn't help smiling at the way her dear sweet face glowed with pride; she was clearly thrilled to be on stage with a microphone of her own, doing her best to keep in time with the music.

Then there were her poems.

My parents are really cool singers
They perform on the stage,
They write some of their own songs,
We hope one will become all the rage.

Mummy has blue eyes, Daddy has brown,
Sophie has violet eyes
And her head is on upside down.

Andee could easily imagine the girlish laughter that had no doubt accompanied the silly rhyme and little drawing that went alongside it.

Browsing on through she found many diary entries charting their day-to-day lives. *Got up, went to school, had singing lesson, came home. Got up, Daddy made omelettes for breakfast, Mummy took me to school, my best friend Millie came for tea. Mummy bumped into a lady in town and knocked over her shopping. Mummy had a headache so I did the singing with Daddy, everyone said I was very good, wish Mummy could have seen us. Daddy says he really likes singing with me. Mummy's birthday today, Daddy gave her flowers and I gave her a necklace I saved up for, she says it's her favourite one ever and she's going to wear it all the time. Me and Daddy got loads of applause at Pontins tonight, Daddy cried he was so happy; we wished Mummy could of been there. Mummy not very well again, I wish she'd get better.*

As the date of Jilly Monroe's death came closer Andee decided not to carry on reading, since Sophie's struggle to understand what was happening to her mother was already affecting her deeply. *Mummy says I have to be brave because she won't be here for much longer. I don't want her to go away. Please Jesus, don't take my mummy away from us. I promise I'll go to church every Sunday and say my prayers every night.*

Closing the photocopied book, Andee put it on the seat next to her and reached for her wine. She felt overwhelmed by sadness as she considered the way Sophie, out of loneliness and despair, had eventually transferred her trust and affection from the parents who'd so tragically and blamelessly let her down, to Tomasz Sikora – another singer, another man whom she looked up to and who she'd clearly thought could make her feel safe. Towards the end of the book his scribbled name was all over the place, scripted inside love hearts, or featured alongside hers as a part of a *he loves me, he loves me not* game. Even when writing about other men or boys she almost always compared them to Sikora, and Sikora always came out on top.

. . . there's no one to beat Tomasz.
Would love to have Tomasz's baby.
Really, really love T, and I know he loves me.
Going to tell T how I feel about him. I know he'll

say I'm too young, but I don't see how age makes a difference.

Wish I could run away with him so we could be together and I wouldn't have to put up with the WSM any more.

So had Sophie talked him into taking her away? She guessed there was even a possibility she'd blackmailed him into it, though Andee was far from convinced about that. More likely, she thought, Sikora, Perkins too, had been subtly grooming her, allowing her to think they were friends when their intentions had been . . .

Looking up as her mother came into the room, she said, 'Are you off to bed?'

'In a minute,' Maureen replied. 'I'd like to see you eat something before I go.'

Andee smiled. 'Once a mother,' she teased.

Maureen was serious. 'I know you're tormenting yourself with this case,' she said, glancing at the diary, 'and you must try to find a way to stop.'

'I'll be fine,' Andee assured her. 'I thought you didn't want to talk about it.'

'That was selfish of me, because we both know that on one level at least, you're thinking if you can find Sophie, you'll somehow be finding Penny, but it doesn't work like that.'

'I know it doesn't, and I promise you, I'm not losing sight of reality.'

Coming to perch on the edge of the coffee table in front of her, Maureen reached for her hands. 'I hope you mean that,' she said earnestly.

Andee looked surprised. 'Do you think I am?' she queried.

Maureen shook her head. 'I don't know. It's hard for me to tell when I'm not in your world, but I do know, if I was in your shoes I would be finding this very difficult indeed.'

'More difficult would be to sit back and let someone else take it over.'

'I suppose I can understand that. But you're hardly eating, Andee, or sleeping, and that's not good.'

'If I have something to eat now will it make you happy?'

Maureen smiled. 'Actually, it would. I'll even fix it for you.'

'You don't have to.'

'I'd like to, and perhaps we could have a chat about Martin, if only to take your mind off this case for a while.'

Andee frowned. 'What about Martin?'

'Alayna tells me you're seeing him tomorrow night.'

'Ye-es.'

'Well, I know how keen she is for you two to get back together. I was just wondering if it's what you want?'

Moving restlessly, Andee said, 'Aren't you forgetting something? His girlfriend is here . . .'

'But I happen to agree with Alayna, I think he wants a reconciliation with you.'

'How can you say that when he's blatantly involved with somebody else?'

'That may be so, but . . .'

'Mum, it isn't going to happen.'

'Why? Because you don't want it to? Or are you saying that to try and protect yourself?'

'Either way, it doesn't really matter.'

'*Do* you want it?' Maureen pressed.

Andee started to answer, but realised she

wasn't sure what to say. 'It's complicated,' she managed in the end, 'and as I just pointed out, he has someone else now, so how about we stop all this nonsense and go into the kitchen so you can feed your hungry daughter?'

The following morning Andee was standing at the entrance to Blue Ocean Park, staring across the street to the Leisure Park. She'd spent the past hour with Gould, DCI Spender, DCSI May and a battalion of CPS advisers, trying – and failing – to persuade them to involve Interpol in the search for Tomasz Sikora.

'As there's nothing to suggest the girl's been taken out of the country,' she'd been told, 'or to say that she even left the campsite with Sikora, we cannot sanction your request.'

'So what you're saying is we have to wait for a body to turn up before anyone's going to take this seriously,' she'd cried.

They'd already been getting up to leave the room; for them the decision had been made, and they weren't prepared to stay and argue it further.

'I tried,' Gould told her as soon as the door closed behind them, 'but getting them all round the table so you could make your case was the best I could do.'

Now, as she dealt with the frustration of it, her eyes remained fixed on the funfair as though somewhere in all the mayhem was an answer she should be seeing, but was somehow missing. She'd woken early that morning with too many questions niggling away at her, though one at least had now been answered.

'Suzi Perkins moved into the Kesterly flat

yesterday,' Leo told her. 'It's owned by a company called Manifold Properties, which happens to own Blue Ocean Park.'

'Yesterday,' Andee repeated. 'Presumably after Perkins was arrested, but before his lawyer realised there was no chance of getting him out on bail.'

'Seems a safe presumption.'

So the Poynters were helping Perkins, in spite of Jackie Poynter expressing disgust at his criminal record during her interview with Leo and Barry. She'd gone on to blame Heidi for not carrying out the proper background checks.

Leo had returned to the Poynters to question them further, while Andee drove here to prepare the Monroes for their televised appeal.

Though no one from the press camped outside the bungalow had spotted her yet, as soon as she approached they seemed to come alive.

'Have there been any breakthroughs overnight?'

'Does Perkins know where Sophie is?'

'Was she in Bristol?'

'What can you tell us about Tomasz Sikora?'

'Is he a suspect?'

Managing to get through the crowd with the assistance of two uniforms stationed outside the bungalow, she turned as she reached the front door. 'So far there's no evidence to suggest that Sophie was in Bristol,' she informed them, 'however our colleagues from the Avon and Somerset force are still updating us on that. As for Tomasz Sikora, we've been in touch with him and he has expressed a willingness to help us with our inquiries.'

'Does he know where Sophie is?'

'Is it true you're trying to get him brought back to this country?'

'What about the things they're saying on the Internet about him being involved in . . . ?'

'I'm afraid I can't comment on any of that.' She was looking across to the CCTV camera trained on the park entrance.

'Has the diary been of any help?' someone asked.

Curious to know how news of that had leaked out, Andee ignored the question and was about to knock on the door when it opened.

'No Lauren?' she asked, as Gavin led the way down the hall. His head was bowed, his shoulders slumped, reminding her of the news they'd received about the baby.

'She's taken Heidi and Archie for a drive to try and settle him,' he replied. 'They should be back any minute.'

When they were in the kitchen, she said, 'Lauren told me about the Noonan syndrome. I'm sorry. This is a very difficult time for you.'

Though his eyes came briefly to hers, he said nothing as he went to put on the kettle.

She looked around, noting how the place had been cleaned up since her last visit and wondering if Lauren had done it.

'He's in front of the magistrates this morning, isn't he?' he said, without turning round.

'Yes, he is.'

'Do you think he knows where she is?'

'At the moment he's claiming not to. He says he spent the night she disappeared in a golf buggy under the Entertainment Centre, and Rafal, one of the wardens, has confirmed that he found him there on the morning of the 18th.'

As Gavin registered the information he turned around. 'You're no closer to finding her, are you?' he asked, looking bleakly into her eyes.

'Actually, I think we are, but I understand it probably doesn't seem that way to you.'

His attention drifted.

'You mustn't give up,' she told him. 'She's out there somewhere and we're going to find her.'

'How do you know that?'

She started to answer and found she couldn't.

'You don't, do you?' he challenged. 'You know what it's like to lose someone and never find out what happened to them.'

Realising he must have looked her up online, or perhaps one of the papers had run the story that morning and no one had told her yet, Andee was about to reply when her mobile rang. Seeing it was Leo, she excused herself and stepped into the back garden.

'The Poynters are saying they gave Suzi the flat because she was being harassed in her caravan at the campsite,' Leo told her.

'How kind. Do you believe them?' She was staring at a small square of old carpet that had been left on the grass.

'I think it's part of the truth, but not the whole truth. Trouble is, I've got no idea how we prove they were intending the apartment to be some sort of bolt hole for Perkins.'

She hadn't, either. 'OK,' she said, allowing her eyes to trail along the flattened grass next to the carpet. 'Can you remember when the security camera at the campsite entrance went on the blink?'

'Apparently it was working up until midday on the 17th.'

'Do we know why it wasn't repaired immediately?'

'It was a Sunday, the parts they needed weren't available until the next day. What are you thinking?'

'The same as I have all along, that someone could have tampered with it to make it look as though it went out at midday, when the actual purpose was to erase the footage of Sophie leaving the camp.'

'The security guards would have to be in on it if that's the case.'

'Perhaps they are. Or they're covering for someone.'

'Such as Tomasz Sikora?'

'Indeed.'

'What do you want me to do?'

'Get the camera looked at again. I'm at the camp-site now. I'll see you here in an hour. The press conference is being held in the ballroom,' and clicking off the line she went back inside to find Gavin sitting at the table with two cups of tea. He looked as forlorn as a beggar who'd lost everything would look, and considering what was happening to his children he had every reason to do so. At least for now.

Going to join him, she picked up her tea and took a sip.

'Are you going to tell me what she wrote in her diary?' he asked.

Having prepared herself for the question, she said, 'There's nothing to indicate where she might be now, but there are a lot of mentions of her crush on Sikora and time spent with Perkins.'

He winced and looked away.

'She's written some lovely things about her

mother and how happy you all were when she was alive,' she told him. 'They're very moving.'

He nodded slowly. 'I was looking at these before you came,' he said, pushing an album across the table. 'It's pictures of her when she was little, with her mother. It could break your heart to see them together, how perfect everything was back then. They had no idea anything was going to happen to shatter their world. None of us did.'

Opening it to the first page, Andee found herself staring at the shining, joyful faces of a young mother and her beautiful newborn baby.

'She was about ten minutes old there,' Gavin said. 'I took the picture myself. I'll never forget how it used to make me feel when I looked at them, it was like all the missing pieces of my world had finally come together.'

'They're lovely,' Andee murmured, meaning it.

The following pages showed many of the same sort of shots found in her own family albums, holidays, birthdays, Christmases, mostly of the children, but plenty of her and Martin. It was rare these days that she looked at those from her own childhood, but she remembered how she used to watch her father going through pictures of Penny laughing, or pulling silly faces, sitting on his shoulders, pretending to drive his car, or simply being the Penny who hadn't felt let down, ignored, rejected by those she loved.

'Why didn't she take the diary with her?' Gavin said shakily. 'Or this album? I wish she had. It would be like her mother was with her, you know, watching over her.' A smile was twisting awkwardly at his mouth. 'That's a daft thing to say, isn't?'

'Not at all,' Andee replied. 'But at least this way they're safe until she gets back.'

He turned away as though afraid to connect with the words. It was a while before he said, 'I want to believe we'll find her, that she'll come home, and most of the time I do, but then I start thinking what if it's already too late?'

Understanding the fear only too well, Andee said, 'This is why you need to speak to someone who can counsel you on the best way to cope with what you're going through. Have you looked at the brochures I left? Lauren should have discussed them with you.'

'Yes, she has, but we don't want to be a bother to anyone.'

'You're not a bother.' She was watching him closely, trying to see past her own father, but it was hard. 'That's why the organisations are there, to help you deal with everything that's going on in your head. It can be terrible, the things we tell ourselves when we're under this sort of stress. We make up stories that have no bearing on reality, no grounding in truth, only in fear, and that's no help to anyone, least of all you.'

His eyes almost came to hers, but not quite. 'I know you're right, but what difference can anyone make if she's already . . . ? If they've done something to her . . .' Swallowing hard, he said, 'I'll want to kill them if they have . . . If I was to see that Perkins, or Sikora . . .' His voice trailed off as though he wasn't even listening to what he was saying.

Hearing the front door open and close, Andee turned round and got to her feet as Lauren came into the room.

'He's asleep,' Lauren announced, sounding as relieved as if she'd been up all night with the baby herself. 'I think Heidi needs to be, too.'

Turning to Gavin, Andee said, 'How would you feel about doing the appeal on your own? Obviously we'll be with you, but if Heidi's not . . .'

'I can do it,' he interrupted. 'Let her have some rest. I've already made some notes.'

Andee glanced at her watch. 'Shona should be here any minute,' she said. 'She's from our Corporate Communications Department, or press office as we usually call it. She'll explain how everything's going to be set up, exactly what sort of thing . . .' She broke off as the doorbell rang. 'I'll go,' she told Lauren.

After letting Shona in Andee spoke quietly with her in the hall, explaining that she was going outside to make some calls and would be back in time to help finalise Gavin's statement.

'Yes, I know they've charged him with rape,' Suzi was saying to Jackie Poynter on the phone, 'and the magistrate's bound to remand him in custody.'

'Have the police questioned you since his arrest?' Jackie asked.

'Not yet, but someone's coming round here later.'

'Well, all you have to do is keep a level head and remember that you were there when he was supposed to be committing this rape, so you know it's not true.'

As she registered the advice Suzi's blood turned cold. 'Are you asking me . . . ? Are you saying I should . . .'

'You know what I'm saying. We both want to

help your brother, and I think it would be good for him to know that. I have to go now. Call me after you've spoken to the police.'

As the line went dead Suzi rang off too and began pacing the sitting room of the fourth-floor flat she'd moved into under Jackie's instruction. She hadn't seen or spoken to Gary since his arrest, nor did she want to. If she had the courage she'd contact the police and tell them everything she knew, but she was too afraid of what the Poynters might do to her and Gary if she did so.

Quickly dialling her mother's number, she blurted, 'They want me to give Gary an alibi, say it wasn't true, that he . . . you know . . .'

'Then do it,' her mother said tiredly. 'You don't want to see him go to prison again, do you?'

'He will anyway, for breaking his protection order.'

'But not for as long as he would if they make these charges stick. He's family, Suzi, and families stick together, you know that.'

'But what about me? I don't want to lie . . .'

'I understand that, but sometimes you have to. If you won't do it for him, then do it for me.'

Not knowing how to answer that, Suzi clicked off the line and sank to her knees. None of this was making any sense. She'd come here to try to make a new life for herself, and it was all turning against her.

'Mum, can you talk?'

'Not for long,' Andee replied, glad to see the press had decamped for the conference as she headed back to the Monroes. 'Are you OK?'

'Yeah, I'm cool,' Alayna assured her, 'I just

wanted to make sure that you are. Have you heard anything from Dad today?'

'As a matter of fact I had a text earlier about the trust funds Grandpa Dougie's set up for you and Luke.'

'What about them?'

'He wants me to go into the lawyer's office when I can to sign some forms.'

'Cool. You're still seeing him tonight, aren't you?'

'I am. Is Luke home yet?'

'I haven't seen him, but if they had a late night partying he's probably still asleep.'

'Do me a favour and try calling him.'

'What do you want me to say?'

'I just want to know where he is, that's all.'

'OK. Any more news about Sophie?'

Touched that she'd remembered to ask, and wishing Sophie knew that people were concerned about her, Andee said, 'There have been a couple of developments, but nothing I can discuss. I should go now. Don't forget to ring Luke,' and clicking off her end she took a call on the Airwave. 'Jemma, speak to me.'

'Kasia Domanski just called,' Jemma told her excitedly, 'apparently Sikora's on his way back, due here sometime on Monday.'

Really wanting to believe that, Andee asked, 'So he's driving?'

'Sounds like it.'

'OK. We need to be ready to pick him up as soon as he comes into the country. How's he going to do that? Through Calais?'

'That's the most obvious route.'

'Put all the ports on standby. Does Gould know about this yet?'

241

'No, but . . .'

'Don't worry, I'll tell him when he gets here. We don't want the press to know, you understand that, don't you?'

'Of course.'

'Are you going to the mags' court with Leo?'

'Yeah, we're just about to leave.'

'OK, call me when you're done.'

Kasia was in Henryk's Polish food shop in Kesterly's old town, where she came every week to buy Tomasz's favourite treats from their country. It didn't matter that he'd be having them regularly at the moment, she still wanted to prepare something special for when he came home.

He'd texted earlier to let her know that he was starting back in the morning and should be with them by midday on Monday at the latest.

Please get in touch with the police and tell them I am coming, he'd said at the end of his message. *But do not tell anyone else, not even Olenka or the children.*

So, in spite of bursting to share her relief, Kasia was managing to keep it to herself. She was so happy to know that he was going to help the police to sort out the terrible mistake everyone was making about him. And it was a mistake, she was in no doubt of that. Just because he worked at the camp and he knew Sophie didn't mean that he was some kind of predator or pimp, who went round tricking girls into believing he was going to help them find a better life. He'd never do anything to hurt anyone, especially not a young girl, and soon everyone would know how wrong and cruel they had been to think him capable of all the dreadful things that were being suggested.

If anyone had hurt Sophie, and Kasia was praying every day that no one had, then she felt sure it was Gary Perkins, who, they'd said on the news just now, had been remanded in custody. He was the one who had a past, a criminal record even, proving that he had done bad things with young girls before. In spite of what Olenka said, Kasia felt certain that there was no friendship or even association between Tomasz and Gary Perkins. She would know if there were. Tomasz would have mentioned it, if only in passing, but he never had.

'You're too trusting,' Olenka had told her. 'You have to face up to the fact that even the best men are capable of doing bad things for money.' *And let's face it, Tomasz is doing very well for money*. She hadn't said those words, but Kasia had heard them anyway.

She didn't know why Olenka was so ready to believe badly of Tomasz, nor did she care. All that mattered to her was that Tomasz was on his way home to clear his name.

After filling her basket with Henryk's best *pierogi* with sauerkraut and mushrooms, a box of six *paczki*, delicious doughnuts the children adored, some challah bread and a few bottles of Tyskie beer, she went to the checkout.

'I am sorry,' Henryk said, his tired old eyes seeming sore today, 'to hear these things about Tomasz. People, they come in here talking about him all the time. They think everything that is on the Internet or in their newspapers is the truth. I tell them, you know this man, you sing and dance with him at parties, you drink vodka with him and you let your children play with him, so how can you believe these things of him?'

'Thank you, Henryk,' she whispered, aware of the heads that had turned to stare. 'I will tell Tomasz what you have said. It will mean a lot to him. It does to me too.' Taking out her purse she offered him some money, and found it being pushed back into her hand.

'I will pay for this,' the man beside her said. 'Please tell Tomasz when you speak to him that many of his Polish friends are with him.'

'Yes, please tell him,' a woman joined in. 'My name is Joana, my husband is Franz. We know Tomasz is not what they are saying.'

As Kasia looked at their gentle faces, she felt her eyes filling with tears of gratitude.

Leaning towards her, Henryk said, 'Tell him, from Henryk, that it is better for him to stay where he is. Here, there will be too many problems for him with the police and the lawyers. Problems it will be too difficult for him, as a foreigner, to overcome.'

'Now they have labelled him this terrible kind of person,' the woman Joana added, 'the people here will always suspect him. That is how it works. *Nie ma dymu bez ognia* they will say, because that is what the British believe.' No smoke without fire.

'*Niewinnego do czasu udowodnienia winy,*' her husband added. Innocent until proven guilty. 'But it is not true. *Dla nas jest Winny az udowodni swoja niewinnosc.* This is the truth.' For us it is guilty until proven innocent.

As she left the shop Kasia could feel them

watching her, their sympathy and counsel weighing more heavily in her heart than the smoked sausages and potatoes in her bag. Should she do as they said and tell Tomasz not to come?

Chapter Eleven

It was past four thirty by the time Gavin, together with Heidi, who'd insisted on coming for the appeal, were led into the dance hall at Blue Ocean Park where the press was waiting.

It had taken no time at all for Penny's disappearance to make headlines; with their father being who he was the scrutiny had been fierce from the start. Andee would never forget the conference that had ended with two of his colleagues taking him in for questioning. She knew her mother would never forget it either – nor had her father ever really got over it. If Penny had been found maybe he would have put it behind him, eventually, but she hadn't and so he'd always wondered if people, the press, continued to suspect him.

In front of the stage two long tables had been set out with a clutch of microphones at the centre, and a large blue board with the Dean Valley Police logo providing a backdrop. An official camera was set up amongst the many others to record proceedings.

Now that Gould had finished briefing the gathering on the investigation so far, he and two press officers were vacating their chairs ready for the Monroes to sit down. As requested by Gavin, Andee took up position one side of him, while Lauren sat the other side of Heidi.

'Are you OK?' Andee murmured to Gavin. He had the deer-in-the-headlights look that so often overcame people in this position.

As her words reached him he blinked and said, 'Yeah, I'm fine.' At least he sounded more confident than she knew he felt. He was wearing a shirt and tie for the occasion, while Heidi had combed her hair and dug out a pale pink summer dress. Andee knew, because Heidi had told her, that it would mean something to Sophie if she saw they'd made an effort for her.

Her parents had dressed for the cameras too, though she couldn't remember now what her mother had worn, only that her father had wanted to appear casual with an open-neck shirt and pale grey pullover. No one had advised him against it; no one had seemed to know if it would make a difference.

As the cameras focused on Gavin and Heidi, Andee could see Gavin's hands starting to shake as he took out the statement they'd prepared. He cleared his throat and began to read aloud, but had to stop and start again. 'Sophie,' he said quietly, 'if you're watching this, we want you to know how desperate we are for you to come home. I realise things haven't been easy lately, but we love you very much and we miss you . . .' He swallowed hard and took a moment to recover. 'You're not in any trouble, I promise,' he continued. 'I just want to know that you're safe.' His head went down as he fumbled for Heidi's hand and the cameras zoomed out to include her.

'Sophie, if you're watching this,' Heidi said softly, 'please get in touch.' She took a breath. 'If someone out there is holding her, I beg you, please bring her back to us. We need her home. *Pl-please* bring her home.'

After returning the Monroes to their bungalow and sitting with them for a while going over everything that had been said, and helping to deal with the calls as they came in, Andee finally got into her car. Instead of driving back to the station, she pulled into a quiet spot at the edge of the Cove.

For a long time she sat gazing out at the sea, watching gulls diving and soaring, lazy white horses dissolving and small children paddling. It seemed such a normal world, but she knew from experience that things were rarely as they seemed. There were too many meanings behind the simplicity of one glance to make it as harmless as its apparent innocence, too many thoughts left unspoken, truths still untold when a story was over. It was as though everyone was an actor, doing his or her best with the part they'd been given, but no one else would ever really know how happy, or sad, afraid, hopeful, ashamed or guilty they were feeling inside. It simply wasn't possible to read someone's mind or to feel their pain. There was only instinct and empathy and the intangible, but often powerful, links they provided.

But even they could be misunderstood.

She needed to think this through, to give herself time to understand the unease she was feeling so she could decide whether she had allowed her own history to impact on this case, as she now feared it had.

There was no time this evening, though. She'd promised to meet Martin at six thirty and it was already six o'clock. Sending a quick text to let him know she wouldn't be there until seven fifteen at the earliest, she turned the car around and started the drive home.

By the time Andee pulled into the car park of the White Hart at seven thirty she'd managed to push the unease that had overwhelmed her earlier to the back of her mind. This evening was about her family, no one else, although her Airwave was with her in case anything broke as a result of the Monroes' appeal.

As she turned off the engine she took a deep breath and braced herself. Actually, she was looking forward to seeing Martin, she realised, though she'd probably rather be seeing Graeme. He'd called while she was getting ready to let her know he was going to Dorset to spend the rest of the weekend with friends. She'd felt bad about not saying much in response, but with Alayna right there she'd been forced to keep it low key.

Maybe she should text to say how much she'd like to be with him.

Maybe she should just get out of the car.

As she walked into the pub Alayna's excitement was ringing in her ears. 'Oh my God, he is going to be so totally blown away when he sees you,' she'd declared when she'd stood back to admire her skilful styling of Andee's hair. 'You look so much softer and gorgeous when you wear it down like this, kind of movie star-ish, and you really ought to wear make-up more often. It totally defines your eyes and makes you look loads younger. *Plus*, you are way, way more attractive than Brigitte.'

Though Andee had to admit she was impressed by how expert Alayna was with brushes, liners, highlighters and glosses, she felt embarrassed now in case Martin thought she'd gone to so much trouble for him.

Trying to pretend there were no jitters clowning away behind her adult composure she looked around the bar, and spotting him at a window table she felt a familiar clutch in her heart. The instant he saw her he rose to his feet, and she had the dubious satisfaction of seeing his eyes widen in approval.

'Wow,' he murmured as he greeted her.

'Wow yourself,' she responded, trying to make light of it.

With his rugged, irregular features, messy blond hair and intense indigo eyes he was without a doubt a handsome man, at least to her mind, but so, in a different sort of way, was Graeme. And Graeme was a better dresser – however, despite Martin's plain pale blue shirt, open at the collar, and his usual tatty jeans, she could tell from his aftershave that he'd made a small effort for the evening.

What had Brigitte thought about that? Was she feeling worried, wherever she was now? Or was she totally secure in their relationship?

'You really do look amazing,' he told her.

Annoyed that he hadn't let the subject drop yet, she replied, 'Alayna's hard to escape when she's at large with her make-up case. You're looking well.'

Arching an eyebrow, as though he was managing to understand more of what was going on in her mind than she was, he said, 'What will you have to drink?'

'A lime soda will be fine. I'll have a glass of wine when we eat.'

As he went to the bar she sat down at the table, and, since his back was turned, she allowed her eyes a quick head-to-toe assessment. He'd always had a good physique, broad shoulders, long legs and narrow hips. He had a natural charisma that drew people to him in a way she'd often found fascinating to watch.

Was Brigitte fascinated by it too? Maybe she too had a similar charm.

What would Martin think of Graeme?

What did she care?

Martin rejoined her. 'There you go,' he said, putting their drinks down and sinking back into his chair.

She noticed he'd ordered himself a beer and wondered if he'd driven here or taken a taxi. Maybe Brigitte had dropped him off and was coming back later to collect him.

'Cheers,' she said, clinking her glass against his. 'It's a long time since we were here.'

'I was trying to remember when it was,' he admitted, 'and I think it must have been the day after your dad's sixty-fifth, when we came, the whole family, for a hangover lunch.'

She smiled. 'You could be right, which means it would be about seven years ago, though I think both our parents have brought the children a few times since.'

He nodded as he sipped his beer.

'How's your mum?' she asked. 'I wish I'd been able to see more of her this week.'

'Don't worry. She's the first to understand that a missing child takes precedence. She wouldn't want it any other way, nor would Dad.'

Knowing that to be true of his parents, she said,

'So how are the funeral arrangements coming along? Will many be going?'

'Let's put it this way, we expanded out of standing-room-only a couple of days ago, so we're trying to find out if we can install a sound system, and maybe a couple of screens, for those outside.'

'It's at South Kesterly crematorium, I take it?'

He nodded.

The same place her own father had been cremated, though his had been a much smaller affair.

'How are you dealing with it?' she asked, knowing it would affect her deeply if he said not well.

He shrugged as his gaze drifted outside. 'It fluctuates. To be honest, I'm finding it hard to get my head round the fact that he's actually gone. I keep expecting him to walk in the door, or that it's going to be him when the phone rings . . . "I've got tickets for the big match Saturday week, are you going to be around?"' he mimicked. '"I need your expert opinion on something you know nothing about."' He laughed and Andee smiled. '"Are you ready to take over the business yet?" I can hear him in my head as though he's actually right here.' His eyes came to hers. 'How do you think the kids are coping?'

She put down her glass. 'Reasonably well, on the surface, but I don't think it's really sunk in for them yet. Having said that, Luke is definitely moodier lately and I wouldn't be surprised if somewhere down the line it hits him quite hard. Have you spoken to him today?'

He shook his head.

She sighed. 'I'm afraid losing his grandpa might be bringing up everything he felt when he lost you.'

Martin blinked. 'But he hasn't lost me. I'm still here.'

'You know what I'm saying. You're not a constant in his life any more, the way you used to be. He can't turn to you at the end of the day when he needs moral or male support . . .'

'He can always call. I've told him that a hundred times . . .'

'It's not the same, and you know it.'

As his eyes went down she could tell by the set of his jaw that the guilt he felt over leaving wasn't even close to abating. He spoke quietly. 'My dad used to say to him, in front of me, "Not all men are like your father, my boy. We don't all walk out on our families. Some of us honour our responsibilities and I want you to be one of our number."'

Surprised, and faintly shocked, Andee said, 'Luke's never told me that.'

'No? I thought he might have.'

'Your dad shouldn't have tried to create a division between you.'

'I'd already done it,' he reminded her. 'Although I didn't realise it straight away. I guess he's been bottling things up for a while . . .'

'That surely can't be a surprise.'

He shook his head. 'Not really, I guess I just haven't allowed myself to see it.'

She frowned. 'You mean you've never stopped to consider how lonely he is without you? You used to do everything, go everywhere together, then suddenly you weren't there any more.'

'I never stopped seeing him,' he protested. 'Or Alayna. Even when I'm away I'm always at the end of a phone . . .'

'You don't have to tell me what I already know, you just have to accept that the day you decided you didn't want to live with me any more you weren't only hurting and rejecting me, you were doing the same to them. Think how you'd have reacted if your father had walked out on your mother. Luke and Alayna are naturally protective of me, especially Luke. He sees it as his role, now you've gone, to be strong for me, and it shouldn't be that way. He should be focusing on his own life, thinking about his exams, uni, girl-friends, his sports, not having to worry about me, or whether you're going to be in touch.'

He was clearly taking everything in. 'I get that,' he told her, 'and I promise you, I want to change it, I just don't know how.'

Being unused to seeing him at a loss, she found herself feeling almost sorry for him. 'Then work it out,' she said firmly. 'He's your son. He needs you to explain why you did, what you did, so that he can at least try to understand it and move on.'

'And how is telling him I felt stifled, that I was losing myself, that I didn't want to live the way I was any more supposed to make him feel better?'

Wondering if he realised how hurtful his words were for her, she replied, 'You need to find a way of explaining it that *will* make him feel better. I can't tell you what to say, because I'm not the one who felt they had to get out of our relationship.'

Swallowing dryly he picked up his beer and stared at it hard, apparently frozen in his thoughts, maybe his guilt, before putting the glass down again. With a hint of irony in his tone, he said, 'To think I've been trying to get you to sit down and talk to me for over a year. If I'd known it was going to go like this . . .'

'Oh come on, Martin, what did you expect? It's not just about us, you know it's about the children too, and as far as I'm concerned they matter far more.'

'If that's true, then how come it's taken you so long to agree to see me?'

Flushing angrily, she retorted, 'Is that your way of trying to say the children don't matter to me?'

'Of course not, but shutting me out, refusing to let me near you, was hardly in their best interests, was it?'

Smarting with the truth of that, she said, 'You'd hurt me enough. I didn't want to go through any more, and nor did I want them to see me going through it. Anyway, we're talking now. It's just a shame it took your father's death to make it happen.'

'Meaning you wouldn't be here now if you weren't feeling sorry for me?'

'Not sorry for you, sad for your loss, though you're right, if it weren't for that I probably wouldn't have come.'

He arched an eyebrow. 'Well, at least you're honest.'

Taking a sip of her drink she said, 'It would be nice to know that you feel at least some regret for what you did.'

'Of course I regret it,' he cried. 'It was never my intention to hurt you, or the children, it was just that when the contract came up I saw how desperate I was to get away. I hadn't realised until then just how much everything had been piling in on me . . . No, listen,' he insisted as she made to interrupt, 'I've tried telling you this before, but you've never wanted to hear it. You don't know what it's like to be a stay-at-home parent, because it's not something you've ever done. If it were, you'd have a better understanding of how bloody soul-destroying it can be at times, not because you don't love your kids, but because you almost stop existing outside of their needs . . .'

'And yet you managed to build up a very successful business while you were not existing, and somehow succeeded in keeping your frustrations to yourself, because I don't recall you ever discussing them with me.'

'Oh believe me, I tried, but you'd always find something else to do, or to talk about, as if the minutiae of my world, my needs couldn't possibly compare to the larger issues you were dealing with outside the home.'

Silenced by that, it took her a moment to say, 'I never felt that way, ever. In fact, I used to take time off when you insisted . . .'

'You took hours off, Andee, and maybe a week here in Kesterly before rushing back to London to solve the next case. And do you know what really got to me about it all? It wasn't only that you'd never actually wanted to join the police in the first place, though that was bad enough, it was how you were behaving like your own parents, shipping the kids off for the summer, focusing on your work, without seeming to realise that you were putting *our* children in danger of going the same way as your sister.'

Andee's face paled. 'If that's the rubbish you've

been telling yourself to try to excuse walking out on us, then you appal me,' she informed him furiously. 'To use Penny's disappearance that way . . . Jesus, I can't believe you even thought it, never mind said it.'

'I thought it, and said it, because it's true. You were doing everything your parents had done, and I wasn't prepared to see our children go the same way.'

'So you saved them by walking out and leaving them? Yes, that makes sense . . .'

'I thought, if I went, you wouldn't have a choice, you'd have to put them first, but what did you do? You got your cousin Frank and his wife to take over, and then your mother.'

'They were thirteen and fifteen. How the hell was I supposed to cope on my own when I have a full-time job?'

'You could have given up work. I was earning enough, I'd have given you anything you asked for, but oh no, you were too damned proud to take anything from me. You were earning your own money and as long as you could do that you could carry on putting your career ahead of your children . . .'

'That is *not* true. Nothing has ever mattered more to me than them . . .'

'But you weren't showing it, you weren't even acting it . . .'

'So how come I have such a great relationship with them now? And if you're trying to suggest for a single moment that either of them could at any time sink into the kind of depression Penny did without me noticing, then you are seriously deluded. No, I'm sorry Martin, you can try all you like to make me responsible for what you did, but in the end *you* are the one who left, not me.'

Since he could hardly refute that, and because he never had been able to argue for long, he swallowed whatever he was going to say next and sighed wearily. 'I really didn't want this to happen,' he said, 'but at the same time I guess it was inevitable, and of course, you're right, I'm the one who's really screwed up.'

Reminded of how gifted he was at defusing a situation, of removing the sting before it went too deep, she found herself thinking that this was one of the things she missed most about him. He'd never been able to cope with bad feeling, hadn't even experienced a grudge that she knew of, though he was capable of regretting his mistakes – and was even big enough to own up to them.

Maybe she ought to try doing the same.

'So where do we go from here?' she asked, not quite able to meet his eyes.

'I don't know,' he replied. 'Obviously I have a lot of ground to make up with Luke.' He regarded her anxiously. 'Alayna's OK, is she? Please tell me there's not something I'm missing . . .'

'She seems fine,' she interrupted. *Apart from being mad keen for us to get back together*, but she certainly wasn't going to say that. 'Something she is finding quite difficult,' she said cautiously, 'is Brigitte being here.'

He nodded slowly, clearly accepting that.

Though she really didn't want to know, she found herself asking, 'How long have you been together?'

Seeming not to hear the question, he said, 'She understands that it wouldn't be right for her to come to the funeral. She didn't know Dad, has barely met Mum and the kids . . .'

'Is it serious between you?' she interrupted, aware of how tense she'd become.

'Mum wants us all to sit together on the day,' he said, again as though he hadn't heard the question, 'as a family. Are you OK with that?'

'Of course,' she agreed.

Reaching for her hand, he entwined their fingers and smiled ironically into her eyes. She wondered what was going through his mind, what he might be about to confide, or ask, and almost smiled when all he said was, 'Do you want to eat here, in the bar, or shall we go through to the restaurant? Apparently there's a band playing in the other room tonight, so we've been advised to get our orders in early.'

A while later, with their food and half a bottle of wine between them, she was aware of falling prey to another of his natural gifts. He was so skilled at putting people at their ease, being a great listener, always seeming to know the right responses, at the same time as being able to make someone laugh, or feel good about themselves or their opinions. Unless he disagreed, of course, but even then he was never combative or pig-headed, merely persuasive, sometimes insistent, though not to a point where he felt he had to raise his voice or hit back by causing unnecessary offence. In fact there were times when his calmness in the face of her frustration had driven her to start hurling things at him, which had invariably made him laugh.

'What are you smiling at?' he asked, as their plates were cleared.

'Was I?' she countered.

He nodded.

She shrugged, in an effort to make her comment seem offhand. 'I guess I was just thinking about how good we were together at times. Very different in many ways, but somehow we used to . . .' She shrugged again. 'I don't know, *fit* I suppose. Or I thought so, anyway.'

'Listen,' he said softly, 'I didn't mean to make it sound all bad earlier, because I swear, it was never that. We had some really good times, the best, and to go with all our wonderful memories we have two gorgeous kids we can feel damned proud of.'

Finding her thoughts straying to Sophie whose family had been torn apart by her mother's death, and by her disappearance, she was about to voice them when she remembered his accusation. She focused too much on her job.

With the sardonic tone she knew well, he told her, 'You can't hide it from me, and you're right to be thinking of her. She doesn't stop mattering because you're out for dinner, or at any other time. So how's the search going?'

She regarded him anxiously, needing to be sure he wanted to hear it before she launched into a detailed account of the past week. This was something else she missed about him, the way he used to listen quietly, patiently, as she talked her way through a case, sometimes nodding his understanding, or frowning his confusion, and more often than not helping her to find another perspective, or even an answer that had become masked by a forest of conflicting information.

It didn't happen this evening, nor did she tell him about the unease that had overcome her during the press conference. Or had it happened afterwards? She really couldn't be sure. She only knew that it hadn't gone away.

'So do you think this Polish guy knows where she is?' he asked as they reached her car.

Putting aside her misgivings, she said, 'I think there's a good chance he knows something.'

'And what about this Perkins bloke?'

'I'm not sure how involved he is, but something's going on behind the scenes at that campsite, I'm convinced of that.'

He nodded pensively. 'If she's got her computer and her phone,' he said, 'then you have to wonder why she's stopped making contact.'

'It's a question we're constantly asking ourselves, and the answer has to be that she's managed to lose them, or someone's taken them from her.'

'Or she didn't take them at all.'

She frowned. 'But we know that she did.' She regarded him carefully. 'Are you thinking her parents lied about that?'

He shrugged. 'I was just trying to see it another way, but I guess we know she did take the phone because she texted – and I'd say my money's on the Sikora connection.'

Sighing, she looked into his eyes as she said, 'Sorry, I'm making it all about me and my work again.'

He simply raised his eyebrows.

She took a breath and tried to think what to say next, but her thoughts were all tangled up in how closely they were standing together, how worried she was becoming about this case, and things she could hardly give voice to in the confusion. 'You didn't answer me earlier,' she began, and stopped as he tilted her mouth to his.

His kiss was so gentle and unexpected that she barely knew how to respond. 'What did you ask me earlier?' he murmured.

'I . . . I was wondering how serious it is with Brigitte.'

Sighing softly, he dropped his forehead against hers as he said, 'Now isn't the time to get into it.'

'Well, it either is serious or isn't.'

'OK, she wants to get married and . . .'

Andee pulled away, so sharply that she almost lost her balance. 'If it's that serious,' she snapped, feeling as though she'd been struck, 'I have to wonder what she'd make of what just happened. I should have known . . .'

'Andrea, I tried to tell you now wasn't a good time . . .'

'Actually, there's no good time to break it to me that you're getting married when you'd never marry me . . .'

'Will you listen,' he cried as she tore open her car door.

'No thanks, I've heard everything I need to for tonight. And for your information, I've met someone else too,' and slamming the car door she started the engine.

As she reversed out of her space he simply stood looking down at her. She couldn't look back, couldn't bear him to see how angry and foolish she felt, so keeping her eyes straight ahead she put the car into gear and drove away.

'Mum?'

Having expected this from the moment she'd heard Alayna letting herself in downstairs, Andee turned on to her back to see her daughter silhouetted like a spirit in the doorway. 'Don't put the light on,' she whispered, 'but you can come and have a chat if you like.'

Kicking off her flip-flops, Alayna climbed up to plant herself cross-legged next to her mother. 'So? How did it go?' she asked excitedly.

Stroking her hair, while feeling for how crushed she was going to be, Andee said, 'Not the way you hoped, I'm afraid.'

'You mean he doesn't want to get back together?'

'No, he doesn't.'

'Oh no! I don't believe it. So what happened? Did you talk about it? You didn't end up rowing, did you?'

Since she didn't feel it was her place to tell Alayna her father was getting married, all Andee said was, 'We had a nice dinner, it was a bit like old times for some of the evening, but I definitely got the impression that he and Brigitte are a lot closer than we'd realised.'

Thumping the bed in frustration, Alayna declared, 'He is *so* stupid. I can't believe he's doing this . . .'

'Ssh,' Andee cut in softly. 'You'll wake Grandma.'

'Have you told her?'

'Yes. She was waiting up when I got in.'

'What did she say?'

'The same as I'm saying, we just have to accept that Dad's moved on and now it's time for us to do the same.'

'But I don't want to,' Alayna protested angrily. 'I want him to come back to us so we can be a proper family again, and I know it's what you want. Oh Mum, are you really upset?' she cried, wrapping Andee in her arms.

263

'I'm fine,' Andee lied. Once she saw Graeme again she'd feel more grounded. 'Where's Luke? He's not in his room. Did he come back earlier?'

'I don't know. I think he's still at Jake's. I'm going to tell Dad that if he's going to be with Brigitte then me and Luke won't want to see him again.'

'Alayna, you need to give her a chance. You might find you like her . . .'

'Never! It's not going to happen. I don't care if he's my dad, I don't have to like her just because he does.'

Pulling her in closer, Andee held her as she wept with frustration and disappointment. A part of her felt like crying too, though she wasn't entirely sure why. Did it really matter that Martin was going to *marry* another woman?

Yes, it did, she realised. It mattered a lot.

Chapter Twelve

The following morning, despite it being Sunday, Andee drove down to the Cove to see the Monroes. There had been no word from Sophie following the appeal, no sightings showing any promise so far, no breakthroughs at all. Remembering how terrible that felt, how vast and impenetrable the world seemed when it had swallowed up someone you loved, she needed to find out how they were coping today.

As soon as she walked in she was aware of the atmosphere in the house seeming sadder, more despairing, and knew it was how her own home had felt after the appeals for Penny. In the Monroes' case they had even more to deal with now that the baby had been diagnosed with this awful disorder. He was asleep, Heidi told her, as she let her in, so she was trying to catch up with some work while Gavin, who'd been awake all night, had a lie-down.

'The firm he drives for got in touch earlier,' Heidi confided as she made some coffee. 'I think someone went sick at the last minute so they were hoping he'd fill in, but he can't bring himself to do it. He wants to be here in case . . .' Her voice shook, and for a moment Andee thought she was going to break down. However, she managed to catch her breath and continue. 'I don't blame him,' she said. 'I can't find it in myself to do much either. All I can think about is where she might be, what might be happening to her, and now, with what we've found out about Archie . . . It's starting to feel as though someone up there has got it in for us.'

How could anyone not feel that way in the same situation?

'We heard on the news that Gary Perkins was remanded in custody,' Heidi went on. 'I feel terrible that I didn't carry out the criminal record check. To be honest I thought Jackie had done it. She said she was going to.'

'Does she usually do those things?'

'Sometimes, but not always.' She stopped what she was doing and gazed out at the garden.

Andee watched her, noticing how badly she was shaking. After a while her eyes drifted on round the room, across the mugs hanging from the front of a shelf and the keys dangling from a spare hook. She was still staring at the keys when Heidi suddenly said, 'I know you can't tell us everything that's going on, but did he give you any idea where he took her?' She was already shaking her head. 'Even if he had, she's not there now, is she, or you'd have found her. How's his sister taking it? I had a bit of a go at her the last time she was here. I feel bad about it now, but she has to see she was in the wrong for bringing him to a holiday camp. A bloke with his track record . . .' Her voice trailed off as the awfulness of everything seemed to envelop her. 'I don't expect I'll have a job at the end of this,' she said shakily. 'The Poynters haven't even come to see us since they got back, although she rang a couple of days ago.'

'What did she say?' Andee asked.

She shrugged. 'I wasn't here, so she spoke to Gavin. Apparently she wanted us to know she was sorry for what was happening, and if there was anything she could do we knew where to find her.' She laughed without humour. 'I suppose it's nice of her, but she's not someone I'd feel right about talking to. I haven't really talked to anyone since all this kicked off, apart from you, and that's not the same, is it?'

'What about Gavin?'

She shook her head. 'It's like we're afraid to say anything to each other in case the wrong thing comes out, so we just sit here in silence most of the time, waiting for the phone to ring, trying to prepare ourselves for the worst.' She took a shuddering breath. 'I know he blames me. He denies it, but I know he's thinking that if I'd tried a bit harder with her, hadn't allowed myself to get so obsessed with the baby . . . Well, I'm paying the price for it now, aren't I? She's gone, he's never going to be right . . . Makes you wonder what it's all about, doesn't it?'

Andee had lost count of the number of times she'd heard that phrase from frightened, desperate people, trying to make some sense of their tragedies when there was no sense to be found.

After leaving Blue Ocean Park she took a longer route into town, past the haulage firm that Gavin occasionally worked for, where she paused for a moment. The yard was all locked up, with not a soul in sight, only an emergency number printed on a board over the chains and padlocks of the gates.

From there she drove on to the Poynters' mansion where she stopped again, though apart from the high pink walls and black iron gates there was nothing to see. After making a few notes, she put the car in reverse and turned around to head back to Kesterly.

'Here are the times of the crossings from Dover,' Leo told her, handing her a printout as she entered the incident room. 'As we're not sure what time Sikora set out from Krakow, and the girlfriend isn't either – this is presuming that he did set out . . .'

'You've tried ringing him?'

'Of course, but he's not answering.'

'You've got Kasia to try?'

'Yes, but he's not picking up for her either, so there's nothing to say that he actually is on the way. We're only going to know for certain once he shows up, and when that's going to be . . . The window's about as big as they come, but all the ports have been alerted, so if he does come through he'll be taken in straight away.'

'Do they know how important the van is? We need to find out if she was ever in it.'

'Yes, they know.' He regarded her curiously. 'Are you OK? You seem a bit . . .' He shrugged.

'A bit what?'

'I don't know.'

'I'm fine. Just listening.' Glancing at her mobile as it rang she saw it was Martin and decided she really didn't want to speak to him now, so left the call to go to messages.

'The boxes you found in the Poynters' study,'

she said, calling up the case notes, 'what was in them?'

Clearly surprised by the question, Leo replied, 'Some new-fangled locking devices. Apparently they're for the higher-end caravans.'

As she found the entry for his first visit to the Poynters her mobile rang again, and again a few minutes later. Accepting that Martin wasn't going to stop until she answered, she finally clicked on. 'Martin, I'm at work . . .'

'I know, Alayna told me, but this won't take long. What I said last night about Brigitte . . .'

'For goodness sake, I really don't want to discuss it now . . .'

'What you didn't give me the chance to say was that if I was ever going to marry anyone, it would be you.'

As the words hit her she froze. Then, getting up from her chair, she marched into the corridor, found a free office and closed the door. 'How dare you?' she seethed. 'That you have the audacity to presume I'd marry you after everything you've done . . .'

'I didn't ask you,' he laughed over her. 'I said, if I was going to . . .'

Her mouth opened and closed.

'That's how you leap to conclusions,' he told her.

'I'm going to ring off now,' she said stiffly, 'and we'll pretend this conversation never happened.'

By the time she returned to the incident room she was trying not to laugh herself. He'd always had a way of doing that to her, taking the wind right out of her sails and leaving her with nowhere to go, or feeling foolish, or ready to throttle him.

What would Brigitte say if she knew that was how he felt?

It wasn't until she started down to her car, much later in the day, that she realised he hadn't commented on the fact that she'd met someone else. Maybe he hadn't heard. Or, knowing him, he'd decided not to take it seriously. He'd tell himself it was simply something she'd said to try and save face, or to get him worried. Maybe he was worried. It could explain why he'd made the call. She wondered what Alayna had said to him, or indeed what he had told Alayna.

She guessed she'd find out when she got home.

'Is Luke back yet?' she asked as she walked into the kitchen to find her mother with a recipe book balanced on a table-top easel and pans every-where. 'I thought we were going over to the pub tonight?'

Maureen frowned as she blinked. 'Did we arrange that?' she asked, seeming perplexed.

'This morning,' Andee reminded her. 'You said you were going to book a table . . .' Noticing that the memory lapse was starting to bother her mother, she quickly said, 'Listen, it doesn't matter. I probably just assumed I'd suggested it, and ended up forgetting. It'll be lovely to eat at home. What have we got?'

Maureen looked at her cooking as she said, 'Stroganoff. Martin's always been keen on it, and Carol's bringing one of her lovely vanilla cheesecakes.'

It was Andee's turn to blink. 'I didn't realise they were coming this evening,' she said, not thrilled by the idea of spending any time with

Martin right now. 'What time are we expecting them?'

Still seeming slightly worried, Maureen glanced at the clock. 'In about ten minutes,' she replied, making it sound more like a question. 'I haven't got the day wrong, have I?'

Sounding more impatient than she intended, Andee said, 'I don't know, because I wasn't there when you made the arrangement. I'm sure you haven't.'

Maureen pulled a face. 'You'd better give Carol a call to check. My memory's definitely not what it used to be.'

'Hey Mum,' Alayna chirped, bouncing into the kitchen and treating Andee to a hug and kiss. 'Grandma, Dad just rang to say he and Grandma Carol are on their way. He hopes they won't be too early.'

'I hope you told him that any time is fine,' Maureen responded.

'Something like that. OMG, Grandma, this is like amazing,' Alayna gushed, as she helped herself to a taste of the fillet steak. 'Is it a Jamie Oliver?'

'Yes, it is,' Maureen replied, seeming pleased Alayna would know that, in spite of the book being right in front of them. 'Your dad told me about it. He said it's very good, so I thought I'd give it a go.'

'Try it, Mum,' Alayna insisted, bringing a sliver of meat to Andee.

Feeling all her tastebuds zing as she tasted it, Andee murmured a note of ecstasy, not having realised until then just how hungry she was.

'Is Luke home?' she asked Alayna.

Shaking her head as she picked at the sauce

again, Alayna said, 'I don't think so. Did he come in, Grandma?'

'I haven't see him,' Maureen replied. 'I hope he'll be back in time for dinner.'

'Oh God,' Alayna gasped, spinning round. 'You don't think Dad's bringing Brigitte, do you?' Her eyes went from Maureen's to Andee's.

'Did he say he was?' Andee asked her mother.

'Not that I recall. No, I'm sure he isn't. It wouldn't be right to bring her here, would it?'

'It's not right that she's here at all,' Alayna put in.

'No, he wouldn't do that to us, or to her,' Andee declared confidently. 'Now will one of you please tell me when you last spoke to Luke.'

Alayna's shoulders went up as she thought. 'I think it must have been Friday.'

Feeling a dark beat of alarm, Andee said, 'Try ringing him now,' and she turned to her mother. 'Did you see him or speak to him yesterday?' she demanded.

Maureen's eyes were wide as she shook her head. 'I'm sure he's still at Jake's,' she murmured.

Andee was already dialling Jake's number.

'I've just got his voicemail,' Alayna announced.

'Hey Mrs Stone,' Jake drawled down the line, 'how are you?'

Not bothering to remind him she was a Lawrence, not a Stone, Andee asked, 'Is Luke with you?'

'No, I've only just got back from London, but I'll tell him you're looking for him if he calls.'

London? 'Jake, when did you go to London?'

'Friday. Why? Is there a problem?'

'I'm not sure, I'll get back to you,' and clicking off the line she tried three more of Luke's friends, only to be told that Luke wasn't with them either, nor had any of them seen him since Friday.

Andee was trying very hard to stay calm. Her son had been gone for two days and she was only just noticing. What the hell kind of parent was she? What in God's name could have happened to him?

'It's not like him to go off without saying anything,' Alayna mumbled worriedly.

It hadn't been like Penny either, at first, or Sophie, as far as Andee could tell.

There's no comparison, she told herself forcefully. *Luke's a boy, a young man, who's in a funk, not a depression, and he knows how to take care of himself.*

Connecting to his number, she spoke fiercely to his voicemail. 'Luke, you are to ring me the instant you get this. You know very well the kind of case I'm working on at the moment, so you'll understand why it's important to me that you make contact. I need to know you're all right.'

Seeing how alarmed her mother and Alayna looked after this outburst, she tried lightening her tone as she said, 'He needs to learn that it's not OK to disappear without saying anything. It's inconsiderate, and causes people to worry when they might have better things to do.'

'That'll be Dad,' Alayna cried, starting down the hall as someone knocked at the front door.

Maureen was still staring at Andee.

'I'm sure he's fine,' Andee said, wishing she believed it. 'He's probably trying to punish me, or his father . . . Actually, I don't know what he's trying to do . . .' She felt sick with fear, unable to think past it.

Luke, her precious boy, her baby!

She hadn't been paying attention.

'What's going on?' Martin demanded as he and Carol came into the kitchen. 'How can you not have spoken to him since Friday?'

Thanks, Alayna. 'I assumed someone else had,' Andee shot back. 'He's seventeen, for God's sake . . .'

'I know how old he is, and I also know he's not in a great frame of mind.' He was dialling Luke's number. 'Son, I need to hear from you. Pull it together now and get in touch.'

'Dad, I'm scared,' Alayna wailed. 'You don't think something's happened to him, do you?'

Seeing clifftops, jagged rocks, lonely figures on empty skylines, Andee dropped her head in her hands. 'No, of course it hasn't,' she cried. She had to control her imagination. 'He's probably with a friend we don't know and his phone's run out of battery.'

'Still, he should find a way to get in touch to let us know where he is,' Carol declared, her papery-soft complexion seeming starkly white in contrast to her inky-black hair.

'Have you checked in his room?' Martin demanded.

'Of course,' Andee replied, realising that actually no one had.

Instantly on the case, Alayna flew up the stairs. 'He's not here,' she shouted from the landing. 'Oh Mum, what are we going to do?' she cried, running back down again.

'Sit down,' Carol told Maureen, whose colour had completely vanished. 'It's going to be all right. We'll find him.'

Acutely aware of what this was doing to her

mother, Andee said tersely, 'I'm so angry with him. He knows better than to do this to us.' *He wouldn't do it purposely. He wasn't insensitive that way.* 'Where are you going?' she asked Martin, as he headed for the back door.

'I'll be just a moment,' he told her.

As she watched him run down the garden, seeming oblivious to the sudden downpour of rain, she was aware of Alayna coming to stand with her.

'Why's he going into the shed?' Alayna wanted to know. 'Luke won't be in there.'

Bewildered, angry, terrified, but thankful Martin was there, Andee simply watched, praying that he was going to come back with something helpful.

'He's taken his camping gear,' Martin announced, stamping his feet on the mat as he returned.

More alarmed by that than comforted, Andee cried, 'That still doesn't tell us where he is.'

'But it gives me a fairly good idea,' Martin informed her. 'You guys go ahead and eat. I'll call when I've found him.'

Go ahead and eat! Was he crazy? 'I'm coming with you,' Andee declared, reaching for her bag.

'No, you stay put. He'll be on Exmoor. I think I probably know where, and if I'm right we have this pact, no girls allowed.'

Andee started to protest, ran after him down the hall, but he was driving off before she could reach the car, leaving her panicked and furious and wishing she knew how the hell she was going to cope with the others.

They were looking to her for reassurance, waiting for her to tell them that Luke would be exactly where Martin expected him to be, that he hadn't got lost on the moor, or somehow fallen into a ravine and was even now lying unconscious, unable to let anyone know where he was.

Please God don't let history be repeating itself. He's a good boy and we love him so much. My mother and I will never survive it.

Martin had been gone for over an hour, and though Andee had tried his number several times he still wasn't answering. He'd be on the moor by now and all she could see, almost feel in her bones, were the endless stretches of nowhere, a vast, uncompromising landscape filled with hidden hollows and streams, gushing rivers, rocks, thickets, marshes and some of the highest cliffs in the country on the coastal edge. The wind gusted that rugged terrain like packs of demons on the prowl, while lightning storms tore the sky apart. It would be possible for Luke to walk for miles and miles without seeing another living soul, to shout and scream from the bottom of a gully never to be heard.

Her eyes closed as she tried to hear him. Tried with all her motherly instincts to connect with where he was.

Starting as her phone rang, she quickly clicked on. 'Have you got him?' she asked breathlessly.

'Yes, he's here,' Martin told her. 'Cold, hungry, and ready to come home.'

Unravelling with relief, she cried, 'Where are you?'

'Just coming off the moor, about twenty minutes away. I'd have called sooner, but I couldn't get a signal. Here, I'll put him on.'

'Hey Mum,' Luke said sheepishly. 'Sorry, I didn't mean to make you worry.'

'You must never *ever* go off without telling someone where you're going,' she responded fiercely. 'If Dad hadn't been around we'd never even have known where to look.'

'I was OK, I promise. I just needed to chill for a while.'

'On your own? In the middle of Exmoor? Luke, there have got to be safer places.'

'I knew where I was. Dad and I have been there tons of times.'

'Tell him,' her mother said, 'that there's plenty of stroganoff. We're keeping it warm for him.'

'Thanks, Grandma,' he called out, 'I'm starving.'

Realising her mother was trembling with relief, Andee took her hand and squeezed it tight. Luke had no idea how lucky he was to have so many people who cared about him. He must learn to appreciate this, and realise that such a precious gift didn't come without responsibilities.

By the time father and son walked in through the door, damp from their dash through the rain, and looking ridiculously pleased with themselves, Andee was ready to forgive anything as long as her son was safe in her arms.

'You fool,' she murmured, taking in his dirt-smeared face and malodorous clothes. 'What on earth were you trying to prove? Didn't it occur to you that we'd be trying to get hold of you?'

He gave an awkward shrug and glanced at his father.

'He's got something to tell you,' Martin informed her, 'but let him clean up and have a bite to eat first.'

As Luke left the room with Alayna hot on his heels, Andee's eyes went to Martin.

'He's OK,' Martin assured her. 'He's been having a rough time over losing his grandad, and he's not very happy about Brigitte being here either.'

'I told you,' his mother said.

'I know you did, but what was I to do? She was trying to be supportive, and the way you lot have closed ranks against her . . .'

Carol threw out her hands in protest. 'What does she expect? We're a bereaved family trying to come to terms with our loss, and none of us even knew she existed before she just decided to turn up.'

'It was poor judgement, I admit,' he responded, 'but you don't have to worry, she's leaving tomorrow . . .'

'Oh, well now I feel rotten,' Carol exclaimed. 'It's not that we don't want her here . . . Well, actually, we don't. In case it's escaped your notice we're a very close family and the mother of your children is right at the heart of it. Have you given any thought at all to what this has been like for Andee?'

'It's OK, I'm fine,' Andee assured her.

'That's not true,' Maureen argued. 'It came as a terrible blow when you found out she was here . . .'

'Mum!'

'No, it's high time we cleared the air around here,' her mother insisted. 'You know very well that you two belong together.'

Martin's head was in his hands.

'I thought you'd got over all your nonsense by now,' his mother said sharply. 'It's been long enough. If I were Andee I wouldn't even . . .'

'Stop!' Andee cut in loudly. 'I don't mean to be rude, but this really isn't any of your business.'

'Mum!' Alayna shouted from upstairs, 'Luke wants you.'

Thankful for the timely interruption, Andee ignored Martin's stare, treated their mothers to a warning look and ran upstairs to sort out her son.

'He's in his room,' Alayna told her as she reached the landing. 'Apparently he really laid into Dad about Brigitte and everything . . .'

'Oh God, not him too,' Andee groaned. 'What's going on with everyone? Please go downstairs and get your grandmothers off Dad's back.'

'But Mum . . .'

'Just do as you're told,' and taking off along the landing she found Luke's door open, with Luke himself slouched forlornly on the edge of the bed.

'So what's going on?' she said, putting an arm round his shoulders as she sat down with him. 'I know Dad . . .'

'It's not about Dad,' he interrupted. 'Well it is, but that's like . . .' He shrugged. 'It's about something that happened just after the end of term. I've been trying to find a way to tell you, but I thought . . . I was afraid if it all came out it would be bad for you, for me too, and there was nothing to it really . . . I mean, there was, but it wasn't me who did it . . . I was there, for some of the time . . .'

'Sweetheart,' she came in gently, 'you're not making a lot of sense, so let me remind you that you can tell me anything and no matter what it is we'll find a way to work it out.'

He nodded distractedly. 'That's what Dad said.'

'You've told him?'

'Yeah, I told him. I was going to tell him before, you know when everything first kicked off about

Sophie, but then Brigitte turned up and it was all like, you know, weird and stuff, and . . .'

'What does Sophie have to do with it?' she asked carefully, already praying that he wasn't going to admit that the local boys Sophie had written about included him. 'Do you know her?'

He shook his head. 'I mean, I know who she is, but I'm not like . . . Some of my mates met her and her friend on the beach . . .' He turned to her in sudden panic. 'You're not going to make me give you their names, are you?'

'Luke, I need to know what happened.'

He hung his head again. 'There was this party, just after we broke up, in one of the caravans. I found out after that she'd invited us because she wanted to get off with Robin Howell. You know Robin, he's in my class . . .'

'Yes, I know Robin.'

'Well apparently, Chelsey, that's Robin's girl-friend, was mean to Sophie at school, so Sophie wanted to get back at her by, you know, going with Robin.'

Filling with dismay, Andee said, 'And did she go with Robin?'

He shook his head. 'I don't know. I don't think so. It was like she wanted to, but then she changed her mind . . .'

Andee's eyes were stern. 'Please tell me he didn't force her.'

'No! I mean, if he did I didn't see him, but I swear I don't think he did. No one did. All I know is that everyone was smoking dope and getting out of their minds . . .'

'Were you smoking dope?'

Looking down, he nodded.

Her jaw tightened. 'Go on,' she said, deciding that would have to wait until later.

'I just remember that Sophie was crying and her friend was shouting . . . Some of the guys seemed to think it was funny. That was when Jake and I got out of there. It was like crazy, but I don't think anyone else stayed, because we saw them all about ten minutes later in the Leisure Park.'

'Was Sophie with them?'

'No. They were saying she was bad news and needed to grow up and stuff, and then it was like everyone forgot about her until . . . until it came on the news that she was missing.'

Andee stared at him hard as his body began convulsing with sobs. The only good part of this, if he was telling the truth, and he'd better be, was that there hadn't been a rape. 'Is it possible one of your friends might know where she is?' she asked, torn between comforting him and throttling him.

With his head still in his hands, he said, 'I don't think so. Everyone's scared out of their minds in case the police come knocking on their doors, but she didn't go missing until at least three weeks after that party and I swear none of us saw her in that time. I don't think any of us even really knew her name till then.'

Angered by the wretched arrogance of that, Andee was struggling to decide on the best way to go forward. Though she didn't believe any of the boys *were* involved in Sophie's disappearance, there was no getting away from the fact that they had to be questioned.

'You're not going to like what I'm about to tell you,' she warned, 'but I'm afraid I am going to need the names of everyone who was there that night.'

'Mum, no!' he cried. 'Everyone will know it's me who told you . . .'

'Robin's I already have,' she continued.

'Mum, you're not listening. If they think I grassed . . .'

'I'll pass their names to someone else at the station so they can speak to your friends. Luke, listen, you said yourself that the party happened three weeks or more before Sophie went missing, so they should have nothing to worry about. No, hear me out. The police aren't about ruining young men's lives for the sake of it, so if there was no assault, and no one's saying there was, not even Sophie's friend . . .'

'We were smoking dope, Mum. It's against the law.'

'I'm aware of that, but it's not the main issue here. However, I will be taking it up with you again, you can be sure of that, and you can consider yourself grounded for the rest of the holidays.'

'Mum, no!'

'Mum, yes. And I'm sure Dad will support me on it, so don't try getting round him. Now I want those names.'

'Mum, please . . .'

'You're going to give them to me, Luke, and I'll tell you why. If one of your friends does know more than he's telling, is he the person you'd want to protect right now? Or would it be a vulnerable young girl who really needs to be back with her family?'

'But I swear none of them knows where she is.'

'And I probably believe you, but it still has to be checked. Now the names, please.'

As she started to write them down Alayna came dashing up the stairs. 'Mum, your phone,' she gasped, holding it out. 'It's Leo. He says it's urgent.'

Grabbing it, Andee said to Leo, 'What's happened? Have you got her?'

'No, 'fraid not, but Sikora's just been arrested in Dover. A couple of uniforms are driving over there now to bring him back.'

Chapter Thirteen

Though Andee was extremely keen to interview Sikora, she'd decided during the night that there was something she needed to do before going to the station this morning. As it ended up taking longer than she'd expected, it was past ten o'clock by the time a disgruntled Gould came over the Airwave.

'Where the heck are you?' he demanded. 'We were expecting you an hour ago.'

'I'm just pulling into the station,' she told him. 'Has anyone spoken to Sikora yet?'

'He's with his brief.'

'Don't tell me, Piers Ashdown.'

'Wrong. Helen Hall.'

Andee's eyebrows rose. 'Now that does surprise me.'

'She's the duty solicitor. A friend of yours, isn't she?'

'Sort of. Are they ready to talk to us yet?'

'Not that I've heard, and she's been in there since eight.'

Finding that slightly less curious than Gould apparently did, Andee bypassed the custody suite as she entered the station and took the stairs to the incident room, where she spoke quietly to Jemma about the situation with Luke's friends.

'I don't for one minute think any one of them has any idea where Sophie might be,' she concluded, 'but they have to be spoken to and I know I can rely on you to handle it discreetly – and whatever you do, try not to let them think we received our information from Luke. If anything has to be mentioned, say it was the diary.'

'I hear you. I'll get on to it right away.'

Turning to Leo, Andee handed him a Post-it containing a few scribbled notes. 'I want you to check if there was a diversion on this road on the dates I've written there,' she told him.

Leo regarded the information in confusion. 'What's this about?' he asked.

'Just do it,' she replied, and taking out her phone she sent Martin a quick text as she headed for the lift. *Tell Luke a very good female officer going to handle things. Will call when/if any news. X.* To her annoyance she hit send before realising she'd added a kiss. Damn! Still, it was too late to take it back so she'd just have to let him decide what to make of it, and put him right if he got it wrong.

He did, within seconds.

XXXXXXXXXXXXXXXXXXXXXXXXX
XXXXXXXXXXXXXXXXXXXXXXXXX

Trying not to laugh, she tucked the phone away again and pressed a button to go down to the Stress & Mess. The custody sergeant would contact her as soon as Helen Hall and her client were ready to talk. Meantime she had a lot of thinking to do, and some reading.

Once seated at an empty table with her first coffee of the day, she took out her photocopy of

Sophie's diary and turned to the entries at the time Jilly Monroe had died. She was doing this now because she felt they'd lost sight of Sophie as the sweet, confused girl she'd been before her world had fallen apart after the birth of Archie – before she had had to struggle to feel that she still mattered. In a way it was a little like turning back the clock, something she'd done so often in her mind with Penny, needing to remember her sister as the happy, carefree girl she'd been before they'd stopped noticing how she was changing.

Surprisingly, there was only one entry following Jilly's death, written about a month later. *I only have this book left now. It doesn't stop me missing her, but sometimes, when I look at it I feel like she's looking at it with me. I hope she's happy where she is and not missing us too much. Dear Jesus, please tell her I love her with all my heart and I'm doing my best to look after her flowers.*

Having to swallow hard, Andee turned the page to find what she'd thought, during her first reading of the book, was some astonishingly accomplished poetry for a girl so young. Then she'd realised Sophie had meticulously written out the lyrics of some of her mother's favourite songs. 'Just Like a Woman'. 'I Saw Her Again'. 'I Got You Babe'. Andee found it easy to imagine Gavin and Jilly singing together, à la Sonny & Cher, while Sophie glowed with happiness as she watched them.

The last song she'd written out was 'Jesus Wants Me for a Sunbeam', and just like the first time she'd read it, Andee felt her eyes filling with tears. She hadn't heard the song in so long that she'd almost forgotten it existed, but now she was looking at the words it was as though she could hear herself and Penny singing them together at Sunday school.

Penny, where are you? What happened? Will you never, ever come back to us?

Would there ever come a time when she'd stop asking those questions?

Knowing she wasn't going to find any answers in these pages, only a connection to Sophie that sometimes felt like one to Penny, she put the diary aside and picked up her coffee. Almost before she could gather her thoughts, her mobile bleeped with a text from Graeme.

Just letting you know I'm back in Kesterly. Would love to see you. No pressure. Call when you can. Gx

A moment later the phone rang, and seeing it was Martin she clicked on. 'Hi,' she said, 'if you're looking for an update on Jemma's enquiries she hasn't even started them yet.'

Realising Luke must be there as Martin repeated her words, she added, 'Tell him not to worry, please. Actually, put him on.'

'Hey Mum,' Luke said, managing to sound a little more buoyant than he was obviously feeling. 'We heard on the news that you've got this Polish bloke now. If he ends up confessing, or something, will that mean we're all, like, off the hook?'

Sighing, Andee said, 'Probably.'

'OK, cool. I mean, great. Thanks. Here's Dad again.'

'Hey,' Martin said, coming back on the line, 'did you like my text?'

'Very funny,' she responded, trying not to smile. 'I hope you realise that my cross was a mistake.'

'I did, but I hope you realise that none of mine were.'

Finding herself wanting to laugh, she said, 'Listen, I'm sorry none of us were as receptive to Brigitte as we should have been. I hope it hasn't caused any difficulties . . .'

'Don't worry, she was very understanding.'

It was a moment before she could reply, 'Good. So you two . . . You're still OK?'

'We are. That is, she is and so am I.'

Not quite sure how to read that, she said, 'Well, once the funeral's over and the extended family's dispersed it'll probably be a better time for us all to meet her.'

'Ah, speaking of extended family, I had a call from your cousin Frank earlier. He and Jane are arriving sometime this afternoon, so I thought I'd invite you all for dinner this evening. Hilary and Robin will probably come too,' he added, referring to his sister and brother-in-law.

'You want to cook for that many?' she asked incredulously.

'I thought I'd book the Crustacean.'

'*The Crustacean*. It'll cost a fortune . . .'

'Why don't you let me worry about that? Can I count you in?'

'That's going to depend on what happens here, but if I can get away, I'll be there.'

'OK. I'll make the reservation for eight o'clock. If you find that's too early for you, just come and join us when you can. Hang on, Alayna's saying something . . .'

'Alayna was there while you were talking about Luke's friends?' she cried.

'She's only just come in . . . We're at the Seafront Café.'

As she waited for him to talk to Alayna Andee

pictured them gathered around a table, probably one of the banquettes next to the window, and remembered many times over the years when they'd eaten there together, as a family. The café had even been there, on the corner of North Road and the Promenade, when her grandparents used to take her, Frank and Penny for a treat after a ride on the donkeys, though it had been under different ownership then.

'Alayna's just reminded me,' Martin said, coming back on the line, 'that I need to make things absolutely clear. So, here goes: it's over between me and Brigitte, and the reason I'm flirting with you . . .'

'*Dad!*' Alayna protested in the background.

'What's wrong?' he demanded.

'Just say it.'

'I'm trying to, but you keep interrupting me.'

'All right, well get on with it.'

'She is so bossy,' he told Andee. 'It can't be me she takes after. Anyway, as I was saying, I have finally come to my senses and realised what a terrible mistake I made when I left. Actually, I knew it almost straight away, but I was finding it kind of hard to admit, and then you wouldn't listen when I tried to explain . . .'

'Martin,' she interrupted, thinking of Graeme, 'I don't think this is a conversation we should be having on the phone, or in front of the children.'

'But they're on my side,' he pointed out.

Closing her eyes in an exasperated laugh, she said, 'Luke wasn't.'

'He is now. A bit of male bonding on the moor. We're very simple, and fast, us blokes. He got it all off his chest, I took it like a man, and now we're good to go again.'

Knowing that a part of the instant forgiveness was Luke's need for his father's support while the issue with his friends was settled, Andee replied, 'Well I'm glad about that, but I'm afraid it's going to take a bit more than some bonding on the moor and getting things off our chests to sort things out between us.'

'I'll buy a bigger tent and let you bare your chest first,' he promised.

Though she only just managed to swallow a laugh, especially when Alayna injected a *puhlease*, she said, 'I repeat, now really isn't the time, and I should go. If there's anything to report about Luke's friends I'll let you know.'

Glancing at her watch as she rang off, she tried to imagine what was going on with Sikora and Helen Hall that was taking so long. Was he admitting to taking Sophie with him that night, to knowing where she was now? If so, then today was going to take a very different turn from the one she was expecting.

Suzi was sitting in a window seat of the Seafront Café, absently watching a man on the next table with his two teenage children. She knew they were his because she'd heard the girl say *Dad!* a couple of times, in the way teenage girls often did, and the boy was a dead ringer for him. Not as tall yet, or as filled out, but the same tousled fair hair and definite features. It was nice watching a family that seemed to get along so well, though she expected they weren't without their problems, because as far as she could tell nobody was.

She'd come in here on her way to the police station, and had ended up staying after the caff's owner, Fliss, had come to sit with her, saying she looked like she could do with a bit of cheering up. The next thing they knew they'd been telling each other their life stories and not holding much back. It turned out Fliss was no stranger to heartbreak – her only son had been killed in a car crash and because she'd been driving at the time her husband had blamed her.

'He wasn't the only one who blamed me,' Fliss had confessed, the lines on her sweet oval face telling their own tale of suffering. 'I blamed myself, and I don't suppose I'll ever stop. He'd be eighteen now, if he'd lived. How about your girls?'

Feeling the fractures in her heart widening, Suzi said, 'Seventeen, fifteen and twelve.' With a sigh, she added, 'You have to wonder, don't you, why life dishes out these things? You do your best, try to stay out of trouble, and suddenly everything comes crashing down around you.'

'Isn't that the truth?' Fliss responded, shaking her head.

It was around then that the man and his two children had come into the caff so Fliss had gone to serve them, and had brought Suzi another cappuccino once they were settled.

'I came to Kesterly to try and rebuild my life,' she was telling Fliss now, 'and I was doing OK until all this blew up. I swear I don't know what my brother's done with that poor girl, if he's done anything at all . . . I only know that he's got himself in really deep with the people who own the camp-site and now they're expecting me to give him an alibi . . .' She shook her head, too close to tears to say any more.

'You need to get away from that caravan park,'

Fliss told her firmly. 'Everyone knows the Poynters are no good, and it's not your job to get anyone off crimes they've committed, even if that someone's your brother. It's your job to be true to yourself, and if you ask me, I think you should go to the police and tell them everything you know.'

Suzi's heart jolted. 'I was on my way there when I came in here,' she admitted. 'I don't know if I can do it. If I do they'll say I was a part of it . . .'

'Part of what?'

Suzi shook her head.

'Well, whatever it is, there's no doubt in my mind, we have to get you away from those people,' Fliss insisted.

Suzi regarded her with a mix of disbelief and hope. That this woman, a total stranger until half an hour ago, should say 'we' as if this were her problem too, as if Suzi really mattered, was so unexpected that she started to cry.

'There, there, now don't be daft,' Fliss said, patting her hand. 'Like I said, we'll get it sorted out.'

'But I don't understand why you'd want to help me when you don't even know me.'

'I feel like I do now, so you just sit tight. I know just the person to help us, so I'll go and get my phone.'

And with that she disappeared into the back of the caff, calling a cheery goodbye to the man with his children as they left.

On returning to the banquette with her mobile between both hands she told Suzi, 'The woman I'm about to call is probably going to want to know a bit about your background. Are you OK with that?'

Suzi nodded uncertainly. She couldn't imagine anyone wanting to help her once they knew who her brother was, but Fliss was being so kind, and she had to try something.

After leaving a message on her friend's mobile asking her to call, Fliss followed Suzi's eyes to the TV in the corner. Though the sound was down low they could hear it well enough as a reporter announced that Tomasz Sikora was still in police custody, and as far as anyone knew there was still no news on Sophie's whereabouts.

'Do you know him?' Fliss asked Suzi.

Suzi nodded. 'But not well.'

'Do you reckon he took her off somewhere? That's what they're saying.'

'I don't know,' Suzi replied brokenly. 'I swear I don't know what to think any more.'

'The diversion you asked about?' Leo was saying as he and Andee headed for the custody suite. 'The local authority's saying it never happened.'

Though it was the answer she'd expected, Andee felt a cold fist tightening inside her.

'Are you going to tell me what it's about?' Leo prompted. 'I mean, I can guess, but . . .'

'Andee,' Helen Hall smiled warmly as Andee and Leo came out of the lift. She was a short, slender woman in her mid-forties, with a faintly waxen complexion and arresting green eyes. 'Long time no see. How are you? Sorry to hear about Dougie.'

'Thank you,' Andee replied. 'It's taking a while for it to sink in.'

'I'll bet, and I'm sure all this isn't helping.' She glanced at Leo. 'Well, I guess we should get on with it. My client's prepared a full statement, and he's willing to talk to you, but before that happens we're looking for immunity from prosecution.'

Andee's eyebrows rose as Leo choked.

'We have to know what he's going to tell us before we can agree to that,' Andee informed her.

'Of course, but it's important for you to know that he won't agree to tell you anything unless he has the immunity.'

Flabbergasted, Leo looked at Andee.

'Does he know where Sophie is?' Andee asked.

Helen shook her head.

'No, I didn't think so.' Andee's face was pale as she said, 'OK, let's hear what he has to say.'

'The immunity?' Helen prompted.

'Is not in my gift, as you know, but if his story bears out and we're all satisfied it's the right course to take I'm sure the CPS will consider it.'

Apparently accepting that was the best she was going to get, Helen led the way to an interview room where Sikora was waiting. Andee could see right away how anxious he was, how out of his depth and exhausted. He'd probably been awake all night, but there again, so had she.

After the door was closed and everyone had identified themselves for the tapes, Leo began, 'You are a Polish national, but you say you can read and write English. So, are you happy to proceed without an interpreter?'

Sikora nodded.

'You have to speak,' Helen told him.

Sikora cleared his throat. 'Yes,' he said, too loudly.

Andee knew that sometimes you could look into a person's eyes and sense instantly that good or evil ran through them; and sometimes you simply couldn't. All she could feel sure about with this man was that somewhere amongst the anguish, fatigue and fear blanching his Slavic features, he had the kind of looks that many women – and girls – would be drawn to. Very masculine, but tinged with a reassuring hint of beauty that was almost feminine.

She could see why Sophie had fallen for him.

And why Kasia loved him so much.

She continued to watch him as Leo asked if he could explain the meaning of the caution. This was to make sure that Sikora really did understand English, and it was clear from his answer that he was having no problem with it.

Andee's eyes moved to Helen as she began reading the statement she had helped her client to prepare.

'"I, Tomasz Sikora, am making this statement to say that I was not with Sophie Monroe at any time on 17th August, apart from a few minutes after the show at Blue Ocean Park. During that time she told me that she had enjoyed the performance and that she was glad she had come to see it. She also said that she would like to see me after, but I told her that I had to go home. I left the Entertainment Centre some minutes before midnight and I drove straight to my home at number eight Patch Elm Lane, on the Waverley estate, taking the longer way round via Copple Lane. The first time I knew Sophie was missing was about a week later when her parents raised the alarm."' Helen Hall's eyes came up as she lowered the statement. 'That's all there is about Sophie,' she told Andee.

Andee nodded, and gestured for her to carry on reading.

'"For the past seven months I have been forcibly involved in an operation, run by Mrs Jackie Poynter, to remove various electrical goods from stores around the Kesterly area. This is done by using a device, manufactured in China and shipped into Poland, that deactivates the alarm as the goods are taken out of the store. To the best of my knowledge many thousands of pounds' worth of DVD players, TVs, computers, cameras and white goods have been shipped from this country to pre-arranged destinations in Eastern Europe. On 25th August I delivered a shipment to Krakow where I was also due to collect six Latvian girls to bring them back to England to work at the campsites, or in the nightclubs owned by Mr and Mrs Poynter in the Midlands. I didn't collect them because I knew the police were looking for me, so I returned to this country alone. I do not know if the girls are on their way yet . . ."'

Andee held up a hand. 'Would Tania Karpenko and Michaela Reznik have come into the country this way?'

Sikora's eyes were large and sore as he said, 'I don't know for certain, I didn't bring them myself, but it's possible.'

'And after working at the campsite they were transferred to the clubs?'

'Again it is possible, but I don't know for certain. Some girls choose to go because they make more money at the clubs.'

'Are they ever forced to work there?'

'I don't think so, but it is not a situation that I am involved with.'

'Can you give us the names of these clubs?'

As he spoke them Leo wrote them down.

Going back to the beginning of his statement, Andee said, 'You told us you were *forcibly* involved in Mrs Poynter's operations. Can you expand on that?'

Sikora's shoulders sagged as he said, 'The first time I drive the stolen goods to a depot in Portsmouth, I have no idea what is inside the boxes.'

'Didn't it say on the outside?'

'Maybe, I didn't look. I only drive the van to Portsmouth where I leave it and take the train back. It was after this that Mrs Poynter tells me what I have done and said that if I didn't continue she would make us, me and Kasia and the children, leave our home. She also said that she would tell the police that I am the organiser behind all the stealings and that she will send Kasia back to her husband in Poland who is a violent man. So I keep on driving for her, sometimes to Portsmouth or Dover, and sometimes all the way to Krakow.'

Andee's expression was harsh as she asked if Gary Perkins was involved in the same scheme.

'I think so, but we never talk about it. There are many people around the camp who use the devices, some for themselves, but mostly for the European shipments.'

To Leo Andee said, 'Get Hassan Ansari down here.'

Sikora watched in confusion as she and Leo got to their feet. 'One of my colleagues will continue this interview,' she explained. 'My task is to find Sophie and I'm satisfied that you don't know where she is.'

Closing the door behind them Leo said, 'Just like that? You believe he's telling the truth?'

'Yes, I do,' Andee confirmed, taking out her phone. 'I'm asking Gould to come in. As soon as you've found Hassan, get Jemma and the rest of the team and come to the incident room.'

Chapter Fourteen

A flashing rainbow of colours and cacophony of noise from the Leisure Park was washing over the entrance to Blue Ocean campsite as Andee and Gould pulled up outside the red-brick bungalow. Though a drizzle of rain was falling like silvery dust in the afternoon air it was still warm, and plenty of people were around; the atmosphere seemed almost festive as the holiday season began winding to an end. The kids returned to school next week, summer would be over, real life would resume.

Not for Sophie.

Nor for her parents.

As Andee and Gould approached the front door Andee was wondering about the people passing, rowdy, happy, thrilled with the new friendships they'd made this past week or fortnight, full of promises to stay in touch. Many of them glanced curiously at the marked police cars that came to a halt behind Gould's, some even hanging around to find out what was going to happen next. They wouldn't have forgotten the girl who'd gone missing; some had joined in the search, most would know that this was where the parents lived.

Gould knocked on the front door and a few moments later Gavin opened it.

It could simply have been the swinging kaleidoscope of lights, combined with the unexpectedness of the visit and the presence of a man he hadn't seen before, that caused Gavin's face to blanch as he saw them.

Or maybe it was the dread of bad news about Sophie.

Or maybe he'd known all along they would eventually come.

Andee's heart was thudding tightly. 'This is Detective Inspector Gould,' she told him.

Gavin's glance barely made it to Gould. He couldn't move his eyes from Andee.

'Mr Monroe,' Gould began.

Gavin looked at him now and almost shrank from him.

Understanding how formidable her boss's presence must seem to a man with something terrible to hide, Andee said, 'Can we come in?'

Gavin stood aside. After closing the door he started ahead of them down the hall. 'Heidi's lying the baby down,' he managed, having to clear his throat to get the words through.

Andee and Gould followed him into the kitchen, where the TV was on low and something was heating on the stove.

After turning off both, Gavin made himself face them. He should have asked by now if they'd found Sophie, but he seemed incapable of speech.

Taking the lead, Gould said, 'Could you ask your wife to come in here, please?'

Gavin only stared at him. Then, suddenly finding his voice, 'Yes, yes of course.'

As he left Andee looked around. The keys she'd spotted before were still hanging from a hook. She stepped closer to look at them again, but didn't touch them.

When Heidi came into the room she looked as haunted, hunted, as Andee had suspected she would.

'What – what is it?' she asked croakily. 'Have you . . . ? Is Sophie . . . ?'

Andee pointed to the keys as she said to Gavin, 'Are those yours?'

His eyes shot to them in a blaze of fear and confusion. 'Yes, I . . . Yes, they are.'

'Which vehicle are they for?'

There was no colour, hardly any movement, in his face as he said, 'I have a small van that I drive sometimes when Heidi's using the car.'

'Where is it now?' she asked.

'In . . . In my lock-up.'

'Which is where?'

His voice shook as he gave her the address.

After point-to-pointing to one of the officers outside, she said, 'Perhaps we should sit down.'

As they did so Heidi and Gavin seemed, oddly, as though they were turning into ghosts. Their substance was disappearing, their lives, their whole existences were dissolving to dust.

'When did you last use the van?' Andee asked quietly.

Gavin tried to speak, but made a sound like a swallowed cry. 'I – I think . . . It must have been when I did my last job.'

'The one that took you to France?'

He nodded.

'I went to Pollards Haulage this morning,' she informed him. 'Everything was in order with your driver's log,' she continued, 'times, speed, breaks . . . There was just one thing that bothered me, the fifteen-mile detour – or diversion – you took on your way south. We've checked with the French authorities, and there was no traffic diversion in place at that time.'

Gavin's mouth opened, but nothing came out. His eyes were glazed with fear.

Heidi looked between Andee and Gould in panic.

'Gavin, where's Sophie?' Andee asked softly.

He tried to answer, but a terrible, wrenching sob drowned his words. 'She's . . . I didn't mean . . .' he choked.

'Gavin, don't,' Heidi cried, tears streaming down her cheeks.

This was enough; she couldn't allow them to go any further without reminding them of their rights. 'Gavin and Heidi Monroe,' she said, getting to her feet, 'I am arresting you on suspicion of the murder . . .'

'No! No, don't blame Heidi,' Gavin cried. 'She didn't . . .'

Andee continued forcefully, 'You do not have to say anything, but it may harm your defence if you do not mention when questioned something which you later rely on in court. Do you understand?'

Shaking and terrified, he somehow managed a nod.

Heidi's eyes were wild. 'It was an accident,' she sobbed. 'No one meant to hurt her . . .'

'I have to remind you, you're under caution,' Gould interrupted as Andee wrote down her words.

An accident maybe, but there was nothing unplanned about whatever had happened afterwards.

'What about the baby?' Heidi gulped. 'We can't just leave him here.'

'Do you have any family, or friends nearby who could take him?' Andee asked, already knowing the answer.

Heidi was sobbing so hard she was barely able to speak. 'No, no one,' she gasped.

'We've notified social services,' Andee told her. 'Lauren's outside. She'll wait with him until someone arrives.'

'But she doesn't know what to do,' Heidi cried.

'I'm sorry,' Andee said, meaning it, because she truly wished this wasn't happening – that she'd never even heard of Sophie Monroe and her family.

Jesus Wants Me for a Sunbeam.

Gavin's head went down as Gould put a hand on his shoulder, easing him towards the door.

Turning stricken eyes to Andee, Heidi begged, 'Please let me stay with the baby. I can't just leave him . . .'

What about Sophie, Andee wanted to ask. *Who's with her now? Where did her father take her?* However, as a mother, she understood Heidi's despair. 'I promise, he'll be well taken care of . . .'

'*No!* He won't. You know he's different. Lauren can't cope. She doesn't know what to do. No one does, except us.'

'Someone's outside waiting to take you to the station,' was all Andee could say.

'What do you mean? Who's waiting outside? Why aren't you taking us?'

Since there was nothing to be gained from trying to explain the problems of cross-contamination, Andee simply said, 'It's another officer. Her name's Jemma Payne. You'll travel with her and a colleague, while Gavin goes with DCI Gould and DC Wild. I'll follow in another car and see you at the station.'

Heidi looked desperately at Gavin, but he was in such a ragged, broken state that he was barely holding together.

'Please . . . please,' Heidi stammered. 'At least let me go and say goodbye to my baby?'

You mean the way you said goodbye to Sophie?

Andee followed her into the bedroom as Gould walked Gavin outside to the waiting cars.

Watching her kneel next to her sleeping child, not touching him for fear of waking him, while shaking so badly she might have actually fallen on to him, Andee could only wonder how she was finding it in herself to tear a mother from her child. What good was going to come of this for any of them? Punishment would never bring Sophie back.

Poor sweet Sophie, where are you now?

Please God they'd find out during questioning.

After watching the cars drive away Andee closed the door on the fascinated onlookers, and went back inside the house with Lauren to wait for social services and CSI to come and secure the scene. The bungalow at least, possibly the entire camp-site, was now officially a crime scene.

Stepping into the back garden where the square of carpet was still lying abandoned, next to the flattened grass, she took out her phone to call Helen Hall. 'Has your client been bailed?' she asked.

'He has,' Helen confirmed. 'The CPS is considering his request for immunity. I think there's a good chance, provided Sikora keeps his word and gives evidence in court. He knows that and assures me he's willing to do it.'

'OK. Are you still on duty? If you are, there are two more coming your way. I don't imagine they've already got a lawyer.'

'Same case?'

'No. It's Sophie Monroe's parents.'

'Oh dear,' Helen murmured. 'Not what I wanted to hear. I'll get one of my colleagues to help me cover.'

After ending the call Andee rang Martin, while thinking of Graeme and wishing she was with him, planning a trip to Italy, preparing dinner, discussing his business, anything rather than where she was now.

'Hi,' Martin said cheerily. 'How's it going?'

Andee took a breath. 'She – she's dead,' she managed, and almost lost it. *How she had longed and yet dreaded to hear those words about Penny.*

'Oh Christ, I'm sorry,' he said quietly. 'What's happened?'

'Her parents are in custody.' She could hear the noise of their families in the background, each with a sadness over Dougie, but feeling the support of the closeness they shared.

How easily it could all come apart.

One day you were a small girl singing with the Upbeats, the next . . .

'Are you all right?' he asked.

'I will be,' she replied. 'Perhaps you can break it to Mum and the children. I'm sorry if it spoils the evening, but it'll be on the news . . .'

'It's OK, I'll handle it. I guess you're not going to be able to make dinner?'

'I shouldn't think so.'

'Do you want to call me when you're done? I could drive over there and pick you up?'

Appreciating the offer, especially when he had so much else to be dealing with, she said, 'Don't worry, I've got my car. I'll ring you in the morning.'

By the time Andee walked into the custody suite Heidi and Gavin had already been processed, and Gould was talking to Helen Hall and her colleague, Bertie Gifford, a small, wiry young man with a large mole under his nose, like a penalty spot.

'They want to make full confessions,' Gould informed her.

Feeling relief emerging through her sadness, Andee said to Helen, 'Prepared statements?'

Helen shook her head. 'They've agreed to be interviewed and I'd like to suggest we speak to Gavin first.'

'First? Leo can interview Heidi while we're . . .'

'They're both insisting they want to talk to you,' Helen interrupted.

Feeling their dependency, their fear and trust binding her up in their guilt, their tragedy, she said to Gould, 'Are you going to sit in on this?'

He nodded.

'The CPS is here,' the custody sergeant announced, releasing the outer door.

'I'll leave that to you,' she said to Leo, and excusing herself she took off to the Ladies to splash cold water on her face and clean her teeth. The memory of the baby being taken away by a social worker was still proving hard to deal with. He'd screamed and fought, holding his tiny arms out to Andee as if she, a stranger, could save him. Even the social worker had wept, so had Lauren, and Andee was crying now, which was why she'd had to come in here and pull herself together.

She hadn't handled this well, any of it, but she'd have to confront her fears and failings when it was all over.

A few minutes later she and Gould were facing Gavin and Helen across a square, scuffed table in an interview room, with the tape machines running and identities established.

Determined not to engage emotionally with how wretched Gavin looked, Andee reminded him of his rights and said, quite steadily, 'I want you to tell us what happened during the Sunday evening before Sophie disappeared. I know there was a row and she walked out, but she came back, didn't she?'

As his eyes rose to hers there was so much devastation in them that she almost had to look away.

'Didn't she?' she prompted.

He took a breath that became mangled by a sob. 'It was an accident,' he said brokenly. 'No one meant it to happen . . . We . . . We didn't even realise . . . I mean at first . . .' He turned his head away as his voice cracked apart. A moment later he was sobbing uncontrollably. 'She was my baby,' he gasped wretchedly. 'I let her down so badly. Ever since her mother died . . . Oh God, forgive me . . . Sophes, my little sweetheart, my angel . . .'

Struggling to steady herself inwardly as Helen passed him a tissue, Andee waited until he was ready before saying, 'Try to talk us through what happened from the time she came back. What time was that?'

He nodded, and carried on nodding, until finally he said, 'About quarter to midnight, maybe a bit after. I was . . . I was waiting for her. I wanted to see her, try and make up with her, before I went

307

to France, but she was drunk – or she'd had a bit anyway. I hated seeing her like that, and she was coming home like it more and more often. I . . . I told her she was grounded until I got back and she . . .' He choked on a breath. 'She said things I don't want to repeat. They weren't my girl. It wasn't the way she'd been brought up.' He pressed his fingers to his eyes and tried to breathe. 'Everything had gone so wrong for her,' he said shakily. 'She was lonely, I could see that, she missed her mother so badly . . .'

Mummy's favourite things: Sophie, daisy chains, singing, Daddy . . .

Andee could feel so many cracks opening up inside her.

It's not Penny we're talking about, it's Sophie.

'When me and Heidi were first together,' Gavin continued, 'they were that close, her and Sophie, that I thought my girl would be all right, that she'd start getting over it. And I think she did for a while. It did my heart good to see her laughing again. It was like the lights had come back on and she was as sweet and mischievous as ever, and as loving. Then . . . then Archie was born . . .' He swallowed hard as his eyes drifted to what only he could see. 'She was that excited about having a baby . . . She could hardly talk about anything else, and there was nothing she wouldn't do to help out if Heidi was feeling tired. She had all these ideas about babysitting and changing nappies and giving him feeds, but then, when he was there, nothing seemed to go the way we planned. I can see what happened now, but at the time we were so worried about him that we didn't notice what was going on with her. By the time we did, it was too late. She'd turned against us, gone looking for attention elsewhere . . .' His eyes closed as the kind of attention Sophie had received seemed to crush him from within. 'I promised her mother I'd take care of her,' he wailed, 'Oh Jilly, forgive me. I'm sorry . . . I'm so sorry . . . I deserve to be punished. She was our little angel . . .'

As he broke down again Andee's eyes went to Helen. It was clear the lawyer was deeply affected too, and sensing Gould's tension told her that even he wasn't immune to this guilty father's despair.

'Perhaps she's with her mother now,' Gavin went on raggedly. 'That's what I like to tell myself. Jilly will take care of her. They'll sing songs together and play with the angels.'

After a beat, Gould said, 'You still haven't told us what happened when she came back that night.'

Making a visible effort to pull himself together, Gavin put his trembling hands on the table. 'She wasn't only drunk, she was angry, and seemed dead set on upsetting us. She said we were cruel and selfish, and it would serve us right if she ran away and never came back. I tried calming her down, but it must have been the drink, because she wouldn't listen. She kept saying no one cared about her, that she was a waste of space and that she hated the baby more than anything. She called him some terrible names, said he was brain-damaged and ought to be put down and if we liked she'd do us the favour. I got so angry, I hardly knew what I was saying. Then Heidi started accusing her of shaking him, and banging him against the wall to stop him from crying. She said Sophie was responsible for what was wrong with him, that she was the one who was cruel and selfish and maybe she was the one who ought to be put down. Sophie went for her, like she was going to hit her, then Heidi . . .' His eyes closed as the horror of it washed over him. 'I . . . grabbed . . . I pushed Sophie out of the way, and she . . . she fell back against the worktop, hitting her head. We didn't realise . . . I mean . . . It didn't seem like such a bad fall, but then she didn't . . . she didn't get up. I thought she must have been knocked unconscious, so I tried bringing her round, but she just wouldn't wake up.'

His head went down as he said, 'I'm not sure when we realised she was . . . I couldn't take it in. It just didn't seem possible. One minute she was . . . I still can't believe . . .'

'Why didn't you call the emergency services?' Andee asked.

He shook his head, seeming not to know. 'It was . . . We – we thought that if we didn't tell anyone what – what had happened, then everyone would assume she'd run away, and then she'd turn out to be one of the ones that never got found.'

Andee swallowed what tasted like bile. 'Where is she now?' she asked quietly.

When he looked up his eyes were so clouded, so stricken that she wasn't sure she wanted to hear his reply.

'Gavin,' Gould prompted. 'You have to tell us what happened after she fell.'

Finally, looking and sounding as traumatised as he surely must have been throughout the ordeal, he was able to say, 'I . . . There was a roll of carpet in the garden. It was left over from the caravans that had just been fitted. We . . . I wrapped her in it . . .'

Oh dear God in heaven. How had he managed to make himself do it? His own daughter. Why the hell hadn't they rung an ambulance? How had he been able to live with himself since? The answer was clear, he hadn't, because Andee could see now that it had only ever been a matter of time before the guilt would tear him apart.

'The CCTV camera outside the bungalow,' Gould said. 'Did you tamper with it?'

Gavin shook his head. 'I didn't know it wasn't working. I thought it was, so I took my van round the back of the house . . .'

Imagining the scene and wishing it were no more than a nightmare she could wake up from, Andee listened in mute horror as he described how he'd lifted the body into his van, taken it to the transport depot and transferred it to the container part of his truck. From there he'd driven to Portsmouth, crossed the Channel to St Malo and headed south for Toulouse.

'Where did you leave her?' Gould asked.

'In . . . In a lake about twenty kilometres from Clermont Ferrand. I'd have to look at a map to tell you what it's called.'

'We'll get you one,' Gould told him. And for the benefit of the tape, he said, 'This interview is terminated at 19.45.'

As Andee turned the machines off, Gould said to Helen, 'We'll need to take your client to a computer so he can show us exactly where to direct the French police.'

Gavin's eyes were on Andee. 'I didn't mean what happened,' he told her desperately. 'I swear it was an accident. Please believe me, it all happened so fast. When she fell, I tried to catch her . . .'

311

Though she didn't doubt that he had, there was nothing Andee could say to help him now. *The man had driven his daughter's body to a foreign country and dumped it in a lake.*

'There you are,' Jemma declared, setting a fresh coffee and tired-looking sandwich in front of Andee. 'If you don't mind me saying you look just about all in.'

'I don't mind telling you that I feel it,' Andee admitted, deciding to sideline the sandwich and go straight for the coffee. This was only a short break before interviewing Heidi, but she needed it. 'What's happening at the bungalow?'

'CSI are still there. The press have got wind of it now, they're wanting a statement, obviously.'

'Is someone taking care of it?'

'Yeah, DCI Spender's on it.'

Andee sat quietly for a moment. Of course all her bosses would become more visible now; the murder of a teenage girl was big news. 'Where's the CPS?' she asked.

'In his office, I think. Can I ask how it went with Gavin Monroe?'

After treating her to a brief résumé, Andee drained her mug and got up to return to the custody suite.

'What news on the Poynters?' she said, turning back.

'Arrested and bailed,' Jemma replied, 'and Sikora's not the only one round the camp who's decided to sing.'

Andee nodded. 'That's good.' Walking towards the lift, she saw Gould emerge. 'Have you got the location?' she asked him.

'We have. I'm about to contact the French police. Are you sure you're up for talking to Heidi Monroe?'

'I'm sure.'

'OK, let me know when you're done. I'll either be in my office, or upstairs with Spender.'

'Am I going to hear anything different from Heidi?' she asked Helen Hall and Bertie Gifford as she returned to the custody suite.

Bertie shook his head. 'It was an accident, she wishes it had never happened, that they hadn't done what they had. She's desperate for some news about her baby.'

Of course she was, and making the decision to lie rather than tell her how traumatised he'd seemed when they'd taken him away, Andee broke open a pack of fresh tapes ready to begin.

It turned out that the Monroes' stories chimed in every significant way, leaving Andee in little doubt that they'd discussed at length what they would say in case they should ever find themselves where they were now.

'Tell me,' she said, after Heidi had finished describing the scene leading up to Sophie's fall, 'when you realised she was dead, whose idea was it to try and cover it up rather than call the emergency services?'

Heidi flushed deeply as she looked down at her fidgeting hands. 'I – I don't remember,' she stammered. 'I mean . . . We sort of decided it together.'

'Are you sure she fell?'

Heidi's eyes rounded with fear as she said, 'Yes, I'm sure. I pushed her . . . I mean, Gavin did to get her away from me . . .'

'But if it was an accident, I don't understand

why you didn't call the paramedics. They might have been able to save her.'

Heidi was shaking her head. 'They couldn't. She was . . . We knew . . .'

'So one of you, *both* of you, decided to cover it up? Why cover up an accident?'

Heidi regarded her helplessly. 'I don't know. I suppose we were in shock. And we were afraid no one would believe us. Everyone knew me and her weren't getting on . . .' She took a breath and pushed her hands through her hair. 'I know we've made everything ten times worse, but I swear I didn't mean to hurt her.'

'*You* didn't mean to hurt her?' Andee repeated.

Heidi froze. 'Neither of us did,' she insisted. 'It was an accident, I swear it. We didn't mean for it to happen. We loved her.'

'Yet you were willing to let her father dump her body as if she didn't matter at all. I just don't get how you could have done that, either of you. She was a *child*, for God's sake. She depended on you.'

Heidi slumped in her chair, seeming more ashamed than she could bear.

'So you told yourselves,' Andee pressed on, 'that you could report her missing and after all the initial fuss died down everyone would simply forget about her?'

The way Heidi flinched told her that was indeed what they'd thought.

Incredulous and enraged, Andee said, 'Do you know what, Heidi? I don't believe you.'

Heidi's face drained of colour as she stared at Andee in shock.

'I think you and Gavin have conjured up a tale

between you to cover up what really happened that night.'

'No!' Heidi cried. 'I swear it was an accident. We didn't mean for it to happen.'

'We need the truth, Heidi.'

'I've told you, she tried to hit me, Gavin leapt between us and the next thing we knew she was on the floor.'

Andee regarded her coldly. This wasn't the whole truth, and she knew it, but forcing the real story out of her, when she probably believed the fabrication by now, was clearly going to take time. 'Tell me, how did you feel when you watched Gavin wrap her body in that carpet?' she asked. 'I presume you were there.'

'Don't,' Heidi wailed, burying her face in her hands. 'It was terrible. I wish to God we'd never done it. I know we've made everything worse . . .'

'Yes, you've certainly done that,' Andee confirmed. 'And it seems you were even prepared to let someone else go to prison for something you knew they hadn't done.'

'No! I . . . We talked about that and we decided if anyone was charged we'd have to come forward.'

Since she'd never know now if that were true, Andee said, 'Did Gavin tell you, before he left that night, where he was going to take her?'

'Not exactly. He just said he knew a place in France, in the middle of nowhere . . .'

Suddenly needing to get out of the room, Andee rose to her feet. 'I'm going to terminate this interview now . . .'

Heidi broke down sobbing. 'I know we did a terrible thing, but I swear we loved her . . .'

'Enough to let her body moulder at the bottom of a lake,' Andee shot back scathingly.

'Please, you can't make me feel any worse than I already do.'

'Believe me, I can,' Andee assured her, and clicking off the tapes, she removed them from the machines and left the room.

'There's more to it,' she was saying to Gould and Carl Gilbert, the CPS, twenty minutes later. 'Why would they go to such lengths to get rid of her body if it was an accident?'

'They wouldn't,' Carl Gilbert responded, 'which is why they're going to be charged with murder.'

Andee glanced at Gould.

'Even if it turns out it was an accident,' Gould said, 'they still bundled her up in a roll of carpet, packed a bag to make it look like she was leaving of her own accord, stuffed her into a van and then dumped her in a lake.'

Inwardly flinching, Andee told them, 'I think she did it, and talked him into covering it up.'

Neither of them disagreed.

'But how we're going to get them to admit that,' she continued, 'I really don't know. I guess it'll depend on how they plead when it goes to court. Until then, like you say, they both have to be charged,' and deciding to let them handle it from here, she left the room.

Several minutes later she was at her desk in the incident room, gazing at the whiteboard where Sophie's photos were still hanging. She almost couldn't bear to look at them, yet nor could she bring herself to look away. It would feel like a betrayal, a dismissal, when more than anything she wanted to fold this girl into her arms and do whatever it took to make her feel loved.

Sophie's favourite things: singing with Mummy and Daddy, making daisy chains, Daddy.

How could it all have ended like this?

'Are you OK?' Gould asked from the door.

Hot tears suddenly welled in her eyes. 'He's lost everything,' she gulped, thinking of her own father.

Going to her, Gould picked up her bag and put it over his shoulder. 'Come on, I'll buy you a drink,' he said.

Noticing a scrap of paper fluttering to the floor she stooped to pick it up, and seeing what it was she checked the time. It was too late to ring Suzi Perkins now; she'd do it in the morning.

As they rode down in the lift she asked, 'What's happening in France?'

'They're sending divers down in the morning.'

Though she wanted to be there to bring Sophie home, she knew it wasn't possible, not only because the French would have to carry out a post-mortem before releasing the body, but because she simply had to be at Dougie's funeral.

What about Sophie's funeral? Who was going to be there for that?

As they reached her car she said, 'If you don't mind, I think I'll go straight home.' Everyone would still be at the restaurant, and she needed to be alone to try and come to terms with how devastated she was feeling.

If only they could have found Penny.

Poor sweet Sophie.

'I'll see you tomorrow, at the crematorium?' he said.

'Of course,' she replied.

His eyebrows rose, as though he might say more, but in the end he simply wished her goodnight and walked off to his own car.

Chapter Fifteen

The following morning Andee was still at home when she left a message on Suzi Perkins's voice-mail to call back when she could. She wasn't going to work today, her family needed her here, and she had to admit it was a relief not to be involved in dismantling the incident room.

It was miserable outside, misty and rainy, with a feisty wind battering the headland as though to push it back from the sea. She couldn't imagine a good atmosphere down at Blue Ocean Park, either for the CSI team, or the press, or the staff and residents of the campsite. Would the funfair still be spinning and flashing across the street, giant arms rotating like metronomes gone wild, dodgems thumping up against one another, shrieks, laughter, the thrill of the ride, music blaring?

Girls Just Wanna Have Fun.

She wondered what the weather was like in France, how much progress the divers had made. Had they even begun? The thought of Sophie's young body at the bottom of a lake kept stifling her, squeezing down on her chest as though to drown her too.

Except Sophie hadn't drowned.

What had really happened that night? Would they ever get to the truth?

Gould was liaising with the gendarmerie in Clermont Ferrand. He'd no doubt update her as soon as he had some news. By then the Monroes would almost certainly have appeared in front of a magistrate and been remanded in custody.

Leo and Jemma were attending to that.

Andee kept thinking about the baby and the dreadful start he was having in life. She wondered where he was now, and if the foster carers would be able to cope with his condition. Would they even understand it? Though she knew social services would do their best, they were appallingly short-staffed, so it wasn't likely they'd be able to keep as close an eye on him as he needed.

She'd make some enquiries next week, speak to one of the managers, if only to reassure herself that he was receiving the proper attention. If he wasn't, she might be able to put some pressure on to improve things.

'Hey Mum, you're up early,' Alayna said, coming into the kitchen with bleary eyes and mussed hair. 'Even Grandma's not awake yet.'

'She's having a bit of a lie-in,' Andee told her. 'We were up late last night, chatting.'

'About Sophie?' Alayna came to hug her.

'Yes, about Sophie,' and Penny, and how much easier it might have been for them if they'd been told Penny was dead. No, easy was the wrong word, but perhaps the suffering wouldn't have gone on for so long if there had been some sort of closure. 'Are you OK?' she asked, smoothing Alayna's hair.

'Yes, I think so. I just feel so sorry for her. Is it true her parents did it?'

'They're saying it was an accident, but the cover-up that followed isn't helping them.'

Gazing into her mother's eyes, Alayna said, 'I just can't imagine you or Dad . . .'

'Then don't, because it'll never happen.' She pressed a kiss to her forehead. 'Is Luke awake yet?'

'He stayed over with Dad last night,' Alayna reminded her. 'We thought you should have one each of us this morning, you know, for a bit of moral support.'

Touched by how sensitive her children were, Andee turned round as Maureen padded in to join them.

'We were just talking about Sophie,' Alayna said, going to her. 'It's terrible. I can't believe it. What sort of accident was it?' she asked her mother.

'Apparently it was an argument that got out of hand. It's tragic all round, because her parents are never going to forgive themselves, especially her father.'

'It's what's concerned Mum the most,' Maureen told Alayna. 'She saw what Aunt Penny's loss did to her own father . . .'

'Please, don't let's dwell on it now,' Andee interrupted, knowing today was going to be difficult enough as they gathered to say goodbye to Martin's father. It was going to remind her so much of her own father's passing, and how truly terrible it had been to let him go with Penny's disappearance still unresolved. 'Today is about Grandpa Dougie, remember,' she said to Alayna, 'and I should call Dad. Have you spoken to him yet this morning?'

'No, but I texted when I woke up. I think he'll be pleased to hear from you.'

Andee couldn't help but smile, and noticed that her mother had found the comment amusing too.

Connecting to Martin, she said, 'Hi, it's me. Are you OK?'

'Sure,' he replied, sounding tired. 'Can't believe the day's actually arrived, or that it's even going to happen. What time did you get home in the end?'

'Late, then I sat up chatting with Mum for a while. How's Carol today?'

'In a flap because her hairdresser's late, and the caterer's just informed us that they haven't sourced enough chairs.'

'Are they doing something about that?'

'Yes, but yours truly has to go and pick them up. Luke's coming with me. Luckily it's not far. Are you going to make it today? I'll understand if . . .'

'I'll be there,' she promised. 'We all will.' Finding herself alone in the kitchen, she said, 'I haven't put the TV on yet, have you?'

'I have and it's making headlines.'

'Have they criticised the investigation?'

'Not that I've heard.'

'It'll come. Anyway, let us know if there's anything we can do at this end, otherwise we'll see you at yours . . . What time are the cars turning up?'

'Twelve.'

'OK, we'll be there by eleven thirty at the latest. I'd better go now, someone's trying to get through,' and clicking over to the incoming call she said, 'Andee Lawrence speaking.'

'DS Lawrence, it's Suzi Perkins.'

'Suzi. You wanted to talk to me?'

'Yes, but only on the phone, if you don't mind. I'm not at the salon any more, or the flat in town, and I don't want anyone seeing me going into the station.'

Curious, Andee went to pour herself a coffee as she asked, 'So what can I do for you?'

'It's about all the trouble my brother's in. I know he's stuffed anyway, because of breaking his order, but I thought you should know . . .' She took a breath. 'You have to promise me you'll never tell anyone where you heard this.'

'You have my word.'

'OK, well the Poynters are running these shop-lifting scams with some Eastern European connection. I don't know exactly who's involved, but my brother was. He won't tell you himself because he hates the police . . .'

'Suzi, when did you last see the news?'

'I have to admit I've been avoiding it.'

'Then if I were you I'd go and turn on the TV. A lot's happened in the last twelve hours. But before you do, can we get you on this number if we need to speak to you further?'

Suzi fell silent.

'It might not be necessary,' Andee assured her, 'but . . .'

'I want to start again,' Suzi interrupted. 'I've been offered a job at a new spa in Dorset. I don't want this following me.'

'I understand that, and there probably won't be any reason for it to, but just in case . . .'

Reluctantly, Suzi said, 'OK, you've got my number, but I swear I don't really know anything.'

'All right. Good luck in your new job.'

After ringing off Andee called the custody

sergeant. 'How are the Monroes this morning?' she asked.

'Quiet,' he replied. 'Neither of them ate breakfast. The van's just turned up to take them to court.'

Day one of a journey they'd never planned, and would never come back from. The irrevocable often made her feel panicked and helpless, and it was happening now.

'So no changes to their story overnight?'

'Not a word out of them, although she was crying a lot.'

Unsurprised, she said, 'OK, thanks. I should go.'

Taking her phone upstairs she closed the bedroom door and scrolled to Graeme's number. Instead of pressing to connect, she stood staring at it for a while, wanting to speak to him, but not sure what to say. Today was all about her family, which didn't mean she should carry on as though he didn't exist, because that wouldn't feel right at all. He did exist and she was glad of it. Were it possible she'd go to him now, if only to look into his eyes as she told him what she was already typing into a text.

Thinking of you. Missing you. Will call as soon as I can. Ax. After hitting send she sat where she was for a moment, imagining him picking up the message, and feeling relieved that she'd finally been in touch. She thought of other things about him, and her eyes closed as her breathing became shallow.

Then, putting the phone aside, she went into the bathroom to start getting ready for Dougie's farewell.

*

324

By the time everyone had assembled at the South Kesterly crematorium it was past one o'clock, making it a late start for the service, but no one seemed to mind. If anything the atmosphere was almost merry as various luminaries from far and wide gathered outside the red-brick hall, along with over two hundred friends from the town, which was exactly how Dougie had wanted it. He'd left a detailed list of instructions concerning this day, from who he wanted to carry his coffin, to the celebrant he'd chosen, to who was to do the readings and what they should be. No flowers, he'd insisted, only donations to various local charities; no tears, only funny memories; and no hymns, just a few of his favourite songs.

Although everything went off more or less as he'd planned, there weren't many dry eyes by the time everyone started to file out of the hall. He'd been a popular man, and now he was no longer amongst them Andee could see how keen everyone was to talk to his son. Watching Martin as he accepted their condolences and listened good-naturedly to their stories, she was still feeling the warmth of his hand in hers, and the tightness of his grip during the more difficult moments of the service. Though his voice had faltered once or twice as he'd read the tribute he'd written, on the whole he was keeping it together well. The time for proper, private grieving wouldn't begin until today was over.

With Alayna and her mother either side of her, Andee took her turn to greet their friends as they spilled on to the forecourt, while keeping an eye on Luke, who was doing a magnificent job of supporting his father.

How proud Dougie would have been of them.

How fortunate her children were to be a part of this family.

Though the sadness of Dougie's parting was weighing on her, and memories of her own father kept swamping her, she still couldn't stop thinking about Sophie, and how she too had once been at the heart of a loving family. How swiftly things had changed for her, how randomly, even cruelly life had thrown out its challenges with no direction on how to cope, or apparent care for how young and vulnerable she was.

Catching Gould's eye, she felt her heart turn over as she nodded to let him know that the news had reached her – Sophie's body had been found and brought to the shore. Sometime within the next forty-eight hours they should know how she'd died, and soon after that she'd be brought back to Kesterly. A lonely, final journey with no one to meet her at this end. Andee was already dreading this.

'Are you OK?' she asked Martin as he came to join her.

Nodding, he slipped an arm around Alayna and pressed a kiss to her forehead. 'Party time,' he murmured, his eyes a little too bright as he managed to sound and look very like his father. Andee could tell how close he was to the edge and wanted to hold on to him, but she knew that any show of emotion on her part would only make it harder for him.

Giving her a wink as though he might have read her mind, he said, 'We won't have much of an opportunity to talk today, but I was hoping I could see you sometime tomorrow, or . . .' he shrugged, 'whenever works for you.'

'Of course,' she replied, suspecting she knew what it was about. She had so many decisions to reach over the next few days, questions to ask herself and answers to find, but she wasn't going to think about any of them now.

'A lovely service,' Gould commented, coming to join her. 'I get the feeling Dougie was in charge.'

'Of course,' she confirmed. 'It made things a lot easier knowing what he wanted. Maybe we should all do the same.'

He arched an ironic eyebrow. 'The Monroes should be in front of the magistrate any time now,' he said, glancing at his watch.

Nodding soberly, she found herself feeling for their fear, until the thought of Sophie sucked up every ounce of pity in her heart.

'Sikora's disappeared,' he told her.

Her eyes widened.

'Barry found the place deserted when he went round there earlier. Apparently the care home, where Kasia works, are saying she rang late yesterday to let them know she wouldn't be coming in again.'

'So they've done a moonlight?'

'It would appear so.'

Though not entirely surprised, she felt the frustration of not having Sikora's evidence to help convict his employers.

'He's not the only one who's turned against the Poynters,' Gould reminded her. 'And it isn't your case, so not your problem.'

True, but Sikora probably knew more than most

about how the operation had been run, and besides she'd never be comfortable with people simply disappearing, no matter who they were. 'Are you looking for him?'

'Of course, and I'm sure we'll find him.'

Knowing she had to leave it there, she said, 'I still haven't watched the news today, but I guess the press are having a lot to say about how long it took us – *me* – to get round to the parents.'

Gould didn't deny it. 'You weren't the only one on the investigation,' he reminded her.

'But I was leading it, and I let my own issues . . .' She took a breath. 'If I hadn't kept seeing my own father every time I looked at him . . . Monroe put on such a good show and I just didn't want it to *be* him . . .'

'Maybe not, but it was you who got us there in the end.'

'It should have been sooner.'

'It wouldn't have saved her.'

No, it wouldn't have.

Nevertheless she could feel something opening up and screaming way down inside her. How desperately she'd wanted that girl to be alive. It was as though if she had been, then maybe Penny would be too. Such nonsense, but nothing about what had happened to either of them came anywhere near making sense. 'I'm prepared to take full responsibility for how long it did take,' she told him. 'I should have . . .'

'We can discuss it another time,' he interrupted, as her mother came to join them, 'your family needs your attention now,' and shaking Maureen's hand he said, 'It's good to see you, though I could have wished for better circumstances.'

'Indeed,' Maureen agreed. 'It's kind of you to come.'

He looked round as the stewards began ushering everyone towards their cars.

'You're coming to the reception?' Maureen queried.

'I'm afraid I have to get back,' he replied, 'but I didn't want to miss the service.' To Andee he said, 'Can I have a quick word?'

Following him to the edge of the crowd, she looked expectantly into his eyes.

'I think you should take a few days off,' he told her, 'spend this time with your family.'

'But Sophie . . .'

'I'll keep you up to speed with everything as it happens,' he assured her, 'but it's unlikely she'll be back much before the beginning of next week.'

As she watched him walk away, threading through the crowd and finally disappearing from view, Andee was aware of a disturbing nervousness beginning to stir inside her, a strange, almost frightening sense of things changing in ways she wasn't sure she wanted to face.

It was much later that day, as she kicked off her shoes and sank on to the edge of her bed, that she received a text from Tomasz Sikora. *This is my new number. I don't want anyone to know where we are, but when you need me to give evidence I will come. Tomasz.*

Realising he probably didn't have a number for anyone else she forwarded the message to Hassan, and scrolled to the text she'd received from Graeme earlier in the day.

Thinking of you and missing you too. There will be time for us when this is over. Call if you need to talk. Gx

She'd have dearly loved to talk now, or even go

over there, but she wouldn't, not while she was feeling so emotional, nor when her mother and the children needed her. This was where she belonged tonight, and it was very probably the only place she really wanted to be.

The following afternoon, leaving everyone else at home, Andee and Martin strolled through Bourne Hollow, past the pub and around to the sloping banks of the headland to climb the rocky outcrop of Seaman's Spit. Though the rain had stopped during the night and the wind had relaxed into a gentle wafting of salty air, a bilious mountain of cloud was rising over the horizon like a threatened invasion from another world.

Finding an empty lookout bench they sat down together and watched a family of rabbits bobbing in and out of burrows, while glossy white gulls swooped and soared around the bay.

'It all feels a bit strange now everyone's leaving,' Martin commented, as he rested his elbows on the seat back. 'It was quite a party though, wasn't it?'

'One of his best,' Andee agreed. 'How many bands played in the end?'

'Four. He'd have loved every minute of it.'

'What always mattered to him was that everyone should have a good time, and I don't think anyone can say they didn't.'

Martin's smile was wry. 'Not if the amount of booze we got through was anything to go by – a goodly amount of which was consumed by our children, I noticed.'

'They're paying for it today,' she assured him. 'How are you feeling?'

'A bit rough round the edges,' he admitted, 'but I expected to.'

They sat quietly for a while, as though allowing the memories of Dougie's final farewell to catch in the breeze and connect them to wherever he was now.

Could he be with Penny and her father, she wondered. How she longed for her sister and her father to be together.

In the end Martin was the first to speak. 'Have you heard when they're bringing Sophie back?'

'Not yet. The French don't act quickly, and they still have to carry out the post-mortem.'

'I see. And what'll happen when she gets here? I mean about a funeral.'

Andee's head started to spin. 'I'm not sure. I need to talk to someone about that.' She turned to look at him. 'Tell me what you're planning to do next?' she said, needing to get off the subject.

Taking a breath, he let his eyes drift out to sea as he replied, 'I guess that kind of depends on you.'

Though her heart contracted, it was more or less the reply she'd expected.

'Is it serious?' he asked, bringing his eyes back to hers.

Though she understood his meaning, she found herself unable to answer.

'Is it someone I know?'

She shook her head and glanced down at her phone as it signalled the arrival of a text. 'It's a message from the vicar at St Mark's,' she told him.

He looked baffled.

'Sophie went to the church a few times after

her mother died,' she explained. 'I thought . . . I needed to talk to someone who knew the real Sophie. Discuss what should happen.' Pushing her hands through her hair, she inhaled deeply and closed her eyes. 'I want to see her when she comes back,' she said. 'I feel she needs me to be there for her.' She glanced up at him. 'Does that sound crazy?'

'Not at all, but is it wise if she's been in the water for so long?'

Maybe not wise, but it was something she had to do. 'What do *you* want to happen next?' she asked.

His eyes dropped as an anxious look tightened his face. 'I think you know the answer to that.'

Yes, she did, but she still didn't know how to answer it. Her thoughts were with Graeme, in his shop, his home, travelling to Italy . . . She'd always wanted to go to Italy.

'Before you turn me down,' he said gruffly, 'will you at least hear me out?'

Feeling his unease, perhaps it was dread, fluttering about the beats of her own heart, she squeezed his hand as she said, 'Of course.'

'I realise you've made a life for yourself and the kids in Kesterly,' he began. 'I know you're happy here and wouldn't want to move, but that's not what I'm asking. Actually, I'm not really asking for anything, apart from the chance to try and win you back.'

There was a self-mocking light in his troubled eyes that touched her deeply.

'I never stopped loving you,' he told her, 'even when I was going through my middle-aged melt-down and thought the answers to my crisis, or whatever it was, were out there somewhere away from you all. I can hardly believe I did it now. It doesn't make any sense to me . . . I mean, the contract was one thing, it was an opportunity I'd have been crazy to turn down, but there was no need . . . I didn't have to do it the way I did. I wish I could tell you what got into me, what madness tricked me into thinking the way I did back then, but I can't. I only know that it was short-lived, because I saw early on that I'd made a monumental cock-up of everything. The trouble was, by then the damage had been done. You were as mad as hell, justifiably, and I couldn't think of a single good reason why you should forgive me. Nor could you, and it was pretty obvious that you didn't even want to try.'

He took a breath and let it go slowly. Probably he was hoping she'd say something, but the right words weren't within her reach.

'And so we find ourselves where we are now,' he continued, 'still all wrapped up in each other's lives, mainly because of the kids, but for me it's also because you're the only woman I've ever loved, that I've ever even slept with apart from Brigitte, and what an unholy mess I've made of that. Being with her made me realise just how wrong my life was without you, but then I could see I was hurting her, and the worse I felt about that the deeper in I seemed to get.' He shook his head, clearly exhausted and exasperated with himself. 'I've managed to sort it now,' he said. 'More or less, anyway. She says she wants to give us another chance if you're interested, but I've told her that even if you aren't, it still can't happen for me and her.' His

333

eyes followed a gull as it swooped off the cliff edge and caught an air current. 'You can stop me now if you like,' he told her, 'I mean before I say the wrong thing, which is presuming I haven't already and I'm really not sure about that.'

Unable not to smile, she watched the breeze tousling his hair as unsteady and difficult emotions coasted through her heart. It was impossible to imagine her life without him, nor did she really want to try, but at the same time life had moved on. 'I won't lie to you,' she said softly, 'my feelings have changed towards you, which isn't to say I've stopped caring about you, because I don't think that will ever happen. You're the father of my children, my first love, my best friend. You hold some pretty special places in my world, and I want you to stay in every one of them, but I don't see how we're going to make things work when . . .'

'. . . you've stopped trusting me,' he came in quickly. 'I understand that, and I've been trying to figure out a way to convince you to believe in me again. The trouble is, all I've been able to come up with are promises, and only time will prove that I can keep them. I know I can, but I realise you might find it hard to take my word for it.'

'I know you mean it,' she responded, 'and I believe you'll do everything you can to prove that we can find the trust again. What I was going to say was, I don't see how we can make things work when you have to be in London, or Cairo, or Singapore . . . To be honest, I can hardly keep track of where you are these days. I rely on the children to tell me, and sometimes even they don't know.'

'It's true, it's been crazyville since I took the contract with the US government, but it's all changing. My lawyers are in the process of negotiation even as we speak, and I'll probably have to go to Washington sometime in the next few weeks to finalise things, because they're buying me out.'

She blinked in surprise. 'Is that what you want?' she asked warily. 'You spent a lot of years building up that business.'

'It's what I want,' he assured her. 'And the offer's more than fair.'

Sensing he really did mean it, she said, 'So what will you do once it's gone through?'

'I'm not sure yet, but I thought now might be a good time for us both to start considering our options. With the kids growing up fast . . .' He shrugged helplessly. 'To be honest, I haven't thought any of this through, and for all I know you don't want to make any changes in your life. You always used to be open to change, but I realise that sometimes dreams can only be dreams, or can go in different directions . . .'

Starting to feel slightly overwhelmed, she said, 'So what are your dreams these days? What options will you consider?'

'I could run Dad's business. It's what he always wanted . . .'

'But is it what you want?'

His eyes came to hers. 'What I want is to be with my family again,' he said softly.

She had to look away. 'I . . . It's not . . .' she began.

'Why don't we leave it there for now?' he came in hastily, as though sensing she was about to turn him down. 'I realise I've given you a lot to think about, and if it is serious with this other bloke . . . Well, if it is, then I guess none of this is sounding very attractive.'

She only wished she knew what to say.

'Can we at least agree to talk again when you've had some time to consider things?' he asked.

Knowing how challenging the next few days and weeks were likely to be, she readily seized the delay and said, 'Yes, why don't we do that?'

Chapter Sixteen

Sophie's body was brought back to Kesterly the following Monday, a day before she'd been due to return to school, two days after the post-mortem results showed that her death had been caused by multiple blows to the head.

Not one, which could have been brought about by a fall.

Multiple, which meant someone had deliberately and repeatedly attacked her. Though Andee felt sure it had happened in the heat of the moment, hitting the child more than once and so hard that the impact had ended her life could only have been the act of someone so enraged, so out of control that they had, in that moment at least, not cared whether Sophie lived or died.

Did Gavin have that sort of temper?

Did Heidi?

She'd seen no sign of it in either of them, but she knew that didn't mean anything.

'I've just been talking to the CPS,' Gould was telling her on the phone as she drove up Blackberry Hill towards the Kesterly Infirmary, 'and I thought you'd be interested to know that the Monroes are now admitting, thanks to the PM, that it wasn't an accident. However, they're both claiming to have done it.'

Andee frowned deeply.

'She's saying she used a rolling pin,' Gould continued, 'he's saying he had a wooden hammer.'

Either way, the brutality of it was unthinkable, unbearable. It never failed to shock, even frighten her the way lives, futures, entire worlds could be destroyed in just a few short moments. 'Where's the weapon now?' she asked.

'Apparently it was burned.'

Of course it was burned.

'I believe her,' Andee stated. 'A rolling pin is something you'd find in a kitchen, which is where forensics have confirmed it happened. What would a wooden hammer be doing there?'

'He could have just finished a spot of DIY. Or maybe he went somewhere to get it, in which case we'd be looking at a premeditated act.'

She couldn't see it, but maybe that was because she didn't want to. 'It's not up to me to defend him,' she said, 'but frankly I wouldn't be surprised if he wasn't even in the room when it happened. I think, in her drunken state, Sophie either physically threatened the baby, or maybe actually hit him, and Heidi, being as stressed as she was, completely lost it.'

'And by the time the father rushed in to break it up it was already too late?'

Yes, that was what she thought, but of course she couldn't know for certain. 'Gavin Monroe loved his daughter,' she said, 'I'm in no doubt about that. Doing what he did, covering up the crime, taking her to France, has completely broken him. Now he's trying to take the blame so his wife can get back to their son sooner rather than later. He's telling himself she's a better parent than he is.'

'You're getting no argument from me,' he responded, 'but it's for the briefs to sort out from here. We need to discuss other things.'

'You got my email?'

'I did. It's not a conversation for the phone. I know you're still on compassionate leave, but can you come in?'

'Maybe later, but I have to tell you, my mind is made up.'

'So is mine. Where are you now?'

'Just driving into the infirmary.'

His voice darkened as he said, 'You're going to the mortuary?'

'That's right.'

'Is anyone with you?'

'I don't need to have my hand held.'

'Andee, I'm not sure this is a good idea. You've seen bodies after they've been in the water.'

'It's something I have to do.'

'Then call me when you leave.'

After promising she would she clicked off the line before shutting down her phone completely.

A few minutes later she was inside the morgue, feeling strangely distanced from herself, as though she'd stepped into another world – an in-between world – as Omar, a technician she'd met before, led her through to the chill inner chamber. The metal storage containers were lined up like file cabinets along one wall, and the faint scent of something flowery lingered in the air. Presumably someone had been here recently for a viewing; it was rare, if not unheard of, for medical professionals to wear perfume.

After sliding open the shelf of a temporary resting place, Omar gently lowered the shroud covering Sophie's face and looked to Andee for guidance.

Andee's throat was dry. She was finding it difficult to move any closer. Sophie had been identified from the computer and mobile phone they'd found with her; surely that was warning enough that she ought not to be doing this.

Yet how could she not?

There was no one else for this girl.

'Can I stay with her for a few minutes?' she asked, still not looking at Sophie yet.

After Omar had gone she remained at a small distance from the body, feeling as though she was about to walk into a space where there would be no ground to support her, or substance to hold on to. It was a place of no return for those who were already in it, a place of unworldly feeling for those who stepped near. Her eyes slowly closed as a gulf seemed to open inside her. Her breath seemed to have lost its rise and fall, her mind was like an empty sea.

As she finally moved in closer she allowed her eyes to alight with a butterfly's gentleness on the tragic devastation of Sophie's once beautiful features. The clench of shock in her heart was a physical pain. Apart from the purple hair there was no way to tell it was Sophie, and yet, as she continued to look, she was able to see past the damaged eyelids to the violet-blue eyes that were probably no more. She could imagine them twinkling and crying, watching with surprise and awe. Emerging through the decayed layers of flesh was the perfect smoothness of her cheeks before they had started to come apart. Her luscious lips were ragged, yet her eyebrows were as immaculately plucked as they'd have been the day she died. There were no signs of the fatal injuries, but the blows had been to the back of the head. Noticing the way her purpled hair had been combed neatly to one side, nothing like the spiky madness displayed in the photo-booth strip, made Andee feel sadder than ever. Whether someone in France had arranged it that way, or a technician here, it hardly mattered. What did, was that someone, albeit a stranger, had cared enough to bother.

She spoke silently in her mind, as though Sophie could hear her thoughts. *You might be wondering who I am, this strange lady standing over you, staring into your face as though I'm expecting you to be who you once were. It would be wonderful if that could happen, but I know it can't. My name's Andee. I wonder if you have any idea how much I hoped we wouldn't meet like this. I wanted to find you so badly . . .*

She paused, breathing softly as so many words came pouring into her heart she hardly knew which ones to choose first.

I went to the campsite this morning. There aren't many people there now, just a few staff, but you'll never guess what I found. More flowers than you can begin to imagine, and they were all for you. People had left them outside the bungalow, along with candles and teddy bears. Do you remember your rag doll? The one your mummy gave you? We've kept her for you – and your book. I had to read it, I'm afraid, but I'm not sorry, because it helped me get to know the real you, and gave me an understanding of how very hard things have been for you since your mummy went. It's difficult enough being a teenager, isn't it, but with all you had to put up with . . . You know, you've been making me think a lot about my sister. Her name's Penny and she was your age the last time I saw her. I don't know where she is now, no one does . . . She . . . She . . .

Suddenly torturous sobs were tearing through her body, annihilating everything else. She sank helplessly to her knees, her hands trailing down the side of the casket. *Penny, Penny, Penny. Why did you go? Why did you never come back? How could you not have understood how much we loved you?*

She couldn't think any more, she couldn't speak, she could barely even breathe. The grief was too painful, too consuming. It was as though she was drowning in it, being swept away by its relentless force. She was trying to pull herself free, but she was only going down deeper. Down and down, past the bottom into the blackest, cruellest despair.

Penny, I'm sorry. I never meant the things I said. I should have listened, tried to understand . . . I loved you so much, but I took you for granted, treated you badly, like you didn't mean anything, but you did . . . I miss you every day. You're always in my mind. Have you ever forgiven me for being so mean? I don't blame you if you haven't. I've never forgiven myself. Oh Penny, how could you have left us that way? It broke Daddy's heart. He never recovered, and Mummy's never been the same either. We loved you so much . . .

It was a while before she realised there was a hand on her arm, that someone was gently easing her to her feet and sitting her down. Her chest was still heaving; she couldn't see through her tears or hear past the cacophony of guilt, grief, longing and despair.

'Drink this,' Omar said softly.

Taking the water, she sipped and put a hand to her head. 'I'm – I'm sorry,' she whispered, hardly able to get the words out. The hopelessness, the need for answers, *for her sister*, was closing her down. It was as though she'd become lost in a place that had no meaning, no beginning or end. Nothing made any sense. How could a young girl simply vanish from the face of the earth? *Why* had it never been possible to find her? It was like a death, worse than a death, because it was a living hell.

An hour later, still feeling shaken and completely drained, Andee left the mortuary and started for her car. Her eyes were sore, and the devastation of her grief had left no colour in her face. She felt light-headed, strangely detached from herself and the mizzling rain sweeping gently into her hair and over her clothes. She wanted desperately to see her mother, to wrap her in her arms and feel thankful, blessed, that she still had her. She'd never tell her what had happened at the morgue, couldn't imagine she'd put it into words for anyone, though she knew she should. She still needed help with Penny's loss, even after all these years.

She was almost at her car when she came to a stop. Leo and Jemma were getting out of the vehicle next to it. Her heart thundered to a halt as she immediately thought of the children, then Martin and her mother. *There had been an accident. Something had happened . . . Gould knew where she was, he had sent them . . .*

'Is everything all right?' she asked, as she reached them.

'Yes, yes, it's fine,' Leo said reassuringly, apparently realising where her mind had gone. He glanced awkwardly at Jemma. Clearly neither of them had expected to find her like this.

She must pull herself together, put on a smile, try and take control.

'We wanted to talk to you,' Jemma said. 'Gould told us you were here.'

They looked so uneasy that she couldn't think what to say. 'I just needed to see her,' she managed in the end. 'It brought back . . . opened up a lot of things from the past.'

'Of course,' Jemma responded tenderly.

Andee smiled. 'I'm going to organise her funeral,' she told them.

'We'll be there,' Leo said firmly.

Knowing they would be, as much for her as for Sophie, Andee nodded her gratitude. 'So now, what do you want to talk to me about?'

'We should get out of the rain,' Leo suggested. 'Do you have time for a coffee?'

Andee glanced across the road. 'There's a WVS caff over there. Or did you have somewhere grander in mind?'

'Over the road is fine,' Leo assured her. 'My treat.'

Andee gave an exaggerated blink, and enjoyed his grin.

A few minutes later they were settled at a table next to a half-empty vending machine, three cups of Maxwell House between them all dressed up with liberal shots of froth and sprinklings of chocolate.

'I have an idea I know what this is going to be about,' she told them. 'Gould has recruited you to persuade me to change my mind about resigning.'

Jemma bunched her hands together as she sat forward in her chair. 'No one's blaming you for not suspecting the parents earlier,' she insisted. 'None of us did.'

Andee eyed them sceptically. 'Actually, I think we all did,' she corrected, 'on one level anyway, because we know it's almost always the parents in situations like this. It was the way it went when my sister disappeared. Everyone suspected my father. The press wrote some terrible things about him, even though there was never a shred of evidence to say he was involved. It was hell for him, for us all. I just didn't want it to be like that again so I . . . Well, I guess I refused to see what was staring me in the face in case it landed me right back in the middle of my own nightmare.'

'But what was staring you in the face?' Leo demanded.

'Well, to begin with I should have done a far more thorough vetting of Gavin's driver's log as soon I knew he'd been in France.'

'It was done,' Leo cried.

She eyed him meaningfully.

'OK, the guys who did it took it at face value . . .'

'And we know we should *never* do that.'

'You can't blame yourself,' Jemma protested. 'Especially not when it was you who got to the truth of it in the end.'

'Maybe, but much later than I should have. And it wasn't the only instance where I let my personal issues get in the way. My questioning should have become tougher when I found out about the baby. That sort of tension in a home, even without a proper diagnosis, is often a recipe for disaster, especially when an explosive and insecure teen-ager is at large. It was . . .'

'Whatever you say,' Leo interrupted, 'you weren't in this on your own. There was a whole team of us . . .'

'But I was leading the case, influencing the investigation . . .'

'That's still no reason to resign.'

Andee's eyebrows rose. 'I happen to think it is, but it's not only the oversights, mistakes, misleads in this case that have brought home to me the fact that I've never really been cut out for this job . . .'

'What are you talking about?' Leo protested.

'Please, hear me out. I've always known it in my heart, and other things have come together lately to show me that it's time to make some changes in my life.' She gave a wry sort of grimace. 'Please don't ask what kind of changes, because I honestly don't know what they'll be yet, but a new direction, new horizons are definitely needed.'

As they stared at her, apparently lost for words, she felt almost sorry for her decision. She was going to miss them, a lot.

'What if we say we don't want you to go?' Jemma finally managed.

Andee smiled. 'I'd be flattered, of course, but I'm afraid it wouldn't change my mind.'

After a while, Leo said, 'Gould told us not to come back until we'd talked you out of your madness.'

Andee laughed. 'Is that what he's calling it? Well, don't worry, you can leave him to me. Now, let's change the subject. Has anyone been able to track down Tomasz Sikora yet?'

'As a matter of fact, we have,' Leo told her.

*

'Are you still sure about this?' Tomasz was asking as he and Kasia strolled along the beach at Kinsale, wrapped up against the wind, ready for the rain. Ahead of them the children were running patterns into the damp sand, while behind them, back on the gentle mound of an emerald-green headland, the small white cottage that was theirs until they found somewhere bigger sat huddled cosily amongst its neighbours. 'I know you loved the house in Waverley . . .'

'Not any more,' she assured him. 'Knowing what I do now, I'm happy to be away from there.'

Pulling her to him, he gazed into her eyes and said, almost incredulously, 'You never doubted me, did you?'

'No, never,' she promised. 'I was only afraid for you.'

'But not any more?'

She shook her head. 'You've done the right thing. The police will help you.'

As he turned to watch the children aeroplaning down to the waves she felt her heart expand with love. Tomasz was back, for them that was all that mattered, and even though they'd fled their home in the dead of night and were now in a strange country where they didn't always understand what people were saying, she could tell they were happy to be here.

Tomasz was starting work at the marina on Monday where his cousin Artur was the manager. Ireland had been kind to Artur, and he was certain it would be kind to Tomasz and his family too. Artur's wife, Shavon, who was from Kinsale, and a teacher at the local primary school, was going to take the children next week to enrol them, while

347

Kasia rang the local care homes to see if they needed help.

They were so lucky to have escaped the nightmare that had been trying to swallow them up in Kesterly, so very fortunate to be blessed with this new beginning. Soon, when the time was right, Olenka and Glyn would join them, and maybe, next summer, her parents would come for a visit.

'Tomasz! Come and look at this,' Anton cried excitedly.

'It's treasure,' Ania shouted, jumping up and down.

Planting a kiss on Kasia's nose, Tomasz trotted off to make the inspection while Kasia strolled along after him, her fingers going to the *rue du Bac* pendant at her throat. The Medal of the Immaculate Conception that her mother had given her before she'd left Poland.

Though she knew it was too late to ask for special graces at the hour of Sophie's death, she'd prayed for her every day since discovering what had happened to her, and she would continue to pray for her. Especially tomorrow, which was to be the day of her funeral.

'Divine Mary Faustina, Apostle of Mercy, fold thy kindness round sweet Sophie and guard her with love, Softly sing songs to her of heaven above.'

Chapter Seventeen

'Are you sure you won't have something stronger?' Graeme offered as he passed Andee a coffee.

'This is fine,' she assured him, going to sit in an ornately embroidered armchair that wasn't unlike an Egyptian throne. They were in his gallery at the heart of Kesterly old town, a place of endless fascination for her with all its hidden treasures and histories. Even before meeting him she'd longed to know more about this world of old masters and antiquities, how to understand values and vintages, or to unravel the mysteries of time. It felt so distanced from her own world, more romance and fantasy than harsh reality.

'So the funeral's tomorrow?' he said, sitting at his desk and fixing her with his concerned grey eyes.

'Actually, it's more of a memorial,' she replied. 'She was cremated yesterday with just a few of us present. Tomorrow will be a bigger . . .' She broke off as his phone rang and waited as he told the caller that he'd ring back. As he replaced the receiver she decided not to tell him any more about Sophie's farewell. It wouldn't be right to burden him with how emotional and yet cathartic she was finding it to be involved in the arrangements. They hadn't gone far enough in their relationship for her to expect him to understand what it might mean to her.

'I read about your sister in the paper,' he told her. 'I'm sorry. This must have been a very difficult case for you.'

Her eyes went down as she felt disappointed in herself for underestimating him. 'We've found Sophie. That's what matters,' she said quietly.

He didn't disagree, and seeming to realise she didn't want to discuss her sister, he said, 'So were her parents at the cremation?'

She shook her head. 'They didn't request it, and it wouldn't have been allowed anyway. They won't be there tomorrow either.' He didn't need to know that she'd had a letter from Gavin, or that she'd decided to carry out his wishes. In truth, she'd rather not think about Gavin at all.

Putting her cup down, she said, 'I'm making my resignation official at the end of the week.'

Though he seemed surprised, he looked slightly puzzled. 'Is that a good thing?' he asked.

She nodded. 'I think so.'

'So what will you do?'

Wondering if, like her, he was thinking about Italy and the house he was hoping to buy, she said, 'I'm not sure yet. I guess you could say I'm considering my options.' She gave a wry sort of smile that he almost returned. 'Actually, there is one decision I've reached,' she confessed, deciding she must get to the point.

The way his eyebrows rose told her that he had an inkling of what was coming.

Though she was trying hard to find the right words, they seemed to have vanished, or maybe

350

they were rearranging themselves to emerge in another way. A way that would change her whole reason for being here.

'You've decided to make a go of it with your husband?' he said gently.

As her heart caught she replied, 'He isn't my husband, but yes, I have. He . . . He's my children's father. It's what everyone wants, for us to get back together. I mean, I want it too . . . It's just . . . Well, there's you and what we have and . . .' She fanned out her hands as she regarded him helplessly.

His eyes were full of the kindness she could so easily have come to love in him. 'I can't really say I'm surprised,' he told her ruefully, 'and I think you probably know how sad it makes me, but I understand your decision, and I respect it.'

Her eyes closed as she tried to convince herself she was doing the right thing. It didn't feel as though she was.

'Are you planning to stay in Kesterly when you leave the force?' he asked.

She nodded. 'For the time being, anyway. My mother's here, and both the children are still at school. Martin's probably going to take over his father's business.'

He smiled. 'Then I hope we can remain friends. Apart from anything else it'll make it easier if we run into each other, which I'm sure we will from time to time.'

'Yes, yes of course. I hope we can too.' She took a breath. 'Graeme, I . . .' She stopped, knowing that if she said any more it would almost certainly be the wrong thing.

He waited, until seeming to understand how

difficult she was finding this, he got to his feet. 'I guess there's no point in drawing this out.'

She stood up too and felt a terrible rawness inside as she looked at him.

'I've enjoyed our times together,' he told her softly. 'I hope Martin realises how lucky he is.'

She wouldn't answer that, as there was nothing to be gained from telling him how much it meant to Martin that they were going to be a family again. How much it meant to the children and their grandmothers too. And to her. But that wasn't making letting go of what she and Graeme had shared, the hopes and dreams they'd given one another, any easier.

'Thank you for coming,' he said, as they reached the door. 'You could have done this on the phone . . .'

'I wouldn't have. I wanted to see you.'

He touched a hand to her cheek. 'Take care and be happy,' he told her, looking into her eyes.

'You too,' she whispered back. 'And thank you for . . .' She shrugged. 'For being you.'

His eyes twinkled as she smiled.

Moments later she was walking down the cobbled street, each step feeling heavier than the last as the longing for what might have been tangled ever more tightly with the doubts of her decision. In her mind she could still hear the bell over the gallery door as he opened it for her to leave; at the same time she was seeing the relief and concern in Martin's eyes when she'd told him why she was coming here today.

'Are you sure?' he'd asked uncertainly.

'Of course,' she'd replied, knowing it was what they'd both needed to hear.

And she was sure. She truly wouldn't have done it if she weren't, but she'd hurt a man she cared about deeply, a man who deserved to be happy, and who she could have been happy with if things were different. She could never feel good about that.

On reaching the car she turned on her phone and was relieved to find no messages from Martin. It wouldn't feel right to speak to him now, and knowing him as well as she did she suspected he understood that. She needed this time to herself, to allow the goodbye to feel as certain in her heart as the decision to leave her job.

That was going to be another wrench, another resolution she must come to terms with as she allowed new directions, new horizons to open up for her. She still had no firm ideas of what she might do next, although she hoped to travel before making up her mind. She had an urge to visit places she'd never been to before, and though she knew she'd enjoy exploring them with Martin, she couldn't help thinking of how different it would have been to explore them with Graeme.

Different, but not better, she reminded herself.

Starting the car, she began heading out of town in the direction of Paradise Cove. There was no point trying to second-guess the future when she, of all people, knew how unpredictable it could be. It was as unreadable as a closed book, or a door that sheltered the secrets behind it.

Or the reasons why some children were found when they disappeared, and others weren't.

Thank God some were.

'Hi,' she said, when Estelle answered the phone, 'I'm going to be a little earlier than I expected. Is that OK?'

'Yes, yes, it's fine,' Estelle assured her. 'I think I've got everything ready. I can't wait for you to hear it.'

The following day no one was moving in the Woodland Memorial hall; everyone was listening as the Reverend Fern Gosling addressed the gathering.

'It isn't unusual to fear death,' she was saying, her tone seeming both comforting and curious, 'most of us do, because we have no real idea of what it means, where we go from here. It's especially difficult to understand when someone as young as Sophie is taken away. We feel that she hasn't had her time; that her whole life was still stretching out ahead of her waiting to be fulfilled. I can't tell you that it wasn't, but I can tell you what I believe, which is that when Our Lord calls it is because the time He wants us to be here on earth is at an end. He wants us to join Him. You might wonder why He wanted Sophie after such a short and latterly difficult time here, and why He chose to take her the way He did. It's very hard for us to understand what His reasons might be, and yet, in a way, it can be quite simple. The shock of how it happened, the very real tragedy of it, will have made each one of us pause in our hectic lives to think about Sophie, and other children like her who are afflicted by bereavement, and become desperately lost along the way. Perhaps we will also remember how important it is to appreciate and cherish those we love while they are with us.'

As Andee listened, absorbing each word as though it were a balm for the grief and confusion of the past twenty years, the buried guilt and devastation that Sophie's passing had shown her she must now start to deal with, she was holding on to Martin's hand and remembering the memorial service her parents had held for Penny seven years after she'd gone. They'd thought, truly hoped, that it would bring some sort of closure to their suffering, but it never had.

Was her mother thinking about Penny now as she sat here saying goodbye to Sophie?

Of course, she must be, and Andee squeezed the hand Maureen had tucked into her arm.

Though Andee had feared that asking her family to attend two funerals in as many weeks would be asking too much, as it turned out not one of them had stayed away. Even Frank and Jane had made the journey from London, and Martin's sister Hilary and her husband had also come.

In fact the quaint candlelit hall of the Memorial Woodland was full to capacity. Most of CID were somewhere near the back, while Leo, Jemma, Gould and DCI Spender were in the row behind Andee and her family. Taking up most of the pews, however, were those from the campsite who'd wanted to say their goodbyes, and sixty or more pupils from Sophie's year at school with half a dozen teachers. Whether or not the bullies were amongst them Andee had no idea; if they were she hoped they were taking some pause to reflect, and perhaps to ask for forgiveness.

Sitting on the other side of her mother were Luke and Grandma Carol. Estelle and her mother, Marian, were at the end of the row. Alayna was with the school choir getting ready to sing.

The gentle humour and compassion Fern Gosling

was injecting into the service now was turning out to be as moving as the thought of how surprised, and probably delighted, Sophie would have been if she could see how many had come to say farewell. Maybe she could. Maybe she was watching from somewhere, with her mother, feeling quietly elated by how wonderful it was to be at the centre of all this.

We planted a tree for her mother at the Memorial Woodland, Gavin had written in his letter. *I'm sure Sophie would want to be with her, and perhaps she could have a Christian ceremony if you're able to arrange it. There is a white dress of her mother's that she always kept in her room; if it's possible perhaps she could wear that.*

If it's not too much to ask, do you think someone might read the following poem.

If tears could build a stairway
And thoughts a memory lane
I'd walk right up to heaven
And bring you home again.

It's much longer than that, of course, but I will leave it to you and the minister to decide how much more to include.

Thank you, DS Lawrence, for caring about her. It's good to know she has a friend at this time.

Yours, Gavin Monroe

Gould had read Gavin's chosen poem at the cremation two days ago, when they'd tucked the rag doll and original diary into the coffin to go along with her. The ashes were now on a candlelit table in front of the Reverend, contained in a white marble urn and next to a school photograph of Sophie.

It soon came time for Estelle's reading, and as

she walked to the lectern Andee felt for how badly she was shaking. It was so brave of her to do this, but she'd insisted.

'I've written a poem for Sophie,' she told everyone, speaking quietly into the microphone. 'It doesn't always rhyme properly or anything, but . . .' She shrugged awkwardly, and looked down at the page in front of her.

'Sophes, it's not going to be the same without
     you
No more laughing at things we're not supposed to
No more shopping for stuff we can't afford,
Please take care of my friend dear Lord.

Sophes, when I look around at everyone's face,
Where yours should be there's only a space
You're in my heart though, be assured,
Please take care of my friend dear Lord.

Sophie, when I think of all the dreams we had
And the fun we shared, it makes me glad
And I'll always be glad that you were my best
     friend,
Please keep her safe, dear Lord here at the
     end.'

As she started to break down Marian went to bring her back to her seat, and Andee knew without turning round that, like her, the entire gathering was deeply moved by the awkward but heartfelt tribute.

'Before we go outside to plant a tree for Sophie,' Fern Gosling was saying as she returned to the stand, 'the choir from Kesterly High School is going to sing a song that was chosen by Estelle. Apparently Westlife was one of Sophie's favourite bands, and the song we're about to hear was also one of her favourites. So it seems very fitting that we should enjoy it now and perhaps, as we're listening, we can allow the beauty of the words and melody to help us imagine Sophie being carried to our Lord's, and to her mother's, side.'

There was a moment before the music teacher struck the opening chords. When she did Andee felt emotion stirring in the hall as though it were a small flock of birds preparing to take flight. Her eyes found Alayna, and her heart swelled with more feeling than she could contain. It wasn't that she'd never been aware that anything could change at any time, and that only a fool took their blessings for granted, but being here today was reminding her of just how important it was never to forget.

Then her head went down and she thought of both Sophie and Penny as the choir began to sing 'In the Arms of an Angel'.

ACKNOWLEDGEMENTS

For their invaluable help with the research and crafting of this book I would like to express my sincere thanks to Carl Gadd, Martin Williams, Dr Helen Lewis, Joanna Miller in Poland, Ewelinaz Edruszczak, Paulina Fiedorow, Ian Kelcey, Rev David Russell, Dr Julia Verne of the South West Public Health Observatory, and Andy Hamilton of the Bristol Coroner's office.

Please note, should there be any discrepancies in police procedure the responsibility is entirely mine.